'It's a strange feeling for me, a m... ...-century man, to identify so strongly with a teenage girl from ... 7th. But such is the brilliance of Antonia Senior's writing in *Treason's Daughter* that I genuinely felt that I was inhabiting her heroine Hen's mind as she falls in love with a young penniless friend of the family. Senior's prose is crisp and clear, fresh as a country walk in spring, and arrestingly original...The religious and political fault lines in 17th-century London in the run-up to the English Civil War are skilfully and unobtrusively woven into a gripping narrative and the atmosphere of a city simmering with fear and violence is beautifully drawn... This is a compelling book that truly gets under the skin of its characters, and does so with compassion and passion. Bravo! This is an exceptionally good historical novel and I predict a glittering future for its hugely talented author.' **Angus Donald, bestselling author of *The Outlaw Chronicles***

'This study of a family divided by the Civil War is powerfully engaging. Senior brings sharply to life the experiences of ordinary people, both fascinated and horrified by the escalation of violence; her grasp of history is impressive and she is equally convincing on the fast-moving, 'male' world of politics and war and the more pragmatic (but equally painful) battles fought by the women who must somehow live with the results. Hen is a delightful heroine; I was rooting for her right up to the novel's heartbreaking conclusion.' **Maria McCann, bestselling author of *The Wilding***

'This big, rich feast of historical storytelling is set in the 17th century, during the (far more fascinating and sexy) English Civil War... Senior's fresh, force... ...into the most destructive, ...pping.' **Kate Saunders, ...**

Antonia Senior is a writer and journalist. After many years at *The Times*, she is now freelance. She writes columns, book reviews and features for various national publications, including *The Times*, the *Guardian* and the *Financial Times*. Antonia lives in London with her husband and two children.

TREASON'S DAUGHTER

ANTONIA SENIOR

CORVUS

First published in trade paperback in Great Britain in 2014 by Corvus, an imprint of Atlantic Books Ltd.

This paperback edition published in Great Britain in 2015 by Corvus, an imprint of Atlantic Books Ltd.

10 9 8 7 6 5 4 3 2 1

A CIP catalogue record for this book is available from the British Library.

Paperback ISBN: 978 1 78239 266 8
E-book ISBN: 978 1 78239 265 1

Printed in Great Britain.

Corvus
An imprint of Atlantic Books Ltd
Ormond House
26–27 Boswell Street
London
WC1N 3JZ

www.corvus-books.co.uk

For my mother

PART ONE

CHAPTER ONE

January 1640

*H*ENRIETTA KNOWS WHAT IS COMING. SHE WATCHES THE candle's shadow dancing on the dressing table. She looks for the familiar patterns in the wood panelling on the walls, the knotted whorls that can be made into maps. Concentrate, she tells herself. Find the mountains, the valleys, river gorges, the great seas that stretch to America. But she cannot do it; she cannot block out the woman behind her and the eyes she is trying to avoid in the mirror.

Here it is, the relentless voice. Her mind scuttles sideways, trying to escape. But she is pushed into the chair by a firm hand, her limbs made heavy by a familiar misery. At last, as she always knew she would, she meets the eyes in the glass and watches them widen with triumph.

'It was just there, young mistress, in that bed,' says Nurse, jerking her head backwards to the bed behind them. 'Oh, how she screamed and wailed, your mother. Didn't bear it well, not like some I know. Hours she was at it, a'screaming and a'crying, and your poor father pacing and pacing down while the

3

screaming ran up and down the whole house. Never heard the like, we hadn't. And then at last the middy came down to tell him – a boy! She shouts it out. "A boy!" he shouts, and his happiness ran up and down the corridors where the screaming had been afore.'

She is well practised in this bedtime story, and she winds herself towards the crescendo. Henrietta tries to escape again, into the gnarled patterns on the wall. That pitted panel is the desert, Sam says. Uncle crossed it on a camel, which swayed like a boat and turned to spit at him. Great green spit that slid down his face, Sam said, giggling. Henrietta smiles at the thought of his laughter. Nurse sees the smile in the mirror and she responds with a ferocious pulling of the hairbrush that snaps Henrietta's head backwards.

Leaning in closer, so her breath creeps on Henrietta's ear, she says: 'And they thought she was fine, your poor mother, and delivered of a lil' boy. A lil' boy, Samuel, to grow in the shadow of his big brother, Edward, God bless his godly heart, and be a great merchant like his old daddy, with a doting ma to love him and a'cuddle him on his way. But something wasn't right. "How's my wife?" your poor father cried, and he saw the answer on the face of the middy, and he ran and knocked on the door, hollering for his love.

'The screams didn't die like they should have done, but stretched and stretched on and on, till your poor daddy was sobbing in sympathy, and his new minted boy all forgotten in a corner. And then they said to him, "There's another coming".'

Nurse stands up and moves over to the bed, pulling back the blankets. She gestures impatiently at Henrietta, who walks over

4

to the bed and climbs in. Nurse pulls the blankets up around her, tucking them under her chin. She bends down and kisses Henrietta's forehead with cool, dry lips. Bustling around the room, snuffing out lights and folding up clothes and prodding at the fire, she finishes her bedtime story.

'"Another?" your poor daddy shouts. "But I got me beautiful boy and I want me beautiful wife." But then there came another scream, a different one. The boy twin came in the world with a big smile on his little face, but this one came out crying and screaming. Perhaps she knew she were a girl. Perhaps she knew what were coming next.'

Henrietta pulls the blanket up over her head, but Nurse yanks it back. She folds the edges under the mattress, so the girl is held tightly in bed.

'"A girl!" the middy shouted. "A girl?" your dad said. All quiet, like, and confused. "Yeh, a girl." "Twins," he said, wondering. "Yeh, twins." One a bonny smiling boy, the other a screaming girl, all covered in little red blotches, like her skin's in a rage from meeting the air. Then there's another big old scream from your mother. Then there's a rushing about. And then your old daddy hears wailing from his wife's mother, and he knows then, my darling, that you killed your mother, you did. Dead, she was, with blood all over the mattress and some spattered up onto this old canopy.'

Nurse pats the roof of the four-poster.

Don't look, don't look.

It is too late. Hen looks up at the fat fingers lingering on the green silk. Nurse has won; they both know it. Yet she can't resist a last shot, a final malicious dart.

5

'Milly, little Milly as she was then, scrubbed and scrubbed, but the stains, they wouldn't never come out. Never.'

She blows out the candle by Hen's bed and picks up the last light. She carries the flame to the door, where it throws its golden glow on her face, softening it and rubbing out the lines.

'Goodnight then, my darling child,' she says as she closes the door, leaving Henrietta in the darkness.

She has looked for the blood in the daylight and never found it. She has inched all over this bed, half hoping, half fearing to see the stains. But at night-time, in the darkness, she knows the blood is there. She can feel it pressing damply through her nightclothes. Great ribbons of glistening blood cling to the roof of the bed, dripping down from the frame and onto the covers in soft, regular exhalations. Henrietta, fifteen years old and brave enough by daylight, lies in the darkness, trapped.

A scrabbling at the door; a whisper. She recognizes the voice and feels the misery lifting. The door opens, and Sam's thin body flits into the room.

'Don't cry,' he whispers. 'Pox on her, the witch. Attack, Hen. Attack!'

'How?'

'That thing we've talked of. Sebastian and Viola. Sebastian and Cesario. I've brought clothes.'

'We can't.'

'He's out. She's down in the kitchen talking about the Greatness of our Ned's Blessed Soul.'

She grins, and he squeezes her hand.

~ ~ ~

Hen jumps from the ledge first, landing in a suck of mud. Sam lingers behind, wedging the window open with a knotted cloth. While she is waiting, she looks down the dark alley towards Fetter Lane and the bobbing lights beckoning them on. I spend hours waiting, she thinks. Waiting for Sam to come home, for Father to talk to me, for Grandmother to be like she used to. Waiting for the end of the day, and waiting for the morning to come, and all the while measuring out time, filling days, chopping the hours into bite-size chunks, like the gobbets of stale bread Cook leaves out for the birds. Not tonight. Not now.

A sense of limitless freedom fizzes inside her.

Sam lands beside her with a squelch, breaking into her reverie. He grabs her hand, pulling her towards the lights. They round into Fetter Lane and on into the hubbub of Fleet Street. A carriage creaks past, the horses' hooves scraping on the stones. Beyond it, a huddle of apprentices, arms linked, pull back from the mud-spattering wheels, laughing. The linkboys jostle for business, their torches jumping and shaking. A pie-seller calls, 'Hot and fresh', and the smell of the stewed meat rises above the hum from the nearby piss-alley. A tub-preacher shouts his disapproval to indifferent drinkers, who spill in a jovial froth from the open doors of the packed-out Crown. There is more laughter and singing, and somewhere a voice raised in anger. After the quiet of Hen's house, it is shockingly busy. Bewildering.

She stands for a pace, reaching out a hand to the brick wall to steady herself, letting the noise and the life wash over her. She is a pebble on the foreshore wanting to be sucked up by the mighty tide. It trembles in her again, this freedom, this fear-edged joy, and she turns to let Sam read it all in her wide grin.

He grins back at her, a mirror. They begin to run, feeling the call of a London night, its promise of adventure and danger, and the fug of coal and booze and chatter. After an initial stunned muteness, she hollers and whoops as she runs through the city's glorious, rancid streets. Her call is lost in the mix, swallowed up in a London burr that rises to the coal-smeared sky.

They run and run, Sam ahead of her, showing her the way in the dusk. They follow the curve of the Thames as it wraps around the raucous city. Along Fleet Street, up Ludgate Hill, Henrietta inhales swirls of coal smoke as she fights for breath. Down Watling Street, past the spilling-out drunks at the inn at the bottom, past the shifty punters emerging blinking from the stews, past the scavenging urchins of the Blackfriars slums.

They run until her chest heaves, and she has to fight to keep Sam's back in sight as he threads in and out of people, of horses, of carts, of puddles. Through the shadowy gaps in the torchlight, skipping through the pigs rooting in the filth that froths over the banks of the Wallbrook. The pigs squeal as they scatter, flicking mud and worse onto Hen's stockinged legs. Still she runs, wanting to laugh, but too short of breath; wanting to stop, but desperate to run on and on. Until, at last, they come to the great bridge, and Sam stops, halfway across, and flings out his arms to catch her.

They lean over a low, soot-black wall on London Bridge, looking up the river towards home. At their backs, the masts of trading ships moored in the Pool jostle and sway, black against the darkening sky. The wind blows up the shivering river, bringing with it the smell of pitch from the shipyards and the fierce creaking and clanking of the working rigging.

Hen and Sam perch between rows of crooked houses in the space left by a fire – a sooted gash handmade for boys to hang out over the river and jeer at the boatmen's attempts to shoot the bridge. No boats now. This late, they won't attempt the bridge's currents, but gather at the steps either side to fight and tout for customers. Hen leans over, a little too far, peering into the darkness of the river. She can just make out the flow and eddy of the water, and the bubbling white ferment where the Thames fights the legs of the bridge. The river is more beautiful than she has ever seen it. But she has rarely seen it by night, and always before she has been hurried past, swept along in a sedan chair or a coach. Now, revelling in the anonymity proffered by the city at its night-time play, she can savour it, dawdle, just look. Filthy and utilitarian by daylight, by night the great river reflects London's tipsy beauty. Torchlight dances across its choppy black waves, and the cold night air subdues its stink.

Behind them, the Tower squats malevolently on the river's edge. But in front of them the city stretches all the way to Temple, where lights dance in innumerable windows, at unimaginable cost. They can hear the roar of the crowd at one of the theatres on their left. The south side of the river is a place of the night: of artifice and theatricals, of punks and their pimps, of vicious dogs and fighting cocks. A man's realm. And yet somehow, straddling the river between the raucous south side and the tumultuous north, Hen feels at peace. Her heart has stopped hammering in her chest. There is space to relish the beauty of the dark river and the torchlight. And there is Sam.

'Is it always like this, at night?' she asks him. He hears the barely suppressed excitement in her voice.

'It is, it is!' he cries, dropping into a low bow. She laughs and curtsies, and they both collapse to the squelching floor, helpless with happiness.

'Oh, Sam,' she says, when the laughter subsides. 'Thank you for bringing me.'

'S'all right. I shall get such a beating if we're caught.'

'Well, we must not be caught then.'

He rises to his feet and pulls her up from the floor. 'We'd best get back.'

'Yes. Slowly though, Sam. The long way round.'

'You'd better let go of my hand. You're supposed to be a boy, remember.' He squeezes her hand before he drops it.

Sauntering home again, they are quieter. The wild joy has faded, and they find the time to stop and stare at small novelties: the gleam of a great glass vase in a shop front; the pendulous breasts of a doxy hanging out of a window, trying to distract potential customers from the syphilitic rotting of her nose; a dwarf lying drunk in the mud while two barefoot boys strip him of his silk-edged coat.

'I hate to see you crying, Hen. Was it her again?' he asks as they walk, the tower of St Paul's guiding them home as they meander through narrow streets.

Hen nods. 'Why does she hate me?'

'You should tell Father.'

'I did. He took her side. Said she was his nurse, and she loved all of us, and I should be grateful to her. The old bitch.'

'Hen!'

10

'She is.'

Hen explores the unfamiliar sensation of a boy's clothes. She takes wide strides, watching her brother. She jumps over dark puddles and kicks at loose stones, delighted by her freedom from heavy skirts, which trail in the mud and filth. How she hates dressing in her best dresses, and the measures needed to protect the precious fabrics from London's oozing streets. Dressed in her finery, she is forced to sit entombed in a sedan chair, heavy curtains blocking out the urban hubbub. Forced to totter on wooden platforms, which slip and slide in the mud, threatening to throw her to the floor. Free from all that, she jumps and lands with a delicious splash in the mud. Sam's boots are encased with mud to the ankles.

Bells ring out from church towers all around them. Nine o'clock.

Sam grabs her hand suddenly. 'I know something you'll love,' he says, pulling her down Fenchurch Street, in the opposite direction to their house. He ducks into an alley.

'How do you know all these little streets?'

'I explore by day, so I'll know them by night. Rough, you being a girl. I'd howl with boredom if I sat at home all day. Here. We need to climb that wall. Can you hear anything yet?'

Hen can hear a low hum of chatter coming from the big building next to the wall Sam is now perched on top of. She scrambles up next to him.

'Now, Hen, you have to lean over, holding out your arms, making an arch over the alley. Do you see?' He falls away from her, his weight leaning on the wall opposite. Hen copies him and finds that she can see into the window of the building she is

11

leaning against. Below her, a procession of rats stalks under their arched bodies.

Inside, at long benches, sit lines of men and women, red with warmth and wine, talking and laughing.

'What is this place, Sam?'

'Clothworkers' hall,' he says. 'Wait, though. The best bit's coming.'

The roar of scores of conversations suddenly dies to a hum. At the top end of the hall a man and a woman are standing, arms outstretched, demanding the attention of the diners. They are dressed ornately, and the woman's hair is piled on her head in waves. Her dress is low-cut, aping the fashion at court. Unfashionably large breasts threaten to breach the scalloped edge of her bodice. She opens her mouth, and a sound of extraordinary beauty floats over the heads of the diners, across the hall, and through the gaps in the window, leading to where Hen, astonished, gazes on.

'Is she an angel?'

Sam sniggers. 'Of sorts. An angel of the punks. One who'll let any rich, old man poke her. 'Tis just singing.'

Hen elbows him in the ribs. 'Don't laugh at me!'

Hen thinks back over the singing voices she knows: her grandmother's creaking lullabies; her father's bellow as he sits in the tin tub by the fire; apprentices, arms linked and weaving drunk beneath her window, singing of women and wine; Lucy Tompkins, sitting at a virginal, singing smugly in French. But this is a different sound entirely. And then the man joins in.

'It's like they're dancing with each other, but just with their voices. Oh Sam, I've never heard anything so lovely.'

Sam is sitting on the wall, and he smiles up at her rapt face. 'I thought you'd like it.'

They stay for the rest of the song, and the next. Hen realizes she is getting cold, and that the forehead she is pressing against the glass is numb. Sam is now lying on the wall, and she feels his impatience to be off. Reluctantly, she pushes herself back upright. Jumping down, they frighten the rats.

'You have to promise me we can do this again, Sam, that I can hear it again. Or else I can't bear to leave.'

'I promise. You are a funny one.'

'It's better when you're at home, Sam. Just four days until you go back to school. I can't bear your leaving.'

'Hush, Hen. You must bear it. I'll write.'

'You always say that, and then your letters stop. Who are your friends? What are you learning? What of the masters? You have all that is novel and exciting thrown at you, and I must sit staring at the walls, waiting for a letter that never comes.'

'You should have been born a boy too, Hen. There was your error. You have the soul of a boy.'

'Perhaps. But I'm not one, am I? I'm useless. A pointless thing.'

They turn a corner and a body hurtles itself from the darkness, pushing Hen over. She is on her knees, staring at Sam's boots, shocked by the suddenness of it and the cold sliminess of the mud on her hands. Above her there is shouting, and she looks up to see a red-haired man raising bleeding fists, his legs planted wide in the filth.

A second man, the one who knocked her over, rushes at the fists, swearing in a continuous roar. Hen sees the punch coming, hears the crunch of fist on bone. The roar becomes a splutter of warm blood that falls on her upturned face.

Sam pulls her upright, back away from it. A small crowd has formed, goading and spitting. God is called upon, Jesus sworn to bear witness. The two men pound each other as Hen steps back against a wall. She has never seen blood gush with such venom and anger before; never seen how vivid it looks on pale skin, how dark it seems pooling on the floor. She watches the big man crumple, the spread of a battered triumph on the red-haired man's face.

'Come away,' Sam says, but she shrugs him off. Repulsed? Mesmerized?

Sam peels her away, holding her by the wrist. As they pass a silversmith's window, lit by a dozen lamps so that the wares sparkle and beckon in the gloom, she looks down at her shirt. Sam's shirt. The material stretched across her bound and flattened breasts is spattered with blood and mud, and grimed with coal. She carries the marks of her adventure, of a life lived at the gallop, and she bounces on the balls of her feet like a dancer.

CHAPTER TWO

*T*HE AIR IS HEAVY, FLAT. THE TINKLING OF SUGAR TONGS breaks the silence of Mrs Birch's richly furnished hall. Hen sits still in the chair, knees pressed together. Her collar and cuffs feel too tight, and her hair is scraped back, pinching at her forehead. The teased ringlets at the front, which still smell a little acrid from the irons, are falling out of their curls and into her eyes. Mrs Birch watches her from above the hand that hovers perpetually over her ruined mouth. Henrietta can hear the crunch of Mrs Birch's black teeth breaking into a sugared nut.

Lucy Tompkins is there, of course. Another motherless waif collected by Mrs Birch from among her husband's business associates. Lucy sits by Hen, with perfect blonde ringlets, smiling sweetly at Mrs Birch. Her eyes only occasionally swivel sideways to find herself reflected in the window.

There is a strange woman present. Older than Lucy and Hen, nearing twenty, she is pale and plain. Her name is Mrs Price, and she is Lucy's aunt, apparently. She is clearly godly. Hen notes her plain dress and severe hair.

'Henrietta, do sit straight,' says Mrs Birch. Hen stiffens her back and lifts her chin, eliciting a smile from the older woman.

'Henrietta's dear mother died while delivering her,' Mrs Birch says to Mrs Price. 'We, her father's dear friends, do what we can to fill the void. Her grandmother lives with them, but she, poor wretch, is not much use, is she, Henrietta?'

Hen shifts in her seat, unwilling to agree, too polite to voice her disagreement. She will not betray the grandmother who was once so buoyant, so loving, before the last of her children died and she came to believe that she was one of the damned. Her poor grandmother. To hear, like perpetually pealing bells, the summoning of your demons.

'An interesting name. Henrietta.' The strange woman rolls the word around in her mouth, filling the syllables with venom. Her dark eyes narrow as she looks Hen up and down, trying to place her, to label her correctly.

'I was born as His Majesty was courting the queen. Nearly sixteen years ago. Father named me after Her Majesty.'

'A black day, indeed,' says Mrs Birch, leaving sufficient ambiguity in the statement to make Hen uncomfortable. Lucy smirks. 'The marriage, I mean, of course.'

'That Catholic slut.' Mrs Price spits out the words. Lucy nods.

How does Lucy manage, wonders Henrietta, to be pompous and simpering at the same time?

Mrs Birch reaches for another tart. 'Of course, we all wish that our beloved king had married a good, godly girl. A German princess perhaps. All these years have scarcely blunted the pain of it, and those poor children to be raised by a papist,' she says, between mouthfuls of burnt sugar. 'But perhaps your words are a little harsh, Mrs Price?'

'Harsh? My beloved brother, who some people call a great

poet, although I leave such matters to God, is much at court, as you know. He tells me that just this January gone she put on a grand masque, dancing and acting the whore with her ladies.'

'The poet?' asks Hen.

Mrs Birch leans forward and speaks over her. 'Tell us more, dear Mrs Price.'

'I hardly like to, with young girls present.'

Mrs Birch, shifting in her seat with anticipation of the scandalous gossip, says: 'They must face the horror like all of us. Papists fighting for the soul of our beloved king and his church. Let them hear the worst.'

'Well,' says Mrs Price, leaning forward, taut with a relished disapproval, 'my brother, Edmund Waller, tells me that, at this masque, they went beyond the usual evil. The ladies of the court, led by our hussy queen, had a special finale. They bared their breasts to the men of the court.'

She is rewarded by a sharp inhalation from Mrs Birch and Lucy.

'No! Oh, the papist hussy. She must be damned!' Mrs Birch's mouth falls open, revealing the rotting teeth she so assiduously tries to hide.

'Of course she is damned, following the whore in Rome,' says Mrs Price, eyes shining.

'Mrs Price,' says Hen, 'Lucy and I were at the dress rehearsal. Lucy's father took us – do you remember, Lucy? There were no breasts bared there. Although to be sure the costumes were low cut.'

'And would my brother lie, miss?'

17

'Would I? Lucy, you were with me.'

Lucy blushes, and mutters something about not daring to look at the scandals unfolding on stage. Hen remembers her eager, shining eyes at the masque, watching the queen and her ladies dancing, and the king's grave face.

Silence settles, and Hen retreats into herself. The windows are covered with drapes, to protect Mrs Birch's furniture from the evil rays of the sun. Only one sharp beam has found its way into the room, and small flecks of golden dust dance in its light.

If I could paint the voice of that lady from last night, thinks Hen, it would look like that.

She lets her mind drift back over the songs, trying to recreate the beauty in her mind. Dimly she is aware that Lucy is talking of embroidery.

'And you, Henrietta?' says Mrs Birch loudly.

Hen jumps out of her reverie. 'Sorry, I . . .'

'I was asking, Henrietta, if you had any little projects on, like dear Lucy.'

'Yes,' says Hen, eagerly. 'That is, I've been working on a new translation of Ovid. In the vernacular, you see. I got the original in St Paul's churchyard, and I just thought . . .' She trails off, realizing from the expressions on the faces around her that she has committed yet another solecism she doesn't understand.

~ ~ ~

Down the road, in the Swan, Sam is deep into his pint of wine, encouraged on by the two Birch boys, Robert and Thomas.

Oysters are piled high on the table in front of him, wobbling white in their shells.

Richard Challoner, his father, drinks slowly. Sam watches how he raises his mug and tries to copy the motion. Tompkins and Birch, Challoner's fellow merchants, are listening quietly to Oliver Chettle, a lawyer known as a rising man, despite his comparative youth.

'I tell you, he has eroded the independence of the judiciary beyond bearing. He may be king but, for time immemorial, the judges and lawyers have been the lions checking the throne. He has made them into lap dogs. Yesterday, I tell you, yet another judge was bought off with a high office and a fat pension.'

The lawyer sits back in his chair.

Birch, who had been nodding his vociferous agreement, breaks in. 'He's not called a parliament since he made Laud his archbishop. They are pressing him to call a parliament, the godly peers. But will he listen? He listens to Strafford and that papist wife. A sliver of water between us and the powers of Europe bent on destroying our faith, yet she prances around Whitehall with a phalanx of popish priests.

'He's trying to fight the Scots with no money, and refusing to call a parliament to listen to the legitimate grievances of his people. Without Parliament's money, how will he pay for this war? You, Tompkins, you, Challoner – you are men of the City; you know how the money works. Would you set off on a trading voyage with no money, no goods, no credit and a mutinous crew?'

'I would not,' says Challoner. 'My Sam was barely breeched when he last called a parliament. Now look at him.' The older men peer down the length of the table to where the younger three sit, playing an elaborate game of spinning coins. Sam looks up, disconcerted by the stares directed at him.

'It's all right, boy,' says his father, smiling at him. 'And your boys, Birch, were still in dresses. I agree he must call a parliament to raise the funds, but he must fight the Scots. They are rebelling against his authority.'

'With reason,' Chettle says, slamming the table with an open palm. 'They are standing up to that papist Laud, and his attempts to corrupt the soul of their church. They show courage that we lack.'

'So he wants them to love their bishops and pray at an altar rail? We may not agree with it, but what if that is the king's will? Imagine I am back on that hypothetical ship. Imagine I tell the crew to sail past a port they have been longing for, full of doxies and wine. They may not like it, but I'd expect them to do it, and I'd flog the bastards if they refused.'

The boys, drawn from their game, are listening to the conversation at the other end of the table, wine and fire mingling in their veins.

'Christ save me, and are we ignorant sailors to be flogged and abused?' asks Birch, his face florid, oyster juice gleaming unnoticed on his chin. 'Or are we Englishmen, who consent to be governed?'

'Where has this idea come from?' asks Challoner. 'This idea that somehow the king needs our consent to govern us? The king's mandate to be king comes from God, not man.'

'Even more reason, then, for him and his advisors not to abuse that mandate,' Tompkins says. He is calmer than the rest, and his even temper moderates the passions at the top end of the table.

Suddenly, at the bottom end, Sam lunges across the table, falling on Robert Birch. They tumble backwards, collapsing onto the floor, the wine following them and splashing the rushes. Sam, pinning his adversary to the ground, lands a punch before he is hauled off by the older men.

'Samuel, you forget yourself!' shouts his father. 'What was that about?'

'Nothing,' says the boy, his eyes fixed firmly on the ground.

~ ~ ~

Later, as Sam emerges from his beating, white with pain and the effort of not crying, Hen asks the question.

'What happened?'

'Robert. He called Father a papist.'

'You were right to hit him.' She hugs her brother. 'I'd have hit him if I'd been there, and not shut in that room with those terrible women. Why didn't you tell Father?'

'Tell him that's what people think when he defends the king? He'd beat me harder. He's in there sinking another bottle.'

When the bottle is gone, Richard Challoner is still furious. The children can hear him through the closed door.

'God damn you, stop your spinning!' he shouts, waving a fist at the churning fireplace. 'God damn you to hell! D'you think I don't know what you're up to, you fox, you wolf?'

Harmsworth, his manservant, comes in with a small glass of wine. Hen slips in behind him and watches him bristle and mutter to himself as he hears his master's words, the blasphemy grating on his ironclad godliness. Harmsworth says nothing as he places the tray at his master's side, but his simmering anger seems to pierce Challoner's wine fog.

'Plague take you, Harmsworth. You hate me, don't you?' Challoner says, smiling and jabbing his finger at the man. 'You think I'm a fucking papist. That I'm a Laudian grates on you. You think Archbishop Laud and his evil acolytes are out to get you.'

Harmsworth says nothing, but his hands shake as he places the glasses on the table.

''Tis a constant and nagging torment to you that I have the effrontery to breathe the same air as you,' says Challoner. 'Because I believe that Laud's in the right. That a little pomp and a little ceremony are good for the soul.'

The manservant kneels down to pick up a napkin that has fallen to the floor. With slow, deliberate actions he folds it back along the crease and returns it to his master's lap. As he bends over, Challoner grabs at his lapel, pulling him in. Their faces are close; Challoner's red and triumphant, Harmsworth's white and taut.

'Hail Mary, eh, Harmsworth? God bless all bishops. God love the Pope in all his purple glory.'

Harmsworth brings up a hand to wipe away a fleck of his master's spittle, but still he says nothing. Challoner lets him go. Harmsworth straightens and takes a step backwards, putting some distance between them.

'Will that be all, sir?'

Cheated by the old man's refusal to react, Challoner raises a grumpy hand. 'I'm no God-cursed papist, plague take you,' he says to his servant's retreating back. 'God rot the whore in Rome,' he says as the door closes behind Harmsworth.

There is a thud and a whispering from beyond the closed door.

Harmsworth has fallen to his knees and is praying for forgiveness. The sound makes Challoner laugh, the ripples of his amusement quivering through his belly. Then he looks up at the walls.

'God damn you. Did I tell you to spin? Did I?' He ignores the water and reaches for the wine. 'God damn you!' he cries again.

Henrietta crosses the room and slips her hand into his. 'Why, Hen!' he says, happy-drunk at once. 'Oh, my darling, why are you up? 'Tis late.'

'Harmsworth is crying in the hall.'

'Crying, is he? And praying, I'd wager.'

She nods as she sits on the floor by his chair, then lays her head on his knee. 'Why do you tease him, Father?'

'Godliness. I hate it. Snivelling cullys. Foolish scabs. So pleased with themselves, the scrubs. I'm elect, they say, long-faced and so smug. What if you're not, eh? What then? Harmsworth's been through all the self-loathing, all the repenting. It's funny, to make yourself so miserable for God. Does He demand that of us, pudding? That we hate ourselves?'

'We're sinners, Father.'

'What have you ever done, child? I'm a sinner, maybe. At least I had some fun while I sinned.' He smiles; remembrance trumping repentance. 'Does the Lord begrudge me that, hey, pudding? But Harmsworth, the goat. Hates me, wants to see me burn. Wants to get paid too, and fed. So he squirms and mutters, and I laugh at his dilemma. Otherwise I'd have to fire him, or hit him. Loathing each other on parallel tacks!'

She puts her arms round his legs, glad that he's smiling, whatever the cause.

23

'Does he think I love my God any less than he his?' her father says quietly, his hand stroking the hair back from her forehead in slow, rhythmic movements.

'Are you a papist?' She tenses, fearing a slap. But the question is out now.

'No, Hen, I am not.' He sounds sober suddenly, and subdued. 'For all that you're a clever cat, puss, we don't talk overmuch about these matters. I'd wager you know more about the Niceaen Councils than the current strife. All those ancients bashing each other about the head with theology, hey, Hen, and not so much about the current japes?'

'Tell me then,' she says, looking up at him.

'Well then, I shall sing, my angel, of the wrath of the godly. Now you know, of course, that across the Channel the papists have been waging a long and nasty war with the true believers. The Spanish and the Holy Emperor set against the various armies of the Palatinate, with the Danish and Swedes swinging in and out as the mood takes the bastards, and the good Protestants of France keeping their king busy with rebellions here and there.'

Hen nods impatiently. 'And you were with Sir Horace de Vere in the Palatinate, to support the king's sister and her husband in their claim to the Bohemian throne.'

'Aye, some twenty years ago now, little one.'

'So it's history,' she says with a shrug.

'Well, keep it in your noddle, for you will need it. Without it, the rest makes no sense.' Challoner stands up, less unsteady than he should be given the quantity of wine he has taken. He pokes at the fire with sharp, vicious actions.

'So to now. When the old queen died, God bless her, we looked to the Scottish king to be ours because he was a good Protestant with healthy Protestant sons. All to the good. One Protestant son died and, between you, me and the walls, Hen, he was the better prince. But here we are with King Charles and he likes his church with bells and whistles. He likes the Latin, and the priest to be one step removed from the people, with an altar rail between them. And Laud, his archbishop these seven years, likes these things even more. And the whiff of incense to the godly is like musk to a maid, little one: drives them to Bedlam and back.'

'Why?'

'The outward forms of worship are important, pudding, in part because they just whiff a bit of popery, but in the main for what they represent: the Church as arbiter between man and his God. Throw predestination into the mix and the godly are wild with fury.'

'You mean the Arminian question?'

'Aye, that's it, puss. So the godly believe that you are marked from the start, elect or non-elect to join Christ in heaven. Arminians – and I count myself one – believe 'tis all gammon. A man's deeds must tell in the reckoning. Lord how we fight about it, as if our places in heaven were settled by rhetoric and noise alone.'

'All played out against the example, in the Continent, of how it could all turn to ruin.'

'Exactly, clever puss.' He pats her head, and she pulls back, annoyed by the gesture. 'So we fear the foreign wars and hurtle towards them, because our fearing them makes us fight with each other all the more. It's a pickle, puss, and it's coming to a head over the prayer book.'

'Why is Laud so insistent on everyone using it, Father, if it's so unpopular?'

'He wants a common church, love. Total uniformity across the two nations. And the Scots ain't happy. Crawling with godly and insects, that place. So though it looks like we're fighting the Scots over a book, it's about a whole heap more.'

'But if the Scots are willing to bear arms against the king over the book, what about our godly?'

'That's what the king's party is fearful of. Some of the godly want to paint their faces blue and join the mad bastards. But mostly they want to bring down Laud, for all the king loves him. Even those not so caught in the theology are cross with the midget Laud. The king's not called a parliament since he was made archbishop. Without Parliament, the king can't raise taxes like a Christian, but must creep about like a Moor, taking levies where he can. Forced loans and arbitrary levies for his ships, all aided by his favourite counsellor, Strafford. So those with God in their hearts curse Laud, as those with imps rootling in their coffers curse Strafford. And some call the no-Parliament years a personal rule, and some call it a tyranny.'

'And what about you, Father? Where do you stand?'

'On my own, largely, puss, with a glass in hand.' He laughs at his own joke, an infectious, rolling sound. He drinks again. 'Well, but I am no papist, love. But neither am I strict in following Calvin, you know that. Each man must find his own path to God, and mine is one that avoids extremes. A higgledy path to salvation. But I'll get there, perhaps.'

He stands quickly. 'Pudding cat, we're too serious, you and I,' he says, and he picks her up and whirls her round in a circle, their hands clasped tight. She laughs as they spin, round and round, until at last they collapse into a chair, Hen sitting on his lap as she used to. She lays her head on him, sinking into the familiar perfume of wine and tobacco, timing her breathing to match the rise and fall of his chest.

CHAPTER THREE

April 1640

THE CROWD IS CLOSELY PACKED AND RAUCOUS. BEHIND HER, a group of tipsy apprentices sing. They lurch to one side, and the people surrounding them are forced sideways, like fish haplessly caught in the current. There is a feverish air. A new parliament has been called at last. At last!

'Sorry, pudding,' shouts Challoner. 'I tried to find a place in a window. But it was no good. All gone.'

She shrugs and grips his arm more tightly. She hears Sam's voice shouting overhead. She looks up to see him perched with assumed nonchalance on top of the sign for the Swan, his feet dangling over the bird's fading beak.

'They're coming,' he cries, and points over the heads of the crowd. She can't see much, wedged in the third row. She peers through gaps in the tightly packed bodies to where the king's men are marching past, from page up to privy counsellor. There is good-hearted cheering from the crowd. But then the whistles and boos erupt, and she thinks it must be the archbishop, or perhaps Strafford stalking past, the crowd's fury breaking on his head.

Now a full-throated cheer, and here is the king. He is mounted, and she can see his head, strangely disembodied, bobbing above the crowd. His face is a mask. In the masque it could be worn to play Dignity or Disdain. She looks up to see Sam cheering, waving his hat in the air, the Swan sign swinging wildly as he kicks it with his feet.

As the king passes, the cheers move along with him. The crowd is subdued for a little while, until another roar builds away to their right. It ripples along with the procession until it engulfs them.

'Hampden!' roars Hen's father in her ear. It must be the MPs then, thinks Hen – John Hampden, the hero of the remonstrance against ship money, and his colleagues. The crowd thins now, as the last of the procession wanders by.

Hen's father sees Sam now and shakes a fist at him. 'God's lid, boy, you'll break your neck!' He stands under the sign and Sam slips down onto his shoulders. Challoner gives a theatrical stagger, and then kneels for the boy to climb down.

'Small, the king, ain't he?' says Sam. 'But what a horseman! Oh my blood, did you see how he had that great beast calm and high-stepping through the shouting?'

'We don't see enough of His Majesty,' says Challoner, an arm round each twin, shepherding them through the remaining people. 'Not like his father, always pimping himself out to the mob. I daresay we made a radiant spectacle for James after the bow-backed Scots.'

They make their way home, stepping over the detritus of the thinning crowd, the piecrusts and the empty flasks.

'But it wasn't his choice to parade for us, was it?' asks Hen. 'The king had to process for the opening of a new parliament, did he not, Father?'

'It is tradition. Mind, it is tradition to call a parliament before now. Eleven years since the last.'

'Why did he have to call it, Father?' Hen threads her arm through his.

'Because, my darling, he's broke. Utterly, miserably lean of pocket. And all the little tricks and teases he's been using to winkle money out of us are wearing thin. So, at last, he's going cap in hand to ask for the proper raising of taxes.'

'And then,' says Sam, 'he'll smash the Scots. Huzzah!'

'Perhaps,' says Challoner, smiling at him. 'But it won't be so simple as he thinks, I fear. There's scores of MPs lined up to say their ha'penny worth, and they've been bottling it all up for eleven years. We've some fun in sight.'

~ ~ ~

Challoner doesn't look as if he's enjoying the spectacle over the coming days, as Parliament stutters. One morning, with the new parliament barely two weeks old and clearly failing, he finds Hen sitting, as usual, in the library.

'Pudding, how do you fancy a trip?'

'To where?' Lord! To escape these walls, just for a while. The thought is intoxicating. She grips her father's sleeve. 'Where, Papa?'

'My brother, near Oxford. The family came here once, if you remember. There's a girl your age, and a boy Edward's, and sundry others whose ages I forget. Perhaps you were too young to remember them.'

'To Oxford? Yes, Papa, yes! When shall we go? How shall we get there? What about Grandmother? For how long?'

He throws up his arms as if she is striking him.

'Whoa there, my pudding. I thought you would be pleased. I'll take you, just the two of us. Sam cannot come – he must pretend to be at his schooling. Not a bad time to be out of the city. Have you felt the mood?'

'I have.'

'There's a fever abroad, and it's too godly and too streaked with chaos for your father, kitten.' She watches him force himself to brighten, and she smiles to help him.

'No matter,' he says, his answering smile growing easier. 'We leave at dawn. So go to it!'

~ ~ ~

'So, Grandmother, I'm to be away. For a month, probably.'

The old lady watches the fire. Hen sits beside her, taking one dry, thin-boned hand in her own.

'To meet the cousins. On my own. Somewhere new, Grandmother – can you imagine that! No nurse.'

'You should be married,' says the old woman abruptly.

'Oh? And who to, exactly? Besides, I am not sure I want to be married.'

Her grandmother turns at that, as she hoped she would, looking at her and not the flames.

'Don't be stupid, Henrietta. It doesn't suit you. Of course you

31

must have a husband. It is boring enough, and miserable enough, to be a woman married. Try being a spinster, my darling child.'

'It doesn't sound so bad. No one to tell you what to do.'

Her grandmother smiles. The fire is warm, and Hen settles contentedly, her head resting on the old woman's shoulder.

'And how would you live? On your brothers' charity? Edward is more godly by the year, my posy. He would demand a high price in conduct to look after you. You would argue.'

'Sam – he would see me right.'

'A second son? He will have enough to do to keep himself. And what of his wife?'

Hen smiles to think of Sam married.

'She may not like you. My love, she will doubtless hate you for your closeness to Sam. And he will be hard-pressed then to help you. No, child. There is little joy to be found in poverty.'

'Well then, Grandmother. What must I hope for?'

'A widow,' says the old lady, smiling down at her. 'Yes, my lovely face, that's the best thing for a woman to be. Unless she's a poor widow. So fall in love with a young pauper if you must, my darling, but marry a rich, old man.'

'Grandmother!'

The old lady laughs, but then a cloud settles over her. Hen watches her grandmother shrinking. 'But don't have children,' the old lady says, her voice quivering. 'You'll lose them, and it will break you. Five I've lost. Five. Not counting the ones that died in me, or died leaving me.'

Hen holds on tight to her grandmother's hand, as the old lady begins to cry. 'Grandmother, you must sleep,' Hen says.

'Sleep? How can I sleep? Oh, I am damned, my darling,

damned to hell. And Judgement Day will come, and I will beg and plead, and I will be told "no". It has been destined.'

'But Father says that predestination is absurd,' says Hen, desperately paraphrasing her father's measured doubts about the orthodoxy, trying to pierce her grandmother's faith in her own damnation. 'He says that our place in the afterlife must be governed by our actions.'

'He would think that, my darling. But are all the preachers wrong, and he is right? Is the faith I have worshipped all my life wrong? Did my grandfather resist the bloodlust of that papist bastard Mary for no reason? It is the great whore in Rome talking through your father. The devil whispers in his ear. Don't listen to him. It has already been decided, and I am chosen.'

The old lady pulls a blanket up round her chin, wrapping herself up into a bundle. Her hands work at the edges of the fabric, pulling it in tighter round herself.

'I hear it in my heart, child. I am damned. Damned to the place of the weeping and gnashing of teeth. And the smoke of my torment will rise for ever and ever.'

The tears roll down her cheeks, and she looks earnestly at Hen, as if the child can convince her that she is wrong.

'Why must you dwell on it, Grandmother, on death and damnation? You are alive now. Can't you concentrate on that? Why do you think on the rest?'

'How can I not? What else matters? This is all a poor rehearsal for the everlasting life to come.'

Hen wipes away her grandmother's tears with the corner of her dress. The old lady doesn't register the action; she just stares at the fire with wide, frightened eyes.

'Don't look at the fire, Grandmother. Look at me. Please.' Hen pulls her grandmother's face round by the chin until the old lady is facing her. But her eyes slide past Hen, so she lets go, watching as her grandmother's head swivels round again to face the fire.

'There are demons, darling child, and monsters. I will sit with the witches and the papists and I will burn. You have never been to a burning, have you, child? You smell the hair first, and then the skin crisping. And all the time you hear the screaming.'

'But how do you know that is what you face? You are one of God's chosen people, Grandmother.'

'Child, He knows my heart. He tested me. He killed my children. And He knows how I cursed Him. And it was decided at my birth that I would be damned, and that He would take my children from me. One by one, He took them.'

Her voice rises, edging towards the point of hysteria where there will be no soothing her. 'And He is so good, so loving, child. He has made a hell of this life, so I may better endure the fires of the next one. Oh, but I am still so frightened of the fire, child. So frightened.'

'Shh, shh.' Hen begins to repeat the litany, her voice rising and falling rhythmically. 'Listen, Grandmother, to the children you will meet in heaven. First there was Auntie Georgiana, the youngest, who died of the fever, just five. She was beautiful as the sun, and spirited as the moon.'

'Yes, yes!' Her Grandmother nods.

'Auntie Sarah, who was beaten to death by her husband, though he was a man of God, and he claimed it was an accident and that she fell down the stairs. She too was beautiful, like the first crocus of the year, full of hope and life.

34

'And then Uncle George, the merchant, who sailed off towards the rising sun carrying your heart and who was never seen again by an Englishman, dead or alive. And he was handsome, and strong, with a laugh so beautiful it would make angels weep.'

'And then my mother, who died bringing Sam and me into the world, and who loved us enough to fill the oceans with her tears when she had to leave us. And she was beautiful, like a star, and I must watch for her in the darkest hour of the night, watching me.'

She strokes her grandmother's hair. The old lady is leaning on her now. She hates doing Uncle Charles. She remembers him, and how he was running to fat, and laughed too long and too loud at poor jokes, and had a defeated air. It makes her question the rest of the litany her grandmother has taught her.

'And then Uncle Charles, who was taken by the evil sickness, though he had been so strong and hale. And he was the handsomest man who walked through the Exchange, and was fair set to become the richest merchant in all the City.'

Her grandmother is calm now. She turns away from the fire and leans on Hen, breathing quietly. Beyond the window Hen hears the bellman walk past jangling his bell insistently. 'Past nine of the clock, and a cold night ahead.' I am leaving all this for a while, thinks Hen, and her relief is mired in guilt.

She steps from the dusky carriage, limbs aching from sitting for so long. She can see a pretty brick house with a lawn in front of it. Somewhere near, a river rushes past. The door of the house opens, and a red-faced man spills out, followed by a woman Hen guesses must be her aunt. A couple of smaller children run about, whooping, and a dog chases its tail round and round in an ecstasy of excitement. Standing sullenly on the steps of the house is a girl of Hen's age.

'Aha, aha!' shouts the red-faced man. 'Richard, dear one.' They clasp each other in a fierce hug, drawing back and looking into each other's face. There is a reckoning of new lines, of hair greying and hair lost, and then another delighted clasp.

'Robert, Robert.' Hen's father says the name like a benediction. 'And Martha, good Martha.' He turns to Hen's aunt, smiling still.

'And this, dear brother, dear sister, is my little pudding cat, all grown up, or very nearly.'

Hen sees the girl at the top of the steps smirk. She feels her cheeks turn crimson. To hide her confusion, she drops into a bow, murmuring: 'Henrietta, ma'am, if you please.'

'Well, well,' says Uncle Robert loudly. He seems incapable of any other vocal register. 'Well, well! Such a beauty. So like her mother.'

His wife shoots him a maddened look. 'Never mind that, Robert. Come here, child. You must be tired after your journey. I'll show you where you can tidy up. And this, my dear, is your cousin Anne. I am sure you will be great friends.'

Hen looks up to smile at her cousin and sees only disdain.

'What news, what news from London?' Uncle Robert's voice booms behind her. 'The parliament, brother. How we're longing to hear of it.'

'Give me a glass of your finest claret, Robert, and you shall hear all the news.'

'So good to have visitors. Such a raising of the spirit you bring,

36

such a quickening of the temper, and you shall fill this country air with news from London. What joy!' says Robert as they walk through the hall.

Anne sullenly shows her cousin up the stairs.

'You're to share with me,' she says, pushing open a door to a small wood-panelled room. 'Smaller than you're used to, I expect, compared to London. And you'll have to sleep on the trestle.'

Hen just nods. She walks to the window, where cushions make a seat of the broad sill. The last of the afternoon sun glows gold around the black leading of the pane. Outside, a perfect lawn runs down to a small river. A willow tree curls over the water, the wind ruffling its leaves.

'What a wonderful room.' She turns to her cousin and is surprised to see the hint of a smile.

'I like it,' Anne says. 'Not grand enough for you, I should think.'

Hen shrugs. 'It's the quiet that worries me. Is it always so quiet?'

'I suppose so. I hadn't thought about it.'

'I can't imagine sleeping with all this silence for background noise.'

'How can silence be background noise?'

Hen shrugs again, and they are silent. They look each other up and down, weighing each other: the young girl's automatic reckoning of relative prettiness. Anne is shorter than Hen, and fair. Her curves show up Hen's lean frame. She has the Challoner green eyes, set in a round and dimpled face. Pretty, thinks Hen. Prettier than me?

'You're fifteen,' says Anne.

'Yes. You?'

'Sixteen. Ever been kissed?'

'No.'

'I have.'

'Who?'

'Have you read *Romeo and Juliet*?' Anne sits down next to her at the window, pulling a cushion into a close hug. 'He quoted it to me. "It is the East," he said, "and my Anne is the sun."'

'What's it like?'

'What's what like?' Anne laughs. 'I can't tell you more. You might tell. You must earn the rest of the tale.'

'How?'

'Come.' Anne stands up and walks towards the door. 'Let's go down. We've been waiting for you to eat, and I am starved.'

The girls walk down the stairs, towards the sound of Uncle Robert's big laugh. Hen can smell roasting meat, and suddenly she realizes she is famished. They sit – Hen and her father, Anne and her parents – at a long table, and Hen lets the talk fade to a hum while she sets about the food. Her aunt sits at the top of the table, triumph and worry fighting over her stern features. The table is spread with dishes: fruit tarts, two whole roasted chickens, a side of beef, stewed carp, a bowl of purslane stalks, and a small dish of salted anchovies. Some buttered new potatoes sit nearest Hen, and a pile of spinach, black-flecked with nutmeg.

She begins to eat, a morsel of beef and a wing of chicken taking the edge off her hunger. Her fingers are sticky with the fat glaze from the skin, and she wipes them on her shoulder napkin, resisting the urge to lick them clean as she would at home. She hears a sharp intake of breath from her uncle and looks up. Her father has the triumphant look of one who has broken news of import.

'Yes,' he says. 'The parliament looks set to fail.'

Uncle Robert lets out a low whistle. 'Yet how long has it been since the last one?'

'Eleven years of personal rule,' says her father.

'Some would call it tyranny, brother.'

'Aye, many do, and indeed have to his face in Parliament. Still, he must hear it. He's desperate for money, they say.'

'Despite the ship money, and the sundry other taxes he's ripped out of us honest merchants?'

'We've not done all badly. Those inside the monopolies have reason to love the king. But the Scots are proving hard to put down, and costly.'

Uncle Robert nods. 'Those bastard Scots, eh? And the Earl of Strafford so determined to punish them. Have you met him, brother?'

'No, and I thank the Lord for it. I have seen him, many a time. His eyes fell on me once, and I thought to cross myself like a papist. He gives the godly ammunition with his very face – it looks like the face Satan borrows to wear for parties.'

They all laugh, except for Aunt Martha.

'Why should Satan borrow a man's face?' she asks plaintively.

Uncle Robert leans forward, waving a chicken leg with excitement. 'To the nub, brother, why is Parliament to fail?'

'You know of John Pym, the MP? He is man of affairs to the Earls of Warwick and Bedford. A connected man, and the Lord bless his courage. He stood there in the chamber and denounced the king's personal rule. It was a clever, measured speech. I brought my copy for you to read. Did not blame the king. Demanded that a number of committees be set up to investigate the abuses of power in the years of tyranny. Pym said the illegal prerogative taxes were as large a threat to our property as popish innovations are to our church.'

Uncle Robert bangs his wine cup on the table, flushed with pleasure. 'Hear him! Hear him!'

Richard Challoner smiles at his brother, clearly relishing the role of storyteller. 'They say the king is steaming with fury, but needs the money so must sit still yet. It's a race to see which wins: the king's hunger for cash, or his fury at little Pym squeaking his demands. The king wants Parliament to vote him the money first, and complain second. The MPs want redress, then they will supply the gilt.'

'Father,' says Anne. They all turn to look at her. She looks so pretty in the candlelight, thinks Hen.

'Is King Charles very wicked, then?'

Uncle Robert's horrified face strikes Hen as extraordinarily funny. She swallows a laugh.

'Wicked? No, no, child.'

'But you're always complaining about taxes, and saying he should call a parliament, and calling his wife a papist whore.'

'Anne!' says her mother sharply. She turns to her husband. 'But she has a point, husband. Tell us what you think of papist whores.'

Something sour settles on the table. Aunt Challoner manages to look both triumphant and sad all at once. Her faded face too deliberately avoids her husband's gaze. For a brief moment, the only sound is the scraping of knives on plates, and the slow, deliberate thumping of a dog's tail on the floor. A spaniel, it lies with its chin resting on its paws, throwing sad looks at the humans who are so provocatively eating in front of him. Mournful eyes track the grease from the chicken skin sliding down Uncle Robert's chin. The dog lets out a plaintive whine, devoid even of hope.

Richard Challoner speaks up, his voice sounding loud in the awkward hush.

'You see, Anne, the king cannot be wicked. He is just badly advised. The Earl of Strafford, for example, is a right hard-horse bully. And yes, the queen is a papist. If he can be brought to listen to the good, honest voice of Parliament, not the strident nonsense of those who whisper poison in his ear, then all will be well.'

Uncle Robert nods with vigour, attracting a new and now malevolent stare from Aunt Martha.

'But,' says Hen, aware of her impertinence at crossing her father, 'are we not just excusing him? If you, Father, ran your business down, it would be easy to blame your advisors, to spare your feelings. But it would be a lie. A kindly lie, perhaps. You are in charge, and your advisors are not.'

'The child has a point, Richard,' says her uncle, smiling at her.

'Aye, she does,' says her father. 'She's a clever puss, this one.'

Hen looks sideways at Anne, but her cousin is looking towards her mother, a half-smile playing on her lips.

Richard Challoner continues to speak, his hand twisting the stem of his wine glass round and round. Hen looks at her mother's wedding ring, which he wears on his little finger. It catches the light of the candles, glinting at her.

'Parliament cannot blame the king directly; it would be unthinkable,' he says. 'So perhaps they say Strafford when they mean "Your Majesty", and Laud when they mean "our Sovereign Lord".'

'Oh, very good! Laud, Lord,' says Uncle Robert, laughing. He looks towards his wife, inviting her to smile with him. But she frowns back, and the smile dies on his face.

Anne says quickly, 'And, Uncle, have you seen the king?'

'I have, child. Hen has too.'

Hen nods solemnly.

'And what does he look like?'

'Like a man too small for his own sense of self,' says Challoner.

'Yes,' Hen says. 'But also, he makes you want to hug him tightly, and tell him it will all be all right. Even though you know he will curse you for it. That's how he looked to me.'

'God keep you from hugging princes, clever puss,' says her father, laughing.

~ ~ ~

Later, lying in bed in the darkness, Hen hears Anne whisper: 'Are you awake?'

'Yes.'

'Clever puss.'

'I can't help what my father calls me. What was gnawing at your parents?'

'Mother caught him tupping the maid. Papist. I heard her screaming from the bottom of the garden.'

'Maid or mother?'

'Clever puss my arse. Turnip head.'

'Stop it!' Hen raises her voice, furious now. 'I'm your guest

42

here, you witch.' She is shaking with the injustice of it. Taken from her books and her home, to be patronized by this short-arsed cow.

'Bitch!' Anne whispers back.

Hen thinks of the boys she's seen fighting on the street, when out roaming with Sam a few weeks before. 'Wind fucker!' she hisses at Anne. 'Cum-twang!'

Anne is silent. Hen hears her sitting up in bed, the old frame creaking. 'Wind fucker?' Anne repeats back. 'Cum-twang? What on earth are you talking about? What is a cum-twang?'

Hen sees her cousin's shoulders shake in the gloomy light. Laugh with her, or hit her?

'I don't know,' she says simply.

Suddenly, they are both laughing.

'Cum-twang!' says Anne again. 'Where, in all that is holy, did you hear that?'

'If I tell, you must swear, on all that is dear to you, that you will keep my secret.'

'I swear.'

So Hen tells her about becoming Cesario, about the joy of pulling on her brother's breeches and sauntering through London. Of seeing the street boys fighting and hollering, of eavesdropping on the watermen, and vaulting walls. Of sitting on a low wall behind an alehouse in Southwark, reeling from its triple strength brew. Of the thrill of nearly being caught when old Mr Birch, slipping furtively out of a Southwark stew, saw her and paused, confused. Of sitting with Sam on the bridge as the sun set over a seething city, dappling the Thames with its blood-red light.

There is a pause when her tale finishes. The moon shines into the room and she can see her cousin's outline, the profile of her face and her knees pulled up under the blankets.

'I won't tell,' says Anne solemnly. 'I promise. My brother and his friends when they swear it, they clasp hands like this.' She reaches out, palm outstretched, and they clasp hands, thumbs entwined. 'Now,' Anne says, 'I swear it on the blood of my mother, on the heads of my brothers.'

Hen smiles and squeezes her cousin's hand.

CHAPTER FOUR

𝓔DWARD CHALLONER WISHES HE HAD NOT BROUGHT HIS friend to meet the family. The coach rumbles towards his uncle's house, and already he regrets his diffident suggestion to Will that they might escape their college for a few days. He sits backwards to the direction of travel, watching his father and Will on the opposite seat talk too companionably, too easily.

His father's coarseness, his joviality, the way his belly trembles when he laughs at his own jokes – all are too much to be borne. Ned feels the embarrassment so acutely it manifests itself as a physical squirming, a twisting away from the joke, from the innuendo, from whatever jollity his father has dreamt of now.

Will, the dear fellow, appears not to be showing the distaste he must feel. He is all affability. Yet what must he think? The ripeness of the atmosphere, compared to the austerity of their college life, is too much. Even the shock of switching from Latin to English, with all its possibilities for vulgarity, all its twists and imprecisions, is grating on Ned. Surely it must irritate Will?

He runs a hand across his pumiced face, feeling for the tender spots where the stone decapitated his pimples. Fewer now than last year, perhaps. The travelling covers are down against the late spring rain, and it is unbearably hot in the carriage. He feels the sweat prickling down his back, an itchiness across his whole body. He has visited the house before, and knows the spot where he will swim in the river later, and he thinks on it with joy. Is it sinful, to anticipate pleasure with such relish?

The rain draws off, and the coachman opens the covers, letting in a delicious lick of cold air as they trundle on. They pull up, at last, and the sound of their approach has brought assorted dogs and children yapping into the driveway. He sees his aunt holding herself stiffly on the steps, and his uncle planting his feet in a wide proprietorial stance. And here is Henrietta, rounding the house, arm in arm with Cousin Anne. There are flowers in their hair, and grass stains on their dresses, and their laughter carries above even the crunch of the wheels on the gravel. Ned knows he should disapprove of their disarray, of their clear frivolity, but he finds an unexpected smile on his face as they run towards the carriage, whooping like children.

Uncle Robert's booming cry greets them as they step down from the coach: 'What news, what news?'

'Parliament is dissolved, Uncle,' says Ned, after the introductions. 'And the apprentices rose. Attacked Laud's palace. All the university talks of little else.'

This is news to be dissected. It comes like an arrow into the isolated house. News to be pored over and pondered. Only Anne seems indifferent, rolling her eyes impatiently as the evening's conversation twists and turns back to the same feverish speculation. What will the king do next? What will the godly peers do? What of John Pym and John Hampden? Will there be more riots? Will we be safe?

At last, Anne and Hen go to bed, leaving the men in their philosophical mood with a brandy bottle near drunk and the fire down to embers. What use a king? Where is God in all this maelstrom? Where does duty lie?

Hen would have stayed to listen, but she sees Anne twitching with impatience. She can sense her cousin's boredom burning brighter and fiercer, until at last it is no longer impolite to leave, and they flee upstairs. It is cold for May, and they undress quickly, race through their prayers, and leap into bed, Anne mock screaming into her pillow, making Hen laugh.

'Who cares? Ship money this and prerogative that – who cares, Hen? Why do they go on and on? Why, why?'

'It's different here. You can't see why it matters, because here it probably doesn't. The king's anger won't make your river stop running or your grass any greener. But at home it matters. What the king does infects everything. There are riots and fights and fires to worry about. And Father's business. You heard Ned – the apprentices have been on the riot in Lambeth.'

'It comes out now,' Anne says. 'We're provincials, and we don't understand.'

'I didn't mean it like that.'

In the three weeks she has been in Oxford, their friendship has grown – close and fierce. But this tone is something new; something unwelcome.

'Then how did you mean it?' asks Anne, pugnacious as a street-boy.

'Do you not care about the king, about his dealings with MPs?'

'Why should I?' Anne's voice is hostile, the words tumbling

out. 'What are they to me? News, my father calls it, and falls on it like a dog on carrion. Rooting about in the entrails. Pulling travellers into conversation. "What news, what news?" he shouts. Yet when Mother and I talk of our neighbours, he scolds us for being gossips. What else is news of the court and Westminster but gossip about people you don't even know?'

'But yet,' says Hen, meeting Anne's hostility with control, 'to be connected to the wider world. Even if, out here, you cannot see the direct consequences of the doings of the great men, does that matter? D'you think that when King Henry fought for the true church, or the witch Mary sought to destroy it, there were women out here who shrugged? Thought, Pshaw, not for me? Did they do the same when the Normans came, or the Romans left? The news, it's just…' She looks around, as if for inspiration. 'Just history as it's being forged.'

'But time filters what's important. All this talk, all that passes as news, is all so much noise.' Anne sticks her fingers in her ears and mouths nonsense. Hen hits her with a pillow. Yet under the mock fight there runs the shock of disagreement.

~ ~ ~

The next morning, when Hen wakes, Anne is already gone. She heads downstairs and finds her father, incongruously still in the bustling kitchen. She kisses the top of his head, and he reaches round, pulling her onto his lap.

'Are you still little enough to give your old man a cuddle, little puss?' She laughs, and pretends to struggle against his arms.

Suddenly Will Johnson walks in, yawning. She hadn't spoken

to him much the night before. He had been passionate when talking, mainly with her father, his arms waving wildly to illustrate his points. Sometimes, turning quickly, she had seen him looking at her, before hastily glancing away on being discovered. He probably thought her a fool. Looking at her, thinking how could she be related to the pretty, vivacious one. Seeing him now, she pushes her father's arms down in earnest and stands up quickly.

'Good morning,' she says.

He looks startled to see her, and runs a hand through his heavy, dark hair.

'Will, my boy,' says her father, levering himself out of the chair.

'Good morning, sir. Miss Challoner.'

'Did you see anything after I left?'

'No, sir. The cloud remained. It must have rained in the night, as it's clear enough now.' Will pours out some of the small beer on the table at her father's wordless invitation, and drinks deep. He sets the mug down and clears the sleep out of his eyes.

'Are you planning to stay tonight, Will?' Her father's tone is one reserved for those few he really likes. Normally it would take a longer acquaintance for its honey colours to soften her father's usual abruptness.

'I am, if your brother has no objections.'

'None, I am sure.' He looks towards the open door, out towards where the cook is throwing seed at jostling hens. 'You are in the right about the weather, Will. It looks set fair.' He rises to his feet, and Hen can tell that one of her father's enthusiasms has settled on him.

'A picnic!' he shouts. 'We shall have a picnic.'

~ ~ ~

Hours later – hours spent by her father in the study, a book open on his lap and dribble leaking from his sleep-slack mouth; by the cook in a frenzy of chopping, packing and muttering; and by Aunt Martha in convulsive, whispered rages to her husband – they set off to follow the river upstream. The little ones are first, abuzz with excitement, then a cluster of adults, Richard Challoner and his brother at its centre, talking loudly of some merchant's disgrace on the Exchange. Last come Hen and Anne, wordlessly reconciled, arm in arm. Their suspension of hostilities is unspoken, but manifest in the way they walk even closer, their arms entwined tighter than usual.

Hen watches as Will helps Aunt Martha over a stile. Her aunt turns back and smiles at the boy from the stile's summit, and Hen thinks how strange it is that a sudden, careless smile can conjure the child in the most resolutely middle-aged of women. How kind he is, she thinks. Why, you turnip, Ned would have done the same. With such grace, though? Now you're arguing with yourself. Fool.

'Why fool?' Anne asks. 'Who's a fool?'

'Did I say it aloud? I'm the fool. Come, honey. Let's run. Let's chase the littleys.'

They arrive, thirsty and tinged with that irritable happiness reserved for hot days, at the picnic spot. The river curves in a wide arc, and a company of willows stands guard over the shining water. The littleys run through the hanging shields of leaves, to paddle and poke things with sticks at the water's edge. Linens are spread on rampant grass, baskets unpacked, and wine wedged between

50

rocks in the river to cool. Then, at last, they are settled and still, the heat heavy on them, with only the laughter and shrieking of the little ones to splinter the summer silence.

Aunt Martha's voice, querulous, breaks the spell. 'Your face is in the sun, Anne dear. All this excitement is all very well, but I'll not have you looking like a peasant.'

'Nothing wrong with peasant girls, eh, brother?' says Hen's father, watching Martha sideways.

Ned blushes. 'Never mind my father, Will,' he says. 'He likes to tease.'

'He's pure Benedict,' says Will, grinning.

'You puppy. Quit your yapping, boy,' says Challoner. 'Pass me a piece of that cheese before I whip you for impertinence.'

Will rolls over onto his front, his hair falling over his eyes. He tucks it behind an ear as he cuts a slice off the cheese. Hen finds herself mesmerized by his ear; the way it curls and tucks in on itself, the delicate peach of the lobe's skin. Why have I never thought about ears before, she wonders, about how miraculously odd they are? Were William Prynne's ears so beautiful before they cut them off for writing that pamphlet about the queen?

Fearful that he will catch her looking, she pulls her eyes away to stare at the grass. But they stray back again, as far as his hand where it grips the knife. Big hands, capable hands, with bitten, ink-rimmed nails. She traces the veins on the back of his hand, up to his wrist. A strong wrist, with fine hair on his arms visible up to where his shirtsleeve is pushed back.

As he passes the cheese to her father, Will looks up and catches Hen watching him. Both look away quickly, both turning red, neither seeing the other's confusion. But Richard Challoner sees.

51

With more than usual tenderness, he says: 'Ah, my pudding cat. Look at you there. All grown up. Where has my life gone that you, my baby, are all grown?'

'Lost in wine, brother?' Uncle Robert passes him a glass with the mockery.

'Indeed, brother.'

'Will? Ned?' Uncle Robert asks, holding out the wine.

'No, Uncle, thank you,' says Ned, as Will holds his hand out.

His father bristles. 'None for you last night, Ned? Are you turning temperance on us?'

'If I say yes, you will mock me.' Ned picks a daisy, pulling at the petals.

'So say no.'

'I cannot lie to please you, Father.'

'Clearly. Where, boy, does it say in the Bible that you should renounce pleasure? When our good Lord turned the water into wine, did he put a cork in the blasted bottle?'

Ned says nothing. The silence spins out over the company, until Will clears his throat and says, with precision: 'Forgive me, Mr Challoner, but I have not yet invited you to come to the college and view our new telescope.'

'A telescope, boy! What a thing, what a boon. I will come, most definitely.'

Hen finds herself speaking before she can stop herself.

'How much does it magnify, Mr Johnson? What can you see?'

'Well, Miss Challoner, you can see as much as eight times larger than the naked eye. You can see the pockmarks on the moon.'

'How different does the moon look, that magnified?'

'She's as beautiful, Miss Challoner, silver and glowing. But when you look closer, you can see the pits and the craters. She looks like she's ravaged by the smallpox.'

Richard Challoner laughs throatily at this. 'Hear that, Ned, boy? You must take the telescope with you when you're wife-hunting. Check the goods.'

Ned scowls. Will carries on talking to Hen, who feels the tips of her ears burn as she watches his lips move.

'You can see the stars, as if they're in the room with you – whole ribbons of stars, Miss Challoner, strung across the sky. And if the sky is clear, and the time is right, you can see the moons a'circling round Jupiter.'

His voice sparkles, thinks Hen, as she feels herself drawn in by his enthusiasm.

'How wonderful. Can I go with you, Father? To look through Mr Johnson's telescope?'

I sound like a littley, she thinks, hearing the excitement in her voice.

'Perhaps, perhaps. We must go home, child. In the morning, I think.'

'Tomorrow!' Anne and Hen cry in unison.

'Father, what of the rioters?'

'They will have burned their anger out by now, I have no doubt. News travels slower than their fury. I must be home, in case of damage. And you, my pudding, must come with me.'

After supper, as they gather to hear Robert Challoner reading, Ned tries to put some distance between Will and his father, sitting between them. Their friendliness grates on him. How can Will not mind the older man's coarseness? Is Will laughing at them all, on the inside, storing up vulgarities to entertain his other Oxford friends? As Uncle Robert's interminable reading of *The Tragical History of the Life and Death of Doctor Faustus* wends onwards, Ned imagines Will's future betrayal, his mockery, in agonizing detail.

The reading finishes, God be praised, but Ned is horrified to see his father immediately corner Will. The conversation is harmless enough, however, for the moment. They talk of stars and meteors, safe amid the celestial equations. Henrietta listens in, enthralled.

Why, Ned wonders, would his father let her become so unattractively learned? No fellow wants his wife to know her *hic haec hocs*, nor to know more mathematics than him. It amuses his father to have Henrietta perform in public, to preen and primp her learning. Poor girl.

Henrietta catches Ned's eye and smiles; glad that he smiles back. He has been prickly and difficult. Anne pulls her off to the window seat, for pledges of fellowship and last whispered secrets. And while Hen, too, feels the sorrow of their imminent parting, she finds herself looking over her friend's shoulder. As the regrets grow wilder, and the promises to write grow ever more exacting, Hen finds her eyes flit, again and again, to where Will Johnson, talking passionately of his work to her father, draws stars in the air with his beautiful hands.

CHAPTER FIVE

August 1640

A FULL HOUSE. SAM AND NED ARE HOME, AND THEIR CLATTER and clutter fill the corridors. Two new apprentices, too, soon known as Chalk and Cheese. Chalk is tall, thin and pimpled; Cheese, small and verging on spherical. Their nicknames give Sam and his father a reliable source of mirth, inflated by Cheese's hopeless resistance to the name.

'He's John and I'm Michael. Or Chadwick, if you prefer,' Cheese says to Sam. His round face reddens when he's angry, giving him the air of a maddened beet.

'I know your name, Cheese, old fellow,' replies Sam. 'Would you prefer Mr Cheese?'

Even Ned's rare smile makes an appearance during the Cheese-baiting, though he tries to look severe. He has come down from Oxford to start his apprenticeship with his father.

Hen likes the full house. She likes the noise and the laughter, and the sense of being connected to the world as the boys pile in from the Exchange or their carousing. Her father has a reputation as a man strict with business principles, but loose with moral ones, and godly parents do not choose him to shepherd their lambs. Cheese comes home smug and silent, trailing cheap perfume; Chalk more often carries the tang of the groundlings at the Blackfriars or the Cockpit. Ned, the household's sole puritan, disapproves of bawdy houses and theatres, treating both with the same outraged contempt. His disapproval rolls off the boys, intoxicated as they are by being young and loose in London.

Hen fills long letters to Anne with Sam's wit and Cheese's wrath. She chronicles Ned's increasing godliness and his growing estrangement from their father. Both Ned and Challoner believe that there can be no reasoned, sensible route to the other's moral high ground; each sees the devil's whisperings in the other man's argument.

Hen watches this mutual incomprehension spiral and turn fractious. She sees, too, what they cannot – that it is their love for each other which ratchets up the bitterness; neither can bear to see the other become the devil's imp. They draw further apart, pushing each other into ever-stronger intransigence.

Ned spends his spare time reading the pamphlets and lectures that are whipping London's godly into a passion against Laud and his popery. Hen suspects that he creeps into the leather-seller's shop on Fleet Street, abandoning his own parish to hear unlicensed preaching by the layman Praise-God Barbon. She sees Barbon striding down Fetter Lane sometimes, carrying his trade's tools with the air of a man who takes his soul seriously.

She writes:

Ned told Father that Mr Gouge, the godly divine at St Anne's Blackfriars, preached a broadside against covetousness. Sam tried to kick him under the table, but he repeated Mr Gouge's thunderings.

'An immoderate getting is when men spend their wit, pains, and time in getting the goods of this world, and rather than fail, lose their meal's meat, and sleep, and other refreshments, yea, and neglect the means of getting heavenly treasure.'

How Father thundered back. My darling Anne, you must imagine here cursing and the swearing; I should blush to write it. But if you read it back and insert an immoderate word or phrase at every third word, you will have the sense of it.

My father said: 'How can you be a merchant without being covetous? Do you have any sense of what your calling will be? If you must choose between your God and your trade, your conscience and your family's empty bellies, where will you choose?'

They have not spoken since, that I have seen, just mutter at themselves as the other passes. How Ned will stay all these years under Father's tutelage without it coming to violence, I cannot tell. His ally, my grandmother, largely keeps to her room, so Ned stands alone against my father.

Hen writes too, with deliberate lightness, of the news that Will Johnson is to live in London from the autumn, coming to the Temple to study law.

Though Ned says he wanted to stay in Oxford and survey the stars between lectures, his father, it seems, had different notions. Will was placated, Father thinks, by the notion that Astronomy and

Geometry are treated with due reverence at Gresham, although not at Oxford. In London, then, he will have more chance of meeting those who share his passions.

Hen's happiness is tempered only by her father's air of distracted worry.

Hen knows that the Exchange is a cauldron of fear and rumour. The costly Scottish wars drag on. Credit is drying up. Money slips through the City, oiled by confidence, and it is one commodity in short supply. But her father's concern seems to run deep.

'It's London, Hen,' he says, when pressed. 'I don't like the mood. The place is like a feverish colt. Twitchy. Skittish. It can smell the failed parliament still, and it's nervous.'

~ ~ ~

One night, with the first chill of autumn in the air, they gather by the fire. The Scottish army has crossed onto English soil, the king's army is in disarray, and even Chalk would rather talk in sombre tones, with the front door bolted and barred, than venture out.

To Ned, with whom he has a temporary rapprochement in the face of the Scots' threat, Challoner says: 'I am not a defender of the personal rule. Not I. But it was better for our trade than this fog of uncertainty. A failed parliament is worse than a no-parliament.'

'How bad is it, Father?'

'It is not good. The money supply is frozen. Mere scruff available on insulting terms, even for those with impeccable words.

We rely on our own books to keep us afloat. But uncertainty is no bedfellow of household spending. Orders are down. Prices stagnant or falling. The aldermen bleat like sheep and know not where to turn. Our own guild is seething with rows and worries, and the others, I'm told, fare little better. The lord mayor, well, Hen would be more of a man than him.' He reaches for his wine. 'Yet it is good for you boys to see merchandising in shadows, as well as in sunlight. It is all in the nature of huckstering. We are not holding out our caps for poor relief just yet, nor reduced to pedlary. The ship I told you of, from the Levant, is not yet worryingly late. The astrologer Penn tells me the stars are still with it. And the Scots, well, they will doubtless stay holed up in Newcastle. The crisis must break soon.'

Cheese stirs himself from making dove eyes at an indifferent Hen to say: 'I was in Whitehall today, sir, and the soldiers were buttressing the defences round the Banqueting House.'

'And there are chains on the streets at Cheapside, and they are strengthening the Tower,' adds Chalk. 'Do they really think that the Scots will come?'

Hen imagines the Scots of the pamphlets, blue-faced and ferocious, tearing up Fetter Lane.

'No, boy,' says Challoner. 'The defences are not for the Scots; they're for you.'

'Sir?'

'The Scots are not coming. But Strafford knows that there's plenty here, like our Ned, who think the Scots have the right of it in this argument, and that they should be at liberty to pray without bishops and altars.'

'As should we all,' says Ned fiercely.

'Let us fight about this no more, Ned,' says Challoner. 'The Privy Council is afraid of you, astonishing as it may seem. I should get Strafford round here, to watch you ladies lolling by this fire. That would cure his fright. But it was apprentices who stormed Laud's palace not four months ago. You can form a formidable mob when roused . . . And you, well, you boys all think yourselves men when there's violence in the offing.'

Sam says: 'You proved yourself a man when you went to fight in the Low Countries.'

'I proved myself a fool.'

Hen can tell her father is a little drunk. She knows Sam sees it too, and wants to needle tales out of the old man.

'It is manly, Father, to fight for what is right, not foolish,' says Ned.

Chalk, Cheese and Sam all nod vigorously. But, thinks Hen, you all have such different notions of what is right. Who is to judge?

Challoner says: 'So I thought when I set out to fight for the faith. Lord, what a ninny-head I was. It is right, too, Ned, and worthy of a man, to fight to keep himself whole, intact, so he can feed and care for his family.'

Hen looks at the boys, who all wear that curiously uniform face the young assume when they think their elders are talking nonsense.

'Well, boys,' says Challoner. 'If we must do this, we must. Stand up. Let's look at you.'

They stand in a line in front of him, drawing themselves up taller under his scrutiny. Cheese puffs out his chest, soldier-shape, and looks at Hen.

Challoner says: 'Cheese, you are a gambling man, I believe, though you swore to your mother you would not.'

Cheese blushes and murmurs a perfunctory denial. His chest caves inwards.

'So there are four of you. Here are the odds, as my ragtag band of Holy Protestant warriors found them when we fought the devil in the Low Countries. At least one of you will, at the first sign of a battle, piss himself and shit himself. Wars being what they are, you will not find sufficient water to wash yourself or your clothes for at least a week. So even if you survive the battle, you will lie in your own filth. When you finally peel off your putrid breeches, you will find maggots living there.

'Chalk, boy, let us say that this is your fate. Sit.'

'Sir!'

'Sit, boy.'

Chalk reluctantly sits down.

'And then there were three. At least one of you will have your guts blown out by a gun, wielded by a man who never even saw your face, and cares not in the slightest for you, or your soon-to-be-departed soul. You will be trampled on by your colleagues as you lay dying in the mud. Probably calling for your mother. Sam, sit down.'

Hen seats herself beside Sam as he sits, white-faced. She takes his hand.

'One of you will find out that you are a terrible coward. Terrified of the enemy, but terrified of your brethren more. So you will fight and hack at the enemy and be feted as a heroic soldier, while all the time the fear haunts you and the devil dances in your brain, until one day you step under an enemy axe, hoping it will cleave your addled mind in two. Which it duly does. Cheese.'

He taps Cheese on the head.

Cheese grins as he sits, but it is a forced smile, and no one believes in it. Ned stands, eyes level with his father's, waiting.

'Father,' says Hen, trying to head off whatever is to come, but he ignores her. I should stand in front of Ned, she thinks, and goes to move. But Sam grasps her arm, holding her back.

'And one of you,' says Challoner, moving towards Ned until their faces are close, 'will find something else about himself. In my experience, the one who believes himself closest to God. He will find that he likes it. He feels the battle-rage pouring into his soul like molten lead, and oh, how he loves smiting the enemy. He likes watching the light drain out of a man's eyes as he twists the pike. He likes the small grunt some men give as their soul flees. He likes to crush the faces of those he kills under his heel, just because he can. And one day, still raging from battle, he will find himself in the defeated enemy's camp, and he will feel God's fire in his loins as he forces himself into a papist witch. And the fear in her eyes makes him harder and harder, until he bursts, and he tells himself that her cries prove her guilt.'

He stops talking, and the silence echoes. Hen realizes she is clutching Sam's hand. Ned and his father stare at each other. Hen is struck by their likeness; it is there in the set of their jaws, and the high forehead. Ned is white, but controlled; their father, red and agitated. Cheese sniggers, but the rest ignore him.

'And which of the four, Father,' says Ned quietly, 'were you?' But he does not wait for an answer as he turns away and walks slowly from the room, leaving behind him a vast, solid uneasiness.

~ ~ ~

One week later, Ned moves to the Birchs' house to begin his apprenticeship again with a new master.

The house feels unconstrained and happier in his absence, yet still Hen misses him. She misses him when the new parliament is called, and there's no one in the house to argue with her father about its significance. Sam is too callow, too easily distracted; Chalk and Cheese too deferential. She misses Ned's intellectual fervour filling the house, a reheated version of William Gouge's sermon spilling out of him, as he seeks to understand by repetition. She envies him his passion.

One of the radical minister's arguments tumbles around inside her head, repeated in Ned's voice.

'What is the reason that there was so great an alteration made by the ministry of Christ and his disciples, by the apostles and others after them, indeed, by Luther, and other ministers of reformed churches? They did not preach traditions of elders like the scribes; nor men's inventions like the Roman Catholics do. They preached the pure word of God. The more purely God's word is preached, the more deeply it pierces and the more kindly it works.'

She wants to be pierced by the pure word of God. The weekly sermons at St Dunstan's, with their slow and sombre ceremonial – are they, as Ned says, merely the empty traditions of the elders? Is the altar rail, and the minister's long and tedious sermons, merely the invention of man?

The pure word of God. The phrase echoes in her mind. She begins to understand why the thoughtless chattering of Cheese and Chalk, and even Sam and her father, could grate the nerves of a man trying to hear such a thing.

At night, when Nurse has finished her tormenting rituals, Hen lies under the canopy, trying to listen in the stillness. *The more deeply it pierces, the more kindly it works.* She wants the Holy Spirit to come to her. She screws her eyes tight shut and breathes slowly in the darkness. Sometimes, she imagines the Holy Spirit pressing down on her body. It wraps round her in the darkness, and her limbs feel heavy and soft all at once. She realizes that the Holy Spirit looks disarmingly like Will Johnson, even as it covers her limbs with its presence. She lets herself feel the touch of the spirit with the shaggy dark hair and lively eyes, before pushing the vision away in shame.

It becomes a nightly ritual of her own, this quest to hear God, which she knows, but pretends not to, will end in a ghostly embrace.

And so it is with a heightened and almost unbearable embarrassment that she greets Will when he comes to visit.

She walks into the library to find him sitting with her father. She can barely look at him as they exchange formal greetings, so at odds with the whispering of the Spirit Will in her ear the night past.

She becomes acutely aware of her own limbs – their immense size and awkwardness. She is huge, gargantuan. An ungainly giant, stomping on oversized feet. She walks across the room, telling herself she lurches, wishing herself graceful. Her crimson-hot head feels as if it is lolling on her neck. Even her tongue is large and flapping; will she be able to speak, to curl her mammoth tongue round even short, familiar words?

'Hen,' says her father, looking at her curiously. 'Will has brought me a paper I wanted to borrow.'

'On Kepler,' says Will.

'Oh, Kepler,' says Hen, with an unnatural emphasis, as if the astronomer is a long-lost friend resurrected from the dead.

'Yes,' says Will brightly, to ward off the silence both can see rushing towards them.

Challoner, watching in amusement, decides to be kind.

'Come, Hen, sit. You will enjoy Will's explanation of Kepler's book. My daughter is something of a hoyden, Will. I've tried locking her up with a virginal; beating her until she dances like a lady; I've tried bribing her to embroider, even if only a kerchief, God's blood; I've tied her to a chair in the kitchen when the puddings are being prepared. But none of it answers. She breaks away and cants away in Latin, or pesters me to teach her mathematics.'

Hen shushes her father, but is pleased, when she looks at Will, to find him smiling, not recoiling. Nurse has not been shy with her prophecies of spinsterhood for the clever puss of the house.

'I am the only boy, sir, in a family of argumentative sisters. I have often thought that, given the right education, women could master much that men keep for themselves.'

'Now, Will, let's not turn radical. You'll have her ranting on the streets next. Now, boy – Kepler.'

Will shows them the book he has brought: Kepler's *The Harmony of the World*.

'Oh, Mr Challoner, how you will appreciate this book. You know already, I think, of Kepler's Rudolphine Tables, which chart the stars? This book, *The Harmony of the World*, Miss Challoner, will change the world of natural philosophy, not just guide us to the cosmos. You know, I am sure, that Copernicus placed the sun at the centre of the cosmos? Galileo's study of the celestial sciences led him to the conclusion that Copernicus was right and, as you know, proved it with the telescope.

'But Kepler, he saw that for the cosmos to be simple and elegant, there was something missing. He realized that the planets move in elliptical orbits.'

Hen interrupts, not understanding.

Will takes a pen, proffered by Challoner, and dips it into the inkpot. With a steady hand, he draws a perfect circle. 'This is what we thought. Indeed, when the ancients believed that the sun circles Earth, they too imagined perfect spheres endlessly revolving around one another. It made the mathematics ugly, though, Miss Challoner, and that was Galileo's great objection.'

He draws another circle, this time flattened out at each end. 'This, Miss Challoner, is how Kepler envisages the orbits. Now, what you have to understand is that this makes the mathematics elegant and simple. It also reasserts God's place at the heart of the cosmos.'

'How so, Will?' Challoner asks, his face rapt.

'You know, sir, that the Antichrist in Rome was disturbed by the upset to the accepted wisdom.'

'As was I, Will. If you take Earth from the centre of creation, where does that leave us as part of God's design?'

Hen nods. 'The third rock circling the sun. Why not the second, or the fourth? It traduces us.'

'And our Lord's sacrifice. Indeed, Miss Challoner. But Kepler's elliptical vision does two things. One, it allows us to predict with extraordinary accuracy the movements of the celestial beings.

We can anticipate their course across the sky. Second, none of it makes sense without the sun, this perfect ball of fire at the exact centre of the orbits, not near enough to the middle as Copernicus thought. It controls the movement of the celestial bodies and keeps them on their course. And it creates a cosmos that resonates with harmonies and symmetries. Music is harmony. Mathematics is the same. And none of the elegance and beauty that Kepler discovers makes sense without the divine touch of our Lord.'

He touches the book lying between them on the table with the same type of reverence Ned saves for the Bible.

'You cannot conceive of the beauty of the cosmos, Miss Challoner, both in what we can see with the naked eye, and in the underlying structure that men like Kepler reveal to us.'

His eyes are shining as he talks, the words tumbling out of him, and Hen is reminded again of Ned when he is caught by a theological idea. Even as the thought makes her warm to him, she is caught by a sudden envy: that Ned and Will can roam the city and have unfettered access to all that is new and exciting. She imagines them sitting in a tavern, trading ideas, surrounded by argument and liveliness. And she must sit here, waiting for the world's knowledge to come to her through them, when they can spare the time.

Just as the envy threatens to overwhelm her, Will smiles, and says: 'You will understand this passage, I am sure.'

She allows herself to be pulled back into the easy atmosphere.

Hen is sitting in the library, reading, when a tap at the window startles her. She looks up, thinking she dreamed it. Another tap. She realizes someone is throwing stones, and she opens the window. Leaning out, she can peer over the garden wall, and sees her father there in the street, an absurd boyish grin spread across his face and a huge package under his arm.

'Ha! Pudding! I knew you would be there! Let me in at the front, will you?'

'Father, what are you about?'

'I will show you soon enough, pudding, but quick now. Harmsworth should be in the cellars – I set him to count the bottles this morning. And the rest of them in the kitchen. Creep around and open the door, there's a good kitten.'

She does as he bids and opens the door. He holds a finger to his lips and jerks his head mutely, telling her to follow him. He leads the way through to the library, and she closes the door behind them, giggling with the elaborate mystery of it all.

He laughs too, and pulls her into a hug. 'Oh, you will love this, my pudding.'

'What is it, Father?'

He places the object reverentially on the table, peeling off the wrapping to reveal a long wooden chest. Inside, nestling in a velvet cushion, is a moulded wooden stand, with a round and gleaming brass ring perched at the end.

'Look. Our new microscope. I told you of them, I believe.'

'Father!'

'I know, my pud. A ship I had an interest in docked in the Pool yesterday. The factor had orders to stop, if possible, in Italy, and spend an extraordinary sum on this.'

He picks it up. 'I almost can't bear to look through it. What if it is a disappointment?'

'I'll look!' Hen reaches for it.

'You will not! Am I not the master of the house? Am I not the man? Know thy place, kitten. Now, what shall I look at? This pin slides in and out for focus, I believe. But for now, give me your hand.'

He takes it and holds it on one side of the glass lens suspended in the brass ring of the microscope.

'Well, shall I look?' he asks.

She is afraid, suddenly, as if her hand is poised to undergo some terrible ordeal.

He brings his face down to peer through the other side, moving her hand this way and that, until at last he sighs with satisfaction.

'Oh, my pudding!' he says, and raises his head from the lens to grin at her.

'Let me, please? Please.'

He proffers her the scope. Awkwardly, she holds her hand still and peers through the lens. She feels disorientated, dizzy almost. She can see her hand, but not her hand. Pink and fleshy; familiar but unfamiliar. There are whorls and patterns, undreamt of criss-crossings and deep lines laid out like streets.

'What a thing, Father,' she says, as she raises her head. 'To see something so ordinary become so extraordinary.'

'Yes. What a thing!' He laughs again, delighted with his new toy. 'To see the world entirely through a different eye! Quick, let us find leaves and bugs and hairs and crystals, and anything else you can think of. You go, I shall hide here.'

'Why hide?'

'God's lid, child. Think of Harmsworth – this would send him into madness. He is strung taut like lute string now – imagine if he knew such sorcery was in the house. Poor man, I would not see him in bedlam. Or us denounced as witches. This must be our secret, puss.'

~ ~ ~

It is a secret they share with Will at his next visit. There is something wonderful to Hen in expanding their conspiracy to include him. A sorcerer's triumvirate. He is, as she guessed he would be, transported with excitement when they show him The Object, as they now refer to it. He wriggles like an eel in his fever to try it out, and his face, when first he brings The Object to bear on a spider pinioned on the sliding focus rod, is almost comically transported.

Together they study mites, hairs and insects, rhapsodizing about the intricate detail of the infinitesimally small. She likes leaves best; the way their green sheen is revealed to be comprised of an intricate marriage of lines and patterns. She is fascinated by the chasm The Object reveals between things as they seem, and as they are.

Hen and Will talk, awed, of God's creation of the impossibly large and the impossibly small. They marvel at man's ingenuity, that his brain can conceive of these extremes and invent the tools to see them.

The Object brings into focus other wrinkles of God's great mystery. Will's dark hair falls straight down over his forehead as he looks through it. She studies him as he studies whatever they have chosen as the day's source of wonder. She knows his profile better than his full face, now. She knows the planes of it, and where the light will catch his skin. She is still unable to quite look him straight in the face. She teases herself for this quirk. Will I melt, if I look at him, or turn to salt? Will the thunderbolts rain on me? Yet still she cannot look.

~ ~ ~

The opening of the new parliament, and the existence of The Object, both combine to leave her father in a cheerier mood. The king is bound over, this time, to listen to the country's grievances; the terms of the treaty with the Scots demand it. The prospect of a resolution to the political crisis is lubricating the City's credit channels. The Exchange reverberates with a new, brash optimism. The City's swagger is seeping back, and with that comes the promise of profits.

Challoner invites Ned round for his Sunday meal. Will is there too, unusually silent. He drums out a quiet tattoo on the table, occasionally lifting his face to smile at Hen. In the seconds before she looks away, she registers yet again how she likes the way he smiles; the way his eyes crinkle and he tilts his head to one side.

Ned and his father manage to be amicable. Both approve of Charles' decision to forgo a ceremony this time, and slip into Westminster to meet the MPs. Hen watches her father's jaw clench when Ned talks of the new religious settlement this parliament could bring. He catches her eye then, and she tries to throw a mute appeal at him to be kind. He nods, almost imperceptibly, and lets the building tension deflate. Ned, in his turn, manages to last the whole meal without quoting Gouge.

The two men find, to their evident pleasure, that there is much that unites them in the discussion about the fiscal grievances. Ned nods vigorously at his father's summation of Charles' financial mismanagement, that the measures used to raise revenue during the personal rule are an abuse of royal prerogative. It is fertile ground in which to find agreement; a man would have to be mad to love ship money or the tonnage and poundage tax; a lunatic to think the king in the right in his demands for a forced loan from the City. They agree, too, that all men must hope for the removal of Strafford, the king's closest adviser. Laud's name is not mentioned; both are aware that it could spark something vicious.

Will tells them that there is talk, around the law courts, of bringing Strafford to trial. 'There is call for him to be impeached, sir,' he says to Challoner.

'On what grounds?'

'Treason. They say that in his days in charge of Ireland, he grew too close to the papists among the soldiery, and that he advised the king that the army in Ireland could be used against his opponents in England, as well as the Scots.'

'The devil,' says Ned.

'And did he?' asks Challoner.

Will shrugs. 'Does it matter?'

'How can you say that?' bursts Ned.

'Ned,' says Hen, 'Mr Johnson means it does not matter if it is true – it's just a ruse to winkle him out from under the king's protection.'

Ned looks put out at being contradicted, and she has to work at coaxing him back into a better humour. At last, it works. Ned tells them of a sermon he has read about, preached in the new parliament.

'"These are the days of shaking," said the minister. "And the shaking is universal."'

They nod, Ned and his father.

'Across the Channel, too,' says Challoner. 'Still all on fire across the Continent.'

'It is too much to expect, that such a violent wrench from Rome could settle quickly,' says Will.

'Aye, and men must fight for their faith, or they are no men at all,' says Ned.

His father looks at him, something unreadable in his eyes.

'Why do we always have to talk of fighting?' says Hen, anxiety colouring her tone. It's Will she's looking at, not her brother.

Her father's thoughtful gaze flits between the three of them.

Afterwards, when Will and Ned have set off into the darkness, Challoner takes her to one side, gripping her arm and pulling her close to him.

'Henrietta, darling child,' he says, pushing her hair back from her face. He looks full into her eyes, and she turns away, knowing what is coming.

He is merciless. 'You know Will is the son of a country parson? You know his father has a brood of children – girls at that – and no money? You know that it will take him ten years, or more, to establish himself and start to make sufficient money to keep a household? You know that Will's head is so full of stars that the law has trouble gaining any purchase? You know that I have wealth, but not enough to divert too much away from the business if Ned is to inherit a manageable concern? And then there is Sam. You know then, Henrietta, that it is impossible?'

She pulls herself away, feigning hauteur because she doesn't know how else to react. 'I do not know, Father, what you are talking about. I have done nothing to make you talk like this.'

Now, she thinks, I must flounce out, because that is what I should do. So she flounces, and Challoner watches her go, and in the empty room his usual expression of sardonic amusement is replaced by something naked and sad.

CHAPTER SIX

Summer 1641

𝓗ENRIETTA AND WILL ARE SITTING UNDER A TREE IN ST PAUL'S churchyard, watching the booksellers rush to cover their wares from the light rain, which has just sprung, unexpectedly, from a blue spring sky.

They meet here, accidentally, every Wednesday at noon – an unacknowledged custom that started as a genuine accident and is now the centrepoint of Hen's week. Twelve noon on a Wednesday is her sun, the exact mid-point round which her life orbits. She has become adept at telling herself lies of omission. It is coincidence, happenchance, that brings them both there, once a week, just as the bells ring out twelve.

Nurse knows, Hen suspects. She looks her up and down on a Wednesday morning, noticing the unusual care that Hen has taken with her dress, noting the girl's desperate attempts at nonchalance. There is the quiver of a smirk around her mouth, something more than her typical facetiousness in the way she speaks to her former charge. Yet she has not told. Is she mellowing,

Nurse, or just plotting? Hen decides to make no decision on this conundrum. Besides, the meetings are accidental, are they not?

They start the meetings with a lone browsing of books. Then she senses his presence, hovering somewhere behind her. A diffident cough, and she turns, a smile ready-formed on her face.

'Mr Johnson!' she says, as she drops into a curtsy. 'How lovely to meet you.'

Then they must discuss whatever book she is holding, which may or may not end up on her father's account. Mr Rowan, her father's bookseller, is a distracted, amiable man. He is indulgent of her learning, and if he notices Will's habitual presence, he does not register it.

After the book comes a companionable walk, strolling aimlessly around the churchyard, with a week's worth of observations and trivialities to keep the conversation light and amiable.

This time, with the rain pattering on the leaves, and a few stubborn drops falling unheeded on their heads, they talk, as everyone around them must, of the trial of Strafford. Some pretty manoeuvering by his enemies in Parliament has brought the king's favourite counsellor to the law courts, and to trial.

It is the great entertainment of the day, the slow hunting down of Strafford by the godly in the lower and upper houses. Londoners watch him writhe and turn, relishing each twist in the tale.

Treason, pronounce his many enemies with passion. The moderates query the charge in quieter voices than those that lay them. Treason? When he was obeying the explicit orders of the king?

'I saw his face, Miss Challoner, as they led him to the court. A black face. I understand why he frightened people. But he is brave and defiant.'

'Father says, and he got it from his friend close to the queen's faction, that the king is stricken with grief over it all. He twists like an eel, but every turn gets him closer to agreeing to Strafford's death.'

'Aye. But what choice does he have? The mob in the street, the Commons and sufficient peers are ranged against him.'

'He should stand by his friend and counsellor. No matter that Stafford is in the wrong, he deserves the king's protection,' says Hen.

Talking so baldly has one delicious side effect: they must whisper, and move their heads closer to one another. She watches his lips as he replies, and feels a churning warmth in her belly and loins that she does not entirely understand. It surges powerfully, and she fights it to concentrate on his words.

'Nonetheless. He still stands where he did when Parliament was called. Poor, besieged and increasingly desperate. All the world knows it is a show trial, with jumped-up charges. They plan to use an attainder to kill a man; it is scarce legal. King Pym rails against Star Chamber abuses, and he uses Parliament's prerogatives to kill a man with dubious legality. And look at you, nervous, looking over your shoulder as I say it.'

She nods, admitting her twitchiness. He puts his hand over hers, and it rests there. The fire in her belly surges again.

'My father was spat at in the street because he was heard saying as much, too loudly,' she says. 'And what next. I wonder?'

'The Lord knows.' He squeezes her hand, as if to reassure her. 'Once,' he says, 'I saw a mastiff backed into a corner by a group of boys. They had sticks and they beat him, and they thought themselves men. Until, at last, he turned and sprang. Grabbed

77

one by the throat, though he knew it would bring a shower of sticks. He had no choice.'

'My father thinks on similar lines. He says we must give the king space to be king.'

They are silent a time, neither acknowledging his hand lying lightly on hers. A raven hops up to their feet and cocks his head on one side, as if he is watching them.

Declare yourself, she thinks. Tell me. Why is your hand there? What do you want of me? Tell me, Will, my heart.

She says, her voice level: 'Father says, too, that Strafford's trial shows the danger of where we are now. On this, the MPs have pushed and pushed. If they fail now, Strafford will return, looking for vengeance. A mad bull, escaped from a net, will turn on his captors. Father worries that we are reaching that place where the reformer MPs and their friends in the City are in too deep in their pursuit of the grievances; that if they stop now, the king will find his revenge. They must tame him before they can be safe.'

'But if they carry on, he will have more to revenge when at last they do stop. Which they must. Surely.'

'Perhaps some impossible things stretch endlessly on. Or perhaps someone will die, or something will change, and what seemed hopeless will become infinitely possible.'

'Perhaps.' He turns to her, and holds her hand more tightly.

She is dizzy. This is it, she thinks. It is coming, at last, and his now familiar face turns hazy in front of her.

'Henrietta,' he says, and all the tenderness she hopes for is contained in that one word.

Suddenly, there is screaming. The raven flies away, squawking, and Will and Hen turn to face the churchyard, to find a tableau of listening. The screams are loud, insistent. Heads turn this way and that to find the source. Hen feels the panic rising in her throat like bile. Will holds her hand tightly now as they wait to see what is happening. A band of men stalk past, grim-faced and purposeful. They carry cudgels and knives, improvised weapons of all variety.

One of their number shouts the news: 'A papist plot! A papist plot! The whore of Babylon has sent the demons. The country will burn!' He roars again. 'Burn!'

His call sets up a wailing and a chattering in the courtyard. There is bustle and panic now, where before there was all ordinariness. How quickly things can fall apart, Hen thinks, as Will pulls her to her feet.

'Come,' he says. 'I will see you home.'

They find the easiest way is to follow the band as it stalks down Ludgate Hill, gathering followers like a snowball, as the men in front cry the news. 'To Westminster to defend our church! A papist plot, a papist plot! Arm yourselves.'

The ragtag band swells as men spill out of shops, grabbing whatever weapons they can find, arming themselves with shouts and warlike cries. There are men of all hue here, from the prosperous to the ragged. Following in its wake, Hen and Will are close enough to feel the excitement growing like a living thing. The crowd spreads panic as it goes, as if a lion were set loose from the Tower. People scatter in front of it; the traffic on Fleet Street pulls to the side.

'Burn the papists! Burn them! Burn! Burn! Burn! Burn!'

Hen is caught in the living crowd's embrace now. She feels her heart thump with its shout: 'Burn! Burn! Burn!'

The fire pulses in her veins, mingling with the Will-heat from earlier. She feels invincible, alive. She wants to shout with it, become one with the crowd. She opens her mouth to shout, to let the fire in her blood join the crowd's rage. As she begins her call, she turns to Will and sees his face, grim-set and scornful. It is as if he is standing steadfast on one bank of a raging river, and she is on the other, caught up in the caterwauling.

With a terrible effort she closes her mouth and wrenches herself away from it. 'Burn! Burn!' it screams around her, as if at a distance now.

Will nudges her sideways into Fetter Lane, and she sees her familiar front door. As the fire leaks out of her and the shouts recede, she feels flat, and somehow ashamed.

'Henrietta,' says Will, 'are you well?'

She shakes her head. He pulls her into the alleyway beside the house, the one where Cesario and Sebastian jump down for their nightly jaunts. He puts his arms round her and holds her, his hand stroking her hair. She realizes that he thinks she is afraid.

She pulls back to tell him otherwise, pausing as she notices how close they are, how entwined. And suddenly they are kissing; her arms wrapped round his back, his beard tickling her chin, and the fire back in her body with such a surge that she would fall if he were not holding her upright. They pull back, breathless and awed by what they have discovered.

'Oh my darling,' he murmurs. 'Oh my angel.'

And she loses herself in kissing him again. Somewhere above her she hears the scrape of a window, and she pulls away again, looking up. No one.

'I should go,' she says.

'Next Wednesday?' he asks, breaking the unwritten rule.

She raises a hand to his cheek. Decide. Now.

'Yes,' she says. 'Next Wednesday.'

~ ~ ~

Later, Hen lies in a dream-haze. She lives the day again and again, trying to sear it on her memory. She tells herself the story of their meeting, over and over. Then she tries the images without words. A series of tableaux, in each Will's face more idealized than in the last.

Challoner stalks into the room.

'Fucking buffoons,' he shouts.

'Hello, Father,' she says.

'God's blood but they should hang the lot. String 'em up, dangle 'em, and see how damned brave they are when their legs dangle in air.'

'The cutlers, Father? Your vintner?'

'No, not the damned cutlers. Oh, very funny, puss. Another damned riot. This time, would you credit it, a papist plot was apparently brewing. So they abandon their work, the lot of them, as if the City were not already mired in the shit, and march to Westminster. To break things, and shout of burning, and threaten the poor old bishops again.'

'And was there a plot?'

'Of course not. Fucking simpletons. Why does a fondness for altar rails and a Romish wife make the king a papist? Hey? Why does the existence of bishops, who are part and parcel of our church, make papists of all who are not canting, godly buffoons?

They lump us all together, Hen, like a blasted suet pudding. I think Arminius had a point, therefore I am a papist. Laud thinks the Church should be an arm of the state, and that somehow makes him suckle at the Pope's teat?'

'You do the same, Father. You lump the godly together. You tar Ned with the same brush as Praise-God Barbon, and the tub-preachers. You admit to no shades of opinion within their ranks either.'

He stops his furious pacing of the room and stares at her. 'Stop being right all the time, miss. It ain't attractive in a woman. It's priggish.'

'Sorry, Father,' she says with exaggerated meekness, and earns a laugh.

'Did you hear what Barebones Barbon called his son, Hen?'

'No,' she says, smiling in anticipation.

'The little boy, a fat little thing, all ordinariness, labours under the name If-Jesus-hadst-not-died-for-thy-sins-thou-hadst-been-damned-Barbon. His mother, I'm told, calls him Nicholas in secret.'

She laughs with him, and the first taste of a soon-to-be-familiar guilt tugs at Hen's heart. She has a secret now, from her beloved father. And she hugs that secret, and the guilt, close to her.

The year ripens, and Hen's life is punctuated by her encounters with Will. Strafford's execution, and the rumours of the king's plots with loyal militia to control Parliament, barely register with her. Instead, there are Wednesdays in the shadows of St Paul's great spire. He looks at her with angel eyes that seem to pierce her skin. Now they have declared themselves to each other, she remembers her awkwardness as if it belonged to someone else. She is light in his presence, so light it feels as if only custom and habit keep her pinioned to the floor. The merest breath of wind and she would swoop skywards with the swallows, skimming the dean's chimney, circling the spire, weightless and gleeful.

There are other meetings that summer. There is The Picnic, as Hen thinks of it afterwards. Hen, her father, Sam, Ned and Will, along with the Birch and Tompkins families, take the boat upstream to Barn Elms, baskets groaning with food and wine. They wander in the meadows by the river, and sit in the shade as the hot summer sun seeks them out through the leaves overhead. Sam and Will go to swim upriver with the Birch boys, and Hen lies on her back looking at the patterns where the green leaves interlace with the blue sky. She can hear their shouts and laughter, the sound of splashing. She tries to imagine what it must be like to peel off all her layers of sweating clothes and plunge feet first into the cool water.

She imagines Will swimming, pushing the wet hair back from his forehead, the sun glistening on his wet skin.

When the boys saunter back, bright-eyed and damp from the water, Will's eyes seek hers. Their secret is curled inside her like a spring, and she fights to keep the happiness from breaking out on her face.

Mrs Birch, red and damp from the combination of sun and bulk, supervises the laying out of the food. There are cold cuts, slivers of cheese sweating with the heat, fine-milled bread, and pastry cases filled with meat and fruit. They all sit for a minute before the blessing, savouring their wealth made edible, thanking the Lord in their hearts for lifting them above the beggars they passed on the way. There but for His grace.

Ned, her father, Tompkins and Birch talk about the quietening mood in the City, how midsummer day approaches and the tensions ratcheted up by the army plot seem quieter. They talk of trade, how their livelihood is linked to the political machinations of state, the invisible threads which link Westminster to the Exchange. How confidence and trust ease the ebb and flow of money around the City, and how quickly both can disappear.

''Tis like a spider's web,' her father says, to nodding from Ned. 'I sit in the middle, and all the links holding me there sag and spin in the wind. Some purely fiscal, some political, some a curious blend of the two. Any one breaks, and down we tumble.'

'So,' says Birch, 'your response to the crisis is dictated not by your conscience, but by your coffers?'

'Can both not be the same, sometimes? I have children, a household, apprentices, clerks to support. My money fills sails, and my linens stock shops. If I tumble, so do many others. There are already plenty starving in our city, while we sit here in the sun, drinking wine. I'd just prefer it if me and mine did not join them.'

Tompkins nods. 'Conscience is a luxury for those with full bellies.'

'Indeed,' Challoner says. 'Do you think the poor sods lining up for bread at the parish gates give a pot for where the altar rail is? Or how much the king's men steal from us in illegal taxes?'

Ned says: 'Surely, Father, there is more to conscience than self-interest? More to a man's honour than the need to fill his belly?'

'Come to me, boy, and tell me that when you've been hungry and naked.'

Hen fades their voices out, concentrating on Will's approach and the carapace of calm she is projecting.

Will flops on the grass near her. He picks a daisy and pulls its petals off, one by one. Only she knows that he is chanting in his head, 'She loves me, she loves me not.' At the last leaf, he raises his head and grins a puppyish grin, and she can't help herself from smiling back, the delight bubbling in her body.

Later, as they wander through the woods, they lag behind the party, and suddenly he pushes her against a tree and kisses her. The risk-edged kissing intoxicates her, and she wonders afterwards that no one can see its traces in her face. How could such joy not mark her body, somehow, as Cain was marked by guilt?

~ ~ ~

It is The Night of the Full Moon.

'A messenger will come to you, with a surprise,' she had told him. 'Be at the Temple gates at dusk.'

Cesario walks to the gate and sees Will standing in the shadows. She taps him on the shoulder and he turns.

'Sam,' he says.

'No.'

A linkboy passes, and she sees the shock of recognition on Will's as the torchlight falls across her face. She laughs and teases him, but it is only as another linkboy passes that she realizes he is not smiling.

Uncertain now, ugly in her boys' clothes, she stammers: 'The full moon. I thought we could see it from the roof, together, as you told me.'

He says little as they climb up the stairs to his room, out of his window and onto the roof of the Inner Temple Hall. There is a play tonight, and the sound of laughter and muffled declamations drift up the chimney with the smoke. There, hanging low over the London sky, is a huge and creamy moon. The silver clouds scud across the lightened sky, and the spires and stacks of the city glower darkly.

It is mesmerizing. Hen wants to throw up her arms and sing at the moon. She sits down, upwind of the chimney, feeling the chill of the tiles through Sam's breeches. She crosses her legs and settles to contemplate the view.

Will sits a little apart, and she senses his disapproval.

'How else could I come?' she asks.

'You ought not to have. It is not right.'

'Why?'

'What if you were caught?'

'I will not be.'

A pause. 'You are playing the whore, a little, dressed so. Like an actress, or a bawdy boy.'

'I can only be a whore if you make me one.'

God's blood, she thinks. That sounds like an invitation.

She had imagined tonight so differently. They would lie side by side, hand in hand, looking at the moon, talking of the heavens. Instead, there is this sourness, this mutual disappointment.

'I did not mean that how it sounded,' she says. 'I trusted you, Will, to come like this.'

There is only silence. She can see his face in profile, as he looks out over the darkness of the Temple gardens to where the river must be.

How little I know him, she thinks. He is a collection of things I find fascinating: his passion for the stars, his beautiful hands, the way his hair falls, his slightly crooked smile. But I do not know him, really, this boy who sits beside me.

His chin is tipped towards the sky as he looks at the heavens. His face picked out by pale moonlight is beautiful, but entirely new to her in this light.

Who is he? And if I do not know him, why am I made so tumultuous by his presence?

'I should go,' she says, no nearer to understanding.

'Not yet.' He turns to her, his face set in an expression she does not recognize, impossible to read. He shuffles closer. 'It was a shock. Seeing you like this.'

They kiss, and there is an urgency about him. His hands wander further than usual, along her legs and between her thighs, where her heavy skirts should be. She pushes them away, but the longing to respond, to lay her body open to him, is so strong, so intense, it frightens her.

'Will. No.'

'Hen, my darling.' His voice is thick, strange.

She stands up. 'I must go.'

They cannot look at each other as they return to his candle-lit room. It is as if, by abandoning her women's clothes, she has lost her armour.

Both are taut with desire, and shamed by it. They walk without touching down the stairs to the street. At the bottom, she runs off without turning.

Home through the window, and to bed, where she dreams strange, dark dreams of being pinioned to her mattress by the man in the moon.

~ ~ ~

Then there is The Wednesday After. She is nervous approaching the churchyard. Swallows swoop in her stomach. She sees him, and they greet each other stiffly. But the daylight, and the bustle of the bookstalls, and her dress, all combine to make them easier. The dark passions of their previous encounter seem unreal here; only the slight swirl of an undercurrent remains to remind her that it did happen.

They sit on their usual wall, and he makes her laugh with tales of his master – a man who manages to be both swollen by pomposity and shrivelled by pedantry.

''Tis the mark of a good lawyer, I fear.'

'You shall have to learn it, then, Will.'

'On my oath, Hen, I'm not sure I can.'

'I think you can.'

'I shall take that as an insult.'

'And so it was intended.'

'He thinks I am at the library, drowning in law. I wish my life was otherwise, Hen. I'm sure I shall be a very peculiar lawyer.'

'Yet you can't live on stars.'

'Or feed a family on moon-pie.'

They sit in silence, but it is companionable. They both know the hopelessness; why talk of it? Better to sit here, side by side in the churchyard, creating a bubble that neither the city's busy workings, nor their own impossible future, can prick.

CHAPTER SEVEN

November 1641

I N A FIELD IN HOXTON, HEN WATCHES HER FATHER RIDE PAST ON a tall grey mare. There are forty from his guild, marching in order as part of the king's triumphant procession into the city, home from Scotland.

Not much to be triumphant about, Ned crowed on the way there. The king's power is a limited thing in the north now, after the costly failures of the Scottish wars, and the godly Covenanters have the Scots' souls in hand. But Ned is there to wave on his father, not the king. Richard Challoner is a rising man. A City player. He has his health, his hair and his teeth. A man to be envied: rich and prosperous, and blessed with two hale sons and one irrelevant daughter. Today is his day of triumph, chosen from all the guild to ride with the king.

Hen, there with Sam and Ned and the apprentices, cheers loudly and waves back at their father.

Cheese shouts, 'Don't he look the part!' above the crowd's hubbub and she nods happily. She imagines Cheese's head is filled with images of himself, fat and prosperous, riding as a liveryman through cheering crowds.

Ned is smiling too. He seems happier, freed from their father's yoke. The two men are finding ways to be friendly, despite their political enmity.

'You'll be riding up there one day, Cheese, old fellow,' he says.

'Cheese!' cries Sam. 'But he's a beetle-headed halfwit.'

'So, Sam Salad-Brain, are most of those bastards riding there,' says Cheese. 'Half a wit ain't a barrier to a full wallet.'

'Money can't buy you what counts,' Ned says.

'Let's see,' says Cheese. 'Power, women, food, booze.'

'Sounds enough to me,' Chalk shouts.

Ned stifles a smile.

'Look at Gurney,' says Sam, pointing to the Lord Mayor, who carries the city's sword in a position of honour behind the Prince of Wales and in front of the Lord Chamberlain and the Earl Marshal.

'My point proven,' says Cheese. 'Look at the old goat, and the smug grin on him. And him a newly minted baron too. Why? Money. That's why.'

Chalk drapes an arm round Cheese's shoulders, and the two bellow: 'The Lord preserve King Charles!' with the rest of crowd, as the king rides past on a magnificent white charger. Behind him comes a coach carrying Henrietta Maria, the Duke of York and Princess Mary.

'The queen has aged shockingly,' Hen says to Ned. Her small, doll-like face is criss-crossed with wrinkles. An old face sitting unnaturally on a little girl's frame.

''Tis ageing paying court to the whore in Babylon,' he says grimly.

Or perhaps it is the strain of a husband under siege, Hen thinks. Poor woman. Papist or no, the pressure must be almost unendurable. They say she is more of the warrior than her husband; that the queen's influence is behind the king's perplexing oscillations between conciliation and confrontation with his enemies. When her voice is loudest, he turns to fight, standing on his royal dignity to give himself height.

Suddenly Will is standing with them, grinning. Drums are beating and cannons firing. All is noise and thunder. The artillery men rattle their muskets and shout. At the centre of the noise is Will, and he is smiling at her in the weak winter sunlight.

'I thought to see you all here,' he shouts, looking at Ned, but speaking to her.

Ned slaps him on the back and says something that Hen can't hear. Sam, though, looks at her as if to assess her reaction to Will's sudden appearance. She feels her cheeks redden, and turns to shout again to hide the confusion.

'The Lord preserve King Charles!' she shouts, her voice feeble in the tumult. Will stands next to her. And if in the crowd he presses against her, if his hand brushes hers and his thigh touches hers, who is to know it?

~ ~ ~

Richard Challoner, senior liveryman, vestry member, heir apparent to the parish place on the city council, the very definition of a London pillar, is in his library. He is surrounded by papers: seditious ones, loyal ones, ranting ones, mad ones. Petitions and demonstrations, pamphlets and newsletters, scurrilous poems and subversive ballads. All the outpouring of London's white-hot presses piled on his floor.

He looks across at Henrietta, who sits amid the piles, cross-legged and furrow-browed.

'They will burn you for a witch, pudding, if we are not careful,' he says.

'I want to help, Father.'

'It's a Herculean task, kitten. The presses are like the Hydra's head. Burn one, and another springs up. Imprison one dissenting, unlicensed scrivener and another three jump up writing pamphlets martyring the first. We shall drown in paper, pudding.'

She smiles at his vexation. Hen is entirely happy in this work. Her father, a moderate who still keeps friends on either side of the growing schism, is charged by his livery company's aldermen with scanning the output of the presses. It is a whispered commission; some of these scribblings have earned their publishers the pillory, or gaol. But the company's officers want to know what is being said, by whom, and how far the press has escaped control of the government.

Strafford is more than six months dead, condemned by the rhetoric of Oliver St John, and the king's reluctant acquiescence. He was executed at the Tower to a roar of approval that must have reached the king at Whitehall, as he lay shut in his chamber, prostrate with grief and guilt. With Parliament's victory and the blowing of the Strafford-shaped hole in the king's retinue, dissent has become a booming business. The king has been presented with petitions from the MPs, from the people and from the Lords. Some have even been written by women, and the thought makes many a crypto-Catholic compulsively cross themselves. Men have marched on Westminster in their thousands, barracking the bishops and the king's peers. A barrage of grievances is raining down upon the beleaguered monarch – in print, in person and in the snarling voice of the crowd – and there is still no sign of an end to the tumult.

Bewildered by the scale of his task, Challoner has accepted Hen's help in following the crisis as it appears in print. He covers his unease at exposing her to the endless tracts with pious chats about her duty: to him, to the Crown, to her maidenhood. She pretends to take his lectures seriously, and both are satisfied.

'Another one about the Irish. Their rebellion is the first stage in a papist plot,' she says, tossing a pamphlet into the 'Evil Irish' pile.

'Shall we be knifed in our beds, or impaled on crosses?' Challoner asks.

'Neither. The Irish are cannibals, and like nothing more than smearing a Protestant baby on bread with quince jelly.'

'It would be as funny as it should be, were people not believing it all, kitten.'

She nods, drawing another one from an unread pile beside her.

Challoner settles himself in a comfortable chair with a pamphlet calling for a march on bawdy houses. Hen knows that this exaggerated settling presages a slow, head-jerking descent into a deep nap.

'Will you sleep, Father?'

'Sleep!' he cries, all astonishment. 'Not I, pud. There is work to be done.'

Moments later, his head nods for the last time and he is gone.

Hen has grown to associate the radical rhetoric with the rattle and whistle of her sleeping father.

There are tracts about the king's demands for money, and equal wrath about Parliament's poll tax. There are diatribes against the bishops, and eloquent justifications of them. There are papist plots uncovered and Arminians condemned. There are radical sects unearthed, and independent congregations lambasted, their occasional female prophets denounced as whores.

The wild rhetoric fascinates her. Do people believe words more, when they are fixed to paper? She thinks of the papist plot that never was. Do all the printed words that talk of papist plots make those plots real? Where do words and actions meet? Is there a space where it is impossible to tell the difference?

As Parliament opened in October, a pamphlet appeared which set the city ablaze with talk and gossip. '*A damnable treason by a contagious plaster of a plague-sore, wrapt in a letter and sent to Mr Pym.*'

Inside, a dark tale of a letter to Pym, the leader of the reform party in the Commons. He opened it, and out dropped a plaster with a plague-sore stuck to it. The letter condemned Pym as a traitor and promised to kill him: '*I have sent a paper messenger to you, and if this does not touch your heart, a dagger shall, so soon as I am recovered of my plague-sore. Repent, Traytor.*'

The horror of the first reading stays with her now. The word 'plague' is a powerful one; imbued with history and horror and all a crowded city's fear.

'It isn't true, kitten,' said her father contemptuously when she showed him the tract.

'How not?'

'Pym needs a plot to rally his friends and demonize his enemies. It's nonsense. Everyone says so.'

'Everyone with reason to hate Pym.'

'Perhaps.'

But the realization that troubles Hen is that it does not matter, in effect, if the story is true or not. Those who want to believe it do; those who don't, likewise. And the story is so strong, so powerful, that it rises above truth and falsehood, to become something else. It is a heavy-shotted broadside in the war of words, in which people sift the noise to find the nuggets they already believe in.

Ambiguity in words troubles her too. The Protestation, Parliament's attempt to forge new unity, is riddled with ambiguity. Her father swore it, and Ned swore it, both with good faith. All grown men must, now it is enshrined in law. Yet if both could swear it, what use was it?

'I, Richard Challoner, do, in the presence of Almighty God, promise, vow and protest to maintain and defend, as far as lawfully I may with my life, power and estate, the true reformed Protestant religion, expressed in the doctrine of the Church of England, against all popery and popish innovations within this realm, contrary to the same doctrine, and according to the duty of my allegiance to His Majesty's royal person, honour and estate; as also the power and privileges of Parliament, the lawful rights and liberties of the subject, and every person that maketh this Protestation, in whatsoever he shall do in the lawful pursuance of the same.'

Afterwards, she said to him: 'But Father, what is, as you see it, "the true reformed Protestant religion"? What are the "power and privileges of Parliament"? You and Ned have both sworn and vowed to defend these things; yet, if I sat you both in a room for a month, you could not agree on a definition of each.'

Challoner nodded ruefully. 'I know it. We let this document give us succour, and yet . . .'

'It is meaningless.'

'Not meaningless. Desperate, perhaps.'

She stops now, remembering the conversation, and looks across at him asleep in the chair. Now he would not sign. The Protestation has become the symbol of the reformers. The 'true reformed Protestant religion' is now defined by custom and partisanship as a non-Laudian one. It is pared back and Calvinistic. The Laudians rally around the *Book of Common Prayer*, Charles' approved version of church services. The Scottish Covenanters and their English sympathizers believed the book 'emerged from the bowels of the whore of Babylon'. More commonly quoted rhetoric to add to the maelstrom.

There is a notable rise in pamphlets, bills and posters calling for 'No Bishops; No Popish Lords'. As the moderates in the Lords increasingly find themselves backed into the king's corner, the votes of the bishops in the Upper House are carrying ever greater weight. The Commons' reformist zeal is repeatedly punctured by the Lords. While the reforms are blocked by the Lords, the reformers rankle. The more strident they become, the further the moderates are pushed towards the king.

The fire burns fierce in the grate. It is bitterly cold outside, this December. Sam is upstairs, sleeping off last night's outing with his fellow apprentices. She heard him come in, late and stumbling. It is hard to imagine, in this cheerful room, the trouble fermenting on the streets, fuelled by the innocuous piles of paper lying across this floor. She knows her sense of peace is an illusion. In May, not long after Will first kissed her, the family sat huddled at the back of the house while the windows at the front were broken, systematically, by apprentices cheering Strafford's death. She buried her head in her father's arm and realized, for the first time and with a sickening lurch, that he could not keep her safe. That the words he used to whisper to the little Hen – 'Daddy's here. You're safe now, pudding. Safe –' were empty lies. She cried then, and he thought it was fear, and he whispered in her ear more sugar-spun empty promises as the mob bayed outside and the glass shattered.

She wishes now, on this calm winter evening, that she could keep the world at bay, draw an unbreakable line round her family. She wishes she could daub lamb's blood on the doorpost, so the Angel of Death will fly straight past.

Her father stirs and settles again, and she takes up a blanket and tucks it round his outstretched legs. The effort of flogging the business through the weakening of the City's finances is telling on him. He looks old, worn.

She picks up a tract: 'The Justification of the Independent Churches of Christ'. She notes, with a thrill, that it is written by a woman, Katherine Chidley. Chidley opens with an apology for being ill-educated and female, and yet presuming to write of the State and the Church. She lays out her argument with a beguiling simplicity. It is God who grants the right to worship and petition, not Government. The state church may be the 'King's Chappel' but it is not the 'Lord's House'. The Lord's House may be found in separatist congregations, meeting in private houses, anywhere with humble souls and open hearts.

And in those houses, thinks Hen, the women have the right to write petitions, such as this one, and even to preach.

Women have spiritual equality before God, Chidley implies. The thought is intoxicating. Hen dwells on it, turning the proposition over in her mind. She can understand why such a notion would be viewed with fear and suspicion. But is it not true, she asks herself, that the simplest, truest ideas are the ones that make their opponents most afraid?

The door opens, and her grandmother walks in. It is a rare occurrence to see her here, and Hen jumps to her feet. She can see Nurse hovering behind her, and a sudden dread takes hold of her.

Grandmother surveys the scene. Hen is dishevelled, ink spattering her like mud; Challoner is snoring, surrounded by papers piled high on each other in precarious stacks. Grandmother holds out her hand and Hen places the Chidley pamphlet in it. Grandmother reads the cover.

'Henrietta, this is by a woman.'

'Yes.'

Grandmother's fist clenches round the paper, scrunching it tight.

'Christ have mercy on us.'

'But you would like what she says, Grandmother. That the state can have no monopoly on conscience.'

'Henrietta, she is a *woman*.' The word, loud and fierce, brings Challoner spluttering to wakefulness.

'Hey, hey,' he cries, as he sees Henrietta's face, flushed and defiant, facing her grandmother's tight-lipped rage.

'Richard. This is your work. I come here to find my granddaughter, my daughter's daughter, reading this *filth*, corrupting her young mind with this *nonsense*.'

It is an age since Henrietta has seen Grandmother roused to anger. There is terrifying power in one so small, yet so filled with righteousness.

'Come now. Henrietta is sensible enough.'

'For what, pray? To do your work? To read this madwoman's ravings? There are women preaching in this city as we stand here, defying the Lord and their place in the world to stand like harlots in rooms full of men, letting the whore of Babylon enter them. Is that what you want for your daughter? To be the devil's handmaiden? Is that what you want?'

The spittle flies from her furious mouth. 'The devil is at work in this house. The devil. And he is tempting my Henrietta, my child, with your connivance, you vile, drink-soaked, pox-riddled fool!'

She grips the table as if the force of her anger, and the shock of her language, will overwhelm her. Hen and her father stand speechless in the onslaught. They look at each other helplessly.

'And you brought that boy into this house! That creeping boy who talks of nothing but stars, as if he can question the Lord's creation. As if there cannot be perfection without understanding. As if it is not enough to know that His ways are perfect and beyond our reach. Idiot boy. You know, I suppose that the girl meets him in secret?'

Oh Lord, thinks Hen, as she sees her father's face change. Oh Lord, help me.

CHAPTER EIGHT

$\mathcal{T}$HE CRUNCH AND THUNDER OF THE CARRIAGE AND HOOVES brings the family to the door, where they peer into the darkness trying to make out their visitors. Calls this late bring bad news: reasons to be fearful. Out here, by this isolated house under a vast winter sky, the horses' laboured breath and their hooves raking the stones echo in the silence. Their breath billows in moonlit clouds. There is a shriek, suddenly, as Hen steps down, and Anne darts out from behind the bulky form of her father to give her cousin a tumultuous welcome.

They embrace, and Hen fights hard not to cry again.

'Many apologies, Aunt Martha, Uncle Robert, for coming unexpectedly like this,' she says, Anne's arm round her waist. 'This is Mrs Wainwright, who was, is, my nurse,' she says over the questions they all fire at her, from the little ones up.

Nurse drops into a fat bob of greeting.

They are ushered through into the hall. Anne looks into her face in the light of the fire.

'Hen! What has happened?'

'Am I that haggard, honey? No one is dead, nor ill,' she says, to allay the fears manifested in the anxious faces surrounding her.

She hands over the letter to Robert Challoner.

'I would explain, sir, but it would be better, I think, from my father.'

He takes the letter. 'I will read it directly,' he says. 'Martha, find our travellers some food.'

They are taken into the kitchen, fussed over, and fed bread and cheese. Warm spiced wine appears. Hen endeavours to tell Anne with her eyes alone that the bedroom will serve as her confessional. But Anne fails to pick this up, and pesters her with questions, which Hen wearily bats away.

'Miss Henrietta, the poor lamb, is in trouble with her father,' says Nurse, all tender solicitude. 'Not her fault, but that boy's, I told the master, but he was in too much of a rage to pay me any heed.'

Hen thinks about contesting the version of events, but finds that she can't be bothered. The faces around her are set in a masque, and a tediously predictable one at that: Martha all thin-lipped Disapproval; Anne all wide-eyed Enthusiasm, and the cook all Anger, on whose behalf Hen can't quite make out. And all the while, Nurse's fat face in the corner, dwelling on the triumph of her timing.

Hen just wants to be alone. Before her uncle comes back from his study, she escapes upstairs, pleading exhaustion from the journey. Anne comes with her, simmering with questions. Was it Will? What happened? Will there be fighting? What happens now? Hen stammers out some unsatisfactory answers, aware that she is disappointing her cousin. This is a moment of high drama, the disgraced cousin arriving from London in the middle of the night, and Hen knows she is failing to play her part. Her aunt expects contrition, and her cousin high melodrama and romantic gestures; and all Hen can provide is taciturn stonewalling.

~ ~ ~

The discord between the cousins is tangible when they wake up, and remains so in the days that pass. Hen cannot shake off her misery, and she finds Anne's eagerness to share in the drama wearing. She pines for her house, and her library, and Will, of course. But most of all she misses her father's good opinion.

'It's not the loving I mind,' he had said, bundling her into the carriage. 'I mind the lying.'

This house, which the year before had seemed such a paradise, seems now to be a prison. With short days and long nights to fill, and dismal dirty weather keeping them indoors, the walls begin to press in. Oxford is just over the horizon, close enough for her uncle to trot over on his horse for a day's business. Yet out here, they can scarcely see another house.

She feels isolated and trapped. She misses her pamphlets and petitions, the sense of all the tumult of political London piling on her floor to be dissected and discussed. As the first Wednesday of her exile arrives, she awakes almost crushed by the weight of her misery. Does Will know she is not coming? Will he sit in the courtyard anyway, just hoping? She lies in bed, dreaming of how the day could have been and thinking of how the day will be. She will go downstairs for breakfast to find Martha and Robert not talking, with the littleys gabbling in the space their parents leave, and Anne irritably shushing them. Martha is pregnant again – she looks tired, worn. She is more irascible than ever.

After breakfast, Hen will ask her uncle for permission to use his library, as she does every day, only to be told, every day, that he believes unfettered reading is bad for female minds. He will leave the last half of the sentence unformed: look how you turned out. But they will both stand looking at each other for as long as the phrase would take to be spoken aloud.

So, somehow, she will fill the long morning. Embroidery, perhaps. At least when the needle pokes into her thumb, she feels something. She will hear, she knows, laughter from the corner, where Nurse and Aunt Martha sit plying needles. They have found an unexpected sympathy with each other; an answering sourness in each other's soul, Hen thinks.

Perhaps, if the rain lets up, they will go gathering winter greenery, for Christmas approaches and the house remains undecked. At least that would be a form of escape, particularly if she can lose herself from the others, and find some space to be alone.

Dinner will come, and a picking over of the lives of neighbours, which substitutes for conversation here. How Mr Such-and-Such is promised to the daughter of Mr So-and-So, yet the fathers are falling out over the king's cause. Or how young Fellow-me-lad, you know, him with the ginger hair and the nose like a parsnip, wants to go and be a soldier, yet his father would prefer him to be a parson. A parson!

Hen, who has not met the neighbours, and cares even less about their calling than the secrets of their hearts, will be silent as she eats, knowing that she casts a pall on the table and not caring. The afternoon and evening will stretch ahead, interminable.

Murdering time slowly until bread, cheese and a posset signal bed, and at least the comfort of silence and dreams.

Hen turns over into her blanket, and imagines standing under a kissing bush with Will, his hand cupping her cheek, and the frost turning his nose a comic red.

She will have to get up soon and face it, the unbelievable, unbearable boredom. She feels like her limbs are atrophying, stuck inside here. Perhaps, she thinks, hell is not fire as we are taught, but an eternity spent sitting in a cold, whitewashed room, with nothing to read and the same conversations about strangers' tedious lives playing again and again.

Eventually she rises, and the day plays out as she thought it would, and it is only by pushing her nails deep into her palms that she can stop herself crying out at dinner: 'Shut up! Shut up! Shut up!'

~ ~ ~

Christmas comes, and Hen forces herself to be jovial. She is aided, in part, by the arrival of Mathew, her cousin, home from his master's lodgings in Oxford. He is Ned's age, some three years older than Henrietta, and apprenticed to a wine merchant. Mathew acts like a boy liberated from confinement, all jests and merriment. He is cosseted by Martha, softer than Hen has ever seen her, and followed around by the adoring littleys.

Hen finds that the sunnier she pretends to be, the sunnier she feels. Anne is less cloying too, with Mathew around, and they recover some of their old intimacy. On Christmas Eve, the family gathers in the hall, wrapped and muffled against the cold. Robert holds a bowl of cider, spiked with toast, and they process with mock formality out to the orchard to wassail the apple trees. Robert places toast on the branches of the trees, and pours the cider into the roots, while Mathew sings a song with such exaggerated lack of melody that Hen finds herself laughing along with the others.

She feels cheerier for the laughter, and grateful to Mathew. Back in the house, warm spiced cider brings the colour to their cheeks. Her head aswim, Hen excuses herself to find the pot. In the hall, Mathew accosts her under the kissing bush, grabbing at her arm.

'Now, cuz, a kiss,' he says.

She laughs. 'Not if there were a hundred bushes. Kiss Anne.'

'Can you make a fellow kiss his own sister at Christmas?'

'One on the cheek, then, for the season's sake.'

He pulls her in and kisses her on the cheek – a great, boozy smack.

'Now another, and this on the lips, cuz.'

'No, Mathew, one is your limit.'

She tries to pull away, but he grips her arm tighter.

'Mathew, let go. You're hurting me.'

'A kiss, a kiss! My kingdom for a kiss!' He uses his comic song voice again, but this time, Hen does not smile.

'So serious, cuz. Shall I take my kiss, then?'

'No!' she says as he leans into her and presses his lips to hers. She bites down on his lip, and he pulls back, letting go of her arm and swearing.

'You pulled blood,' he says, wiping it from his lip and looking down at his reddened palm, astonished.

'You deserved it.' Hen is trembling, rage and fright strangely mingling.

'I heard tell you weren't so damn choosy about who kissed you in London.'

She runs up the stairs, chased by the sound of carols.

28 December 1641

Darling Hen,

You will be delighted to know I am in disgrace as much as you. We have always shared, you and I, and I thought it only fair that I should have Grandmother bleating at me, and Father furious with me, and the house all in a bedlam-taking and your Sam the villain.

For, you see, I slipped out with the 'prentice boys, and joined the riots in Westminster. And great fun it was, Hen, though if I see you in company with Father, I shall play the Contrite Sinner and claim it was ruffians and madmen setting themselves up in opposition to the king's choice of Lunsford as lieutenant of the Tower.

See, the word went round the taverns and the tabernacles alike that Lunsford, a notorious scoundrel, was in league with the French, and meant to storm our city, placing the whore of Rome as master of our souls. The Commons agreed with us that Lunsford must be removed from his post, before he could set London to flames with his popery, but the MPs' attempts to rid London of his popish plottery were foiled by the bishops and the king's peers, who voted down the MPs' good intentions.

We, not standing for that, rose up and marched to Westminster. 'No bishops!' we shouted. 'No popish lords!' It got a bit rough then, Hen, and they do say the Archbishop of York had his gown torn, and was only saved by Captain David Hyde, a fierce fellow of the Northern Armies, who called us 'Roundheads'. Was the first time I heard the term, Hen, but 'tis everywhere used against us now, just as we call Hyde and his like 'Cavaliers'. We sling them about, Hen, but no one knows who coined the terms. Nonetheless, I shall count myself a Roundhead and proud, by the Lord's blessing. Some take against being called Roundhead, Hen, but I and some of my fellows have cropped our hair even closer about the ears, to better earn the name. Father didn't like it – he's growing his down about his ears. With such things we are known now, hey, Hen?

So, Chalk was with me, arm to arm in the throng, and Robert Birch, though not his brother Tom nor Cheese. Cheese claimed to love the bishops, when Chalk and I sought him out to join us. Rot. He loves his own skin too much, not theirs. Our Ned was in the crowd, I was told, though I don't think Father knows it, so play the mummer if he asks.

So, there we are, shouting and making a fine racket, when Lunsford, the man himself, arrives, leading an armed band of Cavaliers. A plot, we think! A damned papist plot, and here the evidence in front of us. Now we had no arms, Hen, and these fellows all carrying rapiers. So Chalk and I ducked and made to run, but the Cavalier sods had closed the doors behind us. We could only go further into Westminster Hall.

The Cavaliers behind us, swords aloft, we set to tearing up the floor for bats and, waving these mightily, we ran at Lunsford, and he ran away! What a splendid victory it was, Hen! My hands are torn with splinters. Noble wounds, I count them.

So then we set to searching the coaches that ran between Westminster and York House, looking for popish lords. Of all the luck, Hen, I opened one, and there, fat and furious, sat George Benyon. Benyon has been leading protests against Parliament's raising of the protection monies, but he's also been more and more at our house, of late, since you were away, talking to Father since the elections, which you missed. Do you know that Father's appointment to the Common Council was blocked? And all the elections across the city went likewise, so the moderates and the royalists have been weeded out of Council, and only the godly remain. So now, Mayor Gurney and most of the aldermen are ranged up against their own council, and every day the passions are grown more violent.

So Father found out I was there, by word of Benyon, and locked me in my room, with an arse so whipped I am writing this standing, still. He told me it was the shame of being defied in public, me on the streets, while his name is ever more linked to the portion calling for peace and unity. And while I was locked up, I could hear and see the passions swelling in the city, though Father unbent far enough to tell me Lunsford has been removed from the Tower. Praise God. Eventually he let me out, but by then all the fun had died down. Though there was a big running battle in Cheapside that night – the 'prentices ranged up to free some of their fellows arrested in the disturbances. Chalk told me as he crept in after, and I helped him hide his bloody clothes. So proud he was of his wounds, but they were paltry gashes, Hen, on my honour.

So New Year approaches, and we're all of a murther here, and missing you. There's lots been sent out of the city while the troubles rage, though, Hen. I ran into a fellow I know in the law courts,

whose friend Cesario has been exiled to the country somewhere.
How this cove raged and said he missed his friend, but felt honour-
bound to keep the pain of the parting all tucked up inside.

So, my Hen, I hope to see you as the New Year turns. I think I
am done with schooling now. How I hope Father agrees, although
he talks chuff about my rioting, and lack of responsibility, and
general ignorance, et cetera. He talks too of ending my lessons in
the ménage, but how he hopes I can pass as a gentleman without
the art of making a horse skip sideways, He alone knows.

With all my love,
Sam

She smooths down the pages to read it again. Sam's handwriting
is quick and illegible, slanting across the page in its rush to tell
the tale. She understands that for Sam, the principles matter less
than the action – the stirring of blood, the threat of danger. She
remembers how little he cared for his Greek histories, yet some
tales moved him: Alexander and Hephaistion side by side; the
Sacred Band of Thebes – the friends with interlocking shields
walking unafraid towards the enemy. Chalk makes an absurd
heroic companion, though. The thought makes her smile, and
she turns back to the letter again.

~ ~ ~

The day after the letter arrives, New Year's Day, brings her father
himself. She sees him stepping out of the coach, and her heart
flips over. She hangs back, waiting to see what happens. The last
time she saw him, he was calm and precise in his anger – a sure

danger sign that his usual irritated fury had spilled over into something more profound, more lasting.

He scans the family as they pile out of the house to greet the coach, and finds her anxious face. He holds out his arms, and she runs to him, burying herself in his cloak.

'I'm sorry, sorry. So sorry,' she says, tears choking her. She imagined this scene so many times; she would be all proud defiance and calm dignity. But now he is here, his stubble scratching her forehead and his voice in her ear, she sobs and grips onto him like a little girl.

'Shh, my pudding. Oh, my Hen,' he whispers in her ear. The family hangs back, and she senses Challoner signalling over her shoulder. 'Be composed, my pudding,' he whispers. 'We will talk later, you and I.'

~ ~ ~

Later, in the quiet hour before bed, they sit alone by the fire in the parlour.

'I have seen Will,' he says.

She nods, waiting.

'You know I like the boy, Hen. I do. But that is not enough, as I told you many months ago, if you remember.'

She looks down at her hands as they twist in her lap.

'A man has no business marrying before he can support a family, and a maid cannot play with such a youth. You do understand that, puss? Come, you have never been faulted in understanding before; you cannot start now.'

'I do understand, Father. And yet . . .' She trails off.

'I understand you too, puss, and Will, poor fellow. So, when the anger had gone, I made a trip. To see his parents.'

'Father,' she says, all shine and hope.

He holds his hands in a gesture of calm. 'Well now, pudding. I thought that with the little I can settle on you, and a nugget more on Will's allowance, perhaps, perhaps we could wriggle something out. But, and I am sorry, Henrietta, there was no deal to be struck, no contract written. His mother is in a rage with you, child, though she managed to be polite. Ensnaring her firstborn with your fancy London ways. And they are decided that he will not marry until he is a lawyer qualified, and if he does, they will cut him off. Will, being a filial cove, will not go against them.'

She lets herself cry, then, and lets him comfort and shush her.

'Hey now,' he whispers. 'Hey now. When the fever takes you, sometimes it is strong. Why do you think, kitten, that I went off to fight in the Low Countries?'

She looks up into his face.

'Yes. But I forgot her, in time, and I came back and married your mother when I was free of my apprenticeship, and all our families approved of the match. And though it didn't start with a fever, it was full of laughter and joy, and love. Before we lost her.'

Kneeling in front of him, she leans into him and he strokes her hair.

'Now promise, kitten. I have Will's pledge.'

'I promise, Father.' She knows that this vow, given in love and in a room free of anger or bitterness, must be kept. 'I will not see Will again.'

'It will fade, kitten, this pain. Trust your old fool of a father on this. It will fade. And in the meantime, we have enough to fear.' He pulls at his wine, drinking deeply.

'Oh, Hen. Darling girl, darling pudding cat. When I went to fight the papists in the Low Countries, I sailed off, all hope and bragging. Absurdly, stupidly young I was, Hen. And I climbed the main mast. It was a clear day, Hen, and the ship was steady in the water. As I climbed I looked up, as they tell you to, always up. Hand over fist and not looking down. The t'gallant masts were swung up and the royal yards were crossed. Up near the top there, Hen, the ropes that you stand on get thinner, so by the top you're curling your toes like a monkey to keep from falling.

'I paused then, at the top, and looked down. Such a long way down. At the top, though the ship was steady at the deck, the mast was rolling in great arcs, pitching and tossing. And such a fear rose in my gut that I began to shake. And I thought I would shake myself out of the ropes and fall into the sea. And I stood up there, rolling and yawing, the sea rising to meet me, then falling back, and my legs quivering and my heart hammering at my chest.'

Hen watches him as he relives the great fear. His hand is trembling, and the wine in the glass is cresting up into waves.

'And now it's like that in my head. I wanted to learn about the world, and how it worked. And then I learn that everything is arsey-versey. The earth goes round the sun. We're not the centre of the universe, little pudding cat. The stars are not fixed in the heavens, but aswim in the sky. Some men believe there are other worlds aswim up there, peopled like ours, ignorant of us as we are of them.'

Hen sits up at this, entranced by the idea. 'Would they look like us, do you think, Father?'

'Who knows, child. There's the rub. Who knows? Natural philosophy, it turns out, is not a set of rules as I thought when I left it to other, but a set of hopeful theories, brashly claimed yet each as open to error as the next. What is everything we know, compared to everything we don't know?'

'But why does it upset you so, Father? Surely that is a reason to be excited? Think of all that there is left to find out.'

He lays his cheek on the top of her head, as if to steady himself. 'A youth's view, Hen. When all the certainties are gone, what are we left with? Fear. Chaos. We sit here, you and I, and we think we're safe. But we're moving, moving, all the time, hurtling through an endless space. And we're not safe, my pudding. Not safe at all.'

CHAPTER NINE

January 1642

'**W**E ARE HOLDING OUR BREATH, PUDDING. ALL IS COMING to a head.'

'How so?'

The coach rattles towards London, and home. Nurse is staying behind to help with the little children while her aunt's confinement approaches, and Henrietta feels unbound. To home, with Nurse left behind. To streets and corridors, rooms and steps that have known Will's tread.

Her father says: 'It is time for the king to choose. He knows it. We know it.'

'Father, I am woollen-headed from country air. You banished me, remember.'

'Disobedient pudding cat. How could I forget.' He smiles, and she is relieved.

If we can laugh at it, we can be friends, she thinks.

'Here is how the land lies then,' he says, wearily. 'This much you know – there were riots against the popish lords and bishops.

The bishops, too soft and frightful to brave the mob, stayed at home, crying into their chalices. They wrote a wattle-headed protest. Parliament with no bishops is no Parliament, they bleated, so we shall not recognize it. They forgot, pudding, that Parliament with no bishops means a swing of power in the Lords. Without their vote, the king's party is outnumbered. The Commons can send bills up and get them passed once more. So they used their new power to arrest the bishops.'

'Arrest them?'

'They languish in the Tower yet. Treason, apparently.'

Henrietta sits back in her seat. This is news like a hammer blow.

'Father, take me to the starting post. Where does each party stand now?'

'Lord, if I could untangle it I would be feted as a sage. But broadly, taking God from the picture, which one can scarce do, there are three positions forming. Here is the future as the reformers see it: England as a new Venice, with a titular monarch like the Doge, and an oligarchy – Pym, St John and the godly peers, like Saye, Sele and Warwick – pulling the reins. Their king would cede control of the military and government appointments to Parliament. Ranged against them is the king's party, but it splits in two: cooperation or confrontation. Uphold the Constitution or seek retribution – these are the choices before him. Shall he be a monarch bound by a parliament that keeps him on a tight fiscal leash, yet retain the rights to choose his own counsellors, order his own church and run his own military? Or shall he take action to confound his enemies at Westminster?'

He pauses and looks at her, to make sure she understands. She nods quickly.

'But why now? Why are we holding our breaths now?'

'Because with no bishops, the reformers control Parliament again. After the elections in the City, the reformers have built power there. For two years now, since the short parliament gathered, the pendulum has swung back and forth – to the king, to his enemies and back again. From the king's triumph in November, when the initiative was his, it has swung back to his enemies. This time, the pendulum seems to be wedged tight. With Westminster and the City against him, the king must act.

'Digby, the king's adviser, has wriggled like a worm these past weeks to try to suspend Parliament, the king's sorry finances notwithstanding. All the while, Roxburgh, a meddlesome Scot, and that papist, stirring witch who bears your name, are whispering to the king. "To arms, to arms," they whisper. "Show them who is king." As I left to come to Oxford, there was a second reading of a bill to take control of the militia from King to Parliament.'

'He cannot agree to that, can he?'

'No, kitten, he cannot. A lesser man, or a bigger man, than King Charles could, perhaps. He cannot. So he finds a way out. How?'

She thinks. The coach shudders beneath her. She hears a growing clamour outside the window, and it feels like cobbles beneath the wheels. The smell, too, seeps under the canvas, rancid after her stay in the country. She puts a kerchief to her nose, swallowing against the retching. She will grow used to it again, in a few hours. Those not born to it are maddened by it, her father says.

Hen unpicks the edge of the cover and peers out. Icy rainwater runs down the canvas, onto her fingers, trickling down her arm.

Everything looks so normal. The Thames-side mansions stand stately and somewhat forlorn in the rain; liveried servants cower under overhangs; a man runs past holding his cloak over his head to fend off the rain; a couple of barefoot children stand miserably, lethargically, in a puddle, watching her watching them.

'I don't know,' she says.

'Neither does he, I fear. Neither do any of us. He tried a coup in Scotland and it left him with less power than he had before.'

'Where do you stand now, Father?' She cannot remember asking him so bluntly before.

He sits back in his seat, silent for a long minute. He looks drawn in the dark light of the coach. When he speaks, his voice is hushed, and Hen leans forward to catch his words.

'It may sound fat-witted, Hen, but I do not know any more. The king twists this way and that. He is hard to trust. He is prickly, vindictive. I dislike his way of ruling, and were he a merchant, he would have been locked up for debt long ago. He invokes ancient customs, and stands on his dignity to wrest money from us. He has shown scant respect for Parliament. Yet Parliament is asking too much, and there is the godly tinge to it all. I support the monarchy, but not the monarch. I support the fiscal grievances, but not the godly zeal. The question I have to ask is this: can my position remain tenable, or does it become so much nonsense in these modern times? Can a man sit on the fence any more, or will his arse burn with the sitting?'

What about me? Hen wonders. What do I think? She knows her opinion does not matter – what place is there for a woman's stance in what is to come? Still, she knows what she believes. That if it comes to a choice between more reform and a return to the

Laudian personal rule, she would choose Parliament. A tiny voice whispers in her heart, *Father or Ned?* Should I survey the heart on matters like this, too, she wonders, or is that womanish thinking?

She says: 'And all over the city, men like you ask themselves the same question. Can a man play both sides?'

He nods slowly. 'And now, I will be frank with you, my pudding. This is why I came to get you. You may have been safer at your aunt's. But I want you with me. I want to see your face in the mornings, and at night. Because I'm all afraid of what's ahead.'

'Should I be so?'

'You'd be a fool not to be. And you're no fool. You must talk to Sam and Ned, too. You've more sense than both together. A family must stand fast in times like these. There is a violent distemper in the body politic, my pudding. And some believe, now, that the only remedy is a blood-letting.'

~ ~ ~

Later, they are sitting by the fire, just Hen and her father, when a fierce knocking at the door shatters the peace. Hen looks up from her book, frightened. No good news travels this late. Sam and the boys are out; she is yet to see them. She pictures Sam lying broken, a blood crust on his darling face. Harmsworth, rumpled and disturbed, ushers in the visitors.

Tompkins comes first. He is grim-faced but self-important. A messenger. With him is a man Henrietta recognizes as Edmund Waller, the court poet.

'Apologies, brother, for bursting in on you,' says Tompkins. 'May I introduce Edmund Waller? Richard Challoner and Miss

Henrietta Challoner.' They bow, and she bobs back at them, aware of her rumpled, informal clothing.

Waller looks at her over his bow, appraising. She finds his gaze embarrassing.

'So, brother, we're here about the five members.'

Challoner looks blank.

'You haven't heard,' says Waller, and he looks at Tompkins, as if questioning his judgement.

'Clearly,' says Challoner, nettled. 'We returned from Oxford not one hour ago.'

'God's blood,' Waller snaps. 'Briefly, then. Earlier today, His Majesty went to the Commons, armed men at his back, and attempted to arrest five of the most pernicious scoundrels.'

'Who?'

'Pym, Hampden, Holles, Haselrige, Strode.'

'From the chamber itself?' Challoner asks.

Hen tries to sink into the background. She suspects that if they remember she is there, she will be ordered from the room. She watches Tompkins nod in answer to the question, and watches the slow dawning of the weight of the news on her father's face.

'Against all traditions of parliamentary privilege?' Challoner enquires.

'They lost their right to that when they attacked their master.' She starts at the vehemence in Waller's voice.

She tries to remember what she knows of him. An MP, as well as a poet. She knows his verse, of course. She likes it, even though it is heavy on panegyric. His love poetry is forced and formulaic; but no one can doubt its elegance. A moderate critic when Parliament opened, severe on the fiscal abuses of the personal rule. Cousin to John Hampden, the ship money hero. He must be one of those who have turned monarchist now Parliament has become rabid, she speculates.

'And did His Majesty succeed?'

'No,' Waller says. 'They fled like rats from a ship.'

'They were tipped off.'

'How?'

A shrug.

Tompkins says: 'The king demanded to know where they were. The Speaker, William Lenthall, replied.'

Tompkins draws himself up. This is clearly a moment of great drama.

Waller jumps in, and Tompkins deflates. 'He said: "May it please Your Majesty, I have neither eyes to see nor tongue to speak in this place but as this House is pleased to direct me, whose servant I am here".'

Hen's father whistles, as Tompkins says, too loudly: 'Exactly that.'

'How brave!' says Hen, not meaning to speak.

The three turn to her, reminded of her presence.

'Challoner,' says Waller. 'Is this proper for soft feminine ears? I do not want to frighten the charming young lady.'

He bows.

'She's in the right, though,' says Challoner, ignoring him. 'Brave.'

'Insolent!' says Tompkins.

'Perhaps both,' Challoner says.

Waller interrupts. 'The rats are skulking in the City. Tomorrow, the king will come to the Guildhall to talk to the council, and retrieve the rats.'

'We are heading to the City to the king's friends,' says Tompkins. 'To persuade the moderates of the benefits of loyalty to the king in this matter. Your house is one of the first. Can we persuade you out to talk to some of the aldermen of your company?'

Hen's father looks at her now, and she remembers the conversation in the coach. He must make his mind up. The time has come, too soon. Oh, too soon!

Waller and Tompkins look at him, heads cocked, eyebrows raised. The silence stretches too long. A log falls from the fire and sizzles in the grate.

Her father looks across at her once more, and smiles. Then he turns to Tompkins and Waller, and he says: 'Of course, gentlemen. Excuse me, while I dress suitably for the jaunt. Henrietta, chase Harmsworth. Wine for our guests.'

They leave the room together, leaving Tompkins visibly pleased with his judgement in coming to the house, and Waller all impatience to be off.

In the hall, Challoner takes hold of Hen, kisses her cheek and whispers: 'So, my pudding, it begins.'

PART TWO

CHAPTER TEN

October 1642

*N*ED WAKES. LORD, HE IS COLD. WHERE AM I? HE WONDERS. Suspended in ice. His eyes come into focus. The moon, that's the moon. Crescent and new; high in the sky. Why so cold?

Sensation creeps back into his body as he comes to, and with it comes the shivering. He trembles and shakes uncontrollably. It can't be hell. Too cold. Besides, the moon is there, and surely there's no moon in hell? Stiff and trembling, he propels himself upright. Bonfires dance in his head, and he cries out with the pain. He reaches up to his scalp and finds a lump. Dried blood. He's hurt. Why? How?

He sits upright, knees drawn up to his chin. He realizes that he is naked. His skin is pocked with goose pimples, and all the hair on his body stands stiffly to attention. His head is throbbing unbearably, and the relentless chattering of his teeth makes the pain worse. Sleepy. That's it. His head drops down to his chest. If he sleeps, perhaps he will wake up in his own bedroom under the eaves at the Birchs' house. He will wake, as usual with the oystercatcher's morning call. 'Fresh, fresh! Oyster! Oyster!'

What is he sitting on? Mud, cold mud. It squelches as he shifts his buttocks. Cold.

Father. Where are you? Did I say that aloud? he wonders. Which father did he mean, anyway? The celestial one? Or the one with the skin and the blood, and the nose running to redness, and the laugh that used to make him giggle until it began to grate. Where are you, Father?

Don't sleep. If you do, you won't wake. Ned, Ned. Wake up, you fool. He jerks his head upright.

Where are you? In a field. *Why are you here?* Don't know. *Where are your clothes?*

'Hello!' he shouts, or tries to, in a voice that cracks and bends. His ears are ringing, and he can hear his voice inside his head only. Am I deaf? he wonders dispassionately.

Cold. Silence. There are strange, dark shapes in this field. It is lumpy. Why? He squints. I can't stay here, he thinks. He rocks forward until he is on all fours. The mud oozes, wet and icy between his fingers. Crawling, he draws closer to one of the lumps.

'Lord save me!' he cries, recoiling. A man. Or a thing that was once a man. His face is gone, just pulp. Naked, too. His body strangely whole and perfect. Just still and blue-grey in the darkness.

Ned closes his eyes. Shuts the thing out.

He crawls backwards, away from the thing. His feet brush something. Cold flesh. Oh Lord, oh Lord. Another one. He turns to look at it. This time, a serene and unblemished face, but a body ripped almost in two. The guts spill out onto the wet mud. The smell. That's it. Like the butchers' yard at Smithfield. If I could swap their heads, they would make one whole person, he thinks.

All the lumps in this field, are they the same? They stretch away into the darkness. Some big mounds, some smaller, lonely shapes.

I am naked in a field of corpses, thinks Ned, with a strange detachment. I am naked in a field of corpses.

Think. Why am I here? Witchcraft? Devilry?

Where is my father? When did I see him last? An age ago. On the banks of the river. The five MPs returning in triumph down the river, from the City to Westminster, after the king failed to catch them. Cheering, bonfires. The king fled London. Gone north.

That's right. I was cheering, happy. Arms linked with Oliver Chettle, the lawyer. Good fellow. Not one with Christ, but sound. Shouting for Parliament and for the true faith. Then I turned and there was Father. He stood looking at me, I remember now. Sam told me the old man had been to the Guildhall to rally support for the king when he'd come after the MPs. And they'd failed, the king and my father. The king chased out with cries of 'Privilege, privilege'. And now the king gone and the City divided, and we stood there, and we knew we were on opposite sides of a torrent. I was all triumph, then I saw his face. Oh, my father.

I'm naked in a field of corpses, Ned tells himself. By rights, I should think of my mother. But I can't remember her face. I can remember a presence, a great love. I could call that feeling Mother. But it was always him there. He danced with me on his shoulders. When was that? On Twelfth Night. A room with a guitar and lute, and smiling faces, and me jigging on my father's shoulders, and he turning round and round in circles.

127

He chased me in a wood. And I hid behind a tree, and wanted to be found. He pretended to be a bear, growling at me. Where? He kissed me, and told me I'd grow up to be a hero, and now here I am, naked in a field of corpses.

Ned thinks of his father standing there in the middle of a delirious crowd on the North Bank. Open-throated roaring; copies of the Protestation everywhere. Fluttering from the bands in men's hats. Posters and bills proclaimed the MPs' escape from a tyrannical king. The MPs, themselves, sailed down the Thames on gilded barges. Pym, at the fore, standing at the prow of the barge, waving at the crowd.

'The barge he sat on was of burnished gold,' shouted Chettle, and Ned smiled.

Ned remembers how the joy curdled when he saw the look of untouchable misery on his father's normally sunny face. At least, thinks Ned, I did not deny him. Like Peter as the cock crowed. Although I thought of it, God judge me. Thought to turn my back on him. Afraid of Chettle's scorn.

He shivers again. Cold. I have never been so cold. Can a body become frost? When does the blood freeze? Will would know.

How strange it was, at the last, Ned thinks. After all the wrangling, all the fighting, you would have thought we would shout at each other.

Instead, they walked towards each other, wordless, and hugged tightly. The talking done. They clasped each other. Ned realized he was the taller, as his father whispered in his ear: 'Oh, my boy. My Neddy. Be safe. God watch you.'

Then he walked away, and Ned watched his scarlet back disappearing through a sea of dun-clad godly revellers.

God watch you, he said. Is he watching me? Ned wonders. He tries to remember what his father smells like, but all he can smell is the entrails of the boy lying beside him. The smell catches in his throat, picks its way into his skin through the goose pimples. He tries to imagine himself curled up in the warmth of his father's arms, but the make-believe slides off his icy skin.

Then what? Why am I here? Ned asks the moon. I volunteered. That's it. Chettle made Adviser to the Committee for Public Safety, and Pym in charge. The king went riding around the country, securing munitions. He issued a call to arms, and Pym's committee the same. I went to the Guildhall with Chalk, and we signed up for Denzil Holles' regiment. They gave me a red coat. Where is it? My red coat? No money to keep a horse for the cavalry. So Chalk and me – pikemen. Standing beside the butchers and bakers and candlestick-makers.

Old Birch, he was furious. Ned remembers his master's brick-red face shouting. 'Throw your life away,' he said. 'I care not. Soldiery: a fool's errand. Don't think I'll have you back if you break your terms.'

But Parliament had absolved the apprentices that fought of oath-breaking, and Ned walked away, head held high.

So proud we were, me and Chalk, Ned remembers. Marching up the Artillery Ground, and back down again. A summer of drills, and sleeping on cold ground. New words becoming familiar. The long pike becoming less unwieldy, and hard skin forming on soft palms.

At the centre of it all – Holles, the hero of Parliament. He spoke to Ned once. 'Well done, boy,' he said, at his pike work. When Ned was a tot, Holles was already an MP, making his name by holding the Speaker in his chair, to read out the grievances against the king. In and out of the Tower.

So there we were, thinks Ned. Boys playing at soldiers, and up and down the country small fights broke out like boils. All the country bubbling with it, both sides squaring up, till the world tilted on its axis and we all slid to this. The king raised his standard at Nottingham in August, planted it in the mud and looked about him. And it fell down – just a puff of wind and down it fell.

Ned laughs. The joke of the king's standard falling – which had the boys in fits in the summer – that joke will never grow stale. Laughing hurts his head, though, clouding it again. He struggles for lucidity, shaking his head from side to side despite the pounding pain.

There was a battle. 'Edgehill!' Ned says it aloud, triumphant in his feat of remembrance. I am at Edgehill. We are at Edgehill, me and all the corpses. A battle, then. Who won? Jesus, Lord. Maybe the godly lost. Are the corpses Roundhead or Cavalier? Hard to tell when a man's naked and turned inside out.

Taffy told Ned they strip corpses after battle, the camp scavengers. Scum. They must have thought I was dead, he thinks. I will be, unless I can find some warmth. Which way to go? Where are their lines, where ours?

Ned is shivering violently. Gingerly, he stands. His head pounds. He looks around but can see only darkness, and the lumps of the dead. Maybe he should wait until morning. *But you will freeze, Ned,* he thinks in his father's voice.

He walks to one of the piled-up mounds of bodies. He lies next to it. Closing his mouth and his eyes, holding his nose, he tugs at a lolling arm. Flailing cold bodies land on top of him. Too many; he can't breathe. He wriggles and pops his head out the top. They will keep me warm, he thinks, pushing the rising nausea back down into his belly. Still cold. But the shivering dies a little. Don't think about them. Don't look at them. Look up, at the sky.

The stars are out now. He remembers Oxford, and lying on the roof of his college with Will.

'Look there,' Will said, pointing. Up there, beyond reach of the provosts, they talked in English. It came haltingly at first, the unshackling of their tongues from Oxford's compulsory Latin. Will reeled off names that drifted into one of Ned's ears and out of the other. The old names. The English names.

'Hmm,' he said. 'It is beautiful, Will, I grant you that.'

'You can feel the workings of God, in beauty like this.'

'But where is He? Where among the stars is heaven?'

'Mysteries like that I leave to you who talk to Him. I talk to my books and my star charts.'

''Tis all the same mystery, though, Will.'

'True.'

Now Ned can't even remember which one is the North Star. Will would be appalled. It would help to know. He could follow it north. But what's there? A triumphant king, perhaps, and a gaol? Better that than dying.

If I die in this field tonight, thinks Ned, will my soul float upwards? Will I look down on this field of corpses and see my body? Or does it work differently, in ways our brains cannot comprehend? Will says that sometimes the world is composed in ways which confound our common sense. We think the world is flat, because it seems so. Yet it is round, like a ball. What is the name of that Greek philosopher who first supposed that all matter is made of more than we can see? Thales of Miletus. Thought all the world was water.

Perhaps, thinks Ned, we only assume our souls float up, because that's the easiest way for us to understand it. Perhaps we break into fragments to get to heaven. Perhaps I am already halfway there. Naked in a field of corpses. Thales would recognize this as Elysium. Lord, I'm straying into blasphemous waters, he thinks. Forgive me. That's not a prayer. Why am I not praying?

I should pray for the ones I love. For my father, and for Sam and Hen. Oh, Hen.

I wrote to her, he remembers. Told her we were marching under my Lord Essex to meet the king. Poor Hen. How worried she will be. Ned pictures her at home, curled by the fire with a book. What will become of her? She can construe any Latin text you throw her way, but would crumble if left to run a kitchen. Can't see how the old man parades her. A novelty. Like the queen's dwarf. Behold! My extraordinary daughter! Hear her declaim Cicero! Be amazed as this daughter of Eve speaks in tongues! Watch as she talks of philosophy, natural and ancient! A woman!

The old man forgets what counts. What kind of wife will she make? Who would take her? Little Hen. Not so little now. Cheese looks at her with those puppy eyes. Ned smiles in the darkness at the thought. Then he remembers. Chalk. Where is he? Did he make it? Will I?

What then? wonders Ned. Think. Why am I here? We marched and marched. Blisters. Ned runs one freezing toe over his other foot and finds the telltale little lumps. I thought they were sore. Now I know what sore means, he thinks, touching his head.

Evenings round the fire, waiting for it all to begin. Who was in his mess? Chalk, yes. And Stephen Edwards, one of the countless run apprentices in the motley army, who everyone called Turnip on account of his unfortunate nose. And Taffy, the strange little Welshman. Small and tough, and scarred, though he pretends to be a novice like the rest of them. Holy Joe, who prays all day, muttering to himself. And Inky Pete, the eldest at twenty-five, a printer's boy near the end of his term, driven by godliness to quit his bishop-loving master and don the red coat of Holles' regiment.

I never had a nickname, thinks Ned. The only one without. Chalk tried to lose his. It made no sense without Cheese, yet still it stuck. Why not me?

He remembers a meal. The first skirmish of the war had just been won by Prince Rupert's cavalry. First blood to the king. The survivors of the small fight had skulked back to the camp, smeared in blood and shame. The two armies had found each other at least, and battle clearly loomed. The boys were rambunctious and pensive in turn. They couldn't strike the right mood. Ned wanted to ask Chalk if he remembered the old man's warning about battle, but not in front of the others.

'It's a relief,' said Taffy, swigging from his canvas carry, 'that it's finally here. No more talking, no more worrying. Just Cavalier blood on our pikes, and the fuckers lying in a stinking pile.'

Turnip nodded. 'No more thinking: have I chosen right? Is God with us? We've chosen. We're here.'

'Of course God is with us. Are we not fighting for his church?' Ned snaps, to nodding from Holy Joe.

'Our horse lost the first bout,' said Chalk, nervously.

133

'Never fear, Chalk,' said Turnip. 'It was a poxy skirmish. First blood to them, so they come at us with all presumption and arrogance. Then the Lord of Hosts will prove whose shoulder he sits on.'

Taffy had laid back, head on his arms, legs crossed casually. Like he was on a picnic. 'A relief, like I said, boys. A cum-rush after some bitch has been teasing you.'

Taffy was trying to wind him up, Ned knew, so he refused to rise.

Chalk was quiet, looking into the fire.

'Frightened, Chalky?'

'Plague take you, Taf,' he replied.

'Something will,' said the Welshman. 'Plague or pox. Smothered to death by giant teats is how I'd like to go. Not a bastard Cavalier if I can help it.'

Turnip laughed. 'Fat chance you'll die happy, Taf. In a ditch, I'd wager. A cuckold's knife in your back.'

Chalk poked the fire with a stick, and a shower of sparks escaped skywards.

'Why are you here, Taffy?' Ned asked bluntly. 'You do not count yourself as godly. Christ's voice is silent in you. What offended you about the king? His laws? His taxes? His abuse of Parliament privilege? Why here?'

'Why not, laddo? Fancied a rumble, and had to choose a side. Why not this one? If I'd known I'd be stuck with prigs like you, I might have chosen differently. Mind, I like getting your share of the wine.'

The regiment was full of Taffys – men with no ability or desire to articulate their choice. What Ned found unfathomable was that they did not care, the Taffys; that they had no definable cause. It was enough that life had brought them there, to this point. To wield a pike for a reason is one thing, Ned thought. Holy Joe understood that much. No shades or subtlety for Joe; he just wanted to stick his pike in some papists. But to brave death and you can't say why, like Taffy?

Ned thinks about Sam. The boy lacks conviction to go against their father. He is sitting at home, by a fire, no doubt. And I'm glad, Ned decides. Better to choose love over faith, if the one is stronger than the other. Though I wish the Lord's voice were stronger in them, my family, he thinks. Yet where is He? Where is the voice? Why have you forsaken me, oh Lord?

Ned's thoughts keep straying to his gruesome blanket, defeating attempts to drive them elsewhere. He doesn't look around him, but keeps his eyes firmly fixed on the stars. If I did look at their faces, he thinks, I would not be able to tell who is a Taffy, who is a Joe, and who is like me. Your cause dies with you. Does it make your death any more pitiable if you fought for no reason? Or perhaps – and this thought makes Ned squirm beneath his fellows – it makes not one jot of difference. Your eyes stare just the same.

Move on, Ned. Think of something else. A fire. They were billeted in a town, Ned remembers, one of many in that strange, prolonged hunt across the country for the king's army. Every day a march, and the king just over the horizon. Sam and Ned used to play tag in the fields beyond the walls; this strange marching was like a prolonged military tag. With a hefty dose of cold and misery and hunger stirred in.

A Sunday morning in this somewhere place, bright and clear, and the regiment gathered round their chaplain, Obadiah

Sedgwick. He preached with fire in his belly; his thin, pinched face suffused with the power of truth. He was deep in the meat of it. Ned stood with his mates watching, and felt an answering fervour.

Sedgwick wound himself, his voice and his tone spiralling ever upwards. 'There is not such a God-provoking sin, a God-removing sin, a church-dissolving sin, a kingdom-breaking sin as idolatry. Down with it, even to the ground. Superstition is but a bawd to gross idolatry.'

Behind Sedgwick, the church loomed. In its windows stood the coloured proofs of idolatry, the graven images of the modern, Laud-corrupted church. Inside those huge wooden doors were altar rails – set up to divide the clergy from the people.

Impossible to hear the pure word of God in a place of idolatry and popish rails. The regiment sat in Sedgwick's clenched fist, quiet and breathless. Even Taffy, next to Ned, seemed caught up in the preacher's power. Chalk, eyes wide open, stared and shuffled from foot to foot. Holy Joe, eyes closed and muttering, was repeating the words back, committing them to memory.

When Sedgwick stopped speaking and opened his fist, the soldiers flew past him towards the church. They battered at the heavy door, until it splintered into pieces. The clergy of the church sat huddled inside. Only one dared stand, and was swept aside by a fist, as the righteous men marched in. The Laudians crawled like dogs to the corner, and watched as the altar rails were ripped from their place. They watched as the stones flew through the glass images of Christ, as the icons on the wall were ripped from their settings. They watched as Taffy jumped on a pew and pissed on a statue of the Virgin, his urine running down her porcelain face like tears.

Like dogs, thinks Ned. Papist dogs.

Outside, they bundled the wooden altar rails onto a pyre, and then laid the fire. In the flicker of the flames, Ned looked at the faces of his comrades, and thought, 'These are my brothers in Christ.'

Ned remembers the joy of it, and the sense of fellowship. The opposite of loneliness. It was warm, too, near the righteous fire. How strange and abstract an idea warmth is, he thinks now. He feels like his body is suspended in ice. Chettle once told him of visiting the Earl of Warwick's mansion, and the ice cave there. They harvested the ice in winter, stored it in the cave and served it up with strawberries on sun-drenched summer lawns. It must be like this inside an ice cave, he thinks.

What is it like to be warm? Have I ever known such a thing? he wonders. He simply cannot imagine warmth. The moon is clear and severe above him; it looks cold up there. Perhaps the man in the moon does not feel the ice. The sun, he knows, is hot. What does that even mean? Hot sun. He rolls the words around in his head, but cannot grasp their meaning. Empty words.

He drifts on the iciness for a while. He pulls himself back. Think, Ned. Think. About what? The battle. That's it. The battle.

The foot soldiers were in the centre. Holles' Redcoats were stationed near the cavalry on the flanks, sitting tucked in behind the Essex Brigade. The king's army was ranged on the ridge ahead of them. Neither side stirred. Ned could hear the grumble of frightened men's unruly bowels in the silence. He was amused despite his fear: an unexpected sound to accompany the start of a holy war. Then, slowly, they rolled down the hill, and his own bowels gave an answering twitch. A terrible wave advancing towards him. The crash of the artillery; somehow louder and more vicious than the same sound on the training grounds. Then the cavalry charged at the flanks, and the panic gripped the City volunteers.

He saw Prince Rupert, he thinks, leading the right wing of the king's horse. A young face to promise death so implacably. His sword waving, his dog, Boy, prancing at his side. No true dog, that one, but a devil-sent imp. Standing crowded in the middle, they saw their flanks crumble like marchpane, and the fear in the foot regiments stank like piss and wet wool. Ned saw Holles, standing firm in the centre, urging them on, and Ned gripped his pike with shaking hands. Chalk stumbled forward beside him. The two sides came together in a clash of metal and panic. Then... Then nothing.

Ned raises his hand to touch his head, and wonders what happened to the others.

Ned thinks about Taffy, and his provocative coarseness. I am twenty years old, Ned thinks, and I am likely to die on this field. And I have never known what it is to touch a woman. He thinks of Lucy Tompkins, and her soft curls and tempting curves. If I escape this, Lord, can I visit a bawdy house? Just once, oh Lord. Cheese will take me; he knows them all. But I won't get home, he thinks, and even if I do, I cannot sin. Can I? Just once?

The devil is tempting me, Ned thinks. Like our Lord in the desert. But deserts are so very hot, and I am so cold. You didn't know how lucky you were, Lord.

Now, thinks Ned, I am a blasphemer, as well as a man desperate to sin. I am being tested and I am failing. Who am I?

He cries now, at last. In the darkness, he prays. He tries to hear God's pure voice. But there is only the sound of his own sobbing.

'Son of God, shine on me,' he says aloud. 'Shine on me.'

As if to mock him, the moon drifts behind a silver cloud.

He tries to remember the example of the martyrs, who were burnt by fire for the true faith. John Hooper, the Bishop of Worcester and Gloucester, who spent three-quarters of an hour being eaten by an inefficient fire. How did Foxe describe the end, in his book of the glorious Protestant martyrs? How Ned pored over that book as a boy, committing it to memory. Hooper bore it, until: 'having his nether parts burned and his bowels fallen out, he died as quietly as a child in its bed'.

Hooper was always Ned's favourite of Foxe's martyrs; the one he chose to play when the boys played papists and saints.

Is Master Hooper looking down on me? Ned wonders.

Now, alone and naked in the field, he whispers: '"He now reigneth as a blessed martyr in the joys of heaven prepared for the faithful in Christ before the foundations of the world; for whose constancy all Christians are bound to praise God."'

Ned adds a private, silent prayer. He wants constancy and courage now, the strength to bear this trial. Cold is better than fire, he tells himself. Hooper's face turned black, and all the fat, water and blood that fill a man's body dropped out of the scorched ends of his fingers. This trial is as nothing to his, thinks Ned. And yet, a small voice whispers mutinously in his head. And yet. I am me, and not him. And his torment is trapped in the pages of a book, and mine fills the world. All the universe is now turning on my freezing body and faltering mind. And a still smaller voice whispers: Fuck Hooper the martyr, what about me?

He sleeps a little, or at least, he thinks he does. The moon has gone without him seeing its passing, and there is a lightness at the edge of the sky. Christ's blood, but I'm cold, he thinks. Cold, cold. He's not sure he wants it to get light; he'll be able to see the faces of his companions. But if it stays dark, he'll die here. Jesus wept. Make up your mind, Ned. Light or dark, which is it?

Suddenly, he thinks, what have I done?

I stood firm for what I believed was right, I lost my family, and this is where I am. I thought I was making a choice. But was I? Unmanly to shirk the fight, manly to fight; what manner of choice is that? The past few years have seen me backing myself into a corner, so this was the only fate possible. And I thought myself my own master.

And this, he thinks, is what it means to be a man, after all. Lying naked in a field, covered in other men's corrupting flesh, waiting for a dawn I'm terrified of. And suddenly Ned, who has spent the best years of his youth disciplining himself into godly sobriety, is laughing. Alone with the naked corpses, he laughs until his ribs ache. The sun comes up, at last, streaking the sky with warm pink light.

CHAPTER ELEVEN

*I*N LONDON, THE TALE DRIBBLES BACK FROM THE BATTLE. A victory, and Prince Rupert captured, come the first reports, bringing cheering to the street. Then the news travels, from shop to shop, mouth to mouth, kitchen to kitchen. No victory, nor a loss neither. An inconclusive, fractious thing. Both sides amateurishly astonished by the horror of battle.

Birch arrives, unexpectedly, after dinner on the Sunday. The young lawyer, Oliver Chettle, is with him. The family are sitting at the table together: Sam, Hen and her father. And an empty chair where Ned should be.

They are surprised by their visitors; callers are uncommon in these times. Birch has been liberal with his money for Parliament, and if it is pragmatism rather than conviction loosening his wallet, the recipients are not asking. Challoner, meantime, twists his way around the levies where he can. The men bow stiffly to each other from across their political differences.

'We came,' says Birch, 'with news of Ned.'

Hen drops her book. Birch slowly sits down in the great chair vacated by her father. He rearranges himself just so, and seems deliberately to be drawing out the tension. Hen thinks she might fly at him, and scratch out his eyes. Pompous old bastard, just tell the punchline.

'He was at Edgehill, and is well.'

The Challoners seem to let out a collective sigh. Oliver Chettle is watching Hen, and as she puts a hand to the table to steady herself, moves forward as if to offer an arm. Sam is there first.

He pulls out a chair. 'Here, Hen,' he says, and she sinks into it.

I will not cry in front of these men, she thinks, and digs her fingernails into her palms. But Ned, Ned is safe. Thank you, Lord, thank you.

'He was injured,' says Chettle. 'A blow to the head, and deaf for a time. They say he appeared out of the morning mist, bloody and naked, and they thought him a ghost at first. But he is well, and hearing. A runner came to the committee, to bring word from my Lord Essex, and told it as a tale from the battlefield. When I heard the apparition's name, I thought to come and tell you.'

'I take it very kindly, very kindly indeed,' says Challoner. He is visibly moved, discomposed. Harmsworth enters the hall, carrying a wine jug. 'A glass of wine for you, gentlemen,' offers Challoner. 'Harmsworth, tell his grandmother that Ned is safe and well after the battle at Edgehill.'

'Indeed, sir! Very glad to hear it; they'll be in the kitchen too, if I may say so.'

'Well, well,' says Challoner, and drinks deeply, too deeply. His hand is trembling.

'He is much cosseted by his regiment, they say,' says Birch. 'In the symbolic line, it seemed, him looming out of the dawn like that. Alive when they thought he was lost.'

The wine is poured and the atmosphere seems almost convivial.

'And the battle,' says Sam. 'What course did it take?'

Poor Sam, thinks Hen. Like a hunter pulling a miserable plough in the field next to where the other thoroughbreds chase.

Chettle lines the wine glasses up like regiments on the table. 'Imagine both lines arranged so,' he says. 'Foot in the centre, cavalry on the flanks. This is Prince Rupert, devil take him. He charges, and our flank collapses, with barely a whimper. If he'd reined them back, His Majesty would be marching down Ludgate Hill this day. But the ill-disciplined whoremongers chased our fleeing boys, instead of wheeling round to take our middle. All was confusion after that. Pike met pike in the centre. Your brother's regiment, led by General Holles, held their ground, the Lord be praised. They fought until dusk, and then lay down and slept.'

He pauses.

'So no side won,' says Challoner.

Chettle inclines his head. He is rising thirty, now, the young lawyer. He exudes confidence, yet without the edge of arrogance that could spill over. Handsome, too, thinks Hen. Not Will-handsome, but comely enough. His hair curls over his collar as he nods.

'Can we not, then, gentleman,' says Challoner, 'consider this as a duel. Both sides have honourably discharged their pistols, and now we may all go home and consider ourselves friends again.'

Birch says: 'It would be a relief to return to trade as usual, but I fear it will depend on the king.'

Chettle nods. 'In confidence, I can tell you that both Houses are preparing a delegation to the king to talk terms. Essex is withdrawing to Warwick, and at present the roads to London are clear for the king's army. But His Majesty proved intransigent in the summer.'

'Parliament asked too much,' says Challoner, belligerently. 'There is little point offering a man terms he cannot accept, then blaming him for not accepting them.'

'Father,' says Hen. 'It is Sunday. Mr Birch and Mr Chettle did not come here to fight, but to comfort us with news of Ned.'

He opens his mouth as if to disagree with her, and closes it again, almost sheepish.

Chettle looks at Hen, a smile hovering.

'Wise words, Miss Challoner. Perhaps we should include you in the delegation.'

Challoner laughs. 'Send my Hen, and we'd be living in peace within the week. If anyone can cut this Gordian knot, it's my clever cat.'

Birch stirs uncomfortably. 'Not even in jest, Challoner. I was there when the women marched on Parliament last winter to deliver their peace petition. Women! In political discourse. I never thought to see the day.'

Hen opens her mouth to speak, but closes it again on catching Chettle's eye. They smile at each other, almost conspiratorially. She stands and walks to the window, overlooking the street. She looks towards the Temple. How long since I saw Will? she wonders. More than a year.

'Bad enough,' continues Birch, 'when it was the poorer, nastier sort of slattern.'

'Among the godly, there are more reports of women preachers,' says Chettle. 'Women who claim to be moved by the Spirit to speak of God.'

The glass in the window is steaming up. Hen wipes it with her sleeve and looks down into the street. She can guess who is coming next, and sure enough, St Paul's strictures thunder around the room in Birch's nasal voice.

'"Let your women keep silence in the churches, for it is not permitted unto them to speak."'

She knows they will all be nodding behind her, as men do when St Paul is invoked to remind them of their women's weaknesses. 'Wives, submit yourselves unto your own husbands, as unto the Lord,' she thinks. I am my father's property, and then my husband's; and this is how it is and always will be. I must learn to be more obedient, in my heart, as well as in my actions, she resolves, and turns back from the window.

But Lord, if you wanted me to be obedient, why did you make me so questioning?

~ ~ ~

When their visitors leave, Sam, Hen and Challoner sit together, not speaking. Glad of each other's presence.

Sam breaks the silence. 'Have you heard the ballad, Hen, that's doing the rounds?'

She shakes her head.

Sitting by the fire, their arms linked and their heads close together, Sam sings softly, following a tune of an old nursery rhyme Grandmother used to sing. Challoner sits in the chair, watching them.

Lament! And let thy tears run down,
To see the rent
Between the robe and crown.
War like a serpent has its head got in,
And will not end as soon as it did begin.

Challoner repeats the last line in a low bass. And the three of them sing the verse again, in a deep, full-throated lament that carries through the house, up to the attic where the old lady sits, alone.

~ ~ ~

Later, on this day of reckonings and foreboding, there is another visitor. The poet Edmund Waller calls on Challoner. He is silky in his greetings, and professes himself willing to wait for Challoner, who is struggling awake from an afternoon nap. Waller stands by the fire in the hall, legs apart, hands on hips. He holds himself as if acting in a masque.

'My dear Miss Challoner. More beautiful than ever.' He bows.

Hen curtsies, blushing, instantly annoyed with herself for the blush. Odious man.

He stares at her a little longer.

'Yet still so young,' he says. *'And then what wonders shall you do / Whose dawning beauty warms us so.'* He declaims his own lines, wrapping his tongue round the words with relish.

Hen debates with herself. Shall I feign ignorance, or admit to this man that I know his work? Lord grant me humility, she thinks, but not yet. She says:

'Hope waits upon the flowery prime,
And summer, though it be less gay,
Yet is not looked on as a time
Of declination and decay.
For with a full hand that does bring
All that was promised by the spring.'

The triumph curdles halfway through when she realizes how flattered it makes him, how much he is preening. But she is committed now, and limps to the finish of the stanza.

He bows again, deeper this time. 'Never have I heard my words with such pleasure, Miss Challoner.'

Hen notices something interesting now with a strange detachment. Flattery from a man is only as valuable as the man is attractive. She can see how some women would find Waller compelling: he is smooth and polished like a wax candle; he is fashionable and charming; he has fleshy lips and clear skin; and if he's running to fat, his clothes are cut well enough to hide it. But to her, his attentions are off-key. She thinks of Will's naked admiration, and of Chettle's candid smile. Perhaps, she thinks, he is just too polished by the court ways for a simpleton like me. His gaze makes her curve her shoulders to hide her breasts, and clasp her arms across her appraised body.

Her father enters now, and she is relieved to see him. She can stand a little straighter with him beside her.

'Mr Challoner, your daughter was delighting me with proof of her erudition. She is the learned one of the world, I declare.'

Challoner chuckles fondly. 'She is, she is.'

'But perhaps the young lady has business about the house.

I would talk to you alone.'

'Well.' Challoner looks embarrassed.

Hen runs over to kiss him. 'I should visit Grandmother,' she says.

As she walks out of the room and up the stairs, she feels lighter, somehow. Chettle told them earlier that Waller had been picked to join the peace delegation. A good choice, said Chettle. The reformers in Parliament trust him after his stand on ship money, even if he cannot be brought to hate the bishops. Yet the king loves a poet, and this one has spread his courtly flattery thick. He can butter both sides of a slice, that one. But, she wonders, if he's been charged with this urgent mission to the king, why is he here? What business can he possibly have with her father?

~ ~ ~

The next day, Hen is at Hyde Park Corner with Mrs Birch, helping to build one of the series of fortifications Londoners are throwing up against their advancing king. It is a peculiar thing, to build a barrier against your own king.

Hen is set to work carrying away the stones unearthed by the spades of the men. Mrs Birch decided on the Hyde Park fortifications on hearing rumours that a better class of woman would be pitching in at this fort building. Sure enough, each time Hen passes the patch of grass where Mrs Birch has spread herself most of the afternoon, she gains some new whispered intelligence.

'Look, Henrietta! Over there, Lady Middlesex and Lady Anne Waller! There, carrying the carts of soil. What a shame to get such fine linen so dirty. I don't suppose Lady Middlesex owns an old gown for such work.'

Despite the dirt and the shock of physical labour, Hen is immensely enjoying herself. There is a festive atmosphere here, on this first day of digging. Children dodge in and out of legs. Carts laden with food have been pulled up from the City to feed the workers. Somewhere a drum beats, and a small boy with a pure alto sings a simple, rhythmic song to aid the diggers.

Hen enjoys the sense of a universal purpose, and the easy fellowship that comes with a common physical goal. And then, suddenly, as twilight sinks down towards the freshly dug soil, Will is standing beside her.

'Will!'

'I saw you. I was working over there.' He points at random towards the far end of the trench.

Hen spins round, looking for Mrs Birch, but she is too far away to be seen in the gloaming.

'Will, we had word of Ned. He was at Edgehill, and hurt, but not badly.'

'Thank the Lord!' he says, and she loves him for his sincerity.

Silence, then. An awkward, lingering one.

She traces the lines of his face with her gaze, trying to capture it. His dark hair, almost black, falls over his eyes, and he pushes it back in that well-remembered gesture. There is a smudge of mud on his forehead, and he is flushed from the digging. Hen is suddenly aware that she, too, has been grubbing in the mud. What she sees in him as endearing, he could perceive as marks of a slattern. Her hair hangs in ratty tangles down her face. And still the silence lingers like an intrusive chaperone.

'I should not—' she begins.

'I must—' he says at the same time.

They laugh.

'You first.'

'You.'

'I know that it is impossible,' he says. 'I shall not see you again, I promise it.'

'But this was an accident,' says Hen. 'It doesn't count,' she adds, childishly.

He smiles, and his beauty hits her again, punches her in the stomach and catches the breath in her throat. 'No, indeed, it does not count. Oh Hen, I miss you. I miss seeing your face, and hearing you talk. I miss kissing you.'

'And I you.'

Silence, again. But this time, not awkward.

He takes her hand and they stand near each other in the half-light. She feels taller, more lithe, under his gaze.

'I had hoped that this would fade,' she says.

'But it has not.'

'No.'

'I will move to another section of the fortifications,' he says.

She clenches his hand tight.

She hears her name being called through the darkness.

'I must go.'

And she walks away.

~ ~ ~

All through that chill autumn, Hen labours at the fort when she can. She loves it; the work brings a freedom she has never known. The tiredness at the end of each day feels blessed and profound. Each morning she wakes and relishes the absence of the question: How shall I fill my day?

The fort grows higher, even as the hopes of a new peace settlement mount. She is happy. And yet, every time she reaches the new top of the fortifications, and sinks her feet into the freshly turned earth, she scans the ranks of labourers. Hoping. But Will is never there.

CHAPTER TWELVE

November 1642

'N ED CHALLONER. NED CHALLONER.'

Ned thinks he hears his name. It is a cold dawn he wakes into, and he shivers. Taffy, lying close next to him, snores with extraordinary vigour. Holy Joe is curled into the Welshman's side, sharing the one cloak the three have left between them. Ned has somehow wriggled free in the night. Must be your stink, Taf, he thinks, without rancour. He remembers – how could he forget? – another cold dawn.

Ned wakes with the soldier's lament in his belly, in his goose-pimpled flesh and in his heart. Fucking hungry, fucking cold and fucking miserable. Who'd be a soldier? But he listens to his mates' guttural breathing and it softens his morning rage. Their snoring is a loud and rattling affirmation of life.

'Ned Challoner, Ned Challoner.' It comes in a high-pitched singsong. Ned raises himself onto an elbow, and looks across the huddles of sleeping men. A boy, an irritatingly chirpy-looking boy, picks through the bodies. 'Ned Challoner.'

'Boy!' hisses Ned.

'You him?'

'Who wants to know?'

'Who's asking?

'Who is . . . Plague take you, boy. I am Ned Challoner. What do you want?'

'I've a message. From a man says he's your father.'

'Aye.' Ned's pulse quickens. He sits upright, wiping the sleep from his eyes. 'And what does he say?'

'He's here.'

'Here!' Ned, absurdly, looks around his sleeping fellows, as if his father will loom up next to them.

The boy jerks his head.

'Not *here*!' he says with scorn. 'Come, I'll take you.'

Ned nudges Taffy, who stirs from his sleep with a growl.

'Sores on your member, Ned. I was somewhere lovely.'

'Tight and wet, Taf?'

'You know me, boy.'

'Listen. My father's here. I'm going to see him.'

'Rich, your old man? Bring us back something, man.'

Ned smiles, and Taffy closes his eyes again, settling back somewhere lovely.

The boy leads Ned through the sleeping soldiers, towards the river and the road that meanders alongside it and heads into the City. Beyond the sleeping soldiers, there are units of men moving through the darkness. The trained bands on the move, coming up from London overnight to join Essex and his men, Ned guesses. Reinforcements, God be praised.

Then he smells something. Bread, by God. Freshly baked,

warm. The smell makes him almost giddy with desire. There are other smells too, drifting over the dew-soaked grass. Meat pies, he thinks, and sausages. I'm still asleep. Imagining it. Must be.

A cart trundles past, with a linkboy running alongside it. Ned can just see the outline of baskets, piled high with loaves.

'What's all this, boy?' he says, as they wait to cross the road. He fights the urge to jump face down and mouth open into a breadbasket.

'The city's alive with the coming battle. Bakers up all night, goodwives cooking by candlelight. Half the city's turned up to bring you food, or stand with you. I've come to fight.'

Ned looks sideways at the boy, who barely reaches his waist. He says nothing.

'Now,' says the boy, and they dodge between two carts. 'Here somewhere,' says the boy, peering through the crowds in the gloom. 'By this tree, he said.'

'Ned?' A tremulous voice from the darkness.

'Father.'

Lord, Lord, thank you, thinks Ned, as his father's familiar bulk becomes obvious in the half-light.

'Oh, my boy,' says Challoner. 'Your hair! And you so thin.'

Ned has forgotten how he must have changed. The surgeon shaved off all his hair when he came in from the cold at Edgehill, the better to pick the maggots out of his scalp wound. He rubs at the bristles, sheepishly. He knows he is thinner, too. The clothes, such as he has left, hang off him.

The small boy holds out his hand, and his father makes to drop some coins in the outstretched palm.

'Wait. Father, have you any food, and an extra coin?'

His father points to a basket at his feet. Ned rummages. Bread. Pies. A chicken! Cheese. He steadies himself, quelling the desire to stuff himself. He fights for control. The bread is still warm. He breaks it in half, grabs a pie, and a couple of smaller cooked birds.

'For my pals,' he says to his father.

'Of course.'

He wraps the food in cloth, and hands the parcel to the boy.

'Take these back to where you found me. The snoring man. Wake him with these and tell him the birds are poxed and his mother pissed in the bread. Do it quietly, or he'll have to share.'

Pocketing the extra money, and holding the cloth parcel, the boy dodges back across the road.

Ned turns back to his father.

'What are you doing here?'

'We had no news of you since Edgehill, and we were afraid you were victims of Prince Rupert's rout at Brentford. I came to find you.'

'And here I am.'

'And here you are.'

Ned realizes that his father is crying. He shivers, from cold touched with embarrassment.

'Sorry, Ned, I forgot. I brought this. In case.' Challoner pushes a cloak into his hands, and Ned puts it on. It is heavy, warm cloth, lined with soft lambs wool. He wraps it round himself.

'How did you know I'd need it?'

'I was a soldier too, boy, remember. Now, food. And there's ale here. Or wine, if you'd rather.'

'Ale,' says Ned.

155

They sit on the damp ground and, with the cloak heavy on his shoulders, Ned stops shivering at last.

'When we heard some of Holles' men were near the walls and the king's troops on their heels, Hen and Cook took to the kitchen.'

'Hen in the kitchen?'

He senses his father's smile in the gloom.

'All night. She said she could not sit idly by. You can tell her pies from Cook's, I fear.'

He puts one fat pie and one shrunken, misshapen thing in Ned's hands. Ned is curiously moved by the funny little one. But he puts it down, and cracks open the pastry case of Cook's pie. Still just warm, the steam rises in the cold air. It smells of meat and ale and carrots. It smells of the kitchen at home, and Cook's apron. Ned takes a moment to savour it, to enjoy the anticipation, the saliva rushing into his mouth. He bites into the meat at last. This is the greatest pleasure of my life, he thinks. Nothing will taste as fine as this again. Nothing.

His mouth full, he says: 'Tell Hen I ate hers, will you, Father, and it was delicious.'

Richard Challoner chuckles.

'We got your letter, after Edgehill,' he says, while Ned eats on. 'We knew already that you were well. Oliver Chettle came to tell us – he'd heard tales of you wandering into the camp, naked in the morning.'

Ned just nods. He's tearing the leg off the chicken now. Cook has basted its skin with honey as it turned on the spit. She knows that's how he likes it best. He licks the heavenly mixture of honey and skin from his fingers, and thinks he might faint with the joy

156

of it. Gluttony is a sin, he thinks, even as he rips a strip of meat from the bird's breast.

'He's doing well, Chettle. Rising fast. Advising the Committee of Safety on legal revenue-raising to fight this war. None of it legal, in my book...' Challoner tails off. 'I will not talk politics, Ned. I promise it. Mind, I promised it on the way here, and I've broken it already.'

Ned waves a gnawed bone at his father, as he drinks deep from the ale. The warm pie, the cloak and the hoppy hug of the ale are combining to make him almost deliriously happy. The pleasure of small things. I would not have understood that, had I not become a soldier, he thinks. His father had always understood the pleasure of small things, he realizes suddenly, and he looks across at the old man with renewed affection.

'Hen is well, but anxious,' says Challoner. 'If I find you, I'm to give you a hundred kisses. Consider them bestowed.'

Ned, his mouth full to the brim with a ripe cheese, grins, and clasps a hand to his breast.

'And Sam. Poor lad is eating his heart out to join you. Sends his love through gritted teeth.'

'Don't let him,' says Ned, spitting crumbs.

'I shall not. Is it bad?'

Ned nods. 'I was at Brentford yesterday.'

'Jesus wept. We heard of it, last night. Bad news travels on wings.'

Ned looks up at his father. 'Did you, in the Low Countries, know the thing they call the panic fear?'

'I saw it myself, once.' His father's eyes look beyond him, seeing past horrors.

They are silent, and Ned lets the food settle. A warmth spreads through his body. He wriggles his toes, glad to be whole and alive. He feels the shame moments later, alongside the gladness. The unbearable burden of surviving your friends.

'They told us, Father, when we trained. Stand together, and you'll make it. Break ranks, and you're done. A row of pikes can take a horse. A lone man with a pike? He is just a dead man running with a big stick.'

'Aye. But it's one thing to be told it, and another to stand fast,' Challoner says. 'All it takes is one or two.'

Ned nods, remembering.

It was misty, cold. Fear fluttered up, down damp skin. Numb hands gripped slender ash pikes. He stood shoulder to shoulder with his brothers, with more crouching in front and standing close behind. He could feel Holy Joe's breath hot on his neck, and the nervous yammering of Turnip's leg as it hit the back of his thigh, repeatedly. Inky Pete behind him on the other side sang a psalm to himself. He half-sang, half-whispered, so quiet Ned couldn't tell which psalm it was. He smiled to himself, briefly, thinking of Pete's relentless psalm singing. Like the oaths falling from a Cavalier.

His smile faded as quickly as it appeared. He was boxed in. Chalk to the left of him, Taffy to the right. So close that, glancing sideways, he could see the puckered ridges of Chalk's pimples. On the other side, Taf's face was immobile, but his mouth was pursed so tightly his lips had disappeared. The Welshman caught Ned's glance and winked. They all stood together, physically bunched and mentally entwined by training and loyalty and the strong desire not to be the one who cracked, who let the others down. Ned understood, then, the courage that is borne of fear; the fear of failing, of seeming a coward in the eyes of men you respect. He was still detached enough, rational enough, to enjoy the irony as if at a distance from it: that bravery is just fear worn in public view.

Tight in, together, they waited. Hands clenched and unclenched on pikes. Their breath and the heat from their bodies punched through the cold air in clouds. Like a dragon, bristling with pikes, they shuffled and breathed, waiting, listening.

Ned's stomach churned. He heard someone retching, and muffled curses. There's no room to vomit among the pikemen without hitting a brother. The sour smell mingled with the stench of frightened men. I have smelled fear, Ned thought, and it smells of shit and puke. On the wings of the five-deep pike unit, the musket men nervously checked their gear, anxious fingers jumping from barrel to match.

The mist was the worst of it. At Edgehill, Ned had known the battle blindness, as the haze of smoke hanging thickly over the battlefield destroyed all visibility. But battle had already been joined. The enemy was in front, a pike's push away.

This blind, silent waiting was worse. The pike unit twitched at rustling leaves, shuddered at cracking twigs. The scouts' shouts, which sent them running to their gear and into formation, the orders of the office, all had abated, leaving this deep and unsettling quiet.

Then came the rumbling of horses' hooves. From somewhere else came the excited yapping of a dog, like a hound on a scent. Packed in with his brothers, part of them, Ned could feel the chain sag before it broke. The few veterans spoke up. Taf to the side of him growled, 'Hold fast. Fast, you whoresons.'

A high-pitched gabbling came from behind Ned's left shoulder: 'Jesus Lord. Jesus Lord. Jesus Lord. Watch us, Lord.'

'Shut your mouth.' This came grumbled from somewhere behind Ned. His helmet was hot and heavy, and the sweat ran down to catch the chill November air, cold on his cheeks.

'Jesus. Oh my Lord.'

'He can't hear you, boy.'

'Them fucking Cavaliers can, though.'

A laugh, and the unit stood firmer. Ned held his pike so tight he imagined his fingers freezing in that position, claw-like.

Inky Pete's psalm tumbled out, fast and louder: "'For the Lord knoweth the way of the righteous: but the way of the ungodly shall perish.'"

'The ungodly shall perish. They shall perish,' Ned muttered under his breath, and still the rumbling grew, and Ned could feel the tremor of it beneath his feet. He forced himself to listen to his brain, even as his legs twitched with the urge to run.

Stand, you fool. Cavalry can't break pike. Cavalry can't break pike. Can't break pike.

The end of his pike was jammed against his left shoe, its point angled up at horse's head height. He tried to imagine the point driving through a nag's neck, catching it on the soft underside.

He could sense his brothers caught in the same battle between brain and legs. Fear gripped the pikemen, vice-tight.

Stand fast, for Christ's sake. Fast.

Suddenly the horses broke through the mist ahead of them, nostrils flaring and hooves tearing up the turf. They came with a noise like thunder and the crack of pistol shot. A shrill screaming and, in a blink-space, the formation behind Ned collapsed. He heard Taf's urgent, fierce swearing and he found himself running, running. The fear was a demon clinging to his soul. He tried to run from it, but who can run from his own soul? The demon obliterated thought, loosened bowels, gripped his stomach and galloped on his racing heart. He let go of his pike and didn't stop to watch its fall.

Ned ran, tripping over mud, his feet scrabbling for purchase. Men were cut down either side of him, their blood raining on him and running into his eyes with his sweat, so that he could barely see. There was no reasoning left to him, no prayer; just the zigzag flight of a cornered fox. The fierce thrumming of hooves behind him pushed it on, that dumb animal trapped inside Ned's familiar, crazed body. At last, the ground gave under his feet, and he threw himself into the river. The icy water knocked the air from his lungs, punching his terrified frame into a new state of shock.

He wrestled his heavy coverlet, icy hands pulling at the straps. He turned, sensing something behind him, and looked straight into the eyes of a man on horseback, a man whose sword was drawn and pointing at Ned's throat. Ned waited, beyond even fear, at the last. Flooded with a calm emptiness. Cowed. The mute creature gazed at the Cavalier through Ned's wide eyes.

And the man cocked his head and turned away, pulling his sword back from the death stroke.

Ned's knees buckled, and the icy water reached his waist. Then suddenly, Taf's face loomed in front of him, shouting at him. Words Ned seemed to take minutes, hours to understand.

'Can't swim, Ned. Help me, Ned.'

The current pulled at his legs and he launched himself into the river as Taf grabbed onto him, clawing at his back.

Behind them the horsemen were coming, scything down the fleeing soldiers. The water was already swirling red as Ned and Taffy fell forward into the choppy waves. Taffy was panicking, pulling them both down. The shock of the cold pulled Ned back to the fore, pushing the scared beast back into its corner of his mind.

Ned struggled across the water, fighting the current and his thrashing comrade. As he pulled himself up on the far bank, only then did he master the demon. But with his returning self came a rushing shame. For what man can lose himself to the beast and not be tainted?

161

~ ~ ~

Squatting here next to his father, tummy full and wrapped in the warm cloak, the horror is receding. He plays the scene in his head, but it already feels like a tale told by someone else. He remembers how the urge to live bade him drop his friend in the icy river; how close he came to biting Taffy's arms as they wrapped round his neck, pulling tighter and tighter.

His father is looking at him with compassion, the face he has always worn for his children's grazed knees and bruised limbs. Ned fights the urge to cry like a boy.

'I looked back across the river, and it was just one great mass of bodies. You could walk across their backs. On the other side, there was Prince Rupert. I knew it was him – I could see his dog prancing at his horse's legs. The mark of Satan, that imp. No dog, but evil, dog-shaped.'

'A bad day.' Challoner shakes his head. 'It's done him no good, His Majesty. There was a peace delegation with him at Reading. And then reports came back of how Rupert's men sacked Brentford. Brutal, it was – the way they learned it in the European wars. Englishmen sacking an English town, even while the king talks of peace. So now the king's seen as too devious to trust with talk of peace, and his men are feared as demons poised to sack London.'

'Small wonder that most of the city seems to be here, in support of Lord Essex.' In the grey light, Ned can see the crowds of people; the carts and the militiamen; women and children; boys armed with kitchen knives and old men brandishing staves.

'We're better off in a crowd. Standing fast,' says Ned.

'Not always, boy. Not always.'

Ned looks down at the grass and picks a fat blade. As a boy he would have pulled it taut between two thumbs and blown on it, imagining it a war trumpet. Not so long ago, in fact.

He finds the words he's looking for. 'Father, I haven't seen Chalk. Not since Brentford.'

His father sucks in his breath.

'No hope?'

Ned shakes his head.

'Lord, I shall have to write to his parents. When this battle is done, Ned, should you like to join the cavalry? I'll settle enough on you now.'

'Thank you. I will think on it.'

They are silent a while, Ned eating slowly now. Picking at food because he can, not because he is hungry.

'I'm not much of a soldier.'

'You're lucky, Ned. Twice you've cheated death. The only good soldier is a lucky one.'

'I keep thinking about the Cavalier who held the sword to my throat. All that I am, all that I feel – he had it in his power to end it all. And yet…'

'He didn't. Be thankful. The Lord's hand was in it.'

'But Father, do you see? He had the power to kill me, and he chose not to. On a whim? Because he liked my face? Because he didn't? The randomness of it, it terrifies me. Perhaps he had a letter from his mistress, or he has a boy my age and it's his birthday. Chalk dead, me alive. A toss of a coin between us.'

Challoner puts a hand on Ned's shoulder.

'Not a coin, lad. Providence. My poor boy. Soldiering does play with a man's mind. My time in Europe brought me to Arminius.'

'How so?'

Challoner pauses before he speaks, weighing his words. Ned recognizes his father's fear of causing an argument between them here, now.

'Please tell me, Father,' he says.

'Well, then. I saw a man, one I knew, pick up a newborn baby. It mewled in that way they have, like a blasted kitten. He took it by its ankles and smashed its head against a wall. Its brains splattered – some landed here.' He points to his forehead and rubs it, as if to wipe out some ancient stain.

'I saw so many things, but that I could not forget. It made me question what I believed. If God is shaping our destinies, is He a God who guides a man's hands to crush a baby? If it is all predestined, the baby-killer could stand side by side with the saints in God's grace, while the baby sinks into damnation. I know –' he waves his hand as Ned opens his mouth to speak – 'the chosen have a responsibility to deserve God's choice. But I found the argument hollow.

'Then I read of Arminius' teachings, and it felt right for me. That man had free will. He chose to kill that baby, without God's goading. Yet, if Arminius is right, there will be a reckoning. How can there not be? He will be weighed and judged. We will be weighed and judged.'

They are silent, for a space. Ned can't think of a riposte, not now. It is all too abstract. Only his full belly, and the fear churning it into a nauseous mess, is real to him. The coming battle hovers at the edge of his mind, like a malevolent raven.

'We will have this argument for all our lives, Father,' he says.

'One of us will prove the other wrong, at the end. Pray God I find out first, my Ned.'

'I must go back.' It is fully light now. They can just make out the king's army ranged up across the flat marshy fields. All around them, the chatter of the crowd grows, and the screech of sharpening steel rings across the grass. Ned wants to stay, to rest his head in his father's lap, and wrap himself in his heavy cloak.

'I'll look for you after,' says Challoner.

'You should go home. Look to Henrietta and Sam. We might lose.' Ned smiles, as he recognizes the irony of that 'we'.

He turns, and walks back to Taffy and Holy Joe, the last of the boys who set out by his side from the Artillery Ground that summer.

~ ~ ~

In Fetter Lane, Hen paces in the hall. She feels like one of the lions in the Tower, measuring out time and space in an endless, pointless prowling. The house is echoing and empty. Sam has gone. He came to her room in the darkness, and told her he was heading out of the City to Turnham Green. She knew that with the battle so close to home, with his friends all ranged up against the king's troops, that Sam was beyond reach. So she kissed him goodbye, and waited until the door closed shut before crying.

Harmsworth has gone too; bitter, pinched Harmsworth. Perhaps he will curdle the Cavaliers to death with his sourness. Some apprentices she didn't know knocked for Cheese. He left with them, white-faced and silent. A sure beating if he didn't go, a chance of death if he did. Poor Cheese. Not all men are born heroes.

Nurse is still in Oxford, please God to stay for ever. Sally, the cook, after they finished baking, asked if she could go to her sister, whose three boys were all standing against the king. Hen kissed her and blessed her, and she bustled off into the darkness, taking little Milly, the maid, with her. Only Hen and her grandmother were left now, in the rattling old house.

Hen has heard of the sack of Brentford – who has not? She has divided the mountains of pamphlets into royalist and radical. The royalist ones are in the hall, ready to be strewn about, to prove loyalties if such a thing becomes necessary. The radical are buried in a chest in the garden, with her father's best claret, the silver plate and the jewellery her mother left her. Her father, before he left to find Ned, was downstairs in the counting house for the evening; he too buried a full chest under the hawthorn tree.

Hen walks through to the library to look out into the garden. She has scattered dead leaves over the freshly dug soil. The garden looks unkempt, but at least not suspicious. I am the only thing worth plundering now, she thinks. Like Cheese, I face fates I cannot influence.

She goes upstairs to Grandmother, who is lying in bed with the blankets pulled up to her nose.

'Will you come downstairs?' says Henrietta. 'We should be together.'

The old lady nods. When was the last time she left her room? Hen wonders. The summer? The spring, even.

At the threshold of her room, the old lady clings to Hen. With huge frightened eyes, she croaks: 'I can't, can't.'

'Why not? Come, Grandmother. What could happen? Just the stairs.'

But there is a frenzied fear building in the old woman now. 'Can't, Hen. Don't make me. I want to stay here. Safe here.'

Hen is exasperated, furious. She wants to shake the trembling woman, to pick her up, carry her down and shout: 'See! Nothing! No demons, no evil.'

She fights to sound patient. 'Come, Grandmother. Please.'

The old lady pulls herself away from Hen. With surprising agility she pulls back the blankets and leaps into her bed.

With Milly away, no one has emptied the pot, and the room smells high. Hen gives in and pulls the blanket round her grandmother's chin. She opens the window and a rush of cold air smacks her face. The City is eerily quiet; preposterously empty. Will, she thinks suddenly. Did Will go to Turnham Green? Is he there now? Everyone I hold in my heart is miles away, facing guns and pikes and death in all its guises.

She picks up the chamber pot and flings the contents onto the street below. She cannot stir herself to take it outside. Anyway, even the night-soil man is probably at the Green.

Behind her, her grandmother is whimpering. She is becoming ever weaker and more diminished. The flashes of fire that survived her descent into despair have been dampened by time. She is turning childlike. Reduced to the sum of her appetites and excretions. What is it Jaques says in *As You Like It*?

> *Last scene of all,*
> *That ends this strange eventful history,*
> *Is second childishness and mere oblivion,*
> *Sans teeth, sans eyes, sans taste, sans everything.*

A miserable sod, though, Jaques, she thinks. Her father always liked him. She smiles to think of it.

She closes the window and walks back to the bed. She pulls a chair and sits next to her grandmother, pushing the old lady's grey hair back from her forehead. I could get a book, she thinks. But what book can I read with my life in the balance? She lays her forehead on the blanket and closes her eyes. They are stinging; she has not slept. Up all night making pies for Ned, in case her father finds him. She knows they were not very good. Mrs Birch and Nurse are right, she thinks. Who will want me to keep their house? What use am I to Father, to Sam or Ned? I am steeped in all things useless and empty where it matters.

If they survive this, Lord, I will learn to cook, to manage a house. I will become a better servant, oh Lord.

'Grandmother,' she says quietly. 'Will we pray?'

The old lady nods. Hen kneels by her bed and grasps her hand. The familiar words wash over her like a charm, and she feels calmer.

Our Father, who art in heaven,
hallowed be thy name.
thy kingdom come,
thy will be done,
on earth as it is in heaven.

Hen thinks of her father, choosing to conjure his irrepressible smile in her mind. She sees Ned, serious and earnest, striving to find his adult self. She imagines Sam, hailing his friends in the crowd, treating the battle as an enormous, elaborate jape. And she thinks of Will, as she saw him last: mud-spattered and forlorn.

She thinks of Chalk and Cheese, and the Birch boys. And Oliver Chettle; he must be there somewhere too. Is he as good with a sword as with a pen? she wonders.

She kneels next to Grandmother's bed and tries not to bargain with the Lord. Take Robert Birch, but spare Sam. Take Chalk, but spare poor Cheese. Stop, she tells herself. Stop. *Thy will be done, on earth as it is in heaven.* Thy will be done.

~ ~ ~

'For thine is the kingdom, and the power, and the glory, for ever. Amen.'

Even Taffy joins in.

Beside them, the remains of the food lie strewn on the wet grass. There's not much left.

'We should save some for after,' Ned says, when the prayers are done, and the waiting starts again.

'There might not be an after.' Taffy reaches for a slice of heavy plum pudding.

'There will be manna in heaven,' Joe says, eyes raised upwards.

'Couldn't taste better than that pudding,' Ned replies, without thinking. He looks up to find Taffy looking at him, a wide grin on his foxy face.

'Pox take you, Taf,' he says, before grinning back.

A captain nearby shouts, and the men around them draw themselves up into a semblance of rank. Ned, Taffy and Joe are the ragtag hangers-on now; their regiment broken at Brentford, they and the other survivors have attached themselves to Philip

169

Skippon's trained bands. Many of their fellow soldiers are unwilling conscripts, pulled away from their small businesses and their families to face death on a pike's edge. Some are substitutes, paid for by the City's wealthier citizens to avoid taking their allotted place in the line.

And here is Skippon himself, riding past, inspecting his troops. He stops at Ned's cluster.

'You were Holles' men,' he says.

They nod and murmur.

'You shall have a chance to serve your fellows out today, I think.'

Skippon is about to ride away when he stops, and stares at Ned.

'Ned Challoner?' he asks uncertainly. Ned's father served with Skippon under Sir Horace Vere in Bohemia, and Ned had met his new commander in London, before the war.

Ned bows. 'Yes, sir.'

'You here? I would not have thought it.'

Ned nods. 'And proud to be so, sir.'

'I heard your father, my old friend, is not so keen on our cause.'

'You heard right, sir. Hence . . .' Ned gestures to his pike, and the collection of muddy rags which now passes as his uniform.

'Sad times, indeed, when families are divided. But God is with us today, men,' he says more loudly, a rhetorical flourish creeping into his voice. 'We shall face the idolators, and the papists, and the dissipated fornicators who stand against us, and we shall march with the Lord in our hearts against the servants of Baal.'

Quietly, against a background of muttered approval, he says to Ned: 'See me after, boy. Come and find me.'

As he leaves, Ned looks awkwardly at Taffy and Holy Joe.

'Ned, m'boy,' drawls Taffy, aping Sir Philip, 'I need someone to lick my arse. I hear you have a fine, fine tongue, young man.' He turns and waggles his arse provocatively at Ned, making Holy Joe giggle.

'Thy mother,' says Ned mildly.

'And thine.'

'You'll see us right,' says Joe. 'Didn't know you were such a plush fellow.'

'Maybe, just maybe,' says Taffy, 'he might see us get paid.'

'Paid! More chance of a kiss off a Cavalier than a payday.' This from a grizzled man next to them.

His words bring a murmuring assent from the pikemen standing by. 'We do the Lord's work, and what do those bastards give us? Promises, and more promises,' says one boy.

The grumbles are cut short by the report of a gun.

'For what we are about to receive,' says Taffy.

'Will you blaspheme in hell, Taf?'

'That I will, Ned, lad, as you'll see when you're standing there beside me.'

Ned grips his pike, waiting for orders. A ball whistles nearby.

'Look over there,' says the grizzled man, pointing to the flank where the spectators stand – an incongruous crowd of gawpers and followers.

Father among them, thinks Ned.

'It ain't a May Day parade we're at,' says Holy Joe.

The report of the gun sends the spectators milling backwards, their panic evident, even from where Ned stands. When it is clear that the ball came nowhere near, they mill forward again.

'Like sheep when a wolf's in,' says Taffy. 'Stupid bastards.'

It is a comical sight, the play of a fearful yet prurient crowd, and it cheers the boys up as they stand waiting for the off.

'There they go,' shouts Ned, as the crowd pedals backwards.

'Nope, back again,' says Taffy gleefully, as they pull forward.

It passes the time, and they need help with that. The morning drags forward. Still no sign of a move. The boys' feverish energy winds down a little; no one can stay so scared for so long. They've sung psalms, and they've talked chuff at the enemy, and now there is only the waiting.

'I've had more excitement shovelling shit,' says Taffy, to a morose silence. Noon approaches, and still no move. The king's troops stand opposite them; far enough to be faceless, near enough to be ominous.

'What's going on, sir?' says Ned to a passing officer, wearing the orange sash of Essex's army. Before he joined up, Ned had not thought that you could stand in the ranks of an army, yet be blind as to its greater movements.

The officer stops and looks at the faces turned to him.

'We outnumber the papist scummers, but they've got us beat on horses. See there.' He points to a small troop of the king's horses picking its way across the ground in front of the royalist army. 'They're looking at the ground. Our lady friends in the cavalry tell me it's terrible for the horse, this ground.' He shrugs. 'So we play chicken, boys. See who moves first.'

A little while later, the word passes down the lines. Stay in formation, keep pikes near at hand, but tuck in. Carts appear from behind them. More food from London's army of goodwives at their backs.

As they obey the rare, welcome orders, more words pass down the line.

The grizzled man comes over, a big grin sitting uncomfortably on his face. 'Seems those papist bastards over there have no food. And they can smell us.' A cheering rises through the parliamentary ranks. They brandish bread and meat at the enemy. They throw the half-eaten bones of birds into the bleak land between the armies. They blow the steam from the pies they crack open towards the royalists.

Taffy laughs until he weeps at the thought of the royalist boys sitting cold, wet and hungry on the other side of the fields, while they gorge for the second time. He wipes the tears from his eyes and stands tall, waving a great pitcher of ale.

'See this!' he screams at the opposing lines. He takes a deep draft. 'Tastes like fucking nectar, you papist cock-munchers!'

At last, sated, they sit back, and silence settles once more.

'Do you think we'll fight, Taf?' asks Ned, watching the winter sun begin to sink into the layer of cloud that sits obstinately above the horizon.

'I don't know. It's getting late. Jesus wept, but I wish the sods in the sashes would make up their minds.'

The grizzled man cuts across him. 'They're on the move!' he shouts.

Sure enough, the pikemen opposite them are wheeling around. Above the royalist heads, a thin crimson ribbon of sky is trapped between the dark clouds and the horizon.

'Jesus, they're going. They're going!'

The muttering grows along the parliamentary arms. The royalists are leaving. Turning away from London, marching away.

Ned can't work out how he is feeling. Cheated? Relieved?

He drops to his knees, and those around him follow suit. They pray and thank the Lord for their deliverance.

When they are done, Taffy assumes the rasping bark of a sergeant. 'Men, turn round, face back.'

Wonderingly, those near him do as he orders.

'Breeches down!' he shouts.

Almost to a man, they obey him. Ned grins as he pulls his down.

'On three, present arses!' screams Taf. 'One, two, three!'

Skippon's trained band presents a broadside of backsides to the retreating papists, as twilight falls over Turnham Green.

CHAPTER THIRTEEN

'*G*O ON,' WHISPERS HEN. 'DO IT.'

Sam looks around him nervously. At the far end of the great hall, a family wanders about quietly. Three children awed into silence by the grandeur of their surroundings. The windows are grimy, and the sun fights to find its way in. A gloomy place now. The walls are dappled dark and light, the pattern betraying where paintings once hung.

In front of them – majestic, awful – is the king's throne. It is bigger by far than their father's great chair. He must have looked small in it, like a child pretending if you weren't close enough to see his face. The wood is interlaid with gold. Hen closes her eyes and tries to imagine the room full of courtiers, Charles sitting here in state as they bow and scrape to him. But the echoing emptiness of the room defeats her imagination.

'I can't,' whispers Sam. 'You do it.'

Hen grins, darts to the throne and sits down. For the longest second, it seems, she sits in it, appalled and thrilled at the same time. Then she jumps up and walks away. She feels irrepressibly naughty, as if she were a child again and has stolen a pie or broken a prized cup.

'Your turn,' she says to Sam, knowing that he will have to do it, now that she has. He does it quickly, pausing in the chair just long enough to wave his hand and draw Hen into a deep, giggling curtsy.

They amble on through the great empty palace, the royal apartments, the bowling alleys and tennis courts, and the staterooms. Layers of royal history piled up brick by brick in this higgledy-piggledy palace. In the tiltyard, a stake is pushed into the ground where once the bears would have been tethered. Hen wonders what happened to the bears. Surely they have not gone to Oxford too, like the rest of the court?

How peculiar it is, to be sauntering around the palace as if they owned it. Word has rippled throughout the city that the empty buildings are not guarded, that anyone may walk in royalty's footsteps in these strange times.

They are not alone in their amblings. It feels as if half of London is using the break in the incessant rain to visit the palace, empty and forlorn as it is. A skeleton staff gives in to the tide of gawpers, collecting the valuables and the king's collection of paintings in a few, guardable, lockable rooms. The palace resounds with the court's absence. There are no gallants by the King's Gate, no guards. No ladies in wide skirts sweeping along the endless corridors. No gentlemen sauntering with tennis rackets. No musicians hurrying to the Banqueting House. No servants, either, to sweep the floors. Instead, idlers trip through the palace, open-mouthed at the splendour. Even without its tapestries and paintings, the palace awes them. The ceilings are arched and carved, the fireplaces huge and ornate. Look down, though, and the floor is a riot of muddy footprints, the rush matting peeling at the edges to let in the draughts.

In one particularly ornate room, Sam and Hen find a small crowd gathering in front of a mural. There is King Henry, his legs wide and his eyes burning. He looks as if he could stride down from the walls to berate them. 'What are you doing here in my palace, you vermin, you dung beetles?'

There is no laughter in this room, just a hush and a fear-edged wonder. *We sent our king away. We sent him away! What have we done?*

On their way down to the kitchens, Hen and Sam are passed by a ragtag couple carrying great sacks of coal, raided from the scuttles down there. The woman, pinched and grey, stares defiantly at Hen as she passes her. Hen looks away as she steps aside to let the woman pass. It will be a hard enough winter for London's poor with the king holding the great coal towns, and the price of warmth creeping ever upwards. It is icy cold in the kitchens. The great hearths lie cold and black, and the twins' breath hovers in visible clouds as they exhale. The pantry and butter-room are bare. The stark kitchens sadden her.

They move on to the great Banqueting House, built by the king's late father, the first of the Stuarts. They have passed the outside often enough. The startling modernity of its great stone façade contrasts with the ubiquitous red brick; its size, grandeur and glorious classical lines still shock. Londoners mime insouciance in front of it; out-of-towners crick their necks and stare. Once inside, their feet slap loudly on the floor; echoes bounce off the walls. The tapestries are gone and the walls are bare. Above them, though, is Rubens' great ceiling, depicting the glories of James I.

Hen and Sam stare upwards and then join their fellow Londoners who are lying on the floor to get a better view. Above them, kings and gods tumble and pose, their limbs alive with movement, the light playing on their faces, their robes flowing in folds that capture the shadows.

'Ned wouldn't like this,' says Sam, his eyes fixed on an angel's plump breasts.

'Lord, no,' says Hen. 'Let's hope the king took his ladders to Oxford, or the godly will be up there painting some modesty on.'

'Hmm,' says her brother, distracted.

A voice from by her head says: 'Aye, miss, it would be a travesty.'

She swivels to see a small, lined man lying near her, looking upwards with a face of near rapture.

'Ain't it glorious?' he says, still looking up. He points at one of the oval panels. 'Look there. Abundance suppressing Avarice, I believe.' A haloed golden figure pins a miserable creature to the floor.

'And there,' he points again. 'Wise Government holding a bridle above Intemperate Discord.' Wise Government is a bored-looking woman, and Intemperate Discord a naked, cowed man.

Hen finds herself strangely affected by the painting. She looks at the indifference in the woman's face, and the abject humiliation of the defeated. She doesn't see the allegory she is supposed to see at all; instead she sees 'Impartial Death vanquishes Brother'. She imagines Ned, out there with the army somewhere, being defeated, so cold and naked and alone.

She reaches for Sam's hand. 'Let's go,' she says. 'Please.' They leave the little man lying there still, tracing the lines of genius on the ceiling.

They wander on through the maze of apartments and find themselves in the privy gardens. The bare trees lining the walkways give the garden a tragic, unkempt air. Unswept leaves have turned to sludge, making the paths slippery. Carved wooden creatures peep slyly from behind hedges, silently watching the twins as they walk.

'Hard to imagine it in springtime,' says Hen, picking an obstinate russet leaf from a tree and twirling it round in her fingers.

'I'm not sure how long I can last, Hen,' says Sam suddenly.

She adjusts to the sudden swerve in conversation. 'You cannot go for a soldier, too. Father would break.' And I, she adds, silently.

'So I must sit and learn to keep ledgers, and understand linen, and try to keep myself from stabbing my eyes out with a pen? When he was my age he ran away to the wars.'

They come to a sundial standing at the centre of the garden. It sits obsolete under the low grey sky.

'True. But not to fight Englishmen. Do you even know which side to fight for?'

'Ned's. Parliament's.'

'Why? Sam, you are not godly. I do not believe you care in the slightest about the king's divine rights, nor Parliament's prerogatives. Without conviction for one side or the other, what need is there to fight?'

'There is honour. Or rather the dishonour of standing by. Of wandering in pretty gardens with my sister, when good men are fighting and dying.'

'Honour. Your sex's trump card,' she says, turning from him impatiently. 'What a thing to die for.'

'There is nothing else worth dying for, Hen, if you think on it. Why should I die to protest the *Book of Common Prayer*?' He picks up a stick lying on the ground and fences with an imaginary foe.

'Take back your damned altar rail, sir, or I shall spike you!' he cries, lunging. He turns to her and pretends to stab himself. 'Or perhaps you would have me die to rid the world of ship money, or tonnage and poundage?' He falls to the floor and lies thrashing on the cold stone. He cocks one eye open.

'Would you have me lay down my life for the sake of taxation, Hen?' He spits with theatrical disgust and mutters again: 'Taxation!'

She finds her reluctant smile spreading into a laugh. 'Beware bedlam, fool,' she says, and taps him with her foot.

He groans, and rolls over onto his front. 'Kicked,' he says, 'by my own blood.'

~ ~ ~

Once home, there is good news: a letter from Anne. But it was borne by a grumbling Nurse, back to resume her tenuous position in the household. As much as she'd hoped to be harassed by over-gallant Cavaliers or rude apprentices on the way home, the road between Oxford and London proved resolutely dull. Cheated of her chance of being heroic or put upon, Nurse hands over the letter with a growl.

'Trouble, that girl. Mind my words, Henrietta. Trouble.'

She shuffles off, grumbling still, to embellish what little danger there was in her telling to Cook and Milly. Milly sits wide-eyed as

Nurse tells of soldiers and potholed roads, of moments of terror and her own heroic stoicism. Cook, less gullible yet diplomatic, makes the required noises as Nurse whines her way back towards equanimity.

Upstairs, Hen and Sam sprawl by the fire as she reads the letter aloud.

Dearest Hen,

We are, like Their Majesties, in Oxford! Father decided that the house, being outside the city walls, was too exposed to passing ruffians, too isolated. So we are crammed, all of us, into three rooms on top of his counting house, in the city itself. He has managed to find a pass for your nurse. You are welcome to her, odious witch, though Mother much laments her going.

There is no room for her here. Mother is flapping and furious about managing us all in such a small space, with but one servant girl who sleeps on the floor of my room, which I also share with my littlest sister. She snores, and is freckled – the maid, I mean.

Father is never here. He says that having the court in Oxford is supplying him with endless business, but I heard them arguing last night about how the grandest folk are least likely to pay in cash. We have already turned over our plate to the king, and must hide any jewels. Those wearing anything fine on the streets are harangued as traitors for not passing their goods to the king's cause. The king, they say, is light of purse and is trying to prize funds from London using underhand channels. To little purpose, evidently.

Father is forced, too, to spend one day a week out building defences against the rebels. The king decreed it. He did not think that what passes for able-bodied in Oxford may not serve – it is a sight to see the stumbling, crooked old fellows prized from the libraries and set to the earth with shovels!

They are arguing much here. I cannot decide if it is because I hear them more in the smaller space or if it is due to the mere fact of more shouting. The littleys are miserable all cooped up in these little rooms. The baby screams and screams. The older ones are just cross, Hen. Now is the time they would be building towers of dead leaves and jumping into piles of them. Here, they just sit indoors and fight, for Mother is loathe to let them out with all the soldiers and the horses marching up and down the street. Christmas is approaching, and how we will make it happy for them, I cannot tell.

The house next door was lived in by a godly family, who have upped and left for Abingdon with the rest of their kind since the king arrived. Their rooms are now full to overflowing with soldiers: mostly rude fellows, but polite enough to me as I walk past them. I ignore the ones who call out, and step higher. Our area is overrun with Wicked Ladies, now, attracted by the court and the weight of soldiers quartered here. The other night, Prince Rupert led a torch-lit dance down the street outside my window, followed by a troop of women wearing hoods! I didn't, at first, understand, but Mathew told me.

Mathew has joined to fight for the king. Father would have rather he fought for Parliament, if anyone, and Mathew, I think, did not mind much either, but did not want to be left out. But we all talked it out, and it seemed best to join the king, with the court quartered here and Father's business supplied from royalist pockets. And Mathew was pleased, I think. The Roundheads are most frightfully severe, and godly, yet not above appalling barbarity. Everyone here talks about their nastiness in battle, particularly in the late sack of Winchester. To desecrate a cathedral!

Mathew has taken to his new life, and roisters in the taverns enthusiastically with his fellow new recruits, much to Father's fury. He talks often about his pretty cuz, Hen, and I'm sure sends you a kiss.

He will not be happy, he says, until he has a rebel's guts on his sword. (Not poor cousin Ned, I hope.)

The only really happy one, Hen, is me. Oh, how I wish you were here. The excitement! The fun! Did we ever go into Oxford together? Before the court came, it was all serious young men, jabbering in Latin and locked in their colleges come nightfall. But now! The streets throng with gallant soldiers, wearing the sashes of their regiments. The ladies of the court gather in New College's grove, and I go too with my friends, and we wander through the trees as the lutes play and all the men bow to the prettiest of us. I have seen the king, and the queen! And now when I see you, we shall be able to nod wisely about them together, and I shall not have to envy you your sight of them. (Though, Hen, you are in the right of it. How short!!)

They have turned Christ Church quad into a giant slaughterhouse, and as we walked past this morning, a pig squealed so loudly that I jumped. A passing officer, with the bluest, bluest eyes, smiled at me. Then he bowed so low that I thought he would trip!

The weather has been delightful too, icy but bright. There is another early winter sunset, now, and I look out of my little window to see a group of officers walk past, their faces all golden

in the low sun, their swords glinting. How I love it here – it's
making me quite the poet!

The only boring thing is the constant talk of the current
troubles. All the talk now is of new peace talks. How they all
drone on, though! I keep silent, and in my head bless the wars for
bringing all this excitement to my life, and the court to Oxford. I
wish you were here to share it. But as you are not, I can do little
more than send my heartiest love.

Your Anne

Sam stands, pacing the room. 'So I am the only one of the younger Challoners not to go for a soldier,' he says.

'She says there's hope of fresh peace talks. Look, here.' She points to the page. 'Waller told Father that there is agitation in both houses for fresh talks, and it is only a few weeks since the streets were alive with rioters against the war. This cannot last.'

He stands by the window, looking out.

'Sam, wait until the spring at least. They say it might be all over by then. If it is not, then, perhaps, you should go.'

'The spring,' he says. 'If I wait until then, you promise to let me go with no guilt hanging on me, no reproaches?'

'I promise,' she says.

~ ~ ~

Hen lifts her head from her book. She sits curled on some cushions in the window seat of her father's library. Outside, the gardener is at work on their small town garden, clipping leaves and whistling softly. It is quieter this side of the house. The high wall round their garden puts a barrier between their private realm and the street.

The slushy rain falls relentlessly. Hen sees her father suddenly through the smeared glass. She smiles at the sight of him, and watches as he stands under a tree, accosting the gardener, waving a book. Old Benny is leaning on a stick. His gout must be flaring. She sees his shoulders sag as his master's lecture rolls over him. She can't see the old man's face, but she pictures the wrinkles in it furrowing deeper, the rain dripping off his wide-brimmed hat.

Her hair is loose around her shoulders, her stomacher undone to the waist so she can breathe. Her shoes are on the floor, and her cuffs and collar are upstairs, sitting stiffly on her dresser. There are some comforts in having no mother and a distracted father.

The door opens sharply, and she sits upright, guiltily pushing her book under the cushion. Her father enters, shuffling slowly. His face is pink from the freezing air and his remaining strands of hair are damp.

She breathes out, relieved. 'Oh, only you.'

'Only me? Pudding cat!'

'Sorry, Father. I meant, I thought you were Nurse.'

'Thank your stars I am not. Look at the state of you, turtle.'

She scowls, and he laughs.

'No matter, child. You'll do, I daresay.'

'What's your book, Father, the one you were waving at poor old Benny?'

'Parkinson. *Paradisi in Sole Paradisus Terrestris*.'

'And did you convince him that paradise is held in its pages?'

'My dear, I did not. Natural philosophy he sneers at. Parkinson's brilliance he laughs at. All wisdom that is new he baulks at. His grandfather planted sorrel in such and such a way, as did his father before him, and to break the chain would bring the God of the Garden down to rain thunderbolts on his marrows. Beelzebub himself will crouch in the rose hips, and a new Sodom unleashed on Fetter Lane.'

She laughs, and he sits down next to her on the window seat. He winces as he sits. They both look out to where the old gardener is bent low over the rather pathetic winter shrubs.

'Father, I do not, for one second, believe that Benny blasphemed.'

'Perhaps not, but he wanted to. "God rot you master and your books," he wanted to say, but stood there mute instead. Waiting for me to quit his sacred domain. And so I shambled off, quite contrite. Master turned penitent, and Benny reigning supreme. Ha ha!'

His laughter and the rain-stung glow of his cheeks make him look healthier, younger. His wide green eyes crease into slits, and his great belly shakes in a contagious chuckle, impossible to resist. It rolls down the corridors and spills out into the garden, and even old Benny smiles in response, despite himself.

'The old problem, Father?' she says, pointing at his bandaged foot.

'It is. A bad flare-up, kitten. It will keep me housebound to terrorize the servants for a few days.' He lifts his swollen foot onto the chair opposite, grunting a little.

'Well, then. What's the book you're hiding, my ninny-headed miss? One of those dreadful romances? That oaf Tancred and his absurd mistress?'

'No, Father. Am I a fool?' She pulls the book out from under the cushion and holds it out to him.

He reads the cover aloud. '*The Man on the Moon*?'

'I put it on your account.'

'Did you, Miss Mischief?' His green eyes, so like her own yet cobwebbed with age, twinkle at her. 'And did you find your other worlds?'

'It is not quite as I expected. It's more of a satire. It imagines another world, on the moon – a perfect world. And by its perfection it shows us the imperfections in ours.'

'Ah. A utopia. Beware of those, pudding. In my experience, they don't exist. One man's utopia is another's gaol.'

'Such a cynic! Surely we should look to perfect our world.'

'Impossible, my kitten. And always will be, as long as there is sickness and death. Your politicians and bishops and noble lords can't help that. No praying nor speechifying can raise the dead, nor make the bad man good.'

'So we should aim for dull mediocrity?'

'At all times. But enough of this. Why do I always fall into these conversations with you? I came for a purpose. I need you to visit Lucy Tompkins.'

'Father!'

'I know, I know. It will not damn you, my darling, to spend an hour in her company.'

'Why do I have to?' She crosses her arms, holding her book into her chest.

'Is all the pain in the world not in my foot, keeping me housebound? Did I not ask you? Did your old man not prostrate himself to you, begging you for a favour?'

'No.'

'Well, consider yourself begged or ordered or entreated, or whatever it will take to make you bestir yourself and do me this service.'

'Can I at least wait until the rain comes off?'

'Yes, if you must. And Henrietta, you would oblige me by giving this parcel to her father.'

He hands over a small, nondescript package. She knows him well enough to sense the shift in tone, the sudden chill, and she looks at him.

'Well, well,' he blusters, and retreats from the room, his stick thumping on the floor.

~ ~ ~

Challoner is uncharacteristically evasive over the coming weeks, and Hen's questions slide off him. Every few days, she finds herself visiting women she scarcely knows, binding herself into her formal clothes and flogging her small talk. And every meeting ends with an afterthought – a package or a letter for the man of the house, remembered casually and diffidently offered.

She watches them read, sometimes, as their frowns deepen and their heads tilt and their questions die on their lips. She would not be able to answer, anyway. She doesn't know what the messages are about, and he does not tell her.

Soon enough, she stops asking her father, for fear of his answer. For a pattern is emerging. The men are prominent moderates, silenced by the raising of the king's standard. These are the peace party, the merchants, the lawyers and the middlemen, who warned against the war and resisted the slide to a broken realm. These are the men for whom stability, trade and the unhampered wheezing of the law courts trump God and principle.

Hen comes to think of the tracks of her innocent visiting across the city as a silvery snail-trail of the disaffected. She can see the pattern, but she does not fully understand it. What do these men want, now that peace is in a disorderly retreat? The land has been shaken to its roots, and in the settling all men have chosen sides, whether or not they wanted to make that choice. Where are these men now, and why is she linking them together with her visiting?

She chooses not to question too far. What do her inclinations to support Parliament matter, compared to her loyalty to her father? Men have the luxury of a rampaging conscience. Women have duty. At least this is what she tells herself in yet another stifling room, with conversation stuttering around her and the basket on her lap weighed down by another package, heavy as thirty pieces of silver.

CHAPTER FOURTEEN

December 1642

𝒜 WOMAN HOLDS THE DOOR AJAR, GRIPPING ITS EDGES between thumb and forefinger as if it were something foul. She peers out at Hen with reddened, hooded eyes. From somewhere behind her comes the frantic wail of an ignored toddler.

'What?'

'Mrs Pound?' Hen stammers.

'What is it to you?'

'Sorry, I . . . My father is friends with your husband. He—'

'Can go to the devil.' She spits it from behind the door.

'I'm sorry,' says Hen. 'Can I help?'

'Food?'

Hen shakes her head. The door slams violently shut.

She returns later, this time with a full basket. The woman beckons her in, looking behind her on the street.

There is silence as she rummages in the basket and brings out a loaf, tearing into it with her teeth. Children gather, wide-eyed and eerily quiet. Five in all, ranging from about two to ten. They ignore Hen, watching their mother pulling apart the bread and handing it out.

They ravage the bread, falling on it like rats to the slops. Hen can hardly bear to watch it. The children are well dressed, and polite enough to thank her once the edge is chewed off their hunger. The children's mother behaves oddly now that her own hunger is eased. There's a shifting unease in her now, as if Hen has caught her in some secret transgression. The private pain has been laid open to this stranger, and the woman veers between a squirming over-familiarity and a clear resentment.

'They arrested him,' she says. 'Five days ago. He left no money. The servants left. I should go to sell our stuff, I suppose, but I cannot yet… Not yet.'

'I understand.'

'Do you?'

Hen raises placatory hands.

'They say he is a royalist spy. The daft bugger. They'll hang him, I expect. He's to be investigated by a special committee.'

One of the smaller boys begins to cry, and Mrs Pound distractedly draws him into a close embrace.

'I'm so sorry.'

'And how am I to feed my children, miss? My husband's patron, Lord Portland, is already in the Tower, damn his eyes. What will I do?'

'I… That is, I…' Hen falters, not knowing what to say.

'Never mind. Thank you anyway for the food.'

Hen emerges into the street. She feels a sharp relief to be outside, shedding the woman's cloying misery, sloughing off the immediacy of the children's pitiful faces. And that plaintive, unanswerable question: 'What will I do? What will I do?'

A guilty, happy smile on her face. Then, across the road, behind a rumbling cart, she sees a man watching her.

Her skin shrivels, shrinks on her bones. Of course they would watch the house. Of course, of course. Her heart quickens. He is small-featured, sharp: a rat-catcher of a man. Her legs buckle and beg her brain to run. Her stupid, *stupid* brain. Mrs Pound's hunger is not her hunger. Those children are not her children. Her skin is too tight for her body, too tight to hold in place her yammering heart.

Jesus, keep me. Jesus, are you listening?

She struggles to push the fear back down into her gut, to keep from letting it out, betraying her. She forces her eyes to slide away from the man, who raises his face to the sun, his nose to the scent of her fear.

She walks away, risking a look back at the man. He is still watching the house. Perhaps it is a coincidence. Perhaps he is just taking a stroll, selling something, related to the house. Perhaps, perhaps.

He looks at her suddenly, a smudge of a smile on his face, and she knows that she is lying to herself. She feels a ridiculous urge to run over to him, to declare her allegiance to Parliament, to God's pure voice. To name her brother Ned; to call on the name of Sir Philip Skippon; to throw herself on his mercy. The man looks away again, his air deliberately casual.

He has no proof of anything. Her basket is empty of all but crumbs. He does not even know who she is. She is two streets from home, where her father sits, laid up with the gout. His swollen leg is propped on cushions, and he shouts and grumbles at Harmsworth to distract himself from the pain. That man does not know these things. That man does not know who she is.

She sets off at an amble, up Bow Lane towards Cheapside. She has not thought this through. She glances around and there he is; ahead is the busy cacophony of Cheapside traffic. As she approaches it, she will have to slow down, and he will be upon her. Coming up to the corner, she sees a gap and runs to it. A whinnying horse and a shouted curse and she is through. It is busy, even more so than usual.

Her father had warned that there could be trouble today, at Haberdashers' Hall, where the Committee of Both Houses for the Advance of Money is planning to meet. Londoners, wrung dry by Parliament's demand for money, are feeling mutinous, rediscovering their affection for the king they jeered out of the city.

She struggles her way through the crowds. There he is, the rat-catcher, wandering along the other side of the street. Whistling. Looking in shop windows. He pauses in front of one of the fine goods shops, strung between Bread Street and Friday Street, oodles of gilt proclaiming its exclusivity. The bastard. How to shake him? The need to take action helps quell the fear. If she stops, if she falters, it will swallow her.

Suddenly, she thinks of her books. Of the battle of Thermopylae, and how a narrow aperture can change the odds, shake fate off its trail. A reverse Thermopylae. She finds hope enough to smile at the thought.

So how to do it? She thinks of the narrow tangle of lanes that curl around each other, north of Cheapside.

She turns off, up through Gutter Lane. Now she will know – there will be no mistaking his purpose if he follows. She looks behind her, and there he is. Less nonchalant. Their eyes meet, and there is no mistake. And now she must be guilty of something for she is clearly running from him. An innocent would meet his eyes and bob, not turn, as she has done, speeding up to a near run, her shoes sliding on the mud and the cobbles.

She turns into a narrow passage overhung with slatternly buildings that meet in the middle and block out the light entirely. It's barely big enough for two abreast. She can hear shouting through the flimsy timber walls, and a baby crying. Washing flaps down into the alley, waving at her and tugging at her hair like ghostly sentries. She can hear the squelch of his feet in the mud, and she begins to think that this is a terrible mistake. Time slows, like a nightmare, and his breathing is amplified in the closeness of the alley. She pushes aside some washing and there is light at the end, and shouting.

'Peace and truth!' shouts a voice ahead.

'Hang truth,' comes another cry. 'Peace at any price!'

The man senses the danger of losing her and she hears his footfall wind up to a greater pitch, and suddenly she is through, into a packed and raucous crowd that swallows her up, and eddies her about with her feet barely touching the floor. And she crouches low, letting herself be lost in the crowd.

When she is sure she has lost him, when she has doubled back on herself and waited in nooks and scanned the faces around her, then and only then does she succumb to the great, tumbling fall of joy that follows her escape, filling her from the toes up. She bounces and skips. Her skin loosens and becomes sweetly tender, so the cool winter air feels like a lover's kiss.

She is alive, she has beaten her enemy and she is reborn.

At home, she struggles to contain this wild happiness, even as she is telling her father about what happened. She watches the concern on his face, already furrowed with the pain of his gout.

'We must put a stop to your wanderings, pudding cat,' he says.

She looks around the room, at the familiar, safe walls. She imagines going back to how she was before she had tasted love, before she had stood on top of a fortification she had helped to build. Before these new adventures, and the intoxicating combination of fear and joy which was so exactly the opposite of boredom. She imagines going back, and the panelled walls seem to crowd in on her, like carved and polished trees in a sinister wood.

'No!' she cries. 'No, please. Let me help. I want to help.'

'The king?' her father whispers, and it is in the open now, beyond secrecy.

'Hang the king. I want to help you. Please.'

~ ~ ~

Christmas passes sombrely, if not soberly. Ned makes it home for the Twelfth Night feast. He is on Skippon's staff now, and while the army idles at Windsor, waiting for the peace negotiations to bite, Ned's duties are light. Few people expect peace. But, as Challoner says, at least the sides are talking, if not in a language intelligible to each other.

The Twelfth Night feast is a quiet meal, family only. The spectre of past Twelfth Nights lingers; but there is little visiting this year, and the family eats its own minced pies quietly, in front of its own charred yule log. Chalk's absence is raw. Cheese has

195

gone home to the country, pleading a sick mother for retiring from city life. They all expect him to burst through the door when the peace is signed, the mother miraculously recovered and the son eager to re-embark on his path to riches and dissolute living.

But if the party is small this year, it is warm. Richard Challoner watches his three children, all safe and healthy, talk and bicker with each other. The war seems very far away. They go upstairs with the wassail bowl; the old lady refuses to leave her room now. Sam carries it, and the punch sloshes, dripping over the side. Ned and Hen mock him as they reach their grandmother's door.

Hen knocks gently, and pushes the door open. Grandmother is sitting upright in bed, her hair brushed and plaited, her gown clean and snowy white. She has been looking forward to this evening, Hen knows. She reaches for Ned, and he sits down next to her on the bed, holding her paper-thin hand.

'Ned, boy. Ned, my darling one.'

'Well now, Grandmother. Another year, and you still going strong.'

She smiles. 'When it's the fire that beckons, you're in no hurry to meet it.'

Ned frowns. 'God's grace is with you, Grandmother.'

She looks at him as if he is a little boy still. 'He is with *you*, Ned. I am forsaken.'

Just once, thinks Hen, could we move on? Worry about something other than salvation?

But Hen remains silent and, as if doing penance for her unkind thoughts, bustles forward to plump up her cushion.

'You're a good girl,' her grandmother says. 'Boys, you must

look after your sister. Coddle her. She will not be much use on her own, and what man will have her in these times?'

'Any man,' says Sam fiercely. 'Any man would be lucky to have our Hen.'

She snorts. 'Oh yes? Her father a not-so-secret royalist in a city held by Parliament? And she a girl who can't hold two stitches together, or carry a tune. Who gets lost in a kitchen. Who dances like a bear, or not so well, perhaps. Come, Sam, don't be blind – look at her.'

Sam and Ned turn to look at Hen, as instructed. She shrugs and moves away from the bed towards the fire. I will not be needled, she thinks.

'She knows I only say it from love,' says the old lady behind her. 'She knows, as well as I, that this is a bitter world for women, and she cannot change it, only accommodate it.'

'She won't need us,' says Ned gently. 'But if she does, Sam and I will both be there to look after her.'

Hen smiles wanly at him.

'Aye,' says Grandmother. 'You a soldier, and him an apprentice to a dying business.'

They all four sit silent a while. Outside, there is snow falling. Once, when snow fell, the Challoner children would have been wriggling with anticipated joy, desperate to be out in the garden revelling in the fresh falls. Snow marks the passage to adulthood, thinks Hen. One morning, you wake up and see that it is snowing. And you list the inconveniences the snow will bring, and you grumble a little as you climb out of bed. And that moment is the pivot, the exact turning point between being a child and being an adult. The moment when, whether you realize it or

197

not, your life has been drained of its unthinking joy. Happiness is harder to find, as an adult. Father looks in a glass, and Ned in the Bible, and I in my books, she thinks. But we're all doomed to failure, as long as we look out of the window and think, 'Bother that snow'.

'It's snowing,' she says, in her brightest voice.

They all turn to the window and look bleakly at the crystals forming on the glass.

~ ~ ~

Challoner comes into the hall, brushing the snow from his shoulders.

'Move your arse from the fire, Ned, boy,' he says, and Ned vacates the great chair. Challoner's eyes are shining, and his cheeks glow from the cold. He claps his hands in front of the blaze and laughs, as the snow drips into waterfalls from his cloak.

'How I love a good snowfall. Makes the city look almost presentable,' he says, his voice booming.

Sam grins back at him. 'Twelfth Night never seems right without the snow.'

'Where have you been, Father? We were waiting for you to start the games.'

'Bring them up, bring them up,' he says, deflecting the question.

Sam darts out of the room, and then returns with the rest of the household, scrubbed and poured into their Sunday best. Nurse and Cook look as if they have been at the port, while little Milly, not so little, is ramrod straight by the door, as if looking for an escape. Harmsworth stands as if on sufferance by the wall, his face wretched. He disapproves of Christmas, and he wants them all to know it.

They gather round the wassail bowl, replenished and pungent. With great ceremony, Challoner dishes out the punch. He holds a cup to Ned.

'Come, Ned,' says Challoner quietly. 'You may be dead by Easter. Or I may be. When I am, boy, you can make Christmas as drab and as dull as you like. But, for now, for me, take this.'

Harmsworth watches Ned as he reaches out a hand and takes the proffered cup. 'Serpent,' he hisses suddenly. 'Serpent in the garden.'

In the bowl, apples bob and duck. Ned holds the cup, suddenly looking foolish and young. His eyes dart between Harmsworth and his father, both looking expectantly at him. Quickly, as if to take himself by surprise, he drinks.

Sam and Challoner cheer, and Hen smiles. Harmsworth retreats into himself, his face impassive and unreadable.

Hen drinks more of the heady spiced brew. It travels down her body, flooding her with a warmth that is compounded by the presence of her family, whole in body, and laughing together.

A knock, suddenly, at the door. Harmsworth slips out, and reappears a moment later with Edmund Waller.

'Ah,' Waller cries. 'The family gathers! And I, the unwelcome interloper.'

'Not at all, not at all!' exclaims Challoner. 'A cup for you, sir.' He fills a cup with punch and Waller drinks deeply.

'A triumph,' Waller says. 'Most perfectly spiced. Miss Challoner, I salute you!'

Nurse and Cook giggle, and an awkward silence threatens.

'Apologies, Mr Waller, you don't know my eldest boy, Edward. Ned, this is Edmund Waller, poet and Member for Hastings.'

They bow, warily.

'Ned is on Philip Skippon's staff,' says Challoner.

'Ah, Skippon. Wish him well, my boy, when you see him. A fine fellow.'

'He is, sir,' says Ned shortly.

'I am come to take my leave. I travel to Oxford again next week. To open formal negotiations with His Majesty.'

'Let us drink to peace,' says Challoner, and they raise their cups emphatically.

'To peace!'

Ned can't help himself. 'And the proper regard for the true church of Christ our Lord and the due respect for the prerogatives of Parliament,' he says.

'What kind of a toast is that, boy?' roars his father. 'Too long, too much of a mouthful.'

Waller interjects smoothly. 'Confusion to the enemies of the king, and the Church,' he says.

They all raise their cups again. Which enemies are we drinking to? Hen wonders. Which church?

'Now,' says Waller. 'Loath as I am to tear you away from the very bosom of your family, I would speak with you privately.'

'Of course,' says Challoner, filling both their cups and ushering Waller to the door.

It closes behind them.

'What's that about?' says Ned.

'Unctuous man,' says Hen.

'He's always here, locked up with Father,' says Sam. 'Talking quietly in corners. Plotting.'

Ned frowns, and the word echoes in the room.

They launch into the games with a hilarity that begins forced but soon becomes natural. The bowl is filled again from the pot bubbling on the kitchen fire, and more is spilled on its journey back to the hall.

Challoner is back when the singing starts. He is composed and merry, joining in with a booming baritone.

Bring us in no brown bread, for that is made of bran,
Nor bring us in no white bread, for therein is no grain;
But bring us in good ale.

Bring us in no beef, for there is many bones,
But bring us in good ale, for that goes down at once;
And bring us in good ale.

Later, as she stumbles towards bed, the word 'plotting' ricochets around Hen's befuddled mind. She climbs under the blankets and begs the walls to stop spinning.

Ned stumbles on the stairs, and Milly comes up behind him. She offers herself as a steady-board, and together they climb up, giggling.

'Little Milly, not so little,' he says.

'Older than you,' she says.

'But twice as pretty.' He attempts a bow, but finds himself, to his astonishment, kneeling on the floor instead.

'How did I get here?' he asks her, wonderingly.

She moves to lift him up again, and he throws his arms round her waist. 'Little Milly,' he says into her skirts. 'Little Milly.'

She drags him to his feet, and to the door of his room. He pulls her inside and closes the door, scrabbling at her skirts as he does.

'Master Ned,' she says. 'No, master Ned.' But she is small and meek, and he kisses her to stop her talking. 'Oh, little Milly,' he breathes into her ear, hot and heavy. He pulls her down onto the bed, and she goes with him, passive as he clutches at what bare flesh he can find beneath the layers. As he pushes into her, he closes his eyes so the expression on her thin white face won't distract him from this sensation, this soul-burning sense of relief.

~ ~ ~

The next morning dawns grey and confused in the Challoner house. Hen wakes to a dry mouth and a churning stomach. She lies in bed, blankets pulled to her chin, fear of the cold and thirst fighting for primacy.

In Challoner's room, Nurse, naked and pink, drools a little in her sleep. Challoner, jerked awake by his own ferocious snore, wakes to find half his body freezing and uncovered.

'Confound the woman,' he mutters as he pulls the blankets in his direction, and turns his back to her. 'Blasted, blasted woman,' he mumbles, as he tries to go back to sleep again.

Ned wakes, and for one precious minute is conscious yet untroubled. Then the shame floods in. Little Milly's white face, and the joy of entering her. He sits up and his head pounds. He is alone; she is gone. Lord, turn your eyes away. Perhaps he dreamed it. No, not a dream. He falls back into bed and curls into himself.

He whispers, his head under a blanket. 'Know ye not that the unrighteous shall not inherit the kingdom of God? Be not deceived: neither fornicators, nor idolaters, nor adulterers, nor effeminate, nor abusers of themselves with mankind, nor thieves, nor covetous, nor drunkards, nor revilers, nor extortioners, shall inherit the kingdom of God.'

He is hot and cold with the shame and the agony. He has forsaken his God. He is a fornicator and a drunkard. He is possessed. Even as his mind runs over the texts, and he whispers his frantic pleas for forgiveness, he realizes to his horror that his body is betraying him. For every time the image of Milly's white face and thin thighs creeps into his mind, his prick twitches hard. He fights the urge to touch himself, to give in to the thoughts of Milly's body bucking beneath him. Satan sits on his shoulder, whispering lewd words in his ear.

He balls his palms into fists and presses them into his eyes. Aloud, he calls on Christ to forgive him, to help him resist the temptations of the flesh. For did the Lord not say: 'If thy right hand offend thee, cut it off, and cast it from thee: for it is profitable for thee that one of thy members should perish, and not that thy whole body should be cast into hell.'

Lying there, safe in his warm bed, Ned finds himself longing for battle. For the clash of steel. For the certainties, and the knowledge of God's work in your pike thrust, and His breath in your ear. For the purity of cold, and hunger, and dedication. For the chance of a swift path to heaven, and the angels calling you into the safe embrace of His grace.

CHAPTER FIFTEEN

April 1643

*T*HERE IS A SMELL THAT IS ENTIRELY UNIQUE TO A SACKED town. Ned picks his way down the main street in Reading. Smoke predominates, overlaid with the hoppy tang of the pissed soldiers, and the reek of blocked sewers and untended streets. There is an absence of other familiar smells, like bread and stewing meat. The healthy smells of lives lived quietly are only missed when they are gone, subsumed in the putrid.

He holds a kerchief to his nose. Doors swing off hinges and windows are smashed. Furniture lies confusing and incongruous on the streets; the domestic dragged outside. He steps round a broken chair, and smashed glass crunches loudly under his heels. It has been wet and grey, and the town's misery is compounded by a slick layer of slush.

Here and there are soldiers, hanging off each other in drunken comradeship. They wander, dazed, in search of new territory, of cellars left unraided, pantries untouched and chests unrifled. Ned has become too familiar with the befuddled air of soldiers on the sack; eight parts booze to two parts bloodlust. Perhaps some retain droplets of shame, but Ned can see no evidence of it. One pair, arms linked and stumbling, round the corner and weave towards him. Their laughter seems entirely weird to Ned, as if they are clowning at a funeral. They see his officer's sash and give a cheery semblance of a salute.

The inhabitants of the town are nowhere to be seen. Yet they must have lived here once; children and mothers, old folk and petted dogs, and apple-cheeked young girls. Only the rats remain, picking over the soldiers' discarded waste. Are they here somewhere? Ned wonders. Perhaps they are hiding in holes like badgers, waiting for us to go so they can creep out and try to set their world right side up again. To start on the sweeping up of glass, and the cleaning up of the soldiers' filth. The slow job of rebuilding their shattered lives.

As he passes a tavern, packed full and raucous, the door swings open and a young lad falls out. He lies in the gutter, his cheek pressed into the cold, wet cobblestones. Ned thinks about helping him up but decides against it, just as the boy coughs up a torrent of puke. It dribbles down his beardless chin and slides across the road. Ned steps over him and turns into Broad Street. In a gesture that has become habitual, he spits towards the third house on the left. They say that Laud was born here. His house, its inhabitants long fled, has become an open sewer, flecked with the excretions of the godly soldiers. Every window is smashed, and slogans are daubed on its walls. Ned eyes the grand home's degradation with some satisfaction. Ye shall reap what ye sow, he thinks.

At the corner of the street he comes to an elegant, brick-worked town house – Walsingham House. Inside, the hall is overrun with senior officers lounging by a large fire, idly downing wine. He is a cornet now, and attached to Major-General Skippon's staff. He assumes the languid walk of an officer. He has long realized that if you act the part, no one questions the pretence. He nods to a few he recognizes. There is an air of resignation here, of defeat snatched from victory. Shame hangs in the thick, smoky air of the room like a miasma, ricocheting off the screaming and roaring which occasionally pierce the thick walls.

Skippon is in the corner – sober, of course – and surrounded by maps. He looks tired and drawn. All the triumph of breaching Reading's defences has long since been swallowed by the despair of watching his troops run wild and unchecked through the town's streets. Ned feels a surge of protective affection towards his general, this quiet, godly man who does not understand his soldiers' need to run beserk after the strain of the siege.

Skippon is bent low over a letter, and Ned waits for him to look up. A commander beloved and respected by his troops is a rare thing; Essex does not have the knack. Yet Skippon does. They love him for his godliness, his strength and his aptitude for soldiering. In an army officered by gentlemen volunteers, Skippon's professionalism is rare, and prized by the men whose lives he directs. Yet most of all they love him for his quiet dignity. It is this quality which informed his reply to the king's command to join him at York when he raised his standard last summer.

'I desire to honour God, not to honour men,' he had said. Ned remembers the line and smiles to himself. Amid all the wrangling and the rhetoric, is that not the simplest, sweetest summation of why they are all here?

Yet all their love and respect for their general and their God has not stopped them going on the rampage, Ned thinks, just as Skippon looks up and sees him standing there.

'Ned, boy. Glad to see you. Still bedlam out there?'

'Aye, sir. Quietening a bit now, I think. The beer is running out.'

'Sunday tomorrow; perhaps we can bring them to their senses then.'

Ned nods, non-committal.

'I need you to ride to London. You can ride? Of course, of course. Take this chit to the quartermaster for a horse, and here's your pass.'

Ned takes them as Skippon explains. A verbal order, not to be written down. Permission sought from the Committee of Safety to execute a few of the men, to set an example. A verbal summation to the committee's clerk of the rioting and viciousness since they took Reading yesterday.

'You know the clerk, I believe, Oliver Chettle?'

Ned nods.

'Thought so, that's why I'm sending you. We don't want our misdemeanours here too widely shouted about in town. A quiet word with Chettle, and permission from the committee to set aside the law and deal with a few miscreants publicly and sharply. That's what I want you to come back with.'

A boy arrives with a plate of bread and cheese, and puts it down amid the chaos on the table. Skippon gestures at an empty chair.

'Eat something before your ride, Ned.'

Awkwardly Ned sits, and takes the proffered food. There has not been much around for those sickened by the looting, and he is famished.

'Thank you, sir,' he stammers between mouthfuls.

'Sad business, this. Your first siege and sack, I suppose, Ned? I have seen too many now. At least we've no report of rapes or civilian deaths – not yet, anyhow. There's a spark of the godly in them still, beneath the gallons of ale.'

'My father told me it was not so in the Low Countries.'

Skippon smiles ruefully. 'He did not love being a soldier, your father.'

Ned wants to ask why a man such as Skippon likes it, but knows his place. This descent into bestiality has horrified him, despite his father's warnings. He is shocked by the soldiers' easy carousing, and by the officers' resigned acceptance of it. Why am I shocked by man's vile nature, he wonders, as an image of Milly's white face appears in his mind's eye.

'Men are frail creatures,' Skippon says, as if reading Ned's thoughts. 'This vileness is the aftermath of fear. I do not know why God sends us mad after a battle, but He does. It takes a strong man, or a sober one, to resist it.'

'This… this abomination cannot be His will,' says Ned.

'All is God's providence, Ned, you know that.'

'There is a sty of filth in all our souls. We are beasts. Vile, low, unworthy of His love,' Ned says, a little too loudly.

Skippon tilts his head to one side and looks keenly at the young cornet. 'Aye. I do not know a single man who could bare an unblemished soul. If we did not so desperately need God's grace, and the intercession of His son, it would be no sort of a prize.'

Ned is unconvinced, but he nods anyway because he wants to please Skippon. He has thought of little else these two days. God's providence set against this rampaging of the godly.

'But sir,' he says, waving his hand vaguely towards the window, 'all this refutes Arminius. God's salvation is such a gift, such a bounteous, endless joy. And we are so filthy, so vile, such creeping low things. There is nothing any of us could do to deserve the gift; we are too damnable. So salvation cannot be linked to good works, sir, the way I see it. We are too low for any miserable actions that are within our grasp to save us.'

Ned's evident misery and his loneliness amid the pillaging are so evident, so raw, that Skippon is moved to grasp his shoulder. Ned is terrified, suddenly, that he might cry. This small gesture unmans him.

His commander smiles and forces some jollity into his tone. 'A wife, Ned – that's what you need. When all this confusion is reined in, nothing settles the soul so much as an honest woman.'

There is some truth in that, Ned thinks, as he climbs into the saddle and points his horse towards London. A wife. But what wife and when? Pretty, yes, but godly and modest. He remembers something Taffy said once: 'A homely Joan is as good as a lady when the lights are out.' Aye, Taf, he thinks, but best to marry one whose face you can worship. An image of Lucy Tompkins pops unbidden into his mind. A sign, Lord, he asks, as the phantom Lucy pirouettes in his head, smiling up at him shyly with parted, moist lips.

Ned dreams his domestic dreams all the way home, fighting off the intrusion of darker thoughts; a faceless wife spreading her thighs for him, the devil on his shoulder urging him on.

~ ~ ~

In his room in the Temple, Oliver Chettle sits back in his chair and listens to Ned's account of the siege. Ned tells him about the earthworks thrown up around the town, and the ten-day artillery bombardment. He tells of Aston, the royalist commander, who hung out his white flag moments before the royalist reinforcements arrived at the parliamentary rear. The king's troops paused, waiting for Aston to sally out and join them in crushing the rebels in a vicious pincer, and then came the dawning realization on both sides that Aston would stick to his flag. Ned tells Chettle briefly about the desperate fighting at Caversham Bridge to keep the royalists off, as Aston sat miserably behind the earthworks, bound by his own untimely capitulation.

'A noble man,' says Ned, 'to stick to his flag so. He could have hauled it down and come out to play. The outcome would have been very different.'

Chettle nods. 'Noble, certainly. Foolish also, perhaps. It would be interesting to know how His Majesty deems it.'

Ned is in no mood for ambiguities. Aston was noble, he tells himself obstinately, and hang the king's version.

Ned doesn't tell Chettle what else he learned during the siege. That the constant play of the big guns can jangle on a man's nerves until he feels close to breaking. That a ball travelling from a rampart at musket-shot distance will open up a man's body like a knife through mustard – and spatter his brains for up to ten metres. That a horse pinioned in a spike-pit will scream with pain and thirst and hunger for days until it finally lets go of life with just a whimper. These details feel far away, here in Chettle's book-lined office. Ned fights to hold on to them. They are more true than the smooth patter of the Temple. Outside Chettle's window, a fountain cascades.

'And Essex has made no concerted move on Oxford?'

Ned shakes his head.

'He is an old woman. He let them go at Turnham Green, and now he circles round Oxford like a French dancing master. And of course…' Chettle makes the sign of a cuckold.

Ned ignores it. He fights to remember that he likes Chettle. Them and us, he thinks. I have become a soldier; Chettle is the other. Ned sees the young lawyer as if from a great distance, across a mound of bodies and fear.

Briefly, Ned tells Chettle why he has come, the nature of his mission from Skippon. He describes the debauch he has left behind him.

'Animals,' growls Chettle.

Ned bristles. He can think it, but he was there. Chettle sits sleek and smug behind his desk and condemns Ned's fellows out of hand. Come and hold a pike next to Taffy, then call him an animal.

'Do they not realize that we lose our moral advantage if they rampage? Fools. How can we win the hearts of the undecided by behaving worse than the devil Rupert?'

'Perhaps,' says Ned, 'if we paid the men what we owe, we would not have to worry so much about their plundering.'

Chettle looks at him sharply.

'If men like your father paid up without arm-twisting then perhaps we could pay them.'

'I am not my father.'

'No,' says Chettle. A silence falls on them. 'Will you go to see him?'

'I was not planning on it.' I am a coward, thinks Ned. I can face a royalist charge, yet I cannot face a servant girl's sad white face. I am low.

'It might be wise,' says Chettle. 'Tell him quietly that his attitude is noted.' Chettle leans forward in his chair and speaks softly, despite the heavy walls and thick oak door between the two of them and the rest of the world. 'The estates of clear royalists are being sequestered.'

'My father is not a royalist.'

'Is he not? He is not a supporter of Parliament. The time in which neutrality was an option seems to me to have long passed. I have said enough, Ned. I have a fondness for your family, else I would not have spoken.'

Ned thanks him, his thoughts spinning. He does not care about the money, or the house. They are material trappings. A pure soul is above covetousness. What does William Gouge call it? 'A galling sin, which works in continual vexation.' And yet. Have I not always assumed that I will be rich? Ned wonders. That it will all pass to me, and my soul will be untainted by the pursuit of riches, simply because they will shower on me anyway? Oh Lord, he thinks. Every day you find me more unworthy.

Into his confused thoughts comes Chettle's voice again, this time loud and a little too careless. 'If you see her, send my regards to your sister,' he says.

'Of course,' says Ned. It is only afterwards, as he turns into Fetter Lane, that he notes Chettle's words.

~ ~ ~

The lights are on in the windows, and the house looks big and comfortable in the darkness. A sedan chair pulls up, just as he reaches the steps, and Hen tumbles out, flurried by the sight of him.

'Ned!' she cries. 'Ned!'

He kisses her, and then stands back to look at her. What does Chettle see? he wonders. To him, she has always been a funny, adorable freckled thing. She is smiling up at him, green eyes shining in the flickering light from the windows. She is, he realizes, quite beautiful, his little sister. Creamy skin and chestnut hair. Green eyes that shine with life and humour. It is the first time he has ever really noticed it. A strange, but not unwelcome, discovery.

'Hello, Hen, little one. Where have you been?'

'At the Birch house. Ned, it was so tedious I could have bashed my head on the wall a thousand times. I was to have stayed, but I begged off with a sore head. But where have you been, why are you here?'

'We took Reading – did you hear?'

'Yes! The whole town is talking of it.'

They are still standing on the steps and the sedan chair has trundled off.

'Come,' he says. 'We'll go in and I'll tell all.'

Inside, they hear voices from the library. Looking for their father, they turn into the room and stop, disconcerted.

In front of them, frozen in a guilty tableau, stand Challoner and Edmund Waller. The expression on both faces is peculiar, and

213

the silence that greets Ned and Hen's unexpected arrival spins out across the room. Waller stands to one side of the table, and to the other is a lady. She is dressed in courtly fashion, with a low bodice and a deliberate lack of puritan sobriety. She is about thirty, and handsome. She carries that air of careless elegance that must be worked on and burnished regularly to appear artless.

On the table between the three of them lie piles of golden coins, arranged in stacks and mounds. The gold glitters in the firelight. Ned looks at it, and then back to his father.

Challoner speaks first. 'Ned, we were not... That is...' He stumbles to a halt.

'I had business with the Committee for Safety. I thought to see you before returning to Reading in the morning.'

'Of course, of course. Reading.'

There is an awkward pause.

'Waller, you both know each other, I believe.'

The poet bows and murmurs: 'Delighted.'

'Lady D'Aubigny, allow me to introduce my son, Edward Challoner, and my daughter, Henrietta Challoner.'

Lady d'Aubigny sweeps into a low curtsy. Her hands twist nervously round a lace handkerchief, and her eyes dart from Ned to Waller and back again. Ned, though young, looks the soldier. He wears Essex's orange sash about his waist, and his hand rests lightly on his sword hilt. His doublet is spattered with mud and deeper stains the colour of rust.

Challoner walks forward and, laying a hand on each of their arms, says: 'Children, we have some business to conclude. Will you wait for me in the kitchen and have some food, and I will come for you?'

214

Ned shrugs off his father's arm. 'I will go now, I think, Father. Leave you to your . . . business.'

'Ned, please.'

Hen and his father both look at him in mute appeal.

Stiffly, he nods.

~ ~ ~

'Where is Sam?' Ned asks, as he and Hen walk downstairs to the kitchen.

'Probably in the counting house at the books, cursing your name. He's wild to be a soldier, Ned, and I'm not sure he'll obey Father for much longer.'

'Does he know of...' Ned looks for the word. 'This thing, do you think?'

'He has said nothing,' says Hen. She notes Ned does not ask her. Just a girl. Just a girl who ferried those gold coins that sit, heavy and accusatory, on Challoner's desk, from houses across the city. Just a girl who knows now to check if she is being followed, to take precautions. A girl who knows which barges defy the ban on travel to Oxford, and who sells the contraband pamphlets. A girl who has perfected an innocent face, and fought with her own conscience and won.

They enter the kitchen. Sally the cook and Nurse look up, startled. They stand and bustle forward, cooing over their Ned, sitting him down at the table. He unbuckles his sword and rests it against the wall. Wayneman, the house's new boy, stands near it. His eyes are like saucers and his fingers twitch in their desire to touch its glinting edge.

'Look at you, Master Ned!' says Sally.

'All grown up and a soldier,' says Nurse. 'I could quite cry at the sight of you.'

'Do you mind us down here? Father has… guests.'

Hen notices the slight hesitation before the word 'guests'.

'Always welcome, Master Ned, always!' Nurse and Cook compete to nod emphatically.

Ned looks around the kitchen and sees Milly in the corner. She is standing by the fire, stirring a pot, and that flush in her cheeks could just be the heat from the flames. He checks her belly. Flat, thank the Lord. She is not looking at him but stares fixedly into the hearth.

'Milly, child,' says Sally. 'Leave that pot alone, and let's fatten up Master Ned. I've some cold veal and a lovely cheese. Milly, get back to that stove, girl, and get going on a posset. Look at poor Master Ned's hands, all cold and red, they are.'

Hen sits next to Ned and takes one of his cold hands, rubbing it between her own. She wishes they were alone to talk.

'It is lovely to see you, Sally, and you, Nurse, and Milly. I have dreamt about this kitchen and the smell of it, lying on wet grass eating stale bread for my supper.'

'Stale bread,' says Cook, outraged. She stands from the table and bustles some more, stoking the fire and chivvying Milly, until at last the table is laden with food, and a steaming posset cup is laid ceremoniously in front of Ned. He drinks it up quickly, feeling its warmth. He will never take such a thing for granted, not since the field at Edgehill.

Don't think on it now, Ned, he tells himself. Not now. In his mind's eye a grey corpse lolls in an obscene pose. He closes his eyes, but it takes on Milly's frightened face and leers at him.

Harmsworth comes into the kitchen, and Ned rises, thankful to be distracted from his thoughts.

Harmsworth greets Ned with grave formality. 'We think of you often here, Master Ned,' he says, 'fighting in our Lord's name.'

'Thank you,' says Ned, wondering what the pious and serious Harmsworth would make of the godly soldiers now, as they puke and pillage their way around Reading. 'I brought you something,' he says, fumbling in his bag. He pulls out a small, charred piece of wood. 'Part of an altar rail we burned in a popish church. A token of our works, if you like.'

Harmsworth takes it and turns it over in his hands. He almost smiles.

'I envy you, Master Ned. Out there, protecting the true faith. Smiting the Lord's enemies. While I . . .' He waves a hand around the kitchen.

'I carry your words with me,' says Ned. He reaches for some bread and then hacks a chunk of cheese into his plate. He feels strange, vibrant: the same sensation he gets before a fight. There is an added roaring in his head, a Milly-shaped shame tugging at him. It is fogging his thoughts, distracting him. He looks over to where she stands in the corner, her face in the shadows. He is mortified to find his eyes resting on her body, lit by the firelight. He wrenches his eyes away. His blood thickens at the thought of her naked.

As casually as he can manage, he asks Harmsworth: 'Waller, and the lady with Father. Are they here much?'

'Waller, more and more. Sometimes alone, sometimes with others. Tompkins, in the main. None that you would wish to be here, I am sure. As for *her*…' He spits the word. 'It is the first time.'

'Did you see the bezoms on her?' says Nurse.

'You could not miss them,' says Sally. 'I crept up to have a look,' she says in an aside to Hen. 'I could scarce credit how low her bodice is cut.'

'I had to clasp my hands behind my back to save me going over and wrenching it upwards, a little nearer God and decency,' says Nurse.

'I thought she looked lovely,' says Hen, belligerent.

Nurse frowns. Only Ned's presence makes her hold her tongue, and Hen takes a petty pleasure from the knowledge that Nurse will be bubbling with fury inside.

'So elegant,' Hen continues. 'Such poise and grace.'

The door to the kitchen opens and Challoner stands in the doorway, filling it. Not looking at Ned, Henrietta stands. She walks over to her father and kisses his cheek.

'Mrs Birch bids me to send her love. I came home early. With a headache.' She knows his eyes are not on her but look above her head to where Ned sits, glowering and quiet in the corner.

'I smell a posset,' he says.

Milly quickly moves to dole some out of the pot.

'Ned, Henrietta. Come and drink this with me by the fire in the library.'

In the library, empty of its visitors, Challoner pokes at the logs, setting a fresh flame ablaze. He sits in his great chair, leaning back. Hen kneels at his feet, her arms folded. Ned stands, waiting.

'A fine posset, this,' says Challoner.

Ned grunts, impatient. He is still keyed-up, close to boiling over. 'Are we not to mention what we saw?'

'And what did you see?'

'Gold, and guilt.'

'Guilt?' Challoner speaks the word as if he is testing the sound in his mouth. He rolls it around. 'Guilt?' he says again, the interrogative stronger this time.

'Pudding cat,' he says to Hen. 'What did you see?'

'Just Waller. And a lady.'

'Just so.' He turns to Ned.

Ned gestures angrily. He paces the floor, but it does not take the edge off the furious energy rising in him. 'Do not play me for a fool, Father. We know that merchants are smuggling gold out of the city to Oxford. That woman in her whore's weeds had courtier writ large on her. And Waller – we know where he lies.'

'And if you are right, Ned? What then?'

'You are paying for the guns which point at me, and my fellows. What would you have me do?'

'I would have you at home, in peace, in a land which is no longer sliding towards chaos. I left you free to follow your conscience, yet I am not free to follow mine?'

Hen watches the sparks fly between them. Challoner is growing angry, his face red and his knuckles white where his hands grip the side of the chair.

'I fight with honour,' shouts Ned. 'Sword in hand. I do not skulk inside, dealing in Judas coins with fops and whores.'

'You have said enough, boy. Enough.'

'And so, sir, have you.'

Ned turns to leave and, as an afterthought, holds his hands to Hen. She jumps up and kisses him.

'Ned,' says Challoner. They turn to look at him. 'Go, then.

But do not speak of this. It is between us.'

Ned doesn't reply; he can't. He thinks he might be sick, all the nervous tension and the fury spewing onto the floor. This breach feels irreparable. A chasm has opened up between them, too wide to cross. Hen is crying quietly into his shoulder. He grasps the hilt of his sword for courage. He looks at the old man's face and can see only a traitor's mask.

'Father,' he says quietly, 'the devil is talking to you. He is in your heart, and in your head, and in those piles of gold. He is in Waller's tongue and that woman's eyes.'

The door sounds loud as it swings shut behind Ned. Hen and Challoner look at each other, stricken.

~ ~ ~

Will opens the door, and Ned watches with relief as a smile spreads across his friend's face. He did not know where else to go.

'Sorry to come late,' he says.

'Nonsense. Come in!' The room is lit by one guttering candle, by which Will is reading. Ned sits down on the bed as Will bustles around, laying a fire and unearthing some ale and a mouldy-looking cheese.

Will waves a hand at his bare room, and the pathetic fire catching in the grate. 'Much like Oxford, you see, Ned. Father's allowance doesn't stretch far.'

'Still, brother, you'll be a lawyer soon.'

'Aye, so the bastards tell me.'

'I'll swap you for being a soldier.'

'No fear, Ned. I'll not go for a soldier.'

'Can you stay out of it?'

'I keep my head down; no one bothers me. I have perfected the art of the non-committal nod.' He demonstrates, and Ned laughs. 'I find that it serves. If I am quiet, and nod, people are easily persuaded I agree with them, and leave me to my own thoughts. My master is convinced I am puritan to the soul, as he is.'

'And what are you?'

'Ah, you see, only you know me well enough to ask directly, and even to you I cannot be candid. Because the truth is I don't think on it much. I have enough to think about.' He waves at the stack of books balanced precariously against the wall. 'And those,' he says, grinning, pointing to a far smaller stack sitting forlorn in a darker corner, 'are my law books.'

'The country is at war, all our souls are at risk, and you are content with the stars.'

'Yes. I am too simple to understand my own soul, let alone anyone else's.'

'I envy you.'

'You do not.' Will smiles at his friend.

They settle down in front of the fire to talk quietly and companionably about friends and acquaintances. There is a reckoning of who has joined which side, and who has lost limbs or life for the sake of King or Parliament. Ned tells Will about Brentford and Reading, and the searing horror of an army loose on the rampage after a battle. He tells him a little, too, of the night spent in the field of corpses after Edgehill.

'It's different now, already. That first battle was strange, Will. It was as if both sides were boys playing at soldiers, then one drew blood and both ran home crying. Now, enough has passed to make it bitter and personal. We are harder, and tougher, and angrier.'

'Aye, but to what end? Where can it end? If he wins, you are a traitor, a marked man. If you win, he will still be king. The king will always be the king.'

Ned turns the sentence round in his head. He can't find a hole in it.

Will says: 'Let us talk of other things. How is your family? Your sister?'

'Well enough. Poor Hen sat there while we fought tonight. She's a good girl. I think Oliver Chettle has a sweetness for her.'

He notes the sudden stiffening of his friend, a subtle re-calibration of the room's warmth. 'You too, Will?'

'You didn't know?'

Ned thinks of his grandmother's bony finger pointing at Hen, telling her she will die a maid. He wonders at his own blindness and Grandmother's mistake. He remembers, suddenly, that he never passed on Chettle's warning. But you can't creep back in after you've slammed a door in anger, not without losing pride. Chettle is over-worried, he convinces himself. He has a fancy for Hen, yet can't marry the daughter of anyone uncommitted to the side of God and Parliament. That is all. That must be all.

'No,' he says, touched by the look of misery on Will's normally guileless face. 'I didn't know.'

Later, head to toe in Will's narrow bed, Ned cannot sleep. He thinks over the scene he witnessed earlier. How far has it gone? Where does my duty lie? If my father is funding my enemy, does he not become my enemy too? He can tell that Will is not asleep

222

either; he lies there with the too-still mien of a man awake but conscious of his bedfellow. He's probably thinking about Hen.

Hen. What will happen to her if their father's scheming is laid bare? Should her fate inform any decision? He wishes he were alone, to toss and turn as the thoughts jumble in his head. He lies still, and turns to his God. Oh Lord, show me the light. Show me the right path.

CHAPTER SIXTEEN

May 1643

*T*HEY COME AT DUSK. A CLATTER OF SOLDIERS BURSTING into the house, separating into pairs and running at the stairs, barging through doors and shouting. Hen is in the library, reading by the open window. She has been relishing the warm spring air and the quiet that falls on the city between the end of the working day and the start of the evening jaunting.

The roaring of the soldiers breaks in on her dreaming. She struggles to understand it, at first. The crunch of their feet and the bellowed orders make no sense. The house is unused to these sounds. Then she realizes, with sudden desperation, why they are here. She grabs a fistful of papers from the royalist pamphlets pile and shoves them up her skirt, wedging them fast in her stays. She spots the pile of newsbooks, including the *Mercurius Aulicus*, on the table. They are smuggled from Oxford on the rare barges that make it down the Thames, and Hen buys them at three times the cover price from a bookseller's desperate widow who lurks in St Paul's churchyard.

Hen scoops them up and bundles them under the cushions of the window seat, sitting down on top of the lumpy fabric just as the door bursts open and two soldiers tumble in.

They see her sitting there and they halt, with almost comical awkwardness, in the doorway.

'Beg your pardon, miss,' says one, a little sheepish.

Hen remembers the carriage of Lady D'Aubigny, her extraordinary poise. She draws herself up and lifts her chin, and then says in a voice infused with as much steadiness as she can manage: 'How dare you burst into my room like this. Who are you? What business can you have here?'

They mutter something inaudible. Behind them, she can hear her father's voice. Though she can't hear his words, she can tell from his tone that he is blustering. He's turning on the boozy charm, and she prays to God it will work.

The soldiers continue to stand foolishly in the doorway. They look like apprentices from the rougher trades, scooped up from the tanner's workshop or the smithy, handed a sword and told to be fierce. Hen holds her pose. A man comes in behind the pair.

'Miss Challoner?' he says. He is expensively and soberly dressed. His coat is cut from fine midnight-black cloth. His hair is sparse on top but long at the back, where it curls almost foppishly over his gleaming white collar. His eyes are pale and unblinking. There is something at once clammy and fleshy about his skin, like hot-crust dough slipping from its mould.

She nods. The man – around her father's age she would estimate, perhaps a little younger – bows.

'Nehemiah Stroud, Miss Challoner, at your service.'

'If so, my service demands you leave this house immediately, whoever you are.'

He bares his teeth in a semblance of a smile. 'Wit, good lady? We are taking your father.'

Hen feels her poise slipping away. 'Where to?'

'The Tower, of course.'

She closes her eyes. The Tower. Dear Lord, protect us.

'What for?'

'Treason.'

'Against whom?'

'Very droll, again, dear girl.' He inclines his head in a demi-bow. 'And now I must ask you to leave. We must search the house.'

Hen pulls the poise back, tucking herself up in it like a blanket on a cold night.

'And if I refuse to leave my own house?'

'You cannot, I'm afraid.'

'Mr Stroud, is it? I have nowhere to go. One brother lives at home, and is out somewhere. The other is marching with Phillip Skippon. His right-hand man. Ned was at Edgehill and at Reading.'

Stroud smiles again, and she realizes that he knows all this. He knows all about her, and all she has is his name. This imbalance of power unsettles her.

'Your admirable brother will, I fear, be distraught when he hears of your father's betrayal.'

There is something she does not like about the way he says it, something knowing and snide about his tone. Her father has come into the room behind the soldiers and she wonders if he caught the off-key tone in Stroud's voice. His face is impassive; only a nervous adjustment and readjustment of his cuffs suggests he is aware that a troop of armed soldiers is raiding his house and threatening him with the Tower. He can walk, at least. The gout is in abeyance, for now. She wants to run over and stand by him, but she fears the rustling of the paper in her skirts and the exposure of the lumpy cushions.

Challoner's eyes dart to the table where the *Mercurius* had been sitting, and the space where the newest royalist pamphlets were sitting. Others – the oldest ones – are held in a chest he has buried in the garden.

Stroud picks up a murder pamphlet from the table, from amid the towering stacks of papers. It is a lurid account of a crypto-Catholic's slaughter of his wife and child. He looks at the woodcut on the front and turns it sideways, to better establish that it is indeed the child's headless, spurting trunk on the floor. He tosses it to one side.

'I will go through these later,' he says. 'And now, Miss Challoner, you may, if you prefer, wait in the kitchen with the servants.'

'I would prefer to stay here,' she says.

Challoner walks towards her.

'Pudding cat. Do as the man says.'

She tries to speak to him with her eyes. 'I would have a minute alone with my father.'

Stroud, visibly impatient, waves a dismissive hand. 'Miss Challoner. Enough. Move now.'

Challoner holds out a hand and she takes it. Standing, she watches Stroud as his eyes move past her to the lumpy cushions now laid bare. He walks over in short, sharp strides and pulls a cushion away from the seat with one violent motion. The newsbooks tumble to the floor. Loose papers float like leaves and settle on the library's rush-strewn floor.

Stroud stoops down and picks one up. The front page, in bold type, spells out its aims: 'Communicating the Intelligence and Affairs of the Court to the rest of the Kingdom'.

Hen is still holding her father's hand, and he squeezes it tightly.

'Will we have to stretch that pretty neck too?' says Stroud. 'Quite a collection, Miss Challoner.'

'They're clearly mine, Stroud,' says Challoner. 'Now, can we get on with this? Hen, go to the kitchen. Go on, child.'

Hen walks stiffly to the door, trying not to dislodge any of the papers. A sudden thought comes to her.

'My grandmother,' she says to Stroud. 'Please. She's upstairs. She's too scared to leave her room. Please don't make her. She'll be terrified.'

Stroud just slides his face into a strange, bloodless smile.

In the kitchen, Hen sits with Sally, Nurse and Milly at the table. Harmsworth faces the fire, his face hidden from view. The boy Wayneman cries, frightened.

'Stop that noise, you wretched sniveller,' spits Nurse.

Milly holds out an arm and the boy comes to hide his head in her skirts.

'Fool boy,' says Nurse.

Silence again. They listen to the tramp of the soldiers' boots overhead, echoing through the floors.

'They said they were taking him to the Tower,' says Hen.

'Jesus wept,' says Sally under her breath.

'What will become of us!' cries Nurse. 'We shall be turfed out to beg, to pimp, God help us.'

Suddenly they hear screaming. A high-pitched wail pierces through the house.

'Grandmother,' whispers Hen. She stands and walks to the kitchen door, pulling it open. A soldier stands, blocking the way.

The screaming fades into a low whimpering. Hen watches as three soldiers carry her grandmother down the stairs, gripping her thin wrists and ankles. Carrying her like a sack of coal, they toss her into the kitchen, and she scampers into the corner furthest from the fire. There she crouches, her grey hair loose and tangled around her face, her thin arms clutching her knees. Hen can see the purple fingermarks of the soldiers on her skin.

'Grandmother,' she says quietly, and crouches down next to the old lady. She reaches a tentative hand out to touch her shoulder.

Quickly, spitefully, her grandmother twists and spits at her.

'Did you ever see the like?' whispers Sally. 'Wits set adrift by fear, poor thing.'

Hen remains crouching down, not sure of what to do next. Her back is pressed against the wall, and she leans her head against it. Lord, give me strength, she prays. Please, please, give me strength.

'Look at her,' says Nurse. 'Looks like she's right all along. Damned. Clearly damned. Would our Good Lord send one of his own to such a state?'

Hen finds herself standing, fury blinding her. Before she recognizes her own actions, she has slapped Nurse across the face – a full, open-handed slap, which sends Nurse's head cracking backwards, her mouth frozen into an 'Oh!' of astonishment. The noise of the slap ricochets around the kitchen, and even Harmsworth turns round. Milly smothers a smile, and the boy registers amazement amid his still-flowing tears.

Ashamed of her violence, yet fiercely refusing to regret it, Hen retreats into the corner. Nurse puts a hand to her red cheek, looking at Hen all the while. She opens her mouth as if to speak, but then closes it. They look at each other, and then both look away.

The door is closed again, the soldier on the other side. Hen stands up and walks over to the fire. Ignoring Harmsworth, she reaches under her skirts and pulls out the sheaves of paper concealed there. She throws them into the fire in batches. They catch and burn, the black charred edges spreading to devour the words. Rants against rebels and radical plots. Warnings of women preachers and social sedition in all its devilish guises. Exhortations of loyalty to the king, paeans of praise to Prince Rupert and the warrior Queen Henrietta, who shared a ditch with the king's soldiers at Edgehill as the cannonballs whistled over her head.

All the words crumple and burn in the flames. It is a gesture towards helping her father, but it is too little, too late. Destroying the words will not help, she knows that. Stroud knows. And after all, her father is clearly guilty. Of something, anyway. He is not the only one. Fear prickles across her skin in a familiar pattern. Jesus, keep me. Please, God.

Hen feels herself faltering. She could too easily curl into the corner next to Grandmother and start whimpering. If I lose my mind, she thinks, who will help Father? I am to be tested, like Peter at the cock-crow, and I fear that I will fail.

At last, the door opens, and Stroud appears. His pale eyes sweep the room until he finds her.

'Miss Challoner. We are taking your father. I have no doubt he will be given liberty of the Tower soon, and you will be allowed to visit.'

'I must come to say goodbye.'

'Too late, I fear,' he says with a smirk. She feels her fingers itching to deal out another slap.

Hen waits until she hears the front door thud shut before she emerges from the kitchen. The house is turned upside down. Chairs are upended, chests emptied, beds stripped. In the hall, her father's great chair lies tipped on its side, amid the chaos. The chest where the dining service is kept lies open, its contents thrown across the floor. In the library, the books are pulled from the shelves. Loose pages litter the floor; countless spines lay cracked, broken underfoot.

Something crunches under her feet – glass. She looks down and, with infinite care, picks up the broken pieces of The Object, her father's microscope. She sits, cross-legged on the floor, trying to piece the bits together. Behind her, there are footsteps.

'Hen, thank the Lord you're safe. What in Christ's name happened here?'

'Sam! Sam, I can't fix it. It's broken, Sam. I can't do it.'

She breaks then, spilling great, heaving sobs into Sam's shoulder as he crouches on the floor next to her, looking around at the chaos in the gathering darkness.

CHAPTER SEVENTEEN

$\mathcal{H}$EN WALKS THROUGH THE TOWER'S GREAT ARCH, PAST THE guards and the idle gawpers, past the cluster of ravens which gathers at the entrance, past the beggar woman who sits every day begging for coins and lamenting her lost husband. Just a week of this routine. It is incredible how quickly the extraordinary can become commonplace.

She walks under the shadow of the White Tower and ducks into a doorway in one of the further, smaller towers embedded in the wall. Even this place has its hierarchies. Her father is in a small room with a slit for a window and a bare stone floor. But he has the liberty of the Tower and can come and go within its walls. Hen has done her best with cushions and hanging cloths to soften the room. No shelves here, just books in stacks against the walls. A layer of dust is collecting on the surface of the uppermost books – they are horribly undisturbed.

Her father rises to greet her. She hates his forced smile. The light has gone from his dear face, and what's left is a shell, brittle and empty. She lays down her basket of food and kisses him.

'Dear one,' she says. 'How did you sleep?'

'Fair, pudding, fair.'

She looks out of the thin window into the courtyard. A gang of children are playing an intricate game with a ball. Sunlight finds its way through the ramparts in patches; men and women cluster in the dappled light. An old man sits on a bench in the corner, turning his face up to catch the sun. A couple argues in a darker corner, the man waving an angry finger at the woman.

It could be a normal street. If you walk through the cobbled paths quickly, and try not to think about the darker corners, that is. There is talk of the Rats' Dungeon, deep in the Tower's bowels, where high tide floods the cell and draws the rats in, hungry and vicious. There is an old and crooked man who walks the cobbles and tells all who will listen of his time in Little Ease, the four-foot square hole which forces a man into a perpetual bestial crouch.

The Tower is safe enough, for most, above the cobbles and in the daylight. At night, when the ghosts roam, and below street level in its dark recesses, it reeks of evil. Tortured souls wander here, they say. Papists and godly alike, depending on which sister was on the throne. Their souls walk where their bodies were racked and stabbed, pliered and twisted and forced to recant. Every fire, here, carries the echo of flames past, when the kindling was heretics and the spark was a monarch's righteous fury.

They say Archbishop Laud is here somewhere, but Hen has not seen him. The Tower is full to bursting. Thomas Hood, Challoner's warder, wears the perpetual look of a man ordered to feed scores of mouths on two loaves. Not that she pities him; he is an unbending keeper. A man without compassion. He has developed a knack of seeing only the prisoner, and not the man. Perhaps it's a necessary skill for a warder.

She turns back into the room, where her father sits on his bed and gazes at some point in the middle of the room as if it holds some deep significance.

'Have you eaten?'

'Yes, child, don't fuss.'

'What have you eaten?'

'And would you care to know the secrets of my bowels too? God rot it, Henrietta. Leave off mothering me.'

She turns back to the window, waiting for his anger to blow itself out, and the inevitable contrition to set in.

She watches a small, cheerful man walk across the courtyard, waving his arms about to make a point to the younger man who towers over him. Is that Laud? If so, she wonders, does he feel the shame of helping to bring us all so low? Without Laud, would the country be all ablaze?

She runs through the steps they have taken since her father's arrest. Letters have been sent to Ned and Uncle Robert; the Lord knows if they will arrive. Sam managed to unwind at least some of their father's deals on the sly before news of his imprisonment and looming sequestration reached the Exchange. His face was aglow with his small triumph. He converted what little stock he could into cash, albeit at pitiful prices.

Life continued as normal, otherwise. The servants kept on, and in the dark. The house still lit with full wax candles – no tapers or rushes. Meat on the table. Ale brewed and poured. Washing pummelled and scrubbed. Keeping face. And keeping faith that their father will escape this web.

Tompkins and Waller were arrested too. Let them hang. God, please, let them hang, not him.

'I will visit Lucy Tompkins and her father later,' she says, still gazing out of the window. 'Do you have a message for him?'

'No. But thank you. I will see him later anyway, no doubt. The girl never stops snivelling. Grates on a man's nerves. If her godly relatives refuse to take her in, you may have to, after we swing.'

'You will not swing,' she says.

Lord, not Lucy. Hen feels the burden already of Grandmother, old and feral. Her wits have never returned. The servants are edgy, too, and needy. She is weary of maintaining her poise, but to let it slip would sow panic. And now Lucy to add to it, who sleeps on a trestle bed in her father's Tower cell. She veers between tears and whining. Hen prefers, on balance, the whining. At least it sometimes has a measure of wit about it, the occasional flash of acerbic spirit.

'Hen. I will swing, you must know it.'

'I do not.'

'My trial starts in one month. It will be absurd, I warn you now. A mock trial, like Strafford's or Laud's.'

He reaches for his wine glass. The sun is still low: hours to go until noon. He sits here all day and drinks, she knows. Waiting to pass out. These hours before lunch are his most lucid.

'We will be scapegoated. A new Hipponax.'

'Hipponax?'

'The *pharmakós*. There's nothing new in man's history, my kitten. In ancient Athens, at times of strife, the Demos would appoint a scapegoat: a human sacrifice to atone for whatever is rotten in the state. Hipponax, the satirist, was one. I am to be another.'

He stands and paces, waving his free arm for emphasis.

'Sacrificed for the sake of this rotten government, which needs my blood to shore up its waning support. Bastards. And Waller, the bastard, is calling in his friends and favours. Mark this, Hen. His neck will not stretch, while me and Tompkins will dangle like scarecrows. Westminster protects its own.'

'Stop it, Father, please. Stop. Would you have me snivel like Lucy? I am trying not to break, but you are not helping.'

'Am I not?' He turns to look at her. She watches him struggle with some internal strife. 'Aye,' he says, and sits down heavily. 'I am called a traitor. A traitor! To whom, Hen? The ignorant culls. How can loyalty to the king be treacherous? How can loyalty to being at peace be treacherous? This land is bleeding, and they call me the traitor, God blast their souls.'

He pours a fresh measure. 'I have a duty to you, my pudding, with what time I have left. Here's the truth, so you at least shall know it. I did arrange for monies to be sent to the king. I did secretly collect gold, and make contact with those loyal to the king in the city.' He drops his voice. 'Tell nobody of your involvement, Hen. Nobody.'

She nods.

Louder again, he says: 'I was the channel for the money, and Lady D'Aubigny the boat that took it to Oxford. All else, those wild stories of a deeper plot to kidnap the king's children, or to seize the city walls – that is all fantasy. I wish, now that I am to be condemned anyway, that I had gone further.'

'Really? Yet you are not such a friend to the king.'

'Not to the man, perhaps, but to his state. What are we without order, child, but savages? I wanted you to be safe in an ordered world. Instead . . .' He trails off. Then suddenly, rainbow-like, he smiles, and the rarity of that once familiar act brings tears rushing into Hen's eyes.

'The indignity of it, my pudding,' he says quietly through his smile. 'It is cruel to be hanged as a pawn at the start of the game. If I am to be hanged, I could have at least played the knight's part.' He laughs, incredulous. 'I thought I was a rook, pudding, that's the joke. And yet I was a pawn all along.'

He takes her face in both his hands and looks into it, as if searching for something. 'Don't let anyone make a pawn of you. The brightest and best of all my children,' he says. 'And you a girl.'

He kisses her. 'Did Will ever tell you, or show you, how to look at the sun?'

She starts at Will's name on her father's lips.

'No, Father.'

'You cannot look at it straight on. Turns you blind. You must project it onto paper. I have been thinking much of that, in here. No man can look at his own soul, look straight at it with no tricks or artifice, without running mad. So we tell ourselves our own story, and make ourselves heroic, and tell our hearts lies about our baser actions. We project our souls onto paper and garnish the results with bravery or kindness. We have to believe our own stories, pudding.'

He stands and paces to the window, peering out. He stretches a hand through the opening until it finds the sunlight.

'It's a gift, in a way, pudding, to know that death is coming. I can feel it breathing on me. And I'm looking at my soul, as straight as I can.'

He stops speaking, and she sees the fat tears rolling down his face. She jumps up and pushes herself into his arms, pressing her head into his chest.

He whispers into her hair: 'And I've failed. Oh Lord, how I've failed.'

The door opens, banging against the wall, and Sam walks in. He is drawn and pale. He brings with him the stale, hoppy tang of the tavern.

'No word from Ned?' asks Sam at once.

They both shake their heads. The three stand and look at each other. Ned's absence makes a triangle, where by rights there should be a square. We are aligned all wrong, thinks Hen. No symmetry. She thinks of Will, suddenly, sketching out the universe's thirst for harmony, for parallels. The heavens yearn for beauty, and we blight Earth with our ugliness.

'The army is close enough. We should have heard by now.' Sam's voice is heavy, dripping with hurt and anger.

Hen looks at her father, who lays a hand on his son's shoulder.

'It is no great wonder that Ned is silent. You have guessed, Sam, and you, my clever cat, that it was Ned who betrayed me.'

'No!' She shouts it, even though his words speak to some unacknowledged truth that lies hidden in her mind. 'No.'

'Who else?'

'No,' she repeats again, quietly, as if the repetition will make her will become the truth. She looks at Sam's sullen face, and knows that he believes it. And the three of them sit in silence for a time, watching the shadows lengthen on the walls.

~ ~ ~

The next morning, Sam and Hen are waiting outside Oliver Chettle's office when the young lawyer arrives for work. A whistle dies on his lips as he sees them standing there, and he looks nervously over his shoulder as he ushers them inside. He is all courtesy, but his unease is obvious.

'I should tell you I have been asked to help prepare the case against your father,' he says, as soon as he decently can. 'I will decline, on the grounds of knowing the family. But it may not be so easy to avoid.'

Hen sits in a proffered chair. She is light with hunger.

Sam says: 'It is kind of you to see us, sir. We do understand, in these times . . .'

Chettle nods. 'But I'm not sure how I can help.'

Hen breaks in. 'We do not understand what Father faces. No one will talk to us.'

Chettle squirms a little in his chair. If Hen had any space for laughter left, she would raise a smile at his visible discomfort.

'Miss Challoner. How blunt do you want me to be?'

'Blunt.' She pulls herself upright in the chair. 'I am not a child, nor am I a fool. If you sugar-spin your words, I shall not thank you for it.'

'Very well.' He stands and paces.

'This is unofficial, you understand. This conversation is entirely hypothetical.'

Sam and Hen nod.

'It seems, from what I understand, that there is little doubt

239

as to your father's involvement in some level of royalist plotting. The question is how far does it go. And a deeper question is how far does Parliament want it to go.'

'I don't understand,' says Sam.

Chettle looks at him, before continuing slowly and deliberately.

'Stroud is a new man, and ambitious. He has a direct line to Pym's ear. There are some awkward decisions looming. Your father, and Tompkins and Waller, are public moderates. It would be –' he pauses, searching for the right word – '*convenient* for prominent moderates to be unmasked as active royalists, and your father and his friends have played into their hands.'

'You are saying it may not matter how far the plot has gone, but only how far it can be perceived to have gone,' Hen says.

Chettle nods again, his lawyerly mask slipping a little to reveal some unexpected compassion.

She sits back in her chair, closing her eyes. 'Like the plague-sore,' she whispers.

Sam looks confused. 'Plague-sore?'

'No matter. Lay it out bald for us, Mr Chettle.'

'The best outcome? Lengthy imprisonment in the Tower, and a sequestration order on his estates.'

Sam grips the table. 'And the worst?'

Chettle mumbles. 'I'm sorry.'

'It won't come to that,' says Hen firmly. 'Explain sequestration orders, if you please, Mr Chettle.'

'The sequestration committee will issue an order. Your assets – in this case the house and any liquid capital – will be seized for the duration of the order. The house will be leased, and Parliament will take the profit. And any profit from the assets of the business.'

'There will be no profits from the business while Father is imprisoned,' says Sam. 'His business is the sum of his character and enterprise. Without his person, there are no profits.'

Chettle spreads his hands. 'The orders work better on the gentry, whose income derives primarily from land rents. Less messy for the committee.'

'Lord forbid we should make things messy for the committee,' says Sam.

Hen stands. 'Thank you, Mr Chettle.'

'You are going?'

'You have been very helpful. But we must leave you to your business now.'

'I am sorry,' he says as he opens the door.

She looks up at him. 'Yes. Yesterday, we were rich. Today we are homeless, penniless, and possibly fatherless. I believe I am sorry too. Good day, Mr Chettle.'

CHAPTER EIGHTEEN

July 1643

*I*N ONE WEEK, THEY WILL HANG HIM. THEY WILL CUT DOWN HIS still twitching body and pull his insides out in front of his eyes. He will be butchered, like a pig before a feast. All that he is, and was, will be reduced to a pile of still-warm flesh, the skin addled by knives. And what of his soul? Oh Lord, look after his dear soul.

Since the council of war pronounced its verdict, Hen has been struggling to stay standing. She feels as if the world is turning faster, spinning beneath her feet with incredible ferocity to carry her inexorably towards the gallows day. She is losing her balance, and time rushes on despite her prayers.

The gibbet will be built outside their house, so her father can look towards his own front door as the rope drains the breath from his body. Tompkins will be hung outside his house in Cheapside. And Waller? Waller is now standing in Parliament, speaking for his life, as Sam watches from the gallery.

She wanders, listless, around St Paul's churchyard. She tries, now and then, to pick up a book. Books have always been her crutch and passion. Yet now she cannot concentrate. The words swim. Life is too raw, too real, to be forgotten in lines of ink. She wonders, idly, if she will ever recover her love of books. She thinks of the girl who sat, curled in cushions and lost in words, and does not recognize her. A stranger.

Suddenly, as if by wishing it, Will stands in front of her. Will. He runs an ink-stained hand through his hair and grins uncertainly at her. There, under the shadow of St Paul's tall spire, amid the chatter of the customers and the patter of the booksellers, is her beloved. She smiles back at him. They are silent for a heartbeat she can hear pulsing in her head.

'William!' A new voice, sharp and sour.

Will starts and half turns.

'Mother,' he says, and Hen looks over to where a black-clad woman with pulled-back hair is staring at her with naked hostility.

'This is my mother, Sarah Johnson,' says Will. 'Mother, this is Henrietta Challoner.'

Hen notes the absence of explanation, and Sarah's bristling at her name. The women greet each other, wary. Hen looks curiously at the older woman. It's like reading an oracle, which tells her how Will could look when bitterness and time have tattooed their legacy on his face.

'I heard about your father,' says Will. 'I am so sorry.'

'Yes,' she says. 'There are some books he wants you to have.'

'How very kind,' says Mrs Johnson. 'Have them sent to William's rooms, by all means, Miss Challoner.'

Hen drops her head into a bow. 'What brings you to London, Mrs Johnson?'

'Just visiting my boy. Seeing how his studies go. Such a mountain of work he has, Miss Challoner. Such an age before he will be qualified. Such a life of toil and penny-pinching. He needs a mother's care, once in a while.'

Will squirms. Hen tries not to laugh too openly at the older woman.

'He is lucky, I am sure,' she says mildly.

Then, suddenly, it is too much – Will's passivity, his mother's protective hostility. I cannot, thinks Hen, be bothered with any of this. I am too tired. None of it matters. Let her hate me; let him flounder.

'Well,' she says. 'I will send the books. And now I must be home. My brother Sam will be waiting. You have not heard from Ned, Mr Johnson?'

'No, not for an age.'

'No, well. Goodbye, Mrs Johnson. And Mr Johnson.'

Mrs Johnson bobs a slight curtsy. She barely bothers to hide her relief as Hen turns away to walk down Ludgate Hill.

Once, Hen turns back to see them looking at her, Will's mother talking to the side of her son's face, which is set in a mask of hopeless misery. She turns her back on them and walks down the hill, striding under her skirts as if she's wearing Sam's breeches.

~ ~ ~

At home, she sits in the garden, waiting for Sam to return and tell her about Waller's speech. The sun is hot, and the sweat prickles up her back, and in all the folds and creases of her body. Sweat-slick skin. A sign of life. The dead don't sweat.

The garden, her father's pride, is overgrown and thick with weeds. Old Benny has not been seen since the arrests. She plays briefly with the idea of working herself, pulling up some weeds and rescuing the suffocating plants. But to what end? He will not come here again. He will not see the garden from his gibbet. Someone else will sit here soon; someone who pays Parliament rent to sit in her dead father's garden and sleep in his bed. Let that someone pull up the weeds.

She puts her head back and lets the sun burn her face. Silence from Ned. She will not think about Will.

Her father has asked her not to come. He is, she understands, marshalling his courage for a final meeting. He will send for her.

Her stomach rumbles, angry at her listlessness. Cook has gone to a new post, taking Milly and Wayneman the boy. She has known them her entire life; practically grown up with Milly. Yet they slipped out of her life with barely a glance backwards. Only Nurse and Harmsworth remain, waiting for the end. They each keep to themselves, avoiding each other on the stairs, raiding the fast disappearing stores in the pantry and eating alone. Like mice rattling around an empty house. Hen listens at doors to check the corridors are empty before scurrying out. She cannot face seeing Nurse. She saw her face when she brought home news of the trial, and it was different, suddenly: middle-aged, lost, scared. Hen needs to hold on to her hatred; she has no room for this unexpected surge of pity for her tormentor.

In this upside-down house, Hen is looking after Grandmother – badly. She feeds her and cleans her. She empties her bedpan and puts lard on her sores, and tries not to think as she does it. If she listens to herself, she will hear screaming. 'Let go, old woman. Please, let go.'

But Grandmother will not let go. Mute and unblinking, she somehow wills herself to stay alive. Her fear of the afterlife is stronger than her despair at her half-life.

Hen thinks back to the pronouncement of the sentence, and how her father crumpled as if he'd been struck. The case against him had been compelling. Stroud convinced all who listened that Tompkins, Waller and Challoner had been planning an audacious royalist coup. They were to seize the king's children and arrest a clutch of leading parliamentarians, including the Lord Mayor. They were to seize the Tower, and the forts, and the magazines, and arrange to let the king's army through the gates to take London.

'To awe and master the parliament! That was their despicable aim!' So Stroud thundered to the murmured sound of disapproval, no matter how vehement the denials. No matter how much her father shook his greying head and tried to protest.

She remembers Stroud's triumph at the sentence. And with even greater animosity, she remembers Pym's face. Quiet, disinterested satisfaction. The pawns are taken, and King Pym's position bolstered. She wanted to shout at him, to jolt him out of his detachment. In my game, he is not a pawn, but a man. He likes singing bawdy songs, and drinking Rhenish wine. He likes snow, and summer picnics. He loves my brothers and me, and he keeps a portrait of my mother in a locket. He is not fucking moulded from ivory, for you to tip over at your whim.

Then they led her father away, and she heard him shout: 'Be brave, my pudding. And look after your brothers.'

She nodded, holding on to Sam's hand, willing herself not to cry until he was gone.

She cries now, alone in the garden. A light smattering of tears: she has exhausted her well of sobs. Her throat is permanently dry, and her head aches. And still no word from Ned. Ned – a Judas? Please God, no. But why does he not write, at least?

Time passes. She knows this by the lengthening shadows and the gathering chill in the air. Perhaps she sleeps. Perhaps she just sits, trying to hear the world turning.

Sam flops down beside her on the bench. She leans into him. He is so alive, Sam. So warm and pulsing. She fancies she can feel the strength of his heart through his skin. She feels like she is drowning, and the pressure of his skin on hers is all that keeps her from slipping under the waves. She closes her eyes, imagining herself as a river corpse, floating down the Thames to be caught and buffeted by the eddies at London Bridge. What a release it would be. She imagines surrendering herself to the waves, the ecstasy of it.

Sam is silent. The trial has robbed him of his exuberance. He is a quieter, soberer boy. She can see Ned in him now, where once there was only wonder at the boys being related at all.

'Well,' he says heavily. 'It was as we thought. Waller grovelled, bowed and scraped. His tongue was so far lodged up Pym's arse you could see it poking out the man's navel.'

'And?'

'The word is that it has worked. It helps that his cousin is John Hampden, the darling of the House, and now martyr. You heard, Hen, that Hampden was killed by Prince Rupert's men at Chalgrove just weeks ago. Waller wears his dead cousin's shroud as armour. Waller is back to the Tower. But it is reckoned that is only a stop-gap, and a fat fine will see him free.'

'Can we not muster a fat fine for Father?'

'Too late. The council has condemned him, and besides, I heard more talk at Westminster today.'

'Well?'

His voice is harsh and distant. 'Pym is preparing a new oath. One to be sworn by all in Parliament. It will demand allegiance to the reforms, and vilify crypto-royalists.'

'Those who are not with us must be against us? So there will be no place for moderates?'

'No. Those who refuse to vow will be forced out, to join the king, perhaps. Those who would have liked to play pig in the middle will be forced to align themselves with Pym and his people. Once committed, they cannot row backwards.'

Hen digests the news. 'It's as Oliver Chettle warned us. Pym is using this plot for a political surge.'

'Indeed. So someone has to remain guilty. And if it is not Waller . . .'

They sit in silence for a while, Hen fighting to master her anger.

Then, at last, it comes, as she knew it would.

'I must go, Hen,' he says. 'To Oxford.'

'Not to Essex's army then.'

He grunts. 'You joke. Parliament is to kill our father. We all have our scales, Hen. Ned weighed Father's liberty against his conscience. I must use my own measures. Tip the Church, altar rails, Parliament's prerogatives, ship money and the king's weaknesses in one side. Add anything else you like: Catholic plots, evil counsellors and meddling queens. Tip it all in, and place our father's murdered body on the other side of the scales, and see which sinks fastest. No. To Oxford, Hen, to throw myself on the king's side. And one day, I shall stand in Westminster and stick daggers in the bastards' yellow bellies.'

Hen nods. 'Will you not stay until after?'

'After? No. I want to go now. Get stuck in. I want a sword, a pike, a musket. Anything. I want it, so wholly, so completely, that I'm sorry, Hen, but you cannot stop me. I ask only your blessing.'

'That you have, of course, Sam.'

'And you?'

'Someone has to look after Grandmother. How I envy you, Sam. To do something. To fight. What utter bliss. What joy.'

He finds a rare smile. 'They should raise a regiment of women, Hen, and set you at its head.'

'If only that were possible,' she says fiercely. She pauses for a space, before giving her greatest fear a voice. 'What if you meet Ned? In battle, I mean.'

'How likely is it? Besides, when he turned Judas, he set all this in motion.'

'But what if he did not? What if he is playing Peter, not Judas? Coward, not knave.'

Sam snorts. 'Hen, they came for Father first, before the others. They knew too much. About him, about us. If not Ned, then who? What happened, do you think, when he weighed his father against his God? Him and his poxed conscience.'

She sinks a little further into his shoulder.

'I must go to visit Father. When will you leave?'

'At daybreak.'

~ ~ ~

On the way to visit her father, Hen stops at the butcher's shop. Inside, a woman in her early thirties is cheerfully wielding a cleaver. She lifts it deftly and thwacks it down onto the wooden bench as if she's enjoying it immensely.

Hen watches, unseen. There is something comforting about watching this woman, with her capable hands and her sense of purpose. She stacks the portions she's been hacking neatly, and swings the leg round at right angles. She lifts the cleaver but then, as she's about to start the downward stroke, she notices Hen, stopping the swinging action with a lurch.

'Oh, miss,' she says. 'I'm sorry, I didn't see you.'

'Never mind. I was watching.'

'Cutting for pies, miss, begging your pardon. I like 'em all the same size, see.'

'Yes,' says Hen. She walks forward.

'Miss Challoner, ain't it?' the woman asks.

'Yes. Sorry, I…'

'It's all right, miss. I've seen you in church.'

'Oh. And your name…'

'Hattie Smith, miss,' she says, smiling, waving a bloody hand in a cheerful gesture.

The smell of pies permeates the shop, rich and deep. Hen suddenly realizes how hungry she is, and the realizing of it makes it keener. She feels dizzy.

'Are you well, miss?' comes Hattie Smith's voice, as if from a great and unbreachable distance.

'Yes, I…'

Hattie's there, suddenly, holding her by the elbow, guiding her to a chair.

'There now, miss. Don't you worry.'

'Sorry,' says Hen. 'Sorry, I didn't… I mean… Sorry.'

'Well now, you've not had an easy time of it, miss. I heard about it. Your father, I mean. And him such a kind, cheerful old chap. You been eating?'

Hen shakes her head. She thinks about how all her father's old friends cross the street to avoid them; the echoing silence from his business associates. She thinks about all the standing tall she's been doing when all she wants is to crouch.

Then Hattie pushes an oven-hot pie into her hands. 'There, miss. On me, and one for your father too.'

The unexpected kindness is too much, a final push, and Hen finds herself crying fat, inconsolable tears.

CHAPTER NINETEEN

$\mathcal{I}$NSIDE THE TOWER IT IS DARK AND COLD. DAMP CREEPS UP the wall. Hen stifles her regret at leaving the clean sunlight outside. She sits at his feet; he is in the only chair. The room is silent, thick with stale air and misery. The sunlight in the small window is blindingly bright. Sounds drift in from outside. She can hear the big cats in the menagerie roaring in unison – the keeper must be prodding them or provoking them. She can hear the sound of bowls being thrown, the thud and clink of the balls. Someone is singing a psalm, badly. Someone else is laughing loudly.

She can hear the scuttle of an insect across the stone flags, but she can't see it in the gloom. She looks up at him, at the way his shoulders droop, and his head lolls sideways; and always the slow, determined raising of glass to lips. She listens to the clink of the bottle hitting the rim of the glass, the sloshing of the fresh wine, and the rhythmic swallowing, regular as a heartbeat.

She lets herself be entranced by the stillness of it all. Hen has never been good at being still and empty of mind. In normal times, if she is still, she is asleep or reading. Too easily bored, her father said. Too male, Nurse said.

Occasionally he reaches down and strokes her hair. It is simply gathered at the back, unstyled. Who has time to tease out curls and lacquer down partings when the world is slowly shattering?

She watches the light in the window begin to lose its brilliant noon-glare. The game of bowls has stopped. How long has she been sitting here? They must think of food soon.

They have been sitting quietly for so long, she struggles to speak. 'Here, Father,' she says, pushing the pie towards him again. 'Please eat it. The butcher's wife gave it to you especially. Bade me make sure you ate it.'

'Not I,' he says, his voice muddy with wine.

'You must eat.'

'Must I? And why must I, Hen? Does it matter, when I'm up there, swinging, if I've eaten or not?' He looks at her and softens. 'Well now, pudding, perhaps a little wouldn't go amiss.'

'You're just humouring me.'

'Aye. I am.'

'Well, I am not hungry. We'll forget it.'

'Now *you* must eat. You're too thin, darling. Like a bargeman's pole. Not a wrinkle of fat on you.'

She puts her head on her drawn-up knees. Neither of them makes a move; they are gathered in by the torpor again.

'I used to think,' he says, 'when I was young like you, that if I knew my time was coming, I'd pack the intervening hours so full they would explode. Women and booze and laughter spurting out of them for hours like fireworks.'

'And yet,' she says.

'Yet I find I am sitting in the dark like a God-blasted mole. Waiting for judgement. Chalk that one up, pudding. Yet another thing the young, who think themselves so blasted clever, are wrong about. And here's another one, pudding. The young think that the old have cracked the great mystery. That they have learned how to die.'

'Not true?'

'Not at all. We're just as scared of death. We've learned nothing. But it's closer to us. We can hear the whoreson's scythe whistling past our ears in the darkness.'

'So it's the same – young and old.'

'No, not the same. Are you listening, pudding? The fear itself may be the same. But when you can hear Him whistling for you, it just means you are scared all the time. That's what age brings, pudding. No fucking wisdom. Just a nagging, perpetual fear. So stay young, my darling girl. Stay young.'

~ ~ ~

She doesn't wake when Sam leaves. When she does come to consciousness, it is late and the sun has warmed the curtains on her bed too much. She feels clammy and heavy. As she struggles out of sleep, she knows he's gone without having to call or search. The loneliness weighs perceptibly heavier on her. I will not bend, she vows to herself. I will not.

She is hungry. She pulls on an old gown and walks out of her room, forgetting to listen at the door for footfalls first. She nearly trips over Harmsworth, who is walking down the stairs, arms full of linens. He ignores her and carries on down the stairs, placing the linen in a pile next to a basket full to the brim with silver plate. Her father's best wine glasses are there too, laid in a padded chest.

'What are you doing?' She leans over the balustrade.

'Taking what's my due.'

'Your due? How dare you! Put it all back. Put it back, I tell you. Or I shall . . .' She trails off.

'Or you shall what, exactly, miss?' He smiles up at her from the bottom of the stairs. 'Twenty years, miss. Twenty years of abuse, and viciousness, and living in a house with no godliness. The devil dances here, and I've played the pipes too long. A godforsaken dandy-prat. And when the sequestration order comes, I shall be on the street, old and penniless. Just because your father could not see right from evil.'

'That does not give you a licence to steal.'

'Steal? No.' He turns his back on her and tidies up his pile of linens.

'Harmsworth!' she shouts, furious. She runs down the stairs and stands in front of him. 'Put it back!'

'Shut up, witch!' He shouts it at her, spittle flying from his mouth and landing on her cheek, like a slap. 'Vile, unnatural creature. Satan's whore.'

She takes a step backwards.

'I know all about you, witch. Meddling with mysteries. Reading the word of heretics. Cavorting with that unnatural boy. Do you spread your legs for the devil at night, witch? Do you call him in through your window? Does he suck on your witch's teats?'

She shakes her head, frightened by his vehemence. She backs into the wall.

Hen notices that he wears Ned's burnt cross round his throat, and it dangles down over his heart. He turns away, muttering. 'I should have denounced you, too.'

'Too? What do you mean, *too*?'

'What do you think? That I would sit by and let the devil's work go unchecked? That I would let Satan sit on your pig father's fat stomach and cause the ruination of all the godly reforms? All that Master Edward and his fellows fight for. He made me weak, your poxed and pathetic father, but he did not crush me altogether.'

'It was you! You informed on him!'

He smiles and puffs out his concave chest. 'Of course! Who else?'

He bends down and piles all his booty into one sheet of linen. He picks up the ends, twists them, and heaves the makeshift sack onto his shoulders. He makes for the door, and Hen stands aside to let him go. She waits until the door has slammed shut before she sinks to her knees and shouts her gratitude to God.

~ ~ ~

Hen is in Sam's familiar old breeches, her breasts bound against her chest and hidden under a heavy grey doublet. Heavy because she has quickly sewed every piece of her mother's jewellery, every piece of precious metal that Sam bought with her father's liquid assets, into its patched lining. Her pass, begged from a reluctant Chettle, carries Sam's name on it.

She has hired a horse from an inn outside the gate, and she is clinging, with an ungainly desperation, astride its saddle. She remembers trotting round the paddock in Oxfordshire on a horse named Strawberry, learning to sit man-style on the saddle. She can picture Anne's face, bright with laughter.

She is not distracted for long by her thoughts. The physical punch of her journey is starting to tell – already her thighs are feeling the unusual strain. Even though it feels like she has been travelling for ages, she can still see the walls and defensive works of the city if she turns her head.

By the end of the second day riding, her thighs are oozing blood through the breeches. Her skin is rubbed raw, and exquisitely painful. The muscles are screaming for her to stop. Yet still she rides, hour after hour. The latest horse she has hired from the postmaster is skittish. But at least her guide is silent, unlike the curious and garrulous fellow she jettisoned at Uxbridge. She had fobbed him off repeatedly, replying with curt lies to all his probes. There was one thing he said which stuck with her, that long day.

'An army marching through is like a plague of locusts,' he had said. 'It strips the country bare. It don't care about the lives it ruins. Don't care about which side they are on, even. Just destroys. That's all it does.'

She remembers the man's face, his curious stare and his button nose. 'Yup, locusts all right,' he said. 'And the folk with sense don't give a gnat's piss about altar rails or who prances about on the throne when they're weeping over the stripped bones of their pig.'

The words come back to her as she comes to the top of a small hill, and her taciturn guide points down the valley to a field furrowed with rows of tents, ringing a small and besieged town.

'Great Bicknell,' he grunts.

'And that's the army,' she says unnecessarily. It stretches far and wide, clusters of men lolling in the grass, smoke rising from countless fires. The sound of steel being sharpened, and of hammering, reaches the top of the hill. The smell of hundreds of cook-pots reaches her too, and she thinks of how much it must have taken to fill all those pots. All those stomachs to fill, all those thirsts to be quenched. Locusts.

The guide's horse snorts and paces, as if sensing its rider's impatience.

'I will take the horses now, Master Birch,' he says. There is an emphasis in the way he says the word 'master' that she does not like. 'I'll not take them down there, where a quartermaster will sniff them from a mile away, and have them for the cavalry. They're eating the country bare, the sods, and they'll not have these two.'

She climbs down from the horse's broad back, the change of movement bringing fresh agony. She follows the guide's gaze to where blood has seeped through the rough cloth of the breeches. Handing over the balance of what she owes, she sets off down the hill, walking as tall as she can manage, trying to ignore the pain.

It is nearing dusk, and the soldiers are laying fires in small groups. The atmosphere in the camp is heavy, and quiet, despite the golden beauty of the late afternoon. The ground beneath her boots is muddy, the crops trampled into the ground. A few men look up, but their eyes flick on, uninterested, as she moves through the tents.

The officers, she guesses, will be in the town. It's a small, unfortified place, and she approaches it on the main path. Just as the mud turns to cobbles, her way is blocked. A big, ugly man stands in front of her, a musket in his hand. His messmates are idling on the grass by the side of the path, and a couple turn lazily to watch the encounter.

'And where are yóu going?'

'I'm looking for someone.'

'Course you are, pretty boy like you.'

'Step aside.'

He just laughs at her as she tries to sidestep him. He moves too, and they are locked in a parody of a dance.

'Please!' She tries to keep her voice steady, but it cracks.

Suddenly he grabs for her, and grips onto her shoulder.

'Hold still, little eel,' he hisses as she tries to pull away. 'What's all that staining on your legs, hey? Been pissing blood, boy? Just excited to see me?'

He puts a meaty hand on her thighs, moving it upwards while she wriggles, as a few of his friends lolling on the grass laugh.

'Jesus!' He lets go of her suddenly. She tries to dart past him, but he grabs her coat and wrestles her to the ground. She can feel him lying on top of her, his breath like a ripe Stilton, his fat body crushing the breath from her lungs.

'Lads, it's a girl!' he shouts. 'Or a eunuch boy.'

They are interested now, the clutch of soldiers on the grass. They stand and move closer. He heaves himself off her, and she lies on the ground, pressing her forehead into the mud, trying not to cry.

'You sure?' a new voice growls.

'Unless the poor boy's got the paltriest package in Christendom.'

'Remember what we did to that whore we found in the camp before Edgehill?'

'Aye.' They laugh, and she hears the sound of backs being clapped.

With an effort, she rolls onto her back. 'I am no whore,' she says. 'And you will let me go.'

259

'Will we, angel?' says her captor.

They stand in a ring round her. Above their heads a cloud drifts across the circle of blue sky. She closes her eyes for a second, begging the Lord for strength.

She scrambles to her feet and looks the big man in the eye.

'I am a woman, yes, but no whore. I have come to find my brother on urgent family business. He is with the army somewhere.'

'Oh aye,' says the big man. 'If you're no whore, you look like one. Boy's clothes and blooded thighs. Someone else been having their fun with you?'

He reaches out and under her doublet. She steps backwards, but feels someone grip hold of her arms as the man's meaty hands fumble beneath.

'Please, please. I just want to find my brother.' She feels the tears pricking at her eyes.

A new man, sallow-faced and leering, says: 'And who's your brother?'

'His name is Ned, Ned Challoner. He's a cornet, and serves Philip Skippon.'

'An officer,' says the big man. 'Of course he is.'

A man steps out of the circle behind her and looks into her face. 'Ned Challoner?'

'Yes. Do you know him? Please, please take me to him.'

'All right, lads,' says the man, taking hold of her arm. 'Fun's over.'

'She's mine, Taf, I found her.' The big man squares his shoulders.

'Aye, well, you wouldn't know what to do with her anyway, you limp-pricked bastard.' He says it quietly, but she senses that he has authority, this small, wiry man. A few of the others laugh, and the big man spits angrily.

'Here's the deal, Billy,' says the one called Taf. 'I'll take her to the man she says is her brother. And if it turns out she's telling tales, I'll bring her back and strip her for you myself.'

'Come, that's fair,' says another, and the big man, Billy, can tell that he has lost the crowd.

Taf pulls her out of the ring of men, and Hen wants to crumble with relief. Her legs give a little, but she feels herself pulled upright.

'Come, miss,' says Taf, supporting her. 'Walk a little now in front of the bastards, and we'll sit soon enough.'

She nods, forcing her ravaged, trembling legs to walk. A sudden image of her father strikes her, and how he must dread the walk to the gibbet. The crowd watching, his legs trembling. The thought gives her courage, and she walks on.

They come to a brick house in the centre of town, and Taffy sits her on a low wall opposite an inn with dimpled glass windows and a broken sign.

'Wait there,' he says.

He walks into the house, and minutes later, a man runs down the steps and looks up and down the street, his eyes flicking over her.

'Ned!' she shouts, and his eyes swivel back to her.

'Jesus Christ in heaven,' he says, and runs towards her. 'Hen. Jesus. Look at the mess of you. Jesus wept.'

'Blaspheming, Ned?'

He blushes. 'The shock,' he mumbles. He helps her upright, and then turns to the wiry man at his side. 'It's her, all right. Thanks, Taffy. Thank you. I am in your debt, always.'

'Evens, I'd say,' says Taffy. 'Sir.'

Ned grins at him, and then turns back to Hen.

'Come,' he says.

He takes her across the road to an inn, and they duck inside the door. He orders ale, ignoring the open stares at the bedraggled figure beside him, and asks to speak to the goodwife of the house. As a potboy is sent to find her, he sits Hen down, looking searchingly at her.

'Well?'

'Did you get my letter?'

'Yes.'

'And you did not think to answer it, or to come home?'

He looks down at his cup. 'For what? If it were anyone else, I'd rejoice at his capture. He would not want me there, playing the hypocrite. Crowing. But Hen, why are you here?'

'He is to die. In three days.'

He blanches, and then takes a swig of his ale, as if to fortify himself. 'Well. I guessed it would be so.'

'Ned, he thinks you betrayed him. That night we found him with the gold and Lady d'Aubigny. He thinks it was you.'

She watches his face fall as she tells him, watches the horror spreading slowly. 'But I didn't... I . . .' he stammers.

'I know,' she says urgently. 'It was Harmsworth.'

'Harmsworth?' He says the name in a daze.

'Yes. So I've come to get you. To take you to him. You must tell him, Ned, that it wasn't you. Before he... Before he . . .' She peters out. Her hunger and tiredness, the pain and the fear, all catch up with her. She feels the ale that sits in her empty stomach rising, and she vomits it up into a frothing fizz on the floor.

CHAPTER TWENTY

GUARDS SHE DOES NOT KNOW BLOCK THE GATES OF THE Tower. One more night. For one more night he will be alive. But they will not let them pass.

'Please,' says Hen. 'Send word. Ask Thomas Hood, his warder. He will let us in.'

One of the guards, beetle-browed and surly, shouts for a fellow within the gate, who runs off with the message.

Hen looks out over the river. The dull water, pockmarked with rain, meets the lead-grey sky, and a tangle of rotting wood drifts by. Hood finally appears. He is clearly irritated at being disturbed, and greets Hen and Ned shrewishly.

'Your father has lost his privileges,' he says.

'Why?'

'For not telling more details of his wicked crime. Tompkins and his friend Waller have been squealing away. The plot laid bare in all its viciousness. But your father, the old sot, just swears at Stroud. Laughs sometimes, the mad old bastard.'

Ned steps forward. 'Sir, I have come all the way from the army at Thame to see my father. Please, I beg you, let me see him.'

'Look, son. No visitors.' Hood looks at Ned as if seeing him for the first time. 'No visitors,' he repeats. 'Not even Parliament's soldiers. You're better staying away from the traitorous old sod anyway. You'll see him when he swings, and not before.'

They walk away. Silent. Anyone looking would know them for brother and sister. But no one is looking. They are just two bodies wandering in the indifferent city.

Hen and Ned walk home despite the rain, following the river, seeing glimpses of it through gaps in the close-packed houses. Everywhere holds memories of him. Here, the tavern he blamed for a dodgy oyster that kept the chamber pots full for a week. There, the alley leading to his livery company, its arms gouged into the brickwork. There, his wine merchant's well-visited house, and his favourite bookseller. And into Fleet Street, at last. Here is the place where they watched Charles' march into the City, with Sam sitting on the tavern's sign. Ahead, St Dunstan's spire, evoking Sunday upon Sunday of Challoner family life.

Silence, though, between Ned and Hen. Too early to say, 'Do you remember when?' Too raw for reminiscences. Besides, he is still alive. Where there is breath, there is hope.

Breath and hope. Breath and hope. Hen chants it like a silent liturgy as they turn into Fetter Lane.

~ ~ ~

She lies in her bed, waiting for the sun to come up. She imagines the reprieve coming. Pym jumps from the shadows, waving a pardon. The king rides in to cut her father down, a smile of triumph on his foxy, sad face.

Later that morning, her eyes scoured raw from sleeplessness, Hen leans out of the window at the front of the house and watches the gibbet being finished off. It is, to her irritation, a beautiful day. A clear blue sky, and a warm sun bathes the structure in a golden light. Nails are banged in, edges sawn. At last, the rope is swung into place, its frightful hoop swinging mid-air.

The crowd begins to gather. The pie-sellers shout: 'Traitor-pie! Get your traitor-pie hot!'

From her vantage point, Hen can see the cutpurse boys at work, and she wills them a success rooted in bitter hatred of those gathered to see her father die. She spots Chettle in the crowd, talking to a man she does not recognize. He looks entirely too normal, as if he has been sauntering along the Strand and stopped to gossip with a chance-met friend. He turns his face towards the window, and Hen shrinks back out of sight.

Ned stands next to her, and stays in Chettle's eye-line. She sees her brother's face set hard, and his chin tilt upwards. It's an echo of her father's tick, the bullish putting on of his public face. Ned's hands clench the sill of the window, the blue veins clear beneath taut skin.

There is a dreamlike quality to the day. She has not slept, and her brain lags behind her eyes. She cannot make sense of anything quickly. Faces pop out of the crowd. Here, an old woman with stumps for teeth, throwing her head back to laugh; there, a man biting down on a sausage, the grease on his chin gleaming in the sun. There are children below, arguing about who plays Prince Rupert. The biggest boy seizes a wooden crown from his playmate and, newly crowned, climbs aboard his horse-stick to launch the charge. The deposed prince sits in the mud, visibly trying not to cry.

The voice of the crowd swells. It clamours like a mythical beast, demanding its blood libation. The tenor of the noise changes, as if the crowd senses its offering is coming. She sees him, then, pinioned to a wooden post, being pulled out to the gibbet in front of the heckling crowd. He has shrunk. His shoulders hunch over and his hair is no longer speckled grey but is now shockingly white. The midday sun is harsh on his lined face. She hears Ned draw a breath beside her, all his wonder at their father's dramatic decline contained in that sharp inhalation. It must be a shock to see him like this. Ned did not sit with him in the Tower, day after day, as he crumbled piece by piece.

She wonders, for the thousandth time, what it would feel like to face the noose. To know it will score your neck and slowly choke you. To know that your gasping last breaths are just a prelude to more pain, as they carve out your innards and cut off your cock.

She feels faint, suddenly, from the heat and the horror. She forces herself to stay standing; she will not add to his fear, to his humiliation, by crumbling now. She must be there – he needs loving faces in this hostile crowd. But, oh, how she wants to yield to it, to curl inwards like a hedgehog, and close her eyes.

He is in place now, and the crowd is ravenous. They love a hanging, but the prospect of a drawing and a quartering is making them slaver. With gleeful, well-practised prurience, they prepare to be shocked. They anticipate being frightened; they look forward to that small, delicious moment of relief that comes as someone else feels the noose tighten – someone else's father or brother begins to choke.

Children will peep through their mother's fingers, storing the details for the telling to less fortunate, absent friends. Apprentices will jostle to the front to get the best view, and to hope – joy of joys! – that a splatter of blood will hit them, to be paraded from tavern to tavern at sundown. Genuine traitor's blood! The dark-suited godly folk will practise their stoic faces on her father's death throes, murmuring proverbs and thanking Providence for the exposure and the punishment of the Judas.

The Judas looks around him. His chin tilts upwards, and his eyes are wet with tears.

Hen feels a hand slip into hers. Ned. He's trying to shout something to their father.

'It wasn't me. It wasn't me. It wasn't me.' But the bile of the crowd is too strong, and Ned's voice too faint. She sees her father scanning the crowd, looking for them.

'Father!' she cries out. But her voice does not carry. He looks at the house, then, and sees them in the window.

'It wasn't me!' shouts Ned, but it's clear the old man can't hear. He looks up at them, holds his hand over his heart, and nods once. He turns away, looking back out over the many-faced crowd of those who hate him; the jeering, shouting, slavering mob.

They lay the noose round his neck. Still she prays for a miracle. Still she hopes, and lets a morsel of belief live on. And then. Then, they push. And he swings by his neck.

PART THREE

PART THREE

CHAPTER TWENTY-ONE

14 June 1645

'𝓗EY, PUDDING, MY PUDDING.'

Lieutenant Samuel Challoner strokes the horse's soft nose and smiles as she snorts with a juddering pleasure.

'Hey, hey. Puddingy pud.'

It is night, and Sam can only see the whites of her eyes. But he knows her by the way she smells, the way she moves beneath his hands; by everything about her. He came straight to her in the dark stable, past the other officers' horses.

'I couldn't sleep,' he tells her, quick hands stroking her long and elegant neck. 'Not at all. You awake too, my best girl?'

She pushes her head into his shoulder and he smiles again. 'Nothing for you, lovekin. Are you hungry? Wait till we smash those joyless bastards, and you shall have the pick of their baggage train. So you shall, my pudding heart.'

He looks behind her head and through the door of the stable, to where the hint of dawn smudges the horizon.

'Today, they reckon. There was a skirmish last night in Naseby town. We'll meet them today. Do you think Ned's with them?'

He turns back and pulls a pail of water to where she can reach it. She bows her long neck and drinks loudly, water splashing up the side of the bucket and onto Sam's leg. He stays with her as she drinks, running his hands over her in the darkness, checking she's still whole and healthy. Up her right foreleg, over her powerful shoulder, along her back, down her haunch and her back leg.

She lifts her head from the pail and turns, looking for him. She pushes her wet nose into his neck, and he laughs as the icy water trickles across his skin.

'Oi, Pudding, careful.'

He takes his brush and begins to tug it through her mane, feeling his way in the darkness. He talks to her in a low, soft voice to keep her docile.

'Do you remember when we first met, Pudding? Oh, I do, queen of horses, I do. When the king kissed me for my father's loyalty and gave me my commission, and had you led forward to me. And there was I, penniless and friendless among all these potentates; and there were you, all grace and beauty. Oh, my Pudding.'

He moves on to her coat, brushing her down with quick, practised strokes. 'And there I was, dressed in a borrowed coverlet and sporting a dead man's pistol. And they sneered at the tradesman's boy, the city boy, and said I'd never make a king's horseman. But we showed them, my Pudding, we showed them, hey?'

He moves round to the other side of her. There are stirrings in the camp now, low voices and dark figures stretching. A man wanders past the open door, and Sam can hear his happy sigh as his piss rattles a bush. The sky is beginning to lighten, and Pudding is coming into focus. He can see the chestnut shine of her coat where he has brushed it. He leans in to kiss her neck, before brushing again.

'You must look your best today, my queen. Your lovely best. They say they're here somewhere, the traitorous sods, and we shall deal them out today. It's their new army, Piers says. The New Noddle, or whatever they call it. Fairfax, the chief; Cromwell, heading up the cavalry. Shall we be the ones to spit him, Pud, you and me?'

He works on, brushing away the dirt of yesterday's march. Not long now before the morning starts properly. Not long left of just the two of them, close together in the dark lull before daybreak.

He leans in to whisper in her ear. 'You'll look after me, won't you, Pudding? Like at Marston Moor, when you carried me away from Cromwell's Ironsides.'

Barely a sound; more like a rush of breath on her ear which pricks upright and twitches as he moves in closer. 'Don't tell the other horses, lass, but I've a secret.'

Her hoof rakes the fetid floor of the stable. It's not designed for so many horses. She deserves better. He puts an arm across her long neck as he whispers.

'I'm fearful, Pudding. Proper piss-your-breeches fearful. And I miss my father, and I miss Hen, and I even miss that bastard Ned, who's probably there across that hill waiting to kill us.'

A voice from behind him. 'Sam, that you?'

He straightens and twists round, glad of the gloom that hides the rush of blood to his face.

'Aye,' he says. 'Just grooming Pud.'

Piers Langton walks towards him. The rolling strut of a king's cavalry officer is unmistakable, even in silhouette.

'I'll never understand why you called such a noble beast such an ignoble name,' says Piers.

'I told you. After my sister.'

'Pretty girl, is she? Face like a horse, body like a suet pie.'

Sam bristles, and Piers throws his hands in the air.

'Calm it, Samson. I'm sporting with you.'

He moves closer, and Sam can make out his matted long hair and stubble. Even Piers struggles to groom himself on campaign. He stretches sleepily.

'Still, Samson, she's your twin, ain't she? So can't be much to look at.'

'Better than the monkey-woman that spawned you, Piers.'

'Now, Sam. Mockery of a countess – it ain't gentlemanly.'

Sam turns to whisper in Pudding's ear. 'Cuntess, more like.'

She whinnies as his breath tickles her ear, and he takes it for laughter. He smiles, feeling the two them are conspiring against Piers' effortless, aristocratic smugness. Though the two boys are the same age, Piers had been his superior until Marston – a lieutenant to Sam's cornet. Now they are both of equal nominal rank, and Sam struggles with the parity, on occasion.

'Any word on the rebels?' Sam asks.

'No. They're hereabouts, though. I can smell their rotten traitor souls.'

'I thought that was your feet.'

Piers laughs. 'The whores at Mother Goffrey's shall wash these with honey when we make it back to Oxford, Sam.'

'While you're dipping your feet in honey, I shall be dipping my –' Sam pauses – 'tongue in a pie.'

'Are you speaking in tongues, Sam?' says Piers.

'No. It's priorities, Piers. Pie first, girl second.'

He thinks of Sally, his favourite girl at Mother Goffrey's, and her snowy, pink-tipped breasts. Sorry, Sal. A hot meal first.

Piers' voice takes on that dreamlike quality of a man who lives on stale cheese and hard tack. 'Aye, Sam. You're in the right. Hot chicken. Mutton breast.'

Sam says: 'My cook at home made court sops on cold mornings like this one. Bread dripping with ale. Not too much cinnamon. Hot from the fire. Crisp on top, soggy below. Christ's bones, when I think of that grey stink the old woman served us last night.'

'Not our best billet, Sam-boy. I don't believe a word of it. No food, my arse. The old witch is hiding it. Her imp's guarding it, waiting to jump out and suckle on her third teat.'

'Did you have to hit her, though?'

'Not this again. Hell's breath, Sam. We're fighting for the king, and these loyal fucking subjects have a loyal fucking duty to feed us. And if they don't feed us, they ain't loyal.'

Sam shrugs. Light is beginning to leak in through the crumbling walls. They have had this argument too many times, and today he finds himself unable to stir.

'Aye, well, perhaps you are right,' he says finally.

Piers smiles and claps Sam on the back. 'That's it. Come join me for breaking our fast. I have some bread that's as hard as a whore's heart. And some cheese. And, Sammy-Samson, if you are very charming to me, you shall have the maggots which have made a home of my cheese.'

Sam bends into a low, mock bow. 'The maggots? Too kind, sir.'

Piers throws an arm round Sam's shoulder and they saunter back towards the small house where they are billeted. Sam doesn't have to remind himself to strut any more; it comes naturally. He is twenty years old and a veteran of these wars, after all.

It is growing steadily lighter as they walk away from Pudding. He turns to bid her goodbye, and she tosses her head as if in farewell. He pauses as he looks back, forgetting to be scared, and forgetting to be tough – brimful of her beauty in the dawn light.

~ ~ ~

Across the dewy fields, Captain-Lieutenant Edward Challoner comes to a halt. He passes the order back to Sergeant Fowler, who turns to bark at the company.

Around him, men sling off their packs and adjust to the new terrain. A low-level grumbling breaks out: the first sounds since they were pulled out of their sleep and marched across country without warning. Close by, he sees the sails of a windmill looming out of the brightening sky. Ned's joints feel stiff and sore. He remembers, suddenly, how his father used to grunt on rising or lowering into a chair; and how he would blame the rough sleeping of a soldier's lot for his stiff limbs.

Ned tries not to think about his father. Even the most benign of memories soon becomes overlaid with his old man's face as he looked up at them from the gibbet.

'It wasn't me,' Ned mutters to the old man in his head. 'It wasn't me.'

He shakes his head, as if to dispel the image, and looks around.

'Ensign,' he calls.

'Sir.' Ensign Somers bounds up to him, reminding Ned, not for the first time, of an over-familiar piglet.

Keeping his voice quiet, Ned says: 'We missed prayers in the rush to march. Private prayers, at a whisper. Satan's imps may be close.'

Ned kneels, grunting a little with the effort. He prays, long and hard, the dew soaking through to his bare knees. Hen is in his prayers, and Lucy, his wife. Keep them safe, oh Lord. And Sam. He asks his Lord for Sam's deliverance.

Let him be the last boy standing, even as all your enemies are smited by our righteous swords, oh Lord. He is lost and misguided, oh Lord. Let him see Your glory, and bring him back to Your flock. But spare him, please, my Saviour.

He imagines Sam, standing in a mire of traitors' corpses. More than two years since last I last saw him, Ned thinks. The Sam in his mind's eye is still a boy; a shining, mischievous boy who climbs trees that are too high, and jumps streams that are too broad. And yet this same boy rides with the devil Rupert. Will I even recognize him? wonders Ned, as he clambers to his feet.

'Sir!' A voice emerges from the grey gloom of dawn. 'The major-general wants you, sir.'

Ned hurries over to Skippon, who sits eating breakfast, wrapped against the cold in a heap of blankets. It may be hot later, but dawns are cold to men who sleep out the night. And his commander, Ned realizes with a jolt, is getting old for this game.

'Ned, good morning,' says Skippon, with unexpected brightness. 'First rule of war, boy?'

'Know your enemy, sir.'

'Good lad. We know they're somewhere near, God be praised. You know, I expect, that some of Ireton's men had a set-to with some Cavalier boys last night?'

Ned nods. He saw the troop riding past on their way back, sombre and bloodied. Henry Ireton at their head, his name whispered around the watching foot-soldiers. Ned knows the godly cavalryman by reputation. He is a rising man, they say. Close to Cromwell, and, through him, to Fairfax himself.

'Yes, sir, I saw them. Hence this night-time marching, sir?'

'Aye. Now we just need to find the rest of the traitors, God willing, and we can bring them to battle. Lord Fairfax has ridden on in front of us, along the ridge.' Skippon waves ahead. 'Will you go to him, Ned, and be my ears and eyes?'

'Yes, sir. I have no horse at present, sir.'

'Of course, of course, I forgot.' Skippon turns to address another of his men. 'Quartermaster. A mount for the captain-lieutenant.'

Amid the bustle, Skippon beckons Ned closer. 'Second rule, Ned?'

Ned hesitates, unsure of what is expected of him.

'Know your friends, boy. I drew up a plan for the battle for the lord general not two days ago. But that was before Colonel Cromwell joined us. He may have suggested changes, Ned, and I want to know about them. He is wily, Cromwell. I am still at sea as to how he alone, of all the MPs, managed to keep his commission when Parliament made this new army and stripped it of politicos. Off you go, then.'

'Yes, sir.'

Ned is handed the reins of a tall, grey mare. He mounts, a little awkward from lacking the habit, and presses the horse forward with his knees. It responds, and he is relieved, glad that he has not been betrayed as an uneasy horseman in front of his general.

He heads first to his own men. Ensign Somers stands with the colours unfurled: the plain green block denoting the company's pre-eminent standing.

'Somers, Fowler!' Ned shouts, and the two men hurry over. They have learned to be brisk when Ned calls.

'Sir.'

'I know the men have had a long march, and little sleep. Allow breakfast, but stay in loose formation. No fires. Pikes to hand. I have a mission for the general. On an alert, you know where to take the company. Do it, don't wait for me, and I will find you.'

His servant, Wakes, appears behind him, jabbering about breakfast.

'Later, man!' Ned shouts, wheeling the horse round. It follows his command, and Ned thanks the Lord for its biddable nature. He has worked hard to gain his standing as a man of competence and courage; the senior lieutenant of the major-general's own company in his own regiment. Landing on his arse in front of his men would undo months of work.

They hate him; he knows this. They have marched up and down this riven land, hungry and tired. And every time the marching stops, Ned has been there, calling them to their drills. He has drilled them until the blisters pop and their hands run with blood. A martial stigmata. And in the winter quarters, when their training was done and the alehouses and baggage women called their siren call, Ned volunteered them for cavalry training. They have stood too many times in the rain and sleet, being mock-charged by friendly cavalry, to love Ned.

But he has been in a square that crumbled, and felt the panic and fear. He has watched men die because their mates ran. He has been ridden down by Rupert's horse and heard the yapping of his poodle, chased like a fox into a frozen river. Drill, drill and more drill – until, in the cacophony of battle, the men hear only the rattle of their own drums, spurring them on in order. Drill, drill and more drill – until each man is a mindless cog, and safer for it.

I have become a hard bastard, he thinks. But so be it. I will wear this carapace until the job is done.

The horse picks its way through the little groups of men huddled together, and Ned is content to let it lead. The sky is brightening all the time, and the sails of the windmill are becoming ever more distinct. The red coats of the soldiers are bright against the grass. It takes some getting used to, this homogenous uniform. Some of the officers hate the passing of the multicoloured ragtag uniforms of the old armies, but Ned likes the New Model look. He looks down at his own red coat, with the blue sash of Fairfax's colours, and relishes afresh the sense of purpose in this new army. Gone are most of the old officers, and all of the MPs, bar Cromwell. Gone is the Earl of Essex, tainted as he is with the suspicion that he baulks at crushing the king. This now is God's army – His red-coated avengers.

They all hate us. The old women in Parliament, who cling to their hopes of peace, though the king spits in the tureen each time it is offered. The Presbyterians, content with the old Church stripped of bishops, who fail to recognize that the world has cracked open and men can find their own way to God. The nobles, who loathe the lack of titles in the New Model Army, which is commanded by two barons and a squire. The Earls of Essex and Manchester, who have slunk off to polish their coronets and dream of kissing the king's arse. They all hate us, thinks Ned, with satisfaction.

Ned notes with approval the number of redcoats kneeling in morning prayers. God's warriors. He thinks back with amusement to the amateur bands that set off to fight at Edgehill. This new army, dedicated to the Lord's work, will give no quarter to that slippery old sod who calls himself king.

And then I can go home, he thinks, and I can let the shell crack. Home. He retreats from the idea of the old house in Fetter Lane, which conjures itself immediately in his head. He thinks instead of the two rooms above a butcher's shop, where Lucy sits waiting for him.

One year married, and yet how seldom they have seen each other.

It looks as if it will be a fair day. The sort of day that might have heralded a picnic beyond the city walls in a different time, a different life. Ned wants to think about Lucy, just for a little while, as the horse trots on – about her soft blonde curls and her blue eyes. He wants to think about her naked. He wants to think about lying in the darkness, lust slated, and how he will tell her all that has happened. How much he will pour out when he lets his shell crack. What plans they will make, what secrets they will share!

As he trots along the ridge, he looks to the horizon, and there they are. The king's men, arranged on top of a far hill in what seems to be full battle deployment. They are at least five miles away, he estimates. He realizes too that the New Model is drawn up below the crest of the hill behind him. We can see them, but they cannot see us, he thinks. They must have scouts, though.

Ahead of him a small group of horsemen clusters, watching the enemy. At its front are two men talking. It is light enough to recognize them. One slim and long-faced, a handsome but tired face under a tumble of dark curls; the other is broader and uglier. Fairfax and Cromwell. Like a fox and a toad, Ned thinks irreverently, as he makes them aware of his presence, and they turn, unblinking, to stare at him.

~ ~ ~

Hen closes the door of the two rooms above the butcher's shop. She closes the door on Grandmother, and on Lucy, who will sit being prettily vacant all day, as far as she knows, storing up grievances for Hen's return. The room will be too cold, or too hot. Grandmother too silent, or too voluble. Perhaps Hattie will be out the back, enthusiastically slaughtering a pig, and its squeals of fear and explosive death-shits will waft upwards to where Lucy sits at the window, pretending she is still rich enough to be idle.

Hen hopes that Hattie will, indeed, be slaughtering today. She still has not quite learned the knack, since her husband was pulled off to fight in the last levy. They scream more when Hattie wields the knife. The apprentices are long gone: one dead, one run from the levy. Hen hugs the thought of Lucy's discomfort to herself, smiling as she walks, thinking of that pretty nose wrinkling in disgust.

She goes up Newgate Street and turns towards St Paul's, her back to the great prison. She will not look at it. On Sunday nights, when the bellman from St Sepulchre tolls for the next morning's execution, she buries her head in her blanket. Lucy seems unmoved, though her father, too, died on the gallows.

Hattie takes leftover scraps from the shop to the prison, she knows. Offal and eyes and snouts, cooked and chucked down the food chutes to the crouching convicts who have no relatives to feed them. Hattie's husband forbade the practice when he was around. Hen smiles to think of Hattie's florid face and salty tongue.

'He may kiss me arse if he ever comes back,' she said when Hen asked her about the convicts' food. 'Those poor souls may at least taste meat before their necks are stretched out, God love 'em. He can kiss me broad backside and I shall not budge.'

God help John Smith if he does make it back from the wars. Hattie has a taste for independence. As have I, thinks Hen, as she walks past St Paul's to the churchyard and the bookshop.

She passes through the front of the shop into the back room, nodding and smiling at Mr Rowan, who is talking to a customer. She knows enough not to interrupt – Mr Rowan has given her this work for love of her father, and due to a lack of suitable apprentices. But the customers might not like it, a woman loose among the shelves, so she stays hidden amid the stores and reserve stacks.

Once in the back she begins the day's tasks of sweeping and dusting, cataloguing and accounting. But first, she looks to the map that lies on the table in the centre of the room. A map of the British Isles, it shows, to the best of their knowledge, the progress of the war. Chestnuts serve as the king's armies; conkers serve as Parliament's. One chestnut has an S cut in it; one conker bears an N.

She has watched the war develop on this table, as conkers and chestnuts march and meet and retreat from each other in waves. She watched the king's initial victories, and the scrabbling of Parliament to gain a hold. She watched Sam's criss-crossing of the north with Prince Rupert, and learned to hope that the tales dribbling back to London about Rupert's men and their depredations were exaggerated. She hears little from Sam. Three letters in all this time. The first reads a little subdued and lost as it recounts the granting of his commission. The second, a note scribbled as they entered winter quarters last year. The third, received just weeks ago, assumes knowledge of lost letters in the interim. It was written on march to Leicester. The newsbooks say that the sack of Leicester by Rupert's men was a second Magdeburg. Women raped and babies crushed. The tone of Sam's letter was buoyant, more familiar, full of lengthy descriptions of his horse's capabilities. Pudding Cat he seems to have called her. She smiles at that.

She writes once a week and misses a meal to pay for the letters to float about the country on secret channels in the hope of meeting him. But she has no way of knowing what he receives.

Ned is a more frequent correspondent, and occasional visitor. She tracked him on this table last year all the way down to the West Country, to that alien spit of land they call Cornwall, where wild men speak their own tongue.

There is, she admits, a fault to her system. It makes a game of it all, moving these pieces about her map like so many chess pieces. Rowan's friends come in, sometimes, to look at the table, and he tells them what's what. They are mostly old, like he is; the ones left behind. Rowan struggles to get the map in focus, now his eyes are going, but he never calls her forward, except when they are alone. The conkers and chestnuts can be brushed away quickly, if necessary, or laughed away as foibles. Rowan is careful to keep his head low in these times.

But these are real men's lives she carelessly totes across the table. The skin fell off Ned in loose folds when he returned from Cornwall. He was haunted by the surrender of Skippon's troops to the king, and emaciated from the long march back across a hostile country. The Cornishmen followed the column of defeated London boys and picked them off in the night, beating them and taunting them all the way across the border.

He recounted the tale in an even voice, but the horror could be glimpsed through the monotone. For the first time, Ned's certainty seemed to waver. Was God with the king after all? She thinks back to him sitting hunched like an old man by the fire, Lucy at his feet wearing her Dutiful Wife mask. It didn't help that he had become too small for his uniform. Shrunken. She couldn't imagine him commanding a full company. She still can't.

They fed him up – food from the hawkers, mainly. No Cook this time, nor a kitchen. But plenty of cured meat from Hattie's shop, and tidbits from the baker across the way. Fed up on pies and puddings and oysters, and then sent off to fight again.

She watched the Ned conker begin to move again, and watched all the pieces whirling around the map, as the fortune began to smile at last on Parliament's armies. The king's hold on the north was crushed at Marston Moor where, she surmises from an allusion in his letter, Sam rode hard to escape capture.

Marston Moor. That was the turn of the tide. They say that four thousand royalists died that day, for three hundred of the godly. The north was lost to the king, and an implacable, hostile bulwark forged between his strongholds in the south and west and the resurgent royalists in Scotland. The King had lost the North Sea ports that day too, severing his lines to the Continent.

Hen imagines her namesake in Paris, sitting in exile, eyes turned towards the Channel and her husband's desperate fight.

She's waiting for news, just like I am. It's our unhappy fate in the wartime – yet more punishment for that cursed apple.

Marston Moor. A place she'd never heard of, nor had anyone else she knows. Yet now the name reverberates. It was, she recalls, the first time she had really marked the name Oliver Cromwell. He turned the battle that day, with his troops from the Eastern Association and his Ironsides, breaking Rupert's own cavalry.

And yet it's still not done. Everyone thought after Marston that the end must follow. But nothing decisive. She remembers waiting anxiously after the second battle at Newbury last year, looking for hours at the notched chestnut sitting squarely alongside the notched conker. It was an indecisive fight, and neither brother hurt, God be praised.

She looks at the present configuration on the map. She knows about the New Model Army's orders to besiege Oxford. All London is ablaze with this push to end things once and for all. She can't be sure of Sam's whereabouts, nor the king's. Is he returned from the north? Where are they all? Are they close? Are they, as rumour had it last night, both scuttling about somewhere near Market Harborough?

The map is clearer cut than it was last year. To the west of Oxford, the king holds out, into the wilds of Wales and the West Country. The rest is for Parliament, now. From Reading to York, London to Ely and the Fens, the Committee of Both Kingdoms rules. The war must end soon. Surely it must. And here they are, the Ned chestnut and the Sam conker, circling round each other.

Hen thought that nothing could be worse than watching her father hang. But this waiting, this suspended ignorance of the fates of the people she loves, is unbearable. She remembers her father's death with precise horror. She left before the end, not wanting to watch the cutting down, or the rest. She didn't know if he was dead yet, or just dying, and she still feels a deep shame for not being able to stay until the end. Her eyes are for ever burned with the image of his dangling body, his legs kicking hopelessly, his face turning purple.

It was the next day, she remembers, that she sought out the kind butcher's wife, Hattie Smith, to ask her if she knew of any cheap rooms to let. And Hattie diffidently offered her own two rooms going begging above the shop – meant for a nursery, she'd said, but there was never any need.

Dear Hattie, thinks Hen. Strange to have grown close to someone so different. Can she read? I wonder. I have never seen her.

In the bookshop, as the dust dances in the columns of light, she wonders where her father's soul is, and what it looks like. She thinks of his corporeal body swinging on the gibbet, the knife coming in to slice out his organs. Rowan says that her father will be pleased, wherever he is, to know if he was right. A predestined heaven, or an earned one. She can imagine Challoner's soul haranguing the angels.

Hen shivers, though it is not cold. She loathes the idea of Sam and Ned standing against each other. She concocts elaborate daydreams where they pause on seeing each other, embrace like brothers and walk away from the fighting. She imagines them sitting together by the fire in her rooms, sharing a bottle of wine, laughing at their lucky escapes. She will not think of the alternative. She cannot.

At least it's June, not winter. Poor Ned, he hates the cold. No wonder, after what happened to him at Edgehill. Dear

Ned. If they all get through this, she will make sure he is never cold again.

~ ~ ~

Pudding shuffles beneath him, and Sam reaches down to pat her neck.

He hears a voice behind him from the troop: 'Fucking nancies, we look – full battle deployment and no bastard in sight.'

'Maybe we're fighting them cows.'

Sam thinks about ordering the men to be silent, but lets it go.

Below them, in the dip underneath the ridge, a herd of cows grazes, their herdsman leaning on a stick and seemingly unconcerned about the appearance of a full army above him. Sam remembers the herdsman at Marston Moor, his placid surprise at the troops' appearance, and Sam's hurried explanation of the king's quarrel. The laconic reply: 'Himself fallen out with the parliament, then, has he?'

The men laugh at some ribald humour about MPs and cows. Sam smiles at the laughter behind him. Suddenly he hears the signal to form a marching order. Ahead of him, Captain Fenwick appears alongside Prince Rupert himself, the massive bulk of their chief unmistakable next to the slim-hipped captain.

'Explain as we go, man,' the prince instructs Fenwick, and wheels round to set off at a slow trot.

'Right,' says Fenwick, his voice so low they strain to hear him. 'The rebel bastards are here somewhere. Must be. Our boys clashed with them two days ago, and the scoutmaster-general, may God grant the poor blind sod a miracle, has failed to find them. So, like every dirty job in this fucking war, us noble horse must do it ourselves if we want it smartly. If we find the bastards, no heroics. Your lieutenant,' he gestures at Sam, 'may want to take the bastards on without our two-footed simpleton friends in the infantry, but I intend to see my wife's teats one more time before I die, boys. So eyes open, mouths shut, and follow my lead.'

'That what your wife says, sir?'

'Lucky we're going on a forlorn fucking suicide run, Peters, or I'd kill you myself,' says Fenwick.

The men smile through taut, hard faces.

They ride down the hill. A couple of scouting parties are detached and sent ahead. This is strange, tricksy land. It folds and curves in hillocks and mounds. It is pitted with false horizons and deceptive slopes. The bastards could be ten feet away, over a ridge, and you wouldn't know it until you landed in their laps begging to be spitted.

The prince rides back and forth along the line, stopping here and there for a word. He falls back until he is riding next to Sam.

'Lieutenant…' He pauses.

'Challoner, sir. Your Highness, sir.'

'Sir will do in the field,' says Prince Rupert. Their horses walk side by side. Pudding is small beside the prince's mount, and Sam pats her neck in case she feels it. He is confused by the great man's presence. The junior officers and troopers hold him in such awe. Rupert's life is already a legend, and he is barely twenty-six. Royalists tell of his courage, his battle-madness and glory. He is a new Alexander. And yet Sam can remember running with the London apprentices, who sang of Rupert's bestiality, of his moonlit dances with the devil, and of his ferocious coupling with witches that spawned Boy, the imp dog.

Sam watched from afar, last summer, as Rupert mourned Boy's death in the grisly aftermath of Marston Moor. He watched Rupert cry for the companion of his youth, and at that moment had given in to the consuming hero-worship displayed by the other boys in Rupert's horse. The dispossessed and the younger sons and the glory-seekers – they worshipped their wandering prince. Now not theirs alone; he is commander of the king's whole army. To have him ambling alongside is horribly disconcerting – as if Ares himself has tumbled out of Mount Olympos for a natter.

Rupert breaks the silence. 'Of course, I remember. The linen merchant's boy. I hear good words of you.'

Sam can only nod. Say something, you fool.

Rupert speaks first. 'Will your troop change its colours, I wonder, now that the Lord Essex is no longer commanding the enemy?'

Sam thinks of their colours, the streaming banner he used to carry with such pride as a cornet. And the words 'Cuckolds, we come' emblazoned on green-flowered damask.

'I think, sir, the words still hold true. All the time those bastards spend on their knees, their wives must be crying out for red blood.' He regrets the words even as he says them, remembering too late Rupert's reputation for sobriety and propriety. He is relieved to hear a low chuckle.

'Well, then, perhaps it may serve. Now silence, I think. We are near the edges of where the cuckolds may be lurking.'

They ride on, slowly, stealthily. Up hill and through the unnaturally quiet village of Clipston. The only sound is the squelch of their hooves in the muddy path, which doubtless heralded their arrival to the hidden locals. Who'd be an artillery officer? Sam imagines the job of pulling the heavy pieces up and down these rain-drenched, boggy mounds. They clear the last house, then crest the top of a hill, and suddenly, there they are. Thousands of the joyless bastards, beetling across the opposite hill. They look like they are retreating. Are they? Or just repositioning? It is impossible to tell.

Rupert's horse follow his lead and pull up to watch. Nervous men soothe twitchy, panting beasts.

Nearby, the prince takes counsel with his advisers and the locals he co-opted last night in Market Harborough. Sam hears the unmistakable Germanic inflection in his demi-god's voice as he curses the king's council for deciding to confront the New Noddle.

'I told them we should withdraw to Leicester until Goring arrives with his horse.'

A lower voice reminds him of the king's council's view; a retreat could leave them trapped between Fairfax's army and the advancing Scots.

'So here we are,' Rupert says, louder, intending the whole party to hear. 'Outmanned, outhorsed, outgunned. Still, gentlemen, we have faced worse odds. We shall find ways to amuse the rebels.'

Rupert calls out over his shoulder. 'Captain Fenwick, to me. Your two best riders with you.'

Fenwick barks: 'Jenkins, Challoner.'

They move forward. Jenkins is a small boy, younger than Sam. The son of a horse breeder, he is said to have suckled a mare as a baby, after his mother died in birthing him. He is more horse than human. Sam canters alongside him, his back pike-straight, thighs tight, trying not to let this great and swelling pride obscure his concentration.

'Sir,' says Fenwick. 'Corporal Jenkins and Lieutenant Challoner.'

Prince Rupert says: 'This ground is pure shite, gentlemen. We'll break our necks before we can swing a sword at a rebel head. Fenwick, take your troop and ride for the king. Give Jenkins the letter in case of an ambush. He must get through. Tell the king our position. There's Mill Hill for your waypoint. Tell him we must flank the enemy to engage on our terms. Tell him Dust Hill is where we will stand, and hope to God the bastards follow us. I'm sending Challoner here with a flag up Moot Hill, to show the angle of advance. It's all in this letter. The field word is "Queen Mary".'

Rupert takes the letter from Sir Bernard de Gomme, the Walloon staff officer at his side. He squints at it, reading it through, before handing it to Jenkins.

The prince turns to Challoner. 'You understand, lieutenant? The far side of the hill from the enemy, so they can't see the flag, but place it so we can see it at Dust Hill –' he points – 'and the king can see it from the current billet. Do you understand? Your cornet will hold your place in the line until you rejoin, when we're all in place.'

'Yes, sir,' says Sam, accepting Rupert's colours from the aide, and settling the point of the lance against his hip as he used to as a cornet.

'Don't fail,' says the prince. 'This is it, I think, gentlemen,' he says to his small band of horsemen. 'Their way or, God willing, ours – all will be decided today.'

~ ~ ~

The ground is horribly boggy and pockmarked with warrens. Sam can see the rabbits scurrying about, ignoring the lone horse walking though their terrain and its nervous rider. A broken ankle here would be disastrous. Sam whispers to Pudding as she picks her way across the treacherous ground.

'Careful, my Pudding, careful, my darling.'

He wonders if the captain and Jenkins have reached the king. And he wonders about Ned, before cursing himself for losing concentration.

The terrain begins to slope upwards and, for a lurching moment, Sam loses his bearings. Is this the right hill? He imagines the royalist foot following the flag into an ambush, rebel pikes scything them down like wheat. His palms are sweating. Holding onto the reins and the lance becomes difficult. He wedges it against his belt.

I would rather charge pikes, he thinks, than have this responsibility. What stuff must Prince Rupert be made of, to bear the whole army on his shoulders?

Pudding, untroubled, continues her early morning saunter uphill. Sam forces himself to breathe. Think. This must be the right hill. He tries to remember the map they studied yesterday on the march. Only yesterday? If this is Moot Hill, I would have walked through enemy pickets. If it is Mill Hill, I would see the sails of a windmill – and more to the point, I would have a rebel sword in my bowels. Yes. The right hill.

They continue to climb. They aren't big hills, for all that they play with a man's senses. Not like those big sods in the north they gadded about in the summer just gone. Jesus wept, but that was a tough campaign. And you survived that where thousands didn't, he tells himself. Man up, boy, man up.

As he approaches what looks like the top, Sam stops and dismounts. Tying Pudding's reins to a low bush, he walks up the rest of the hill, checking for a false summit, and getting his bearings. He steps on a dry branch, which cracks like a gunshot. His heart thumps so violently it near batters its way out of his chest.

The summit flattens out to a small plateau. It seems like a flat field, and Sam has the sense, for a moment, that he has walked down instead of up. He walks forward, and the edge of the field falls away suddenly. To his right is a deep valley which ridges and folds like a tangle of thighs. Ahead, he can see, far away in the distance, the rebels are on the move. They're marching west on top of a ridge. They're following Rupert's flanking march. There will be a fight today, God willing. The rebels seem game. Fools. Staffed by God-botherers, officered by butchers and bakers; how can they prevail against the king's own? But, God's blood, there are a lot of them.

'More for us to kill,' Sam says aloud, and feels foolish. What use is the Cavalier's fearless banter if nobody is there to hear it?

He looks behind him, and he can see the king's army. Too far to make out any colours or banners, but they seem to be on the move. They are marching, in full battalia, the three or so miles to where the prince stipulated. An hour, then, to go. Less until they pass below him. He slithers back down to Pudding, who tosses her head when she sees him. He plants the banner where he thinks it must be visible, pushing the point of the lance into the earth. Pudding is idly nibbling at a bush, and he pats her neck.

'We'll join them when they pass below, hey, Pud? That cornet best be keeping them in order, or I'll scrag him.'

Reaching into his saddle, Sam finds the last of the dried, salt meat he's been saving. Spreading his cloak on the ground, he sits and stretches out his legs. He starts to worry at the meat with his teeth.

'Like a damned picnic, this,' he says to Pudding. 'Do you think Ned is there?' She reaches across and splutters into the back of his neck, tickling him.

'Do you know, Pud, we used to fight, me and Ned. But not always. We played too, at soldiers, mostly. Ain't that funny, Pud? Me and Ned toting branches at each other, playing at saints and papists. We'd charge with sticks. Build forts in the garden, though Benny would shout at us. He got to be Gustavus Adolphus, with him the elder.' He takes another bite of meat. 'Those birds don't half make a racket up here.' He throws a stone at the tree, with a short prayer to land a songbird. Some fresh meat would be exquisite. The birds flutter out of the tree in a fluster, and the singing stops.

Sam realises he is unused to solitude; a soldier's life does not allow much time to be alone. He finds it disquieting. Talking dispels the sinister edge, but he whispers, and looks around him with nervous eyes.

'Aye, Pud. He drew blood once, with a stick fashioned into a pike. I must have been a little 'un. Five, say, or six. Ripped right through my cheek, it did. And do you know what Ned did, when he saw me bleeding? He cried, my Pudding. He cried.'

CHAPTER TWENTY-TWO

*I*T STARTS WITH THE TRUMPET'S HIGH, INSISTENT CALL.

Sam is back where he should be, alongside his men. They move off slowly, down the slope. The rebels line the hill opposite; between them lays the battlefield. The place where the reckoning will come. Sam busies himself with details. Are they in close order, three foot from nose to tail, knee to knee? He shouts at one trooper whose horse is skittering sideways.

'Keep close!'

Knee to knee, they advance at a slow trot. They can see the bastards lined up against them begin to move. And they, Rupert's own, leading the king's men to battle. There is the prince himself, all brawn and fire, leading the slow charge forward. He should be at the back, behind the lifeguards with the king. That's where the commander-in-chief should stand, and Sam heard the muttering from the old-timers. But the prince will charge with them, and they will break the enemy's right, and wheel behind the rebel bastards, and Rupert will then, and only then, join the old men at the back.

Did Alexander skulk at the back, Sam shouts silently to the sky. Did Hector, or Belisarius? Did King Harry at Agincourt?

'Did they fuck!' he shouts aloud, and Pudding tosses her head at the sound of his voice as it carries over the sound of the trumpet playing the notes of the 'Carga, Carga', the call to charge, and the drum roll of the horses' hooves shredding the turf.

'Rupert! Rupert!' he cries, and the men take it up, and the prince waves his sword in acknowledgement, not wavering, his helmeted head facing ever forwards towards the enemy.

On and on they trot, over flat ground now. Suddenly there are gunshots and screams. A horse falls sideways into its line, felling another, and forcing a crab-like movement to the side. Pudding skips a little, and throws her head skyward, seeking reassurance from the hands she knows best.

'Re-form, re-form!' screams Sam, and the troopers battle with their horses' terror, even as more men and more beasts are caught by unknown assassins.

The bastards are hiding in the bushes to the side of them, picking them off.

'Ignore the fuckers!' shouts Sam. 'Advance, advance.' He can hear other voices shouting the same words, but blocks them out. Concentrate on your own job, boy, and let the rest of the army take care of itself. Captain Fenwick told him that once. He presses Pudding onwards with his knees, back straight. On she goes. God, he loves her, his gallant, noble Pud.

'Swords, swords!' he shouts. 'No fucker draws pistols until we're on them.' He waves his sword, solid and heavy and deadly in his hand. The cavalry in front are looming larger now. The trumpet will give the call any second, and Sam's men will ratchet up the speed. The line ahead looks inviolable. It moves towards them in immaculate close order. We will break on them. Waves

297

on a cliff, shattering into spumey foam. Too late now; too late to stop. I will break, oh God, I will break.

The trumpet calls, and they are off. There comes a shard of fear so sharp it is indistinguishable from joy. He shouts now, the terror and the ecstasy tumbling together out of his mouth in an immortal roar. Oaths and obscenities fly from his lips, spit raining on Pudding's neck and his own white-knuckled hand, which clasps the reins so tight his nails have broken the skin of his palm. Smoke wreaths the horsemen ahead of them as they fire at Sam's advancing men.

'Kiss my arse!' screams the trooper nearest to Sam, as a bullet clangs loudly off his helmet. 'Kiss my godless arse!'

There are barely metres to go.

'Charge!' screams Sam, his throat raw.

He fixes his eyes on one helmet coming towards him, praying that Pudding, gallant Pudding, will not swerve, will not break, and then, in an instant, they are upon the enemy. Among them, and smiting them, and pressing them. And the enemy break; they spin and tumble and run. They are running! We are gods! We are fucking immortal! His body is so fiercely alive it cannot possibly die. Spit flies from his open mouth; his heart pummels his chest. He is a giant! He is Titan, hear him roar: 'Rupert!' he screams. 'Rupert!'

He pulls back his sword and whirls it around his head. Pudding, brave Pudding, canters on. Sam brings his sword down on a rebel neck, and laughs for joy as he finds the soft skin between helmet and breastplate. Blood erupts. Crescents of it shoot skyward, and Sam laughs again. Now who is dead, you bastard? Not me! *Not me.* You. *You.*

He doesn't wait to watch the man fall, but finds another, and another. His sword is part of his arm, and both are coated in blood. Not mine, he screams. Their blood. Theirs! He is so light, and so alive, he might float up to the sky. He grips Pudding tighter with trembling thighs, and again he shouts: 'Rupert!'

~ ~ ~

Ned watches as Ireton's horse gives in front of Rupert's charge.

'Jesus, what arseholes,' mutters a voice behind him.

'Silence,' orders Ned. 'Sergeant, take that man's name. If he lives, I'll flog him myself.'

The men behind him shift at their stations. But they have more to worry them than their hard-horse lieutenant. The horse was first, but here comes the foot.

'Fire in ranks!' Ned shouts.

The frontline of muskets kneels and fires, and the second comes forward, kneels and fires, and on they go. Slowly, in good order. Lord God, thank you for these men, these wonderful men. Their pikes bristle at the enemy, and Ned is so ferociously proud of their courage, he feels as if God's breath is pushing them forward. And then – then they collide with the king's foot in a grunt of pain and relief and terror.

~ ~ ~

Pudding is flying. Like Pegasus, she whistles over ditches; she glides over the churned grass. Sam laughs with the joy of the chase. They are one, Sam and his Pud, and they have unlocked the secret. They know how to do this. They can run for ever. She stretches out her long neck and legs. She is a goddess among horses, his Pud. Blood has dried on his arm, crusting into a cast that makes moving awkward. He finds he wants more, fresh and liquid. And Pud shall help him find it. The rebels run and he shall have their brushes. He will carve them and cut them and stuff them, the bastards. Alongside him, a herd of troopers flies with him, chasing them down.

His brothers! His glorious, beautiful brothers. He can see the fuckers ahead. Frightened and scrambling, as well they might be. Cuckolds, we come!

Behind him, something nags at him. A sound tries to intrude upon him. How dare it? He is an avenging god! He shakes his head, but there it is, the trumpet call. Sam tries to ignore it, but it thrums in his head, until at last he listens to it.

'Halt!' he screams, pulling at the reins, checking poor Pudding's glorious flight. She judders to a stop, tossing her head. He strokes her sweat-slick shoulder, trying to find his mind. He is all limbs and thunder, raging blood and fire.

Orders, Sam. Give some orders.

He calls out: 'Regroup, regroup. Retreat to the colours. The colours!'

Some of the men listen to him. He fights his way back to control and takes stock. Half the troop stands watching him, horses gulping at the air, men clutching at their sanity. A few others are galloping still, heedless and beyond discipline. The ones that remain look confused. They stare around at the field, as if awakening from some extraordinary dream. He looks for the right words to marshal them, but he doesn't know what to say. Words seem stupid, empty vessels. The bloodlust leaks out of him, and he is just a boy on a horse, in a field.

There, over there! Rupert. Unmistakable. Relief floods Sam, and he calls them to him, and they canter towards their chief. Tell us what to do, thinks Sam. Make sense of it.

~ ~ ~

'Hold them! Hold them!' Ned screams, rage fighting frustration. They are being pushed back, slowly, inexorably. They slide and scrabble in the mud. To fall is to die.

'On your feet. Your feet!' Ned shouts, even as his own boots fight for traction. Oh God, how is it Your will that they, these papist scum, will push us backwards? How can we be dying? Where are you, Lord? Where are you?

Ned looks behind him to see Hugh Peter, Cromwell's chaplain, riding behind the lines. A Bible in one hand, a pistol in the other, he is shouting them on, but Ned can't hear him.

A ripple along the ranks. Skippon is hit. Oh Lord, not thy best servant. Please, oh Lord. He feels the men sag around him. Skippon down. The men next to him deflate like a kicked pig's bladder.

Ned tries to rally them. He screams and he cajoles from the middle of his pack of men. But he can see the front pikes sliding away, melting into the mud and gore and blood. On his left, exposed by the flight of Ireton's cavalry, their flank is being energetically stormed. Their muskets are hemmed in by their own pikes, wheeled round in a hasty manoeuvre to protect against the royalist horse. The charge is ferocious, and at the push of pike they are losing. They are being squeezed and pressed, front and left; juiced like summer fruit, their blood puddling in the trenches raked up by their desperate feet.

Beside him, Ensign Somers grips the colours, and the banner still waves. But the boy is crying and shaking with the effort of keeping the flag up. He has lost his helmet in the scrum, and he looks ludicrously young. Snot dribbles from his nose, and Ned, absurdly, wishes he could offer the boy a handkerchief.

'Head up, boy,' he exhorts, instead. 'Show the papist scum how God's anointed die.'

The boy just looks at him, as if through a fog, his eyes unfocused and red-rimmed, tears dropping fast. And then, somehow, a musket-ball finds its way through the pack to punch a hole between his weeping eyes. His head falls forward, chin lolling on his chest, but the press of men keeps him upright. Ned lurches forward to grab hold of the colours from the boy's hand. He drops his sword to catch the pole, and it is lost in the mud.

He holds on to the pole with desperate ferocity. God's banner is our sword. He thinks of the words emblazoned on the six foot of silk above his head.

'In God we trust!' he screams. 'In God we trust.'

And then, from behind him, comes a roar, a rising surge of men and shouting. The men, feeling the reinforcements coming rather than seeing them, stiffen, and in the stiffening lessen the pressure. Ned, for the first time, thinks they might survive this. God has heard him.

~ ~ ~

'Sir,' screams one of Rupert's staff officers. 'We must return to the field, sir.'

There, in front of them, is the bastards' baggage train. Stuffed with food and stores. With musket-balls and cannonballs. Groaning with cash from those rich fuckers in London who fund the rebels. It must be. Why else would they defend it so rigorously? The handful of men guarding it stand firm and shoot decided volleys at Rupert's horse, who circle and pick at it like scavenging crows.

We could take it, thinks Sam. Just a little more time. Just a little more.

As if hearing his thoughts, the prince, nearby, says: 'Not enough time,' and swears vociferously in his thick home tongue. They turn then, back towards the field, following the drums and the thunder of the guns. Up the hill they ride, trudging back the way they had flown. They couldn't get where they wanted to be, round the back of the rebels' right flank to fuck Cromwell's Ironsides from behind. Too few of them have regrouped from the charge, despite the urgent tarantaring of the trumpets. And there are hosts of the bastards this side of Moot Hill's summit, hidden from the king where he stands on Dust Hill. They'd have to fight through all the reserves to get to Cromwell.

No, back the way they have come then. They pause on the great circling route round the field to come behind their own army again. On a ridge of high ground they can see the battle laid out like a chess game; too far to hear individual screams, or to smell the thick mix of blood, shit and gunpowder smoke.

They can see the two hills where the armies faced each other at the off, and the slopes down to the flat field between. It is like a flat-bottomed pudding basin, with the chaos now contained in its centre. And Sam hears the prince swearing again; at least that is what he imagines those thick vowels and vicious consonants must be. For it is obvious from up here that things are falling apart. The charge to the enemy's left with the best of Rupert's horse and foot was supposed to have destroyed that flank, ripping open a route to the New Noddle's heart. And yet the bastards are holding. From the pattern of the ensigns, it looks as if Colonel Pride's regiment has come up from reserve to bolster Skippon.

There is worse. On the rebels' right, Cromwell has clearly stuffed the Northern Horse, and is now assailing the king's exposed left flank. The royalist reserves are all committed now, yet still there are hundreds of the rebel bastards milling away behind the hill or at its crest.

Bizarrely, on the other side of hill, are a herd of cows, munching at bush and grass. One lifts its head to stare at Sam, chewing lazily.

As they pause, taking in the patchwork of the battle below them, Rupert and his men can taste the loss to come. They can see already the looming humiliation. They know, in their warriors' hearts, that this day will end badly. Sam glances sideways at Rupert, who wears a taut, impassive face, his eyes darting to take it all in. This loss will be laid at his door. Sam, for a heartbeat, thinks about turning Pudding round. We could run, my Pudding and I. This fight is lost; we need not be. He almost makes the move. The muscles of his right thigh begin to squeeze, to tell Pudding: Let us live, my darling, let us live.

Then Rupert turns to them, and says as if he is inviting them to tennis: 'Gentlemen, shall we?'

It is not really a question. Sam looks straight ahead, trying not to catch any eyes. *What if they knew what I was thinking?* Despite the fear that courses though him, he presses both knees and urges Pudding on, back to the fray. As he descends back down to the chaos of smoke and death, some instinct makes him look over his shoulder. And he sees the unmistakable form of Piers Langton, mounted on his priceless black charger, cantering away in the opposite direction.

~ ~ ~

There is a respite now. The front line has moved forward, leaving Skippon's mangled regiment some room to breathe and lick its countless wounds. Ned sees a horseman come by, helmetless. He waves his sword and shouts, 'Well done, my brave boys. God our strength!'

It is Fairfax, this apparition, and the men around Ned mumble in appreciation of the general's bravery, of his willingness to get mucky in the heart of the battle.

Ned raps orders at Sergeant Fowler. *Wounded there, we'll deal with later. Get ready for a return. Five minutes rest, and then close order.*

'I'm going to check on the major-general,' he tells the sergeant. He clambers up the hill behind him, slipping once and grabbing onto a gorse bush, which lacerates his palm. He picks at the thorns with his teeth. Suddenly, there is Skippon walking down the hill, chased by a remonstrating lieutenant. The major-general is white-faced, and a bandage on his arm is soaked red.

'Ned!' he shouts. 'Hot work this, hey, my boy.'

'Yes, sir,' says Ned, dropping in next to Skippon and retracing his steps.

Ahead of them, the infantry who crumbled at the royalists' first charge have been regrouped in some sense of order by their officers. Much depleted by death and running, they are ready, nonetheless, to be thrown at the sagging enemy. Beyond them, the royalist foot is stretched and close to breaking, and entirely unaware of this new tide building.

'Well, Ned,' says Skippon. 'Let's finish them.'

Sam and the captain ride among the fleeing Northern Horse, urging them back. But they are too far gone, horses and riders, lost in fear and life-lust.

Behind him, Sam knows, the Ironsides have reformed in calm order and are pressing the royalist flank. We should have done that, he thinks, disloyally. What training it must take to hold fast after a charge, to calm your blood and the raging life beneath you. What conviction and leadership, to hold, to re-form and to wheel back round in order. He thinks of his own mad charge after Ireton's horse.

Aye, but we had to make sure they were cleared, he thinks, determined to be loyal to the last. Rupert was right, he tells himself, as he reins in, giving up the last attempt to quell the Northern flight. Surely Rupert was right.

~ ~ ~

Oh, the glory of it! They harry and chase the king. His Majesty's muskets attempt a covering fire, but they are no match for the remorseless advance of God's own army. Advance, kneel, fire, reload! Advance, kneel, fire, reload! It sings out like a psalm. Advance, kneel, fire, reload. A mighty victory paean to the God who has given this victory. Oh my Lord, Ned sings in his heart. Oh my Lord.

~ ~ ~

Captain Fenwick appears at Sam's side, and together they shout and rally what horse they have left. No sign of their colours. Ten of them. Just ten. They canter up and down aimlessly for a while, rattling their swords. They have lost their bearings but will not admit it, even to each other. Each man secretly hoping that they will stay lost in these cursed and malevolent hillocks.

They mount a slope and see their own baggage train. It is being driven up hill through remorseless gorse, horses and men white-eyed and spit-flecked with effort and fear. Sam's pathetic troop rides to guard their rear. Over a crest comes a party of horsemen. Whose? Hard to tell. Assume it's an enemy. The pistol shots ring out, confirming it. Behind him, Sam hears the sound of dropping axels, of scrabbling feet and swearing. They're running, and God, who can blame them, the poor saps who have to piss about on two feet while the Ironsides advance on thundering four. Sam half-heartedly swears at them to halt their run, but he knows he would do the same, God help him. No better target for a cavalry sword than a single, running man zigzagging across a battlefield like a cornered hare.

On Fenwick's shouted command, they stand and draw pistols. 'No fucker fires till he can see their eyes,' shouts the captain, his voice high and cracking.

On they come, and finally, as they canter forward in a towering line, Sam feels his bladder give, and shame and piss leak from him.

He thinks, suddenly, of his father's face. The old man's creased and smiling eyes. Poor old bastard tried to warn us it would be like this. Oh God, he thinks, Ned. He imagines Ned's face in victory. The smug compassion. He can't bear the thought of it, the bastard's pity and his righteousness. The thought of being humbled before Ned and his implacable God shrivels him.

'Fire!' shouts the captain, and Sam pulls the trigger. He pulls out his other pistol and sets his sights on one Ironside. Something about the way he is mounted, something about the set of his shoulders, makes Sam hate him, violently. He fires and the man falls, and then they are in a mêlée all together – swords swinging, the sound of steel striking armour, and the grunts of the men mingling with the high-pitched whinnies of the frightened horses.

Suddenly, Sam finds that the fury of the little fight has spewed him out of the side. He sees Fenwick, feet still in the stirrups, flung backwards across his horse's haunches, arms out wide, only Fenwick has no nose and no chin.

Sam expands with rage. He wants to chase them, to close in again and to kill the buggers. He presses his knees, but Pudding, gallant Pudding, mutinies for the first and only time in her life.

She refuses to go forward. She turns and runs, and Sam loves her more for taking the decision away from him than he has ever loved any creature in his whole short life.

They crest one hill, Pudding and Sam, and then another, before Sam realizes that she is slow, too slow. Too late he looks down and sees the blood tumbling down her right thigh. He checks her and throws himself to the ground. With his weight gone, she seems to fold, his Pud, and lurches forward onto her knees. They are in one of the dips in this treacherous, benighted landscape, and it feels as if they are all alone. She shudders and then pauses.

'Come on, Pud, my darling Pud,' says Sam.

But she falls horribly, finally still under his stroking hand. He puts his arms round her warm, bloodied neck and buries his face in her mane. The sound of horses' hooves looms apocalyptically behind him. Now, at the end, he weeps.

~ ~ ~

At last, it's over.

The baggage train is taken and guarded; the prisoners are rounded up. A couple of hundred papist drabble-tails, found begging for quarter with whorish mouths, are heaped by some wagons, where his men eye them hungrily.

Too soon to take off his armour. It is hot, this June day, Ned realizes. He feels the sadness that comes after battle, the weariness. But he is used to it now, and knows it will pass. He takes off his helmet, and what breeze there is catches on his sweaty forehead, congealing with pleasing coolness.

He will take his time to thank the Lord later, when the work is done and he can concentrate on his God's pure voice. For now, he mumbles his thanks in a continuous, distracted stream. He searches the prisoners' blooded, distraught faces. He does not know what he will do or say if he finds him alive. He thinks of Edgehill and the towers of corpses shimmering in the cool dawn light. He wonders if he should walk back down to the killing fields, once the men are billeted and sated with the king's stores. He pictures the horror of picking over the bodies of dead boys, one by one, looking for traces of his brother's shining face in the grey skin and glassy eyes. Nevertheless, it is his duty to look, his duty to Hen and his father – and, he supposes, to Sam.

It is early in the reckoning, but this victory seems to be the most complete Ned has known. It is true then, that we are God's army, God's beloved. How can it not be, if He gives us this victory in our first battle, when all despised us?

And they, the Amalekites, the cursed ones – did the Lord not smite them? Aye, and the women too. He mouths the words Hugh Peter spoke at last Sunday's sermon, from the book of Samuel. '"And the Lord sent thee on a journey, and said, Go and utterly destroy the sinners the Amalekites, and fight against them until they be consumed."'

Until they be consumed. He looks over to where the women cower, and beckons the sergeant over.

'All secured, sir,' says the sergeant, red-faced and perspiring.

Screams punch the still air. Ned looks over to the whores' huddle, where a group of New Model foot is walking though the middle, swinging swords like scythes. The women are surrounded; there is nowhere to go. Those that fling themselves at the implacable ring of soldiers round them are bundled up and handed out. A second group of soldiers, with calm precision, is slitting their noses – the mark of the whore – inured to the screams and pleadings.

Ned walks over and thinks about intervening. He turns a questioning eye to his sergeant, who shrugs and says: 'Papists, sir.'

A group of royalist prisoners stands nearby and shoves back, bristling at their captors. But they are unarmed and beaten back.

Undecided, Ned turns away to think, closing his eyes to concentrate without the ravaged faces and punctured bodies of the women clouding his thoughts. And then he hears it, tugging at the corner of his mind. A high, urgent shout.

'Ned. Ned!'

CHAPTER TWENTY-THREE

16 June 1645

A FIST THUNDERS ON THE DOOR.

Hen sits up, her heart jumping violently. The window is open, and the city's warm, ripe air fills the room. The sky outside is dark. It is late, then, this June night. Was it a dream that woke her? Beside her, Lucy breathes deeply, still asleep, the blanket pushed down and curled round her legs. It is clammy and silent.

And then the noise again. A thunderous knocking. Lucy wakes this time, lurching straight from sleep into a frightened wakefulness.

'Who is here?' she whispers.

'I don't know.' Hen slides her legs out from under the blanket. She does not want to open the door. Only bad news travels this late. The word came into the city yesterday of a huge battle in the Midlands and the destruction of the king's army.

Oh Sam, would my heart know if you were dead?

She lights a taper from the embers of the fire and crosses to the door, willing herself to open it. Behind her, Grandmother peers out from her cupboard. Hen has tried to coax her out into a bed in the big room, but she likes the small space. She likes being able to touch the walls and the ceilings. She burrows in, watching from where she feels safe. Sometimes she is lucid. But mostly she mutters to herself, obsessed by her approaching damnation. She has started talking to Satan now, begging him to be kind.

Hen does what she can, but knows it is not enough. She is embarrassed that Grandmother is turning beast-like, but she is rebuffed every time she tries to help. The old lady crouches there now, disturbed by the knocking. Hen can see the whites of her eyes beneath the tangled locks of hair.

She mutters: 'See, He comes! He knows I'm here. He knows what I am. Sees through me. Wants to burn me. Wants me. Eat me. He's at the door. He's coming for me, with fire. Where's His fire? Not yet, my Lord. Not yet. Please don't take me yet.'

The knocking comes again, and the old lady's fear grows with it. Hen shushes her, trying not to let the panic grip her.

'Hen, Lucy. It's me, Ned. Open up.'

Ned!

'Grandmother, it's just Ned, just our Ned.'

Relieved, she opens the door to see Ned's grim, unsmiling face. There is someone behind him, an outline in the dark whose shape tugs at her memory.

'Hen. Is it you?' A familiar voice. It can't be. She is in Oxford. Surely.

Ned walks through the door and the pathetic light from her taper falls on a dirty face framed by a bedraggled nest of hair.

'Anne!'

'Hello, Hen.' She walks into the room, nervousness making her step bouncy, her tone ebullient. 'My turn to arrive dramatically at midnight, I thought, cuz.'

Lucy, now tucked into Ned's arm, looks towards Anne with horror. She is spattered with mud and a rust colour that Hen realizes must be blood. Her hair is wild. And yet Anne, irrepressible Anne, smiles at her and bobs into a curtsy.

'Mrs Challoner, I assume,' she says into the silence. She carries herself like a lady, chin high and shoulders straight, but looks like a beggar, and Lucy is clearly awed by her.

'This is Anne Challoner,' says Ned to Lucy. 'Our cousin.' His voice is odd, and strangely accented on the surname. Hen stores the detail to worry at later.

She kisses her cousin's dirty face. 'Welcome, Anne. Have you come far?'

'Just sauntered in from St James, don't you know,' she says, and struts the width of the room. 'What a hole this is, Hen.'

'Suits you, then,' Hen retorts. They smile at each other.

'What are you doing here?'

'I found her,' says Ned. 'In with the whores by the king's baggage.'

Anne looks at him, a straight and level stare. His eyes slide off to the side, and he hides his confusion by crossing to the jug on the shelf and pouring himself some ale.

'Is that it, Ned? Is that all you are going to say? Tell them what your friends did,' Anne says to his back. 'Tell them how you watched.'

'They were papist whores.' His fist crashes down on the table in emphasis. Still he will not look at her.

314

Lucy looks between them, her face unreadable.

'Am I a papist whore?'

He is silent, and Anne demands again: 'Ned, am I a papist whore?'

He turns to face her, visibly discomfited. 'Not a papist, no.'

'You want to cut my nose? Go on then, cut it, you snivelling turd. Or cut my ear. Not so fucking brave now, are you, with your wife and sister watching?'

'Ned, what is this woman talking about?' Lucy crosses to him.

'Never mind, poppet.'

'Ned,' Hen says. 'Ned.'

He turns to her. 'You don't understand. And anyway, they were papists.'

They stand there, immobile, looking at each other.

Anne breaks the silence. 'Oh, we've had a fine old time hotfooting it down from the Midlands, haven't we, Ned? Riding for hours in silence on borrowed hacks, Ned here purple with the shame of being seen with me.'

'Am I to be blamed for that?' Ned looks at Lucy, his natural ally.

'Aye, for that, and for what your friends did.'

'I did nothing.'

'You stood by.'

Hen walks to Anne and takes her hand. 'Enough, both of you. Come, honey, let us clean you and feed you. All is well now.'

Close to, she sees Anne crumble a little under her kindness, and fight to hold herself upright. 'All is well now? Is it so?' Anne says as she finds her smile again.

Hen turns back to Ned. 'The battle?'

'A glorious victory. God was with us, Hen. The king is destroyed.'

'Sam?'

'No sign. I searched, Hen, but if he was with the dead or the injured, I didn't find him.'

She sags with relief. No news is better than bad. Ignorance frays the nerves, but it is better than grief.

She turns back to Anne. 'We'll get you clean,' she says. 'Ned, you go next door,' she says over her shoulder, and hears Ned and Lucy walk into the bedroom and shut the door.

Anne shivers as Hen strips her clothes off. There are finger-shaped bruises on both her upper arms, and a thick tide mark of dirt at the neck and wrists. She is a gypsy. Her clothes smell high, and are crinkled with a crust of dirt and mud.

Hen takes a cloth and dips it in the bowl sitting in a tripod in the corner.

'We'll go to the bathhouse tomorrow,' she says. 'But we can make you comfortable.' Even by the sallow light of the taper, Hen can see the telltale pockmarks of the fleas that feast on Anne's skin. The dirt has built up, layer on layer, and the water turns grey as Hen rinses the linen cloth out. Even in the warm summer air, it can be cool in these rooms that run to damp, and the cold water draws goose pimples from Anne's skin.

At first they are silent, as if intent on hearing the rustle of linen in water.

A small voice, behind a curtain of matted hair, breaks the silence. 'Thank you.'

'It is nothing. My poor Annie.'

Hen takes up her comb and starts on Anne's hair, which hangs in clumps and tatters down her back. She holds it close to the roots as she tugs, and Anne sits uncomplaining.

'So the king was put to flight? How did it run?'

'Lord, Hen, don't ask me. There's little enough chance to work out what's happening when you're in the thick of it. I tried asking Ned, but when he would talk, he just blethered about Providence.'

'But what were you doing there, honey?'

'There was a boy.'

Hen notices, for the first time, the outward curve of Anne's belly and the fullness of her breasts.

'Oh Lord,' she says.

~ ~ ~

Later, in a thin trestle bed pulled out of Lucy's bedroom into the big room, they talk.

'He was – is – the son of an earl, you see. He promised me marriage. He promised me parks and fountains and curtsies. He promised me horses and servants and a place at the masque. Ice in summer and a dozen fires in winter. Pineapples, even!'

Hen smiles, and reaches across for her cousin's hand.

'Oh, Hen. I followed him. Left Oxford one night when his regiment marched out. He promised me the world.'

'And he gave you that.' Hen nods at Anne's belly, straining the fabric of her shift.

Anne's fingers flutter protectively on her stomach, and she laughs. 'Yes. He gave me this. I forgot to thank him.'

Anne's spirit is infectious, and the two of them giggle

together. Hen says gently: 'But, Anne. What now? Where is he?'

'Dead, I think. But anyway, no matter. Before the battle, he was cross. It was the fear, I think, talking, but he made it clear that the promises were as solid as farts. So, here I am.'

'Here you are.' Hen squeezes her cousin's hand.

'I will try to get rid of it. There must be a wise woman hereabout. Don't look at me that way. What would you have me do? I have no money. My mother and father would see me in the gutter. You must help me.'

Hen nods, muttering a silent prayer of forgiveness. These were dark times – perhaps dark measures were allowed. Ned would not think so, but then Ned was not a woman, and not schooled in compromise from birth.

'Hattie,' says Hen. 'Hattie is the butcher's wife. She is skilled in herbs, and if she does not know herself what to take, she will know where to ask.'

The two of them fall quiet, Hen thinking of how it would be done. She knows the properties of the potions designed to keep a woman's blood flowing; Hattie brews her own concoction of laurel, madder, pepper and sage. Was it enough to increase the dose, to dislodge a life? A life. Was it a life?

As if reading her thoughts, Anne says: 'The minister at home told my mother it is not until the quickening that the child inherits sin. I have not quickened yet. This is not yet a life.'

Her fingers, tapping gently on her belly as if to send a message, tell a different story, but Hen pretends not to notice.

They lie together under a blanket, warming each other. The closeness brings an intimacy. Anne talks of love, of her noble boy's soft lips and lying tongue. She tells of the relief of leaving home,

318

the excitement and the sense of adventure, the night she crept out of the house and into his arms.

Some small part of Hen is jealous, and she thinks of Will as she saw him last: abashed and uncertain, with his mother hovering at his shoulder. The Cavalier of Anne's tale is a hero, a dashing figure. And yet he is gone, and here is Anne. With child and alone.

She tries to tell Anne some small part of this, and her cousin turns towards her and flings an arm over her. They lie close and warm under the blanket.

'Did you meet Sam?'

'I saw him, a few times. He didn't know me. I vowed to wait until I was married before I made myself known to him. He's quite the dashing cavalry lieutenant. I thought it better to leave him be until I was respectable. But each place of safety seemed to withdraw the longer I was with my lover. Richard.

'I did not see Sam at the Naseby fight, though, Hen. He was with Rupert, and they charged off. Richard was with the Northern Horse, and they were cut down or fled. They could both be alive, or dead, or somewhere in between.'

Oh Sam. Where are you? My other half; my brother. God keep you. God guard you.

Anne breaks into her thoughts. 'And you, Hen? This is poverty.'

'Perhaps.'

'Come, tell me.'

'Oh Anne. I like this life. I have purpose. I like working. I remember those days back in Fetter Lane, those endless, stretching days. You know how it is, how it was. Waking up and not knowing why, exactly, you are bothering to rise. Expected to fill a whole day with admiring a new bonnet. I was without the worry I have now. How to feed us all; how to keep us warm. But the boredom! Oh Anne, the boredom!'

'God grant me some of that boredom. You want to try following an army, cuz. God's wounds.'

'Really? You'd prefer to have stayed at home?'

'Home? No. Surely there's some middle ground between boredom and terror?'

'Misery?'

Anne's laughter is loud after their whispering. 'Aye, misery,' she says.

'There's guilt, though, Anne. The price of my freedom, if you like, was my father's hanging. Each time I let the joy of it all fill me, I remember his face.'

'Poor cuz. My father wept when he heard. I never saw him cry before.'

'Not just my father, either. All the boys dead and maimed in the war. They bought me this . . .' She pauses, unable to find the word. 'This rebirth.'

Anne pulls the blanket up under her chin and gazes out of the open window to the black sky.

'It was fun, sometimes, on the baggage train. The women, all in it together, you know. I was frightened at first. They were coarse and salty. But kind under it all. And those that weren't kind were funny, which is, as it turns out, a better cure for blisters than kindness or praying.'

'What happened, Anne? At Naseby.' She wants to ask more directly, but somehow she cannot articulate the words properly: What did Ned do?

The moon is high now, and they can see it through the sloping window. It always makes her think of Will. She looks for the man in the moon, but tonight she cannot make him out.

'It's hard to say. We knew we were losing when the first fleers came by, the cowardly bastards. Then we heard the retreat. But it's a hilly country, that, Hen. And it had been raining, and the ground was chewed up and boggy. The wagons were stuck, and we were scared, Lord, how scared. Me and a few others were set to abandon the train and run when the rebels came over the hill and rounded us up. We thought they were just going to take us prisoner, Hen. So we went towards them with our hands in the air, waving what grey scraps could pass as white, asking for quarter. I was scared of being forced.'

She gives a low chuckle. 'We'd have spread our legs to save ourselves, I'd wager. Many of the girls had children, hiding in the carts or under them. Better a raped mother than a dead one. But they did not want us like that, the unnatural bastards. They set to killing us or maiming us. Screaming, I was: "I'm not a papist. Not a papist, not a papist." But there was so much fucking screaming.'

She shivers and closes her eyes tight. 'Why do they hate us so much, Hen? I've lain with a man now. Remember we used to talk of it? And it's all right. Nice enough. But what is it about the rutting of flesh that twists men? Mad with hatred or lust. And whichever way it takes them, we are the victims. Why, Hen?'

Hen looks at the moon as if, somehow, it can provide the answer. She searches for the right words but can't find any. She feels unworldly, small. She reaches across and brushes her cousin's hair back from her forehead. Anne reaches up and takes her hand, squeezing it.

'Still, I'm here, and whole, and there's too many who are not. Lord, Hen, it's good to be alive. And as for the rest, well, it's your fault, anyhow, Hen,' she says, a smile hovering on her lips.

'Mine!'

'When you came that Christmas, all growling with love and despair. I was jealous. I hungered for it, the passion of it, the excitement. And then, one day, there he was.'

Hen props herself up on an elbow to look at her. 'Yes, but Anne, I did not give myself to Will.'

'True.' Anne pauses, pensive. 'It was not that, I suppose,' she says at last. 'You told me once the tale of Achilles. He had to choose between a short-lived glory or a long life lived in tedium. I turned all on the toss of a coin. Heads I'm a countess. Tails I'm a whore.'

'It's not the same choice,' says Hen.

'How not? Men have their sphere; we have ours.'

'But it was not the toss of a coin you gambled on, just this boy's word. His life too, and him a soldier.'

'True.'

There is silence for a while. 'But I did so want to believe him, Hen. So very much. And by the time I started to realize I shouldn't, it was too late. When you're riding a bolting horse towards a cliff, when do you jump?'

~ ~ ~

In the bedroom, Ned and Lucy lie side by side. They can hear quiet voices next door, punctuated by laughter.

Anne's levity chafes Ned. He turns and twists, oppressed by the sound and the weight of unspoken words pressing on his chest. He remembers how Anne ran to him, wide-eyed like a demon, her hair loose and matted, her clothes torn. He quailed before her, failing to recognize her, puzzled by this creature's use of his name.

'Ned, Ned,' she shouted, again and again, and grime-streaked hands reached out to clutch at his buff coat. He tried to shake her off, but she clung on.

'Anne, Anne,' she sobbed at him, incoherent in her despair, and then he knew her.

He dragged her away from the astonished stares of his men, from the questions that hung like screams in the air around them. Which is worse, he wondered as he pulled her away. That this thing from the papist baggage train is my cousin, or that they think she's been my whore? What will they think of me?

The mortification! He remembers the look on Sergeant Fowler's face. Respect peeling away, leaving contempt, stark and unyielding. He had to ask Skippon for emergency leave, even as the injured general prepared to let the butchers loose on his gaping chest wound. He had to bear his chief's disapproval and the pain-edged crabbiness with which his request was greeted. And yet, somehow, he is the devil in Anne's story! He shudders, appalled anew by the memory, by the fracturing of his carefully sealed carapace in front of his men.

Lucy, disturbed by the movement, stops pretending to be asleep and turns to him.

'How long are you here?' she asks.

'Just tonight.'

'Is that all?'

Ask me about the battle. Ask me about the women.

'Can you leave me some money? I must have a new dress; this one is absurd.'

'Of course, my dear.'

Ask me about the way they screamed as the lads cut them. Ask me whether I would have stopped it, had Anne not appeared. Ask me about Sam.

'Grandmother is growing more impossible, Ned. How long must I live with her?'

'Not long. The war should be done soon. Our victory was a complete one. The king is lost.'

'And then what, Ned? You never finished your apprenticeship. There's no money. What then?'

'I will think of something, my love.'

She sniffs and turns away from him. The curve of her shoulder is lovely. He wants to kiss it, but he is afraid of crying.

Ask me about searching the corpses for Sam. Ask me about turning them over, one by one, the lost boys. Ask me about the maggots, and the rats and the crows and the flies, and all the parasites that eat a dead boy's flesh.

Hesitantly, quietly, Ned asks: 'Are you glad to see me, Lucy, love?'

'Of course, husband. What a question.'

They lie in silence for a while.

Lost in a vast loneliness, Ned reaches across to Lucy's body. Is this all there is, he asks his God, before he sinks, relieved, into lust and the quelling of thought. Is this it? Strangers grunting in the dark?

CHAPTER TWENTY-FOUR

18 July 1645

*T*WO DAYS LATER, ANNE AND HEN STAND WATCHING THE
sorry march of the royalist prisoners. They stumble along under
their captured colours, which hang limply in the still air – a
strange parody of a martial procession. Their mottos smack of
hubris here. God was not watching; the king was not victorious,
nor was his strength proclaimed.

Hen scans the faces as they march past, not daring to turn away
in case she misses him. Anne is beside her, restless eyes searching.
Hattie is there too, solid and unmoving amid the crowd, her face
fierce and arms crossed.

Hen tries to shout Sam's name at the passing boys, but her
voice is lost amid the jeering. All the city's hunger and fear rains
down on the prisoners in a torrent of bile and fury. They attract
that contempt Londoners have for the outsider: the poor fools
who know grass, not brick; who are dazzled by the scale of the
place, its mighty squalor and its heaven-provoking grandeur.

Some prisoners shout back, but most fix their eyes on the

shoulders of the man in front, marching, marching, as they marched away from their homes and into the death pit at Naseby.

She has dreamed that she will find him, and filled the waking gap between dreams with her prayers. Keep him safe, oh Lord. Keep him safe. Warm and fed, and happy. She thinks of the map in the bookshop and imagines all the other desperate midnight prayers across the country – all variations on the same theme, wending their way to heaven. Imagine the cacophony of pleading the Almighty must hear. Perhaps He can't distinguish one name from the other in all the noise.

The queen – does she pray for the king? Does He hear papist prayers? Does He look down on us as we once looked through the microscope at ants? Does He laugh at our antics and ceaseless scurrying?

Such thoughts turn her nights into a looping, wakeful riddle. But her dreams are worth nothing. He is not here. She stares until her eyes hurt, lost in pity for these ragged losers, their unhappiness radiating from their slouched, marching bodies. Hattie disappeared at the start of the march, muttering darkly. Now she returns with a basket of bread, and she and Hen press it into passing hands.

'Leave off, you peageese! Leave off!' a jowly man with a drinker's purple nose shouts at them. 'Don't feed the whoresons. Have you no shame?'

There is muttered agreement from the crowd around him, and Hen feels the fluttering of fear in her belly. She continues to pass out the bread. Anne steps in beside her and helps now, goaded by the jowly man.

'Deaf as well as ninny-headed?' Another man has joined the first, short and bristling with his fury.

Hattie rounds on them, furious. 'Is the manikin your pet, you goddamned looby? Did you get a knock in the cradle? Were these boys not forced to fight as well as ours? Were they not levied out of their hearths and hurled at a stupid war like so many hares to the mastiff? Are our boys not somewhere, hungry like them, tired like them, in want of a rag of kindness?'

'Hold thy tongue, trull,' shouts the first man. 'I know you – the butcher's wife. They're traitors and scum.'

'Aye, and I know you, Jeremiah Weeks. A fumbler, ladies and gentlemen!' She turns to the crowd that has gathered around the commotion. 'Whirligigs the size of oranges, I'm told, but a prick the size of my finger.' She waggles her little finger at the man's face, to laughter from the crowd, and then lets it droop. 'Aye, a fumbler. Has to pay double for the extra time he needs, and to give his hackney-whores time to stop laughing.'

Anne is laughing loudly beside Hen, who watches the man begin to bluster. But he's lost the crowd and he knows it, and he scuttles away, yelling over his shoulder.

'Wouldn't pay a ha'penny to strap you, quean.'

'I'd starve first, fumbler.'

She turns back to the girls, and starts at the sight of them as if she forgot they were there. 'Sorry for my language, Hen, Anne. He made me that angry. I'm all in a tweak.'

'Hattie,' says Anne, 'I think I love you.'

Flushed, Hattie smiles. She is still a bit flustered by her lodger, and this new arrival. They are well spoken, well educated, these girls. In other times she would have bobbed to them, and Lucy is clearly indignant that she does not. But with not a rag to their name, and dependent on her intermittent charity, the relationship between them all is odd. Arsey-versey.

Hen puts her arm through Hattie's spare arm. 'You were wonderful, Hattie. As if it's these boys' fault.'

'The fault lies with the slippery sod who calls himself king, Hen. Beg pardon, Mrs Wells.'

Anne shrugs. She wears Hen's mother's wedding ring; a fake, dead Captain Wells conjured in case the potion Hattie brewed failed. There's no bleeding yet. And no mileage in the lie either. Lucy must have talked, despite Hen's urgent pleas. Anne is condemned in the parish already as a grass widow.

They pass the minister's wife, Mrs Pike, who greets them but pointedly ignores Anne. She bustles past, to a real or imagined urgent meeting.

Hattie, after a pause, says in a voice weighed down by acute embarrassment: 'Mrs Wells, I must advise you against coming to the parish church in the morning. I've been warned they mean to refuse you the communion.'

Hen gasps, but Anne carries on walking.

'There's been tongues off like mill clappers, Mrs Wells, and, well, there we are. When the world turns upside down, some women hold on to their morality all the tighter. As if a stricter grip can flip the world back to where it was.'

'Oh Anne,' says Hen.

'Oh, never mind. I shall have to turn independent. It's like Hattie says: the world's turned upside down, and if the Presbyterians won't have me, there's a sect that will. What shall it be, Hen? Baptist? Particular Baptist? Quaker? Socinian? Latitudinarian?'

Hen smiles, but she can't quite bring herself to laugh. Surely some things are beyond even the reach of Anne's wit?

Hattie, however, is grinning widely. She adds in a voice copying Anne's singsong inflection: 'Arminian? Anti-Trinitarian? Antinomianism? Adamite?'

Anne comes back: 'Brownist? Traskite Sabbatarian?'

Hattie is silent, thinking. 'You've trumped me, Mrs Wells.' They turn into Newgate Street. 'I've got one!' she shouts, actually skipping in her excitement. 'Grindletonianism.'

'You made that up,' Hen protests.

'I did not. There's a couple walked here from the north after the king's men burned their farm. He preaches down behind the Three Tuns. Garnered quite a crowd.'

'What do they believe?'

'Lord,' says Hattie, 'you lose track. I'm all a jingle-brains when I start thinking about it. They are against the established Church and the sacrament, like most the independents. They think the Lord's spirit and the scriptures can bring man to a state of perfection.'

'Antinomian then,' says Hen.

'Is it? Lord.'

They turn into Hattie's closed shop and head to the back, where a broth bubbles on a fire and Jenny, Hattie's maid, is sweeping. Hattie ladles bowlfuls out for the girls, who slurp hungrily at it.

'Anyway, Anne,' says Hen, 'you can't just choose your faith like that.'

'No? What must I do then?'

'You must pray and reflect, and listen to God's guidance.'

'But what if I can't hear Him? Can't I just choose the sect most likely to promise me entry to heaven despite my Great Sin?'

329

'No!'

'Why not?'

Hen is foxed. She searches for her arguments. Hattie breaks in.

'Did you see the news-sheet about the letter from Cromwell purged by the MPs? The letter before they censored it called for religious liberty for soldiers. If for soldiers, why not us? That's what Mary Overton says. You know Mary, Hen? Her husband's the firebrand who acted before they banned it.'

Hen nods. She's seen the Overtons, and heard the neighbourhood mutterings about them.

'Ned thinks Cromwell is a great man,' says Hen. 'He says the army is awash with independent thinking, and the Presbyterians will never be able to contain the outpourings of faith.'

'Well, Hen,' says Anne, 'you are the clever one. Just say you could choose. Where would your clever-puss head direct you?'

'If head alone could choose, I would be a Baptist.'

'Arminian or Particular?'

'Arminian, though Ned would disown me for it. Salvation through good works, no predetermined choice of elect and non-elect. But I cannot choose the workings of salvation. Our God has already chosen how we are saved.'

'And how do we know what He has chosen?' says Hattie.

'My head hurts,' says Anne. 'Too much doctrinal tattling does that.'

She wanders out of the room towards the stairs, doubtless for a lie-down. Hattie says that women with child need more sleep than well women, but Hen is beginning to suspect that Anne's endless sleeping is an excuse to be looked after. Another mouth for Hen to feed, another body to keep warm.

In her absence, Hattie says: 'I am sorry you didn't find your brother, Henrietta.'

'I know. But Ned said he had checked the prisoners, so I did not expect it.'

'Hoped, though?'

'Yes.'

Hattie pours out some more broth, brushing aside Hen's thanks.

'Did I tell you, Hen, about walking with the peace protestors back at the start of all this? We got up a petition, the women of these neighbouring parishes, and we marched to Parliament. Made it all humble. We're only poor women, blah-di-blah, and you so wise. That's the rub with men, dear. You have to grease 'em up like a pig on a spit. Then ask.

'They paid us no heed, of course. Set on breaking out their sabres, the lob-cocks. So the world has turned, and we've all this freedom to think what we like and talk how we like. Women standing on tubs, preaching away, the rest of us making do and running things our way. But it's only because half the whoresons are away fighting and the other half are looking the other way.'

'I know what you mean, Hattie. But none of this upside is worth my father and Sam and Ned. One dead, one lost and one . . .' She leaves the sentence unfinished.

'True. I don't mind if my soldier comes back or not. I lost him to drink before our honeymoon was done. It goes straight to his noddle, and he's top-heavy from the soaking.'

Hen looks at Hattie as she prods at the fire, at her deft hands and broad shoulders. She struggles to imagine her as anything other than this woman alone, running her shop and propping up the neighbourhood women with counsel and herb-skill. She probably struggles to imagine me as a pampered trade princess. Yet that was me too, she thinks. Perhaps we are like jelly: we can set in different moulds.

CHAPTER TWENTY-FIVE

October 1645

𝓗EN WALKS HOME THROUGH THE CITY FROM ST PAUL'S churchyard on an autumn day so golden bright it makes her want to skip like a girl. Her cheeks and hands burn with the cold, but she bubbles with happiness. The low sun gilds the buildings, as if setting a halo on the city. God is good. God is good.

In her pocket are her wages, and Mr Rowan has given her a half-day. Tucked under her arm is the book she has chosen to take home with her. She found it buried in the back stacks: *The Countess of Montgomery's Urania* by Lady Mary Wroth. She has read the title page again and again. Lady Mary Wroth. A woman!

Scribbled across the page is a note written in anger, with splattered ink and indentations like furious pinpricks: 'Vile HERMAPHRODITE. Leave idle books alone: for wiser and worthier women have written NONE.'

She thinks of the lines she snatched before tucking the book away in a hiding hole, to take home later. Not stealing, exactly. Just borrowing.

Come darkest night, becoming sorrow best;
Light, leave thy light, fit for a lightsome soul.

The book promises misery, and love denied. What joy! She will read it to Anne. Poor fat, irritable Anne, with her raging heartburn and sleepless nights. Anne's belly grows bigger, swelling and thumping with life, despite her best efforts. She has drunk potions that make her spew from both ends: 'a thorough fart', Hattie called it, which made Anne smile even as she dove headfirst to the pot. She has jumped off walls, and stood on her head. She begged Hattie to use the needle, but accepted her refusal. Too dangerous for the mother.

Until now, at last, she has learned to accept the life inside her, even to anticipate with pleasure its violent kicks. Now coming to term, it batters at her belly from the inside, demanding its entry to the world.

Lady Mary Wroth will take her mind off the coming event. Lord keep her safe.

'Miss Challoner!'

Hen stops, squinting into the sun.

'Mr Chettle!'

They both begin to talk at once. He looks well. His dark suit is well cut, and he looks healthy, handsome even. There is a pink flush to his cheeks, no doubt from the cold.

'Very well, thank you,' she stammers out to his enquiry as to how she is.

'And your brothers – they are well?'

'Ned is with the army, a captain now. Sam we heard of last at Naseby.' All the happiness she has husbanded leaks away in an instant.

'Forgive me,' he says. 'Innocent questions in these times too often provoke pain. May I walk with you?'

She thinks of her rooms above the butcher's shop with a sudden rush of shame. She starts to make excuses and then thinks, the devil take my lies. I am where I am.

'Yes, thank you. I am going home.'

They turn and walk together. 'And have you spent a pleasant morning, Miss Challoner?'

'I have been at my work.'

'Work!' He stops and stares at her.

'Sorry, Mr Chettle. Did I startle you? Yes, work. It helps to buy food, I find. Useful, too, for paying rent.'

'Well, yes, I . . .' He stops talking and they begin to walk again.

'You know my father's property was sequestered. And the committee for which you clerk is having a terrible time actually paying the men who fight its wars. Ned cannot keep me and his wife and our grandmother on thin air.'

Chettle stammers something non-committal.

Hen thinks of Anne, and starts to enjoy this. What a tale she will make of it when she gets home.

'I'm working in a bookshop. There is only one other career open to women, but though I can take the risk of paper cuts, I prefer not to entice the Spanish pox. I rather like my nose.'

'Miss Challoner!'

'Dear Mr Chettle, I am sorry. Do you have any other notions of how I might earn money for my keep?'

'Respectable women . . .' he begins, but trails off.

' . . . are plump of purse. I, however, am not.'

'I am sorry, Miss Challoner.'

'Curious,' she says. 'I find I'm not sorry.'

And now, she thinks, for the final scene.

'Here we are,' she says.

'Here?' He looks at the shop. Hattie sits on the front step, cheerfully plucking a chicken, pausing to wave at Hen. The chicken's throat is cut, and its head swings back and forth on the flap of remaining skin. Its blood pools at Hattie's feet, and there is a red smear on her face.

Hen points to the upper levels, which hang precariously over the fetid street. The place looks tired, cheap and grimy.

'There. Well, Mr Chettle, many thanks for escorting me. Goodbye.'

It would be too much to sit with Hattie and pluck the chicken. A scene too far. She walks past Hattie towards the stairs at the back of the shop, leaving Chettle gawping like a befuddled guppy.

~ ~ ~

Grandmother's end comes with a whimper. The day before she was raging. Demons danced in her brain, and hell beckoned her. Grandmother clutched at Hen's hands, babbling her fear.

'He's coming for me. Coming. And he is dancing, and they are naked, his imps, child, and they want me. And they will burn my flesh; fry me and roast me and souse me. They'll broil me and baste me with my own blood. Henrietta, they're coming. Oh, they are coming.'

Lucy and Anne leave off their bickering long enough to help. They bring warm water for Hen to bathe her; they take away her soiled sheets and put them in the pot, drawn together by the horror of the old woman's descent into a hell she has long prophesied.

To the girls it seems as if she is hanging on to a cliff edge by her fingernails, the fires below licking at her skirts. It is so real for her, her fear so vast and so palpable, that they can almost smell the smoke, and the crisping of flesh.

They have pulled her out of her cave, but she is beyond caring. She lies, tiny and shrivelled, in the best bed. Her eyes are huge in her furrowed face. She closes them to sleep, at last, sometime around two in the morning, and Hen climbs in beside her. She puts her arm round the old lady's concave waist and feels the shock of time. How strange to be the soother, not the soothed. How infinitely sad to coddle and hush her grandmother like a child.

'Hush, my darling. All will be well. All will be well.'

What lies we tell to the ones we love best, Hen thinks in that long, dark night.

In the morning, Hattie is there, solid and wonderful. Her broad red face is shiny and beautiful to Hen, who has watched the pain and fear flit over her grandmother's ruined face for too many hours.

Behind her is Claire Baker, their neighbour and a cunning woman. She is older than Hattie, and grey-haired. Her face is curiously unlined. She nods towards Hen, crossing the room swiftly. She leans in to listen to the old lady's breathing. Grandmother stirs a little and mumbles.

'From life to death,' says Claire softly. 'She will be gone soon. Caught in His embrace. Come, child. No time to cry. She will be in His arms at last.'

'She doesn't think so,' says Hen, sobbing. 'She thinks the devil is waiting. She thinks she is damned.'

'Shall we pray for her, child?' They kneel, but before they pray, Claire takes Hen's hand. She says: 'In the time of our fathers, they thought that prayers could intercede, could help the departing soul find the light. We know now that was mere superstition; hope triumphing over scripture. But we can pray for her path to be easy, for her expectations to be confounded.'

As they begin to say the words, they hear a whimper from the bed. Hen rises to comfort her, but realizes it is too late. Grandmother is gone.

~ ~ ~

Hattie stands in the doorway, fidgeting.

'A visitor for you, Miss Challoner,' she says. From behind her steps a figure, gorgeously arrayed. The silk rustles as he walks forward; the feathers in his hat shiver as he sweeps it from his head. His face is framed by bouncing curls, and his moustaches are artfully twirled.

'Miss Challoner,' says the apparition as he bows, and the voice is unmistakable.

'Cheese!' cries Hen, and Lucy's head bobs up from her sewing at the cry. She swiftly looks the visitor up and down, and decides he is evidently worth the laying down of her sewing and the bending of her knee.

'Forgive me,' Hen mumbles, seeing the annoyance on his face. 'The surprise. Michael Chadwick, my father's former apprentice, this is Lucy Challoner, my brother Ned's wife.'

338

Cheese rustles forward, and Hen is astonished by him. Still short, he is thinner now, and less ungainly. He is all poise and gallantry bending to Lucy, and she simpers and coos at him, delighted. He turns back to Hen.

'Well now, Miss Challoner. What charming company you keep, even if your living accommodation is less salubrious than when last we met.'

Lucy blushes prettily, and Hen bows her head.

Hattie is peering in behind the doorframe, mesmerized by Cheese's ostentatious splendour.

'Hattie,' says Hen, and she straightens and blushes. 'Could you send Jenny with some small beer and some of those caraway biscuits she made yesterday?'

Hattie nods, abashed into silence, and disappears.

'I am glad I found you, Miss Challoner,' he says, as they settle awkwardly into chairs.

Hen blesses Jenny for seeing to their rooms this morning. Three women in two rooms make for living on the edge of chaos. The trunk she perches on is full to bursting, springing open when she moves.

'I had business with the committee, and Mr Chettle mentioned seeing you.'

She nods, but finds herself oddly tongue-tied. The shift in their relationship to each other is disconcerting, dizzying even.

'And what business is that, Mr Chadwick?' asks Lucy.

'Ordnance, madam. When the war intruded on my apprenticeship with dear Mr Challoner, I returned home. Where once there was room only for one son in the firm, an upswing in our business offered greater opportunities.'

'You are clearly prospering,' says Hen.

'We are. My father was granted monopoly for the supply of cannonballs some years ago, before there was overmuch demand for cannonballs. Now, of course, demand is not a trouble . . .'

'How fortunate,' Lucy cries, clapping her hands.

'Indeed, madam. We supply both sides of the disagreement. Cannonballs, bullets, grenades. If a gun fires it, we made it!'

'How proud you must be,' says Hen.

'Indeed.'

'You heard about Chalk, I suppose?'

He nods. 'Yes, alas. Too many good men have been taken by these troubles.'

'Do you think that one of your bullets may have done for him?'

'Why, Miss Challoner, you tease me.'

Hen laughs mirthlessly. 'Apologies, Mr Chadwick. I have become unused to polite company.'

'She excepts me from that, I do assure you,' says Lucy, her laugh all tinkles and silver. 'She can be intolerably severe, our Henrietta.'

'I remember of old, madam.'

They exchange civil chat. Yes, the troubles are tiresome. Yes, the king is surely defeated. Goodness alone knows what the peace will look like. God pray it brings an easing of the wheat price, and a falling off from the malt highs.

Why are you here? thinks Hen. Why now?

Eventually, he makes his move.

'Mrs Challoner, I must beg a favour. I must talk to Miss Challoner alone, if you do not mind,' he says to Lucy.

Lucy does mind, Hen can tell. She covers her minding with

340

a display of coquettishness, before flouncing out of the room. As soon as she closes the door behind her, Cheese moves closer.

'I am glad to find you at last, Miss Challoner. Or may I call you Henrietta? I have been looking for you. And when Mr Chettle told me of your misfortunes, of your unfortunate circumstances . . . Well, I came nearly as soon as I could.'

He sidles even closer, and she can see under the foppish display the boy she once knew. 'I have so long admired you, Miss Challoner. Henrietta. And now I have some little fortune, and you are but a poor woman living, dare I say it, like *this*.' He gestures wildly around her little room. 'I thought, perhaps . . .' He trails off uncertainly.

'Mr Chadwick, are you offering me marriage?'

She knows as soon as she says it that she has made a terrible mistake. He flushes near purple, and struggles to speak. His first attempts end in throat-clearing and coughing, until at last he manages to say: 'Not as such, Henrietta. You must understand my position. Perhaps a more informal, mutually beneficial arrangement?'

She slaps his face. Hard, sharp and irrevocable. His head snaps back, and he makes a curious 'oh' sound. He stands in silence, looking at her.

'And you must understand *my* position, Mr Chadwick.'

He takes a moment to compose himself, pulling his chest up like a fighting cock. 'Forgive me, Henrietta. But I thought that living with whores was bad enough. Now it seems you brawl like one too.'

'Leave. This instant.'

'Wait,' he says, and turns round to rummage in the bag he

341

brought into the room with him. 'I had another reason for finding you, although you deserve little enough consideration.' He pulls out a wooden box. 'Here. A present from one who cares about your safety.'

She opens the box. Inside is a pair of beautifully rifled pistols. Intricately worked patterns whorl on the handles, and the barrels are long and gleamingly straight.

'The best we do with bullets, and the latest in flintlocks,' Cheese says.

'They're beautiful,' Hen says. Then she looks at the letter tucked in beside the pistols, white against the green damask lining the case. The handwriting strikes her like a punch, winding her.

'Farewell then,' Cheese says, and bowls out of the room, ignoring her pleas for him to stop. 'It's all in the letter!' he shouts as he clatters down the stairs.

Hattie comes into the room moments after he leaves; she has been waiting, it seems.

'Oh honey,' she says as she enters, seeing the tears streaming down Hen's face. 'What is it? Did Captain Huff upset you?'

'Hattie. It's this,' she says, waving the letter. She is crying – great heaving tears that catch in her throat and make it hard to speak.

'It's from Sam. *Sam!* He's alive, Hattie. *Alive!*'

CHAPTER TWENTY-SIX

November 1645

*N*ED PUTS DOWN THE COPY OF SAM'S LETTER HEN ENCLOSED with hers on the table in front of him. The window ahead looks out onto Wine Street, and the entrance to the guard house. The wooden horse is ready, and the Bristol mob and the soldiers are beginning to gather for the punishment. As good as a show for them. Still, the poltroon, David Curtis, deserves it. Fairfax promised the army two weeks' pay in lieu of plundering Bristol if they took the city. But Curtis, bored on his garrison duty one night, ignored the general and set off on a spree of pillaging.

We can only finish this thing if we curb the plundering and the looting, Ned tells himself. He must go out to administer the punishment. Time enough later to reflect on Sam's letter. Alive! Thank the Lord. Yet not redeemed, though. He was at Bristol. Strange that we did not see each other as Rupert's surrendering troops marched out, thinks Ned. Providence. God saved my bullets from hitting him.

Ned reads the last part again.

And so here we sit, idle and bored at Woodstock Castle, waiting to see if Parliament will grant us safe conduct to the Low Countries. The MPs have offered the Princes Rupert and Maurice safe conduct if they promise not to serve the king again, yet though his loyalty to them is wavering, theirs to him is strong and they cannot accept. Yet we know, even if the king does not, that the war is lost. The peace must now be thrashed out.

I will follow Rupert where he leads. I am a soldier now, dearest Hen. I have no other calling. He is not half so black as he is painted, my prince. Indeed, his conduct has been beyond reproach. I send you all the love I can spare him. I had a horse, Hen, to love. She died.

Your loving brother,

Sam

All the news-sheets are abuzz with the falling-out between the king and his nephew. The king blamed Rupert for surrendering at Bristol.

No fan of Rupert's, Ned was softened by the prince's conduct. Bristol's outer walls were breached, the townsfolk terrified and Rupert's remaining men bracing themselves for death when the prince decided to trust in Fairfax's hard-won reputation for mercy and trustworthiness. Trust that slippery minnow, the king, to think his men's lives and those of the put-upon Bristolians worth throwing away for a cause already lost. They say that the king is in thrall to his adviser, Digby, who loathes the young prince and drops poison in his uncle's ear. What is it with the man Charles, wonders Ned, that perpetually drives him into the arms and counsel of men all the rest of the world consider fools or knaves?

Was Sam with Rupert in his mad stalk across the country to find the king and tell his version of the tale? Ned wonders. Probably, if he is with him now. A semi-rapprochement, they say, between king and nephew. The elder has proved himself half-faced though, again and again. Ned thinks of the documents seized at Naseby, which proved the king was negotiating to bring armies of papists from abroad. Wanted to ship them in from left and right, to squeeze poor Protestant England between the papist savages of the Irish bogs and the onion-eyed French.

Ned stands and straightens his jacket, donning his hat and pulling himself straighter. He thanks his God that he has only to fight the last pathetic half-battles of this war, and not negotiate a peace with the man Charles, who lies like a cheap whore and wriggles like a maggot.

He steps outside into the icy air. The drums call for the punishment, and the miscreant is led forward. He looks young and vacant, his mouth slack, his limbs long and awkward. The sawhorse is ready, mounted on a makeshift pedestal. It looks like a hobbyhorse for children, except for the sharpened spines that run wickedly across its wooden back. Curtis is led forward and pulled onto the horse. His mates must have smuggled him some liquor, Ned surmises, for his head hangs groggily and there is little sign of the fear that should be consuming him. Once mounted, though, the pain reaches his fuddled brain.

Ned reads the articles of war which cover theft in the solemn, sonorous voice he saves for Sundays, his voice rising as the whimpering from the man begins to swell. At a nod from Ned, Sergeant Brakes comes forward with two corporals and ties heavy muskets to each of Curtis' ankles. He pulls and tugs at the manacles tying his hands behind his back. Writhing makes the horse more painful; but staying still and bearing the pain is impossible. He wriggles between the agony of inaction and the torture of movement. The poor sap-pate, thinks Ned. The men behind him begin to mutter. He's had enough, they reckon. His testicles chafed to ribbons, he'll be shitting blood for a week.

Ned ignores their murmurings, though the man's screaming is whirling though him. *Thou shalt not steal. Thou shalt not steal. Thou shalt not steal.* Oh Lord, keep me strong. Lord, help me keep to your path. Then, suddenly, a new thought, strong and unexpected.

I want a child. A child.

~ ~ ~

Hattie swirls a ring on a string over Anne's distended belly.

'A girl,' she pronounces. 'Poor moppet.'

Anne pulls her clothes back on, shivering in the November chill. She pulls a blanket up over her belly, tucking its edges in and underneath her, smoothing it down on top.

'Cold, today,' she says.

'Yes, child. But we must save all the coal we can. To keep the moppet toasty when she appears. Keep us all warm at the gossiping.'

From the corner by the window, Lucy says: 'How soon?'

'Just a few weeks,' Hattie says, and Anne grimaces. Lucy bends her head back to her sewing.

Hen comes in and dives under the blanket next to Anne, putting her freezing hands onto her cousin's belly.

'Ow. I can feel that through my clothes, you harpy.'

'Well, if you will lie here under a blanket while I work… Hey, I can feel it move.'

The baby kicks and twists under Hen's hands. A life inside a life; miracle upon miracle.

Anne grimaces. 'I can feel it too.'

'Not it. Her,' says Hattie. 'Look at the way she's carrying.'

'You just want it to be a girl, Hat,' says Hen.

'Of course I do, not being a beef-witted simpleton. Who'd not want a lovely girl to raise?'

Hen begins to feel warmth returning, her fingers melting back into life. 'Hat, did you see Mother Wilkes today?'

'No. I must take her something. She's starving herself to death, poor gudgeon. All three sons lost to the war now the youngest has stopped a pike. She's given up, I think. I did see Goody Simmonds.'

'The midwife?' asks Anne.

'Yes.' Hattie pauses, twirling a strand of hair round her finger. Hen has learned to recognize the gesture: it denotes awkwardness and dislocation. The girls look at her expectantly.

At last, she says: 'We spoke in hypotheticals. She told me that the minister is laying pressure on her about attending to by-blows. That her licence is in his hands, and she needs his good will. That she would find herself forced to question an unwed mother most ferociously during the lying-in.'

'And thanks to Lucy,' says Anne venomously, 'I may find myself in such a position. My word and good name doubted.'

'With cause, *Mrs Wells*,' counters Lucy.

'Aye, well,' Hattie bustles onwards. 'Goody Barker, being an old friend of mine, and me a gossip with her at many a birth in the parish, says that if a young lady were to want to avoid such an interrogation during her labouring, there are places to go. She named a house in Stepney where questions are not asked.'

'And what would happen to me, were I to be officially unmasked?'

'At best, a whipping. The father found and made to pay.'

Anne snorts. 'He's dead, most like. Well, Lucy, thank you. Should we tell Ned, I wonder, about the brew you drink each morning? Does he know you purge his seed?'

'I do no such thing.' Lucy stands and walks to the window, fanning herself with one hand, trailing her embroidery behind her in the other.

Hen watches her. She's unfathomable. If Ned were here, she would cry at the accusations levelled at her. She is hard as a nut, yet pretends to be soft. Soppy, that's the word Hen's father would have used. Whereas Anne, God love her, is all brittle shell when people are watching.

'You could deliver the baby, Hattie,' says Hen. 'Anne should be here, with people who love her.'

'If it's a simple birth, yes. Along with some of the more experienced gossips. The goodwife Claire Barker, for one. And Mary Overton. Have you met her, Anne? Lives the other side of the back, in the house with the green door. She's had a few of her own and, more to the point, she's not the least afraid of the minister's wife. Her and her husband are friends of freeborn John Lilburn. She's gaining a name in the agitating line – freedom of conscience and liberty of worship. You know.'

'Well then,' says Anne. 'As long as she don't preach at me while I'm down, this Mary Overton sounds perfect. So there it is – Hattie shall midwife me.'

Hattie pushes her hair back from her face and paces nervously. 'You understand the risk, Anne, love? I can deliver a sow. But a girl? If aught goes wrong, we may need to call in the midwife, nonetheless. And your lying-in with the new moppet may not be a comfortable one.'

Outside the window they hear shouting. Hattie crosses the room to look.

'Old Joe,' she says, and sure enough Hen can hear the thump of his wooden leg on the cobbles.

His voice drifts up through the ice-flecked air. 'Oh and ye will be damned. Oh and ye will be damned.

'*And I saw three unclean spirits like frogs come out of the mouth of the dragon, out of the mouth of the beast, and out of the mouth of the false prophet.* And they were called Charles and Rupert and Laud.

'Oh and you will be damned. You will be damned. *And I heard a great voice out of the temple saying to the seven angels, Go your ways, and pour out the vials of the wrath of God upon the earth.*'

Anne rolls back her eyes.

'Be kind,' says Hen. 'His wits have been addled since the battle at Newark.'

'London, you are Nineveh. Nineveh. Nineveh. *Woe to the bloody city! It is all full of lies and robbery. Because of the multitude of the whoredoms of the well-favoured harlot, the mistress of witchcrafts, that selleth nations through her whoredoms, and families through her witchcrafts. Behold, I am against thee, saith the Lord of hosts; and I will discover thy skirts upon thy face, and I will shew the nations thy nakedness, and the kingdoms thy shame. And I will cast abominable filth upon thee, and make thee vile, and will set thee as a gazing-stock.*'

Anne lumbers to her feet and crosses to the window, wrenching it open to let in the icy wind and the veteran's lament.

'I will cast abominable filth on thee, Joe, if you don't shut up. I've a full pot here, you clay-brained codpiece.'

'I see you, whore. I see you, wag-tailed punk. Who put that by-blow in your belly, whore? *And he saith unto me, the ten horns which thou sawest upon the beast, these shall hate the whore, and shall make her desolate and naked, and shall eat her flesh and shall burn her with fire.*'

Hen is smiling at the exchange, until she sees Anne's face in the pause before she turns back into the room. She puts on a smile then, but Hen saw the fear, saw the uncertainty in the half-second she thought herself unobserved.

Hattie, ever alive to a room's undercurrents, says to Hen: 'Any word of your brothers?'

'Of Ned, yes. He is still busy at Bristol. Of Sam, no. What of your brother, Anne?'

'He still will not reply to my letters. Sends them back unopened from that sty he guards in the back of the west somewhere. Your husband, Hattie?'

'Not a word. But then he's a butcher, not a scholar. The end is coming though, soon enough, and then we'll see if he turns up,' says Hattie.

They nod and look at each other. Why aren't we happier that the war is ending? wonders Hen. Why this bottomless trepidation?

~ ~ ~

'Hen!'

The shout wakes her, and she sits up, disorientated.

'Hen! I think it is coming.' Anne's voice beside her in the darkness is calm, steady. Hen feels the panic begin to grip her. She jumps to her feet, gasping as her toes meet the icy floor. The world beyond the blankets is freezing; Anne's fat, pregnant body radiates heat and life.

'I'll get Hattie,' she says.

'No, wait. The pains are regular, but not too close or too strong to bear. Let her sleep. Sorry to wake you.' Her voice falters a little.

Hen climbs back in. 'Don't worry, Annie. I'm here.'

Anne reaches for her hand. Suddenly her grip tightens, and her breath becomes jagged.

'Is that one?' asks Hen.

'No. Just wind,' says Anne, and giggles. 'I'm teasing, cuz. Yes, that was one.'

'I thought it was not until after Christmas?'

'Aye, well, the baby must not have heard. She's coming.'

'I bought you a present. New linen, for the lying-in. We'll use this old stuff for the groaning. I'll build up the fire.'

'Not yet. To think – when we were littleys, we were surrounded by linen. How could you afford it?'

'Never mind that,' says Hen, her mind turning to the ever-dwindling stock of her mother's jewels. Just a pair of earrings and a necklace left.

In a small voice shrouded in darkness, Anne says: 'I am frightened, Hen.'

'No need, my honey. God is with you, and I am with you. All will be well.'

All will be well. How many times does she utter that phrase in the endless hours that follow?

'All will be well,' she whispers through Anne's groaning, as the pains move closer together. 'All will be well,' she tells herself as the day advances, and Anne crouches by the fire, lost in a pain that advances and retreats in merciless charges. She does not wail so much as groan, a deep and guttural keening.

The windows are barred and curtains drawn, and the room is kept warm and dim. Womb-dark. Just the light of the fire to witness Anne's labour. They are shrouded in its orange light, Anne, Hen and Hattie – and Claire, who comes and goes as the day moves forward. Mary Overton comes too, a sharp-faced woman with fingernails bitten to the bleeding roots and a harassed air. She seems fierce, but her hands when she wipes Anne's forehead are gentle, and she whispers at her softly. 'Come now, darling. Shh, now.'

There is no sense of time in the room, no notion of their place in the world. It is a place apart, a timeless zone.

The room is sadly empty. If Anne were married and birthing at home in a time of peace, it would be brimming with gossips. The chatter and excitement would fill the room as loudly as the groaning. The room would hum with the steady, matronly presence of women who have sat on the groaning stool and lived.

Instead, there are just the three of them, sometimes five, and the child trying to batter its way out. Why so brutal, oh Lord? Was Eve's sin so great that we are rendered bestial by childbirth? Is this pain our desserts? A new thought creeps into Hen's mind. Are Anne's labours worse because her sin was worse? Do bastards hurt more on their way out?

The day, she believes, has given away to night. None of them have slept. At last, the pains seem to swell together, almost seamlessly. Anne's groans become cries of effort. Hattie exhorts her to push. Anne crouches, legs apart, bracing herself against Hen, who holds her upright with arms wrapped under her shoulders. Clasped together like this, Anne's sweat slicks on Hen's neck, her wails of pushing echo directly into Hen's ear.

'I can feel it!' shouts Hattie. 'I can feel the head! Go on, Anne, my darling, you're nearly there.'

Anne screams with a last, violent effort. Hen looks down over her shoulder and sees a tangle of purple, bloodied limbs.

'I can see it! Anne! Anne! I can see it!'

'Her!' shouts Hattie. 'Her!'

And suddenly there's a thin screaming mingling with Anne's exhausted sobs and Hen's rapid breathing. A twist and a grunt from Hattie, and the cord is cut. It lies, grey and mottled, between Anne's legs.

A new sound. Hattie is swearing. She has wrapped the baby in a blanket and now pushes it towards Hen, who looks with astonishment at its furious old-man face.

'Sit down, my poppet,' says Hattie, easing Anne back to lie half upright. Hen sees the blood then. So much blood.

'Hen, run get the midwife.'

'But—'

'Now.'

Anne's head is lolling onto her chest, grey-white and sweaty. She looks towards the baby with unfocused eyes.

Hen runs out of the room, before remembering she is still clutching the baby. Coming up the stairs is Mary Overton. In relief, Hen pushes the squirming bundle at her as they pass. Outside, the light is dim and the air is freezing. Hen has no notion of whether it is dusk or dawn, and cares less as she runs through the frosted street, her bare feet scrabbling for purchase on the iced cobbles.

She comes to Goodwife Simmonds' door and pounds on it, before spilling out her plea to the woman who answers. Goody Simmonds pauses to wrap on a shawl and shout instructions to an unseen figure within, and Hen hates her for her slowness, as the seconds stretch to minutes. She hops from foot to numb foot. At last, they set off, Hen running ahead, pausing for unbearable moments as the midwife bustles to catch up.

They reach the door and climb the stairs, Hen taking them two at a time. She opens the door at the top, and light spills into the darkened room. Hattie's face turns to the light and all the news is there in her grey, horrified face. Blood pools on the floor, dripping into cracks in the boards, soaking through the second-best linen. Mary paces the room with a crying bundle, and she turns to Hen with pity softening her face.

Anne, her back propped up on cushions, looks strangely peaceful, even as her life leaks out from between her parted thighs. Behind her, on the bed, the new linen gleams ivory-white and spotless.

CHAPTER TWENTY-SEVEN

Winter 1645

HE LETTER TO ANNE'S PARENTS COMES BACK. SCRAWLED
on it, in fierce black ink: 'We have no daughter. We have no
granddaughter.'

The next day, the first of the new year, Hen pushes open the
door of the pawnbroker's. He recognizes her now, greeting her
by name. His shop is stuffed with geegaws and trinkets – the cast-
offs of the war's casualties. When anyone has any money to start
buying again, he will make a pretty profit.

He offers her a ridiculously low sum for her mother's necklace,
but she expected as much. Still, it will be enough.

That afternoon, Hen and Hattie gather up the baby from the
wet nurse in Wapping, who is too drunk to notice or care particularly. She wanders around, bare-breasted and leaking, latching
on whichever baby is screaming the loudest. Hen feels sharp guilt
that she left it this long. She picks up the baby. Beneath its swaddling
she can smell that it is dirty. She peels off its filthy layers and throws
them into the fire, while Hattie curses the nurse for her neglect.

'What do you expect for a penny?' she shouts back. 'Fucking gold milk? I've me own to clean, and the others. Now take it, and fuck off.'

They wrap the baby in Hen's shawl and escape from the room. It feels wrong to leave behind the others, but they have enough work ahead to keep this one.

The baby nuzzles against Hen's chest, as if looking for milk. So helpless. Eyes closed, she sniffs and worries at Hen, who feels too awkward to whisper aloud the endearments crowding her head.

They take a coach up to Highgate. The air is cleaner up here just a few miles from town. From the top of the hill they can see across the woods down to the Thames, the City in the distance and the black tendrils of smoke reaching up to the sky.

They find the house Goody Barker described to them, and the door is opened by a woman Hen's age – Alice Harper. She looks tired, and children hang off each leg, but she smiles and ushers them in, winning them over with her politeness and quiet charm.

As they speak, the baby begins to squall.

'Someone's hungry,' says Alice, and reaches across. 'May I?'

Hen hands her across, watching as Alice eases out a breast and proffers it to the baby.

'There we go, precious,' she says gently, and Hattie nods imperceptibly at Hen. 'Your cousin's child, Miss Challoner?' asks Alice.

'Yes. Poor Anne died birthing her, and the baby's father was killed in the wars.'

Hen tries to say the white lie of omission with conviction, but Alice has no reason to question them. She merely smiles, and they talk of the war – of the king's lost cause and refusal to surrender, and Fairfax's march around the country, mopping up the last of the Cavaliers. All the while, the baby suckles contentedly.

'She don't care about all the nonsense, do you, my darling?' coos Alice. 'Let it all be over, and friends again, I say.'

They murmur their agreement.

'What name does the baby have?'

'She is named for her mother,' says Hen, deciding at that moment the only name possible. 'Her name is Anne.'

~ ~ ~

As winter turns to spring, they visit baby Anne once a week. After church they make the journey up the hill to Highgate, sometimes walking back down when the evenings grow longer. They watch baby Anne grow stronger and fiercer. She is impatient and demanding. Chubby hands grab at Alice's breasts; she wails if her nurse is not fast enough.

'Sucking the marrow out of me, this one,' says Alice, and indeed she looks tired, with three of her own to raise as well as Anne to nurse.

One day in May they burst into Alice's house, impatient with excitement.

'Have you heard the news?' Hattie says, reaching immediately for baby Anne, who sits propped on the floor by cushions, gurgling at the youngest Harper child, one-year-old Peter.

Alice, flour-smeared and haggard, looks up from the dough she's pounding. 'News?' she asks vaguely.

'The king has surrendered to the Scots.'

Alice's jaw drops open, and she runs a floured hand across her face. She looks like an astonished ghost, and Hen and Hattie find themselves laughing at her appearance. Without a word she runs out of the room, and comes back a moment later with her husband, a huge and taciturn blacksmith that Hattie and Hen nod to in passing but have never spoken to.

'What's this?' he demands.

'It's true,' says Hen. 'At least, enough people are saying it. *Rumour is quick of foot and swift on the wing – a horrible monster.*'

She looks at their blank faces. 'Virgil,' she whispers, and Hattie impatiently cuts in.

'Never mind all that. The king has surrendered to the Scots at Newark. Our army is besieging Oxford, which must fall, and then they are done. He crept out of Oxford at midnight, they say, three days past. The MPs are to send the king a proposition for peace.'

'Peace!' says Alice.

'Aye, but on what terms?' growls the blacksmith. 'We fought for our God and our Parliament, and is he to skip back to London as if all the blood be in vain, as if it counted for naught?'

Hen says: 'They want him to confirm all the laws passed in his absence and to turn Presbyterian; to abolish the bishops and purge the Church.'

'And if he will not?' Alice asks.

'Well,' says Hattie, 'who can tell? He lost, but he is still the king. And he loves the bishops.'

Hen says: 'And what of the Scots? Are they our allies in this, as they were in the wars? They hold the king – what do they mean to do with him?'

The blacksmith grunts. 'Nothing is clear. Just a forest of new confusions. I must return to my forge, or it will lose its heat.'

They can hear him outside, hammering in a slow, insistent rhythm. It seems to Hen as if he's beating out time.

She looks at baby Anne, who is practising her newly learned smile on Hattie. Kings fall, nations tear themselves apart, and courts fall into anarchy – but still life beats on.

~ ~ ~

One Sunday, in early summer, they return home to find Lucy sitting on the doorstep. It is so unlike her to sit on the ground that, on seeing her, Hen breaks into a run.

'Lucy! What is it? Is it Ned?'

'Don't be absurd. Our rooms have been overrun by a madman.'

Hen hears shouting from above and looks up to see a head peering out of the window.

'Aha!' shouts the head. 'The return of the sluts! Been cavorting, have we, Henrietta? Been flirting?'

Hen turns to Hattie, who stands beside her looking up at him, her mouth hanging open. 'My cousin Mathew. Anne's brother.'

'He's sozzled,' says Hattie.

'Sozzled! Witch, shall I have you burned? I ain't drunk. Sad is what I am. Where's my sister, Henrietta? Where's Anne?'

'Oh Lord,' Hen mutters under her breath, and makes for the stairs.

Mathew opens the door and drops into a low, facetious bow. Hattie is behind her, and Lucy peers into the room from over her shoulder.

'Did your parents not tell you, Mathew?'

'Tell me what, punk?'

'Be civil, boy,' Hattie snaps.

'Forgive me, ma'am, but I save my civility for those that earn it. My slut of a sister sought refuge in this pushing school, and found it with her own kind. So I shall address this hobbyhorse, this cock-bawd, as I think she deserves.' He takes a long draught from his bottle, looking thoroughly pleased with himself. He is unshaven and filthy, dressed as an infantry soldier, and his boots are held together by string. He carries with him the stench of the losing side, the tang of defeat. More of them arrive in London every day, as each of the remaining royalist positions topples, one by one. The city draws them in, offering anonymity and hope to the disgraced.

He looks as if he has not slept. Beneath his red-tinged stubble, his cheeks are hollow. Hen remembers the gleaming, well-fed shine of the first-born boy he used to wear as his birthright. She pities him. He is shrivelled and musty, like an abandoned apple.

Of course. Oxford is under siege. Where else could he go?

Hen holds on to Hattie's arm. Her friend is still bristling, pugnacious.

'Mathew, I'm so sorry. Anne died.'

The words hit him visibly, leaching the blood from his face. He looks at them wordlessly for a moment, before turning away and violently emptying the contents of his stomach onto the floor.

'Sorry,' he mumbles, catching his breath before puking again.

'No matter, Mathew,' says Hen, and she walks forward, laying a hand on his shoulder.

He pushes it away. 'How?'

'She was with child. The baby lives, but—'

'With child? But...' She watches the realization dawn on his face. His parents' silence explained. 'What did you do to her?' He turns towards her, furious. He lashes out and catches her cheek with his fist. Her head snaps back, and the pain makes her gasp.

Hattie moves forward, while Lucy cowers behind the door.

He draws his sword then. 'Back, witches. Back. You shan't corrupt me. My poor Anne. My poor Anne.'

He moves the sword towards Hen, and she stays very still as the point comes close to her face. She watches it advance, mesmerized by the cruel, jagged point of it. Stay still, she tells herself. Hold me upright, oh Lord. Hold me upright.

'Your doing,' he says. 'Bitch.'

She feels the point of the sword brush her nipple, first one, then the other. It snags on her dress. She watches him weigh up his next move, watches him enjoy how she trembles. Time seems to slow. There is only this moment; the two of them and the sword suspended in infinity. His dark eyes flicker up and down her.

At last, he raises the point of the sword and steps backwards. 'Get out,' he growls, and Hen backs away, shaking violently as all the tension dissipates.

Hattie grabs her waist and they tumble out of the door, which he slams behind them. They collapse in the corridor, holding on to each other.

Kneeling, holding on to Hattie, with a door between them and Mathew, Hen feels a strange, wild joy.

'Did I introduce my cousin formally?' says Hen, and Hattie starts laughing. They try to laugh noiselessly, hands clasped over their mouths. But it's too strong, gripping their stomachs, breaking out in tears and squeaks. Hand in hand they clatter down the stairs, still smiling. At the bottom, they find Lucy.

'Hen!' she cries.

'Yes?' Hen laughs anew at Lucy's terrified, uncomprehending face, and Hattie joins in.

'Yes, very funny,' says Lucy. 'But what are we going to do? That madman's locked in there with two bottles of French brandy.'

'It's not often I say this,' says Hattie. 'But we need a man.'

'I know one,' says Hen.

~ ~ ~

The Temple garden is unnaturally quiet. Coming in from the bustle of Fleet Street feels like arriving at Eden from Gomorrah. The grass stretches down to the glittering river, sinuous in the sunshine. A squirrel hops across to a tree ahead of her, pausing to look at her, its head cocked like an inquisitive schoolboy. The air is still and heavy.

Hen looks for the right staircase and walks to it. Her stomach rolls and rollicks like a butter churn. She climbs the staircase inside, listening to the sonorous echo of each footfall. She feels large, awkward.

At the top, she finds his door. His name is stencilled into the panelling. She traces it lightly with her finger. Then she holds her hand up to knock at the door, and notes that she is trembling. Is it the encounter with Mathew, the fear still coursing through her? She tries to fool her mind; she counts silently to three but knocks on two, a violent spasm of a motion.

'Come in,' shouts a familiar voice, and she half turns to run away, before forcing herself to grip the door handle and turn. She opens the door, and there he is, standing next to the bookshelf, one hand ruffling his unruly hair.

'Hello, Will,' she says.

CHAPTER TWENTY-EIGHT

June 1646

*N*ED TAKES THE STAIRS TWO AT A TIME. HE SPRINGS WITH the joy of being first with the news. He has already delivered it to Parliament. He has allowed them to bathe him in purple praises, he has let the old men shake his hand, and he has knelt with the godly to give praise to the Lord. Such thanks for His glory! At last he wriggled free and ran to the river. He told the boatman, who pulled him towards the bridge for free, shouting the news to the boats passing up river.

In one boat, the passenger leapt to his feet, waving his hat. He staggered, rocking the boat, and then fell head-first into the river. Ned turned and watched him get pulled out, still smiling, and he gave a joyous wave.

He jumped up the steps at the landing pier and then walked along the street, deciding who to tell. He scanned the passing faces to see who best deserved the news from the hero of the hour, the conquering Jove, dispensing joy like a benediction. He whispered it to a godly dressed preacher, who stopped in the street open-mouthed. Two young and pretty women out walking were offered the news as a tribute to their beauty, with a gallant bow and a self-deprecating grin.

Now home. Home! He opens the door with a crash to find Lucy there alone. She half rises and he pulls her to him, kissing her.

'Ned!' she cries, half laughing, half confused. 'What are you doing here?'

He stops her questions with another kiss.

At last he tells the news to the one he wanted to see first. 'It's Oxford, my love. It's fallen. It's over.'

She sits, speechless. Like all the others Ned has told, she knew it was coming. How could it not, with the king a virtual prisoner of the Scots and the surviving royalists in tatters. And yet... Oxford has gone. There is no duopoly of power, no strange and unnatural split in the land. All heat and power emanates again, as it should, from this mighty city. Oxford, thinks a gleeful Ned, I piss on you.

'And you were there?' she speaks at last, looking up at him.

'I was.' He pulls himself taller. 'I was trusted by Lord Fairfax with the news.'

'And what did you get?' Her face, looking up at him, is eager and bright.

'Get?'

'Yes. From the sackings and the sieges.' She pulls a crumpled news-sheet from her work basket. It tells of the sack of Basing House, home to the Marquis of Winchester. It tells of Cromwell's men rolling in jewels, struggling to walk under the volume of plate and silverware lifted. It tells of lowly troopers dressed like kings, pikemen set up for life.

'But Lucy, I wasn't there.'

Her face sours. 'What of Bristol, of Oxford?'

'Bristol, the Lord Fairfax gave us orders not to loot. Oxford, well, I left as soon as the flag was hauled. To bring the news.'

'The *news*.' She spits the word out. 'And what do you *get* for bringing the news?'

His voice is small. He can feel her response coming over the hill like a cavalry charge. But he pushes forward, regardless. 'Duty. Honour.'

'Duty! Honour! Ned, you looby. Can we eat honour? Set up house with duty? I married a Jack-Adams, a God-cursed, sap-pated fool!'

'Lucy!'

'Don't say anything.' She paces. 'Why did I marry you?' She presses balled fists to her eyes. 'Why? I should have waited – someone better would have turned up. Look at me! Look at me, Ned. What is the point of looking like this just to be a cursed beggar? Our affairs are at the lowest tide. Must I wash clothes, Ned? Must I knead? Must these hands scrabble in the gutter, for the sake of your duty?'

The words tumble over him, washing away his happiness. Of all the scenes he played in his head on the journey up to London, this was not one.

'Sorry,' he mutters, seeking to calm her. 'Sorry.'

'Sorry! Were you knocked in the cradle? What use is sorry? Will you be a night soilman? A 'prentice butcher? Sorry, for the Lord's sake.'

Her tirade mounts. He looks at her red face, sees the burning hatred. Suddenly she falls silent, looking over his shoulder.

He turns and sees Hen, with Will, of all people, standing framed by the door, peering in awkwardly.

'Ned,' says Hen into the echoing pause. 'Have you heard the news?'

~ ~ ~

Later, they go out to a nearby inn for dinner. Lucy has pleaded a headache, so it is just the three of them. Even Ned, not a man who prides himself on acuity in these matters, can sense a strange current between Hen and Will. They seem too aware of each other. Will focuses his eyes on Ned with an unusual intensity, as if afraid to let them stray to his sister.

They eat well, and drink a fine claret. All around them are people feasting and drinking, toasting the end of the war.

'How do you two come to be together?' he asks.

Hen blushes.

Will says: 'Last week . . .'

'Tuesday,' says Hen.

'Yes, Tuesday. She called on me. For help evicting a trouble-some visitor.'

'Cousin Mathew.'

'Drunk, he was, and pot-valiant.'

'Ned, he was horrible. But he had not heard of Anne's death.' Her face crumples a little, and Will's hand twitches on the table, as if compelled to seek out hers.

'So Will persuaded Mathew away? And?'

'And nothing,' says Hen, blushing ridiculously. 'We have not seen each other since. I met Will on my way home from the shop; he came to tell me the news.'

There are gaps in the narrative. She doesn't tell Ned of the hours they spent together after Mathew left, staggering and cursing into the night. How Will looked at the bruise on her cheek and brushed it gently with his thumb. How they talked as if time itself had dropped away and she was seventeen again.

She doesn't tell Ned either of their meeting just now. She had not expected to meet Will in the street. They stood looking at each other, senses straining. All the cacophony of life around them, and the two of them in the middle of it, just looking at each other. She doesn't tell of how it feels to be perfectly calm on the outside, while inside a torrent of blood and heart and heat rages.

She can't look at Will easily, not yet. She is twenty-two years old, and giddy as a girl just flowered.

Will steers the subject on, moving it to safer ground of wars and carnage and looming political wrangling. They try to dwell on the upside – the effective end of the armed conflict is reason enough to thank the Lord. But they keep coming back to the obstacles; the dark dunghills strewn between this poor benighted England and safety. The king is a slippery fish to catch; he twists and turns. And yet for all the blood and all the lives lost, a restored king is the only sure way to make the peace safe.

But the man who holds the crown – he must have limits placed on his power to wreak carnage, this they all agree.

It is an accepted notion now that the king and the man Charles are two separate entities. How did it happen, this shift in thought, this splitting out of the man from his office? Hen remembers her father and his brother talking of evil counsel, as if the king could be shielded from his own decisions by the attribution of them to malign outsiders. And now the same ruse, differently worked. It's not the king to blame, but the man Charles. To blame the king

– where could that lead? To anarchy. To the breakdown of order.

Will articulates it best. Hen watches him speak, his face illuminated by the house candles, his hands moving for emphasis.

'For what is order but the law?' he says. 'And what is the law of England without the king?'

'But does that mean the man who holds the office of king can be himself above the law?' Ned puts the question, and Will leaves it unanswered.

Instead, he says: 'But this talk aside, what of the practicalities? Parliament wants to bind the man to rules whether or not he believes himself to be the font of common law or subject to it. The Presbyterian MPs – who last time I looked were still the leading faction – want him to abolish bishops and to cede control of the militia. But here's the rub – what if he will not?'

'He must,' says Ned.

'You would think so, would you not? He has no army, few friends. He is, in effect, a prisoner of the Scots. But he has one card which trumps all others.'

'The king card,' says Hen.

'The king card. So I ask again. They want him to cede everything he would not before the war. What if he will not do so?'

'The army will not stand it,' says Ned. 'You do not understand them, Will. I have marched with them, suffered with them, watched them die like offerings. We were laughed at, and we prevailed. We are God's chosen. We beat him, and he must take our terms.'

'Or what? You will fight him? He has no army.'

'What do you think will happen, Will?' Hen looks at him, relishing the swoop of her stomach. He is grown into himself, the boy she once loved. He is confident and assured. If some of his buoyant good humour has muted, so be it. She is older too. He is still the boy who kissed her against a wall, and yet now he is even more alluring, she finds. She thinks of kissing him and feels her cheeks grow hot.

'Lord, Hen. Look where we now stand. The Scots arrayed against us, their former allies. The army bickering with Parliament. The Presbyterian MPs ranged against the independents. The City fathers siding with the Presbyterians, and their sons with the radicals. Religion and politics all a-jumble. And there is the king sitting at the eye of the storm, clutching his trump card. Do you remember, at the start of it all, Jeremiah Whittaker preached a sermon in Parliament, which your father read to us? "These are the days of shaking," he said. Well, we have shaken and we have fallen. And now we shall see the days of bickering.'

~ ~ ~

Hen and Ned remember Will's words countless times as the year winds down to winter. These truly are the days of bickering. Politicians and soldiers, clergy and divines – all in the right and all exhausted by the other players' wilful intransigence.

Hen comes to think of it like a dance in the masque – each dancer has his own history and his own vision of the future. They can come together for the space of a tune, long enough to step in time and look as if they are a coherent whole. But then the beat shifts or the tempo changes and they break into smaller units again, circling each other warily – murderously.

She tells Hattie her analogy, and the butcher's wife laughs. 'As long as the fuckers stop treading on my toes, Hen, they can dance till the dead rise for all I care.'

On one fine autumn day they are walking in Highgate Wood with baby Anne. She sits on Hattie's hip, straddling her waist and clutching at her dress with proprietorial fingers. Leaves crunch underfoot, and the symphony of reds and auburns and browns is making all of them happy. Hen gulps at the beauty with the glee of one normally hemmed in by sooted brick. She hums as she walks, and suddenly they begin to sing:

Fortune, my foe, why dost thou frown on me?
And will my favours never greater be?
Wilt thou, I say, forever breed me pain?
And wilt thou ne'er restore my joys again?

Hattie hugs Anne and waggles her big toe. 'Fortune, my toe,' she sings, and the baby giggles.

'Hen,' says Hattie, an odd tone in her voice. 'I've been thinking. My old man would have been in touch by now. I think he's dead.'

'I'm sorry, Hattie.'

'Don't be. I'm not. I like it on my own.' She pauses. 'But here's the thing, Hen, love. Before the war, we were together ten-odd years. And not once did I get a sniff of a baby. Him or me, I don't know, but the Lord didn't see fit to bless us. So, I was thinking. The baby, Hen. Anne. Mum dead, dad most likely too. Grandparents not interested.'

Hen can see where this is going, and she panics. She loves Hattie; owes her a profound debt, too. But Hattie is a butcher's wife. Her daughter will be a butcher's daughter. The baby will slither down the social scale, irrevocably. She forces herself to think about alternatives. Baby Anne can't stay with her nurse. Could I take her? But who would look after her during the day? Hattie anyway. Do I even have the right to determine Anne's child's future? But if not me, then who?

Meanwhile Hattie has been warbling about the baby, about her many shining parts. At last she comes to the point. 'So, then, Hen. Can I have her?'

'Yes,' says Hen firmly. If that is the decision then at least Hattie should not know of her hurtful doubts. 'Yes, Hattie.' And she watches, smiling but still racked with uncertainty, as Hattie spins baby Anne round and round in circles, both of them laughing fit to split.

~ ~ ~

Ned thinks of Will's words all that long autumn. 'The days of bickering.' He watches the men bicker among themselves, torn over the best way to approach the impending loss of their livelihood and the crippling arrears of pay. He watches the officers struggling to contain the men's anger, sympathy with their cause jarring with disapproval of their mutinous muttering. He reads about Parliament's increasingly vexatious bickering about the future of the army. The Presbyterian MPs want the army disbanded, spooked by the growing religious radicalism in its ranks, fearful of the power effectively controlled by its two great commanders, Fairfax and Cromwell. And all the while the king bickers with just about everyone – including, so the story goes, his wife. She wants him to accept the bishops' demise as a price worth paying to get his crown back. The king's refusal is at once infuriating and admirable. Ned respects his refusal to compromise on his faith, but despairs of his misplaced religious loyalties.

It is a strange campaigning season. They mop up the royalist strongholds in a succession of small wars. It seems unnatural that men still die in this after-war, when they should by rights be at home recounting their adventures as God's victorious warriors to admiring crowds. Ned stands in front of some ruined, blackened castle, somewhere in a land now defined by its sameness, and looks down at the twisted body of Taffy. His face is shattered and his body crumpled. How strange, then, that this empty husk, this soulless broken thing, should still recognizably be Taffy. That though the eyes are blank, they are still his eyes.

Later, still camped round the blackened castle, Fairfax calls a fast. Ned embraces it. For two days they pray, hunger sharpening their minds, opening their souls up to the Holy Spirit. The army chaplains draw huge crowds. But here, too, some of the soldiers set themselves up as preachers. Ned imagines his father's horror: if a plain soldier can usurp a priest, a buff coat for a cassock, why should he not usurp his betters? Religious freedom and liberty of conscience are but the flip side of social anarchy. And yet Ned is increasingly drawn to the godliness in the independents. He berates the soldier-preachers publicly, yet envies their intense relationship with God. This thought keeps coming to him: if God really is calling us to Him, each of us unbound by a uniform state church, then we must listen and hang the consequences. Why fear the breakdown of man's order on earth, why protect this earthly realm, if in doing so we deny His call?

On the second day of the fast, Ned's thoughts are unfettered. His body is light and slow, but his soul and mind range across the plain, listening to the preachers, searching out the pure voice of God. All the men are imbued with a similar awe. Victory upon victory for this army has shown them the face of God, and He is smiling upon them.

In a clearing behind the orchard, Ned stumbles across a gathered church. He recognizes some of the men from his troop, and he sits behind a tree so as not to disturb them with his officer's sash. The soldiers are not supposed to be preaching to each other. So he hears the words, sitting apart, with his back to the bark. His knees are drawn up under his chin as if he were a boy again. He watches the leaves on the apple trees rustle in the wind, letting the russet colours dance in his mind alongside the words.

'Who has tasted the graciousness of the Lord? Who can desire less? Press on, brothers, press on. Let not time, nor hunger, nor mortal flesh cool thy affection to Christ. You shall participate in the glory of the resurrection, my brothers.'

The voice is low and deep. Ned's longing soul skips along its cadences. I have tasted His graciousness! I am His instrument!

Suddenly, in Ned's spinning mind, a simple problem unknots itself. Providence. This army has won victory upon victory. The Lord of hosts is with them. Ned knows it will drive him mad to seek too far for God's will, but this much is clear: the world cannot be remade as it was before these wars. God's hand is in everything. The world must be made anew – this is His will. We are His instruments. He will show us the way.

Ned imagines his body as a whistle, with God's breath coursing through him. The imagery makes him smile, and the smile takes wing on the preacher's words, sharpening to become joy. I am filled with joy! Ned's happiness is vast. It straddles oceans; it soars skywards. He understands with an extraordinary clarity that his body and his soul are not one, but two. Both belong to Christ. And His love will dispel the loneliness.

~ ~ ~

Hen is not alone. She has breached the City walls with Will. Now the nights are drawing in, he is fulfilling a promise to her. They lie in a field in Dalston, two blankets beneath them, three on top of them. They hold hands under the blanket, and Will guides her through the skies.

'Sirius, of course. And Cerberus – there. Do you see the constellation of the Centaur?' Hen follows his finger, and listens to his voice as it wraps round the names. It's a form of poetry, this naming, and she loses herself in it even if she sometimes fails to follow him. The stars are a jumble to her, and she cannot always discern the shapes that lend the constellations their names. The source stories are sharp and clear to her – Chiron striding across ancient Attica; Andromeda, the chained sacrifice. But she can't see them. No matter, because Will can.

Later, hands still tightly clasped, still looking up and not across, he says: 'I feel less of a man, somehow, for not having fought.'

'But you had no reason to fight, and the levy missed you.'

'Aye, but so many good men are dead, and I'm here with you, lovely you, and I cannot help the guilt. My friend William Gascoine, he died at Marston Moor. Oh Hen, he was barely older than Ned. He would have been an English Kepler, had he lived. His work with telescopes, it would have taken your breath away; yet he never published, and now he's gone. So too Jeremiah Horrocks, who saw the elliptical swing of the moon so clearly.'

'But which side would you have chosen, Will?'

'Both look increasingly ridiculous from here.'

'Well, then. Bad enough to die for something you believe in. You're wasting your guilt, Will.'

He laughs beside her. 'Plenty enough to feel guilty for. You're right, Henrietta.'

'You'll find I often am.'

He pulls her hand across his stomach and holds it with both of his. There is something deliciously transgressive about being here at night, beyond the walls. It's profoundly quiet out here. The darkness is deep and still. Under the blanket is warm, but the air on her cheeks is cold, and the contrast is a humming backdrop to the tension in her whole body. From the ends of her toes to the top of her head she is aware of his presence. She can feel her hip touching his. The casual stroking of her hand with his thrums along her skin, spreading from her hand to her arm and into her belly.

'You will have to outshine the dead, Will.'

There is an even deeper silence. She can feel him weighing his words. His hands fall still.

'Well, now, Hen. When we first met, I could barely keep my eyes from the stars, do you remember? And then I saw in them endless possibilities. I saw my name transfixed to a new discovery. I saw my posterity writ there, Hen. I thought there could be no greater prize for a man than for his name to outlive him. I was such a child.'

'It's not such a childish wish, Will. We're all afraid of being forgotten. Claudio says it in the play: "to lie in cold oblivion, and to rot". No matter how they dissemble, what scholar would not want to find a touch of immortality through his work?'

'Perhaps, but that should not be the sole motive, should it? Besides, I'm beating around the truth like a coy miss. Here's the worst of it, Hen. I'm barely a better astronomer than I am a lawyer. Passion is not enough; aptitude counts for something too.'

'Nonsense,' she says. 'You have both – I know it.'

He props himself on his elbow and looks down at her face. They can only see silhouettes and shadows. He draws a finger along the line of her jaw.

'You are kind. But it's important to be truthful. Truth must be the first mistress of natural philosophers. I can follow other men's work, but they will not follow mine. It's all right, Hen. Don't worry. It's like a grieving, this grappling with your own mediocrity. But I've faced it and I've grieved, and now I'm sanguine enough, I find.'

She stays quiet, distrusting platitudes. He knows more than she does about the limits of his ability. She looks at the myriad stars and thinks of all the countless men and women whose names died with them. Women don't allow posterity to needle them. We're too close to the truth of oblivion. How many Ciceros can there be; how many Caesars?

'And there are some consolations for being mortal,' he says, his voice dropping to a whisper that is nakedly intimate under the huge, star-pricked sky.

He leans forward and kisses her throat. She can't breathe. Her eyes are accustomed to the darkness, but she still can't see him clearly. She can see the outline of him, and he is so familiar to her now, she can fill in the middle with a loving eye.

'So here's the rub, Hen, darling Hen. If I'm not to stand with giants, at least I can stand tall among mortals. Enough pandering to others, Henrietta. We tried to be apart, and here we are. Shall we be betrothed, Hen? I am three months short of my seven years, and then I'm my own man completely. Shall we be together, Hen, you and I?'

'Yes,' she cries into his shoulder. Yes.

His lips are on hers then, and her hips rise to meet him. She thinks briefly of Anne, the big belly and the blood, the broken promises and the confounded hopes. But she shrugs the thought aside, banishing it. Over his shoulder, the stars buck and sway.

CHAPTER TWENTY-NINE

December 1646

*T*HE DAY THEY ARE MARRIED, IT SNOWS. THE CITY IS MUFFLED in white. She walks with Ned towards the church, thinking of her father. How he loved the snow, loved seeing the familiar and commonplace turned magical; how he moaned at its melting, as if each mound of coal-grimed slush piled into the street was a trap laid by God for his foot alone.

Ned strides alongside her, the cold buffing his face and adding sparkle to his eyes. She holds his hand against a tumble. It would not do to fall in this dress, so painstakingly sewn together by her and Hattie, with some lacklustre hemming from Lucy. Her hands are cold; she worries that her nose must be chapped and red. She bids Ned to stop at the door of the church, overwhelmed suddenly. Inside is Will with his father and his mother, and three of his four siblings. She met them briefly last night. Will's father was all affable charm, leaving the disapproval to his tight-lipped wife. Will's three younger sisters were there, ranging from her age down to sixteen, and indistinguishable from each other.

She has been so happy, so content these past few years, shifting for herself. Beholden to no one. Earning her own money to be spent as she pleases. Friends with Hattie, darling Hattie. A butcher's wife may be friends with a pauper, an anomalous single woman making her own way. A butcher's wife may not sit so happily gossiping with a lawyer's wife. Hattie is probably inside the church, baby Anne insisting on standing with that look of triumph on her face and her hands gripping Hattie's skirt. 'Mama,' she says, 'mama,' and a light shines in Hattie's face like steel striking flint.

Hen feels sick. She tries to concentrate on Will's face, to imagine his smile, and the quivering in her skin when she is near him. Panic rises.

'Hey, hey, Hen. What's wrong?'

'Ned, what am I doing?'

She thinks of the bookshop, the smell of it, and the hours of flitting tedium and joy she has spent in the back room. No longer. Mr Rowan has given her a book of housewifing skills as a present and a thank you; he knows her own mother did not pass her one down. A new boy takes her place next week – properly indentured. Mr Rowan is inside the church too, most likely, with his sour wife.

Oh Christ. What if Will and her become a shrivelled couple? What if the yoke is too much to bear? All old and miserable marriages started young and hopeful.

'Breathe, Hen. Look. In through your nose, out through your mouth. In, out. In, out. You look set to face a cavalry charge.'

She thinks of the rooms above the butcher's shop, raddled and damp, but all hers. Will has taken a lease on a new place, nearer the Temple. Near where her father hanged. Oh Father, she thinks. I wish you were with me. She thinks of the scales that Sam uses as a mental trick. On the one side she piles everything she is losing, and throws in her new family for good measure, imagining her mother-in-law's furious squeaking, and the irritating fluttering of her sisters-in-law. On the other side is Will. All alone – just Will. He is high in the air on the mental scales, which are weighed too heavily against him.

She looks up at Ned and smiles at his concerned face.

'Ready?' He asks the question nervously, as if half expecting the answer to be: 'No, let us run. Run!'

Instead she just nods. He pushes at the door, and it swings open. Ahead of her she sees a jumble of faces, and there, brilliant in his scarlet lawyer's robes, is Will. And the scales tip back towards the centre.

~ ~ ~

Afterwards they head to the Mermaid, for food and drink and dancing. Will's father has found some money, and it is his wedding present to them. If Will must marry a royalist plotter's poor daughter, at least he can do it in some style. The wedding party wears bridal ribbons, which flutter colourfully against the fresh-laid snow. One of the new sisters-in-law, Patience, grabs Hen's hand and smiles into her face, eager to show her joy. Will walks next to her, near bouncing with happiness and confidence. They hold hands tightly, anchoring each other amid the chatter and excitement.

When they enter the Mermaid they see someone has gone to extremes with winter foliage. Leaves and berries are wound round tables and chairs; every nook groans with greenery, like a bridal bower brought inside. Steaming spiced wine is doled out, and the warmth courses through Hen.

The food, too, is hot and plentiful. At the centre of a busy table is a great suckling pig, which Hen knew until last week by the name of Fat Peg, as it rooted about in Hattie's yard. At the end of the table are the bride cakes, piled one atop the other. Will grabs her by the hand and leads her to them. Suddenly the old customs seem so new, so exciting, when it is her kissing her new husband above the cakes to whistles and laughter.

After the food there is dancing. Amid the scraping back of chairs and pushing away of tables, Will takes her onto the floor for the first dance. The beat of the drummer makes her want to skip, and she grins furiously at him as they caper across the floor.

'Mrs Johnson,' he whispers each time they come close. Each time she laughs as if her husband is the wittiest man who ever lived. And he laughs at her laughing, until the entire crowd are smiling and joining in the capering in a swell of good humour.

Even the godly caper and dance with the best of them. Hen overhears Ned talking to her new mother-in-law.

'There is a difference, of course, between festivity and excess. And the Lord loves a wedding. Did he himself not feast at Cana?'

Dear Ned. He has set himself to win Will's mother over, to prove that Will's choice is not so entirely devoid of sense.

The afternoon becomes a blur for her; a series of snatched conversations. She whirls away from Will, and fights her way back to him, again and again.

Her new father-in-law pumps her hand with ferocious enthusiasm. 'I was never against you,' he whispers. 'Ah, but be kind, Henrietta, to my poor Sarah. When you have a son, you will understand.'

The music turns and she finds herself with John Cooke,

Will's mentor at the Bar. His face is genial, warmed from its usual earnestness. Next to him, his wife Frances bobs and sways to the music. Both are notoriously godly, and Hen notes with amusement how they react to this licence to enjoy themselves: creeping towards the unaccustomed levity, and then pulling back, before creeping forwards again.

'We were only married ourselves four months ago, Mrs Johnson,' says Mr Cooke. She likes the way he turns to his wife as he says it. She is already predisposed to like him; she read his notorious pamphlet 'The Vindication of the Professors and Professions of the Law' before she knew his relationship to Will, and thoroughly approved of its argument that the law is out of reach of the common man. Justice, he argued, should not be solely available to the deep of pocket.

'The Lord's blessing on you,' says Frances. 'You will need it, married to a lawyer. Your husband will live in the inn during term-time, I suppose, the better to ferret in his law books. You and I can keep company, perhaps, in the long evenings.'

'Yes, I would like that,' says Hen. Ned is passing and she drags him over, introducing him to the Cookes. 'Mr Cooke is General Fairfax's lawyer, Ned,' she says, and watches as the two men fall immediately into a discussion of the general's shining parts.

'The war would have dragged on without him, I assure you,' says Ned, punching his palm with his fist for emphasis. Hen watches Lucy coming over to lay claim – Mrs Cooke is not unattractive – and she leaves them to it, circling away with the freedom a bride expects on her wedding day. Back to Will.

'How beautiful you are, Mr Johnson.'

'Stay, a man cannot be beautiful.'

'And yet you are.'

'Wife.'

'Husband.'

She is pulled away again, this time by Hattie, and forced to be pleasant to the vicar's unpleasant wife.

Mr Rowan joins them and, when the vicar's wife is distracted by something to disapprove of, he whispers to her: 'You are so beautiful, my dear. A very Viola. Your father...' He retreats into an embarrassed cough, flapping his hands.

Hen kisses his faded cheek, and then circles back to Will, passing Ned.

'The essence!' she hears him say. 'The word of God must be preached simply to the common man, as must the word of law!' The Cookes are nodding furiously.

She reaches Will at last, who is being teased by his sisters.

'They are merciless, Hen. They say you are too pretty for me, and altogether too good for such a flummox as I.'

'Your sisters are wise and excellent judges of character, I say.'

The youngest, Patience, who seems to have been named more in hope than foresight, bounces up to her and throws excited arms about her shoulders.

'Sister!' she says, and Hen kisses her warmly.

She meets Ned again on her wanderings and says, unthinking: 'Oh, how I wish Sam was here!'

She watches, saddened, as his face loses its merriness.

'Sam,' he murmurs, in a voice made maudlin by wine that he is unaccustomed to drinking. 'Oh Hen,' he says, looking at her intently. 'I used to think, perhaps, that all the blood between us was as nothing compared to the blood we share. But now... Now

I am not so sure. He is so wrong, Hen. His cause is so misguided, so evil. To seek to deny us the chance of making God's kingdom on earth. How can we be easy with each other?'

'You must,' she says, almost stamping her foot.

'But how?' The misery in his face saves him from her fury.

'Poor Neddy,' she says, and takes his arm. 'Poor Ned!'

He mock punches her arm, and they laugh together.

But Ned's words cast a pall on the day for her. She has, like him, been assuming they will just slot back into brotherhood when all the troubles are over. Now she must face the coming discord, and pray with fervour that she is never asked to choose.

~ ~ ~

The day wends to a close. At last comes the time. Will's few remaining unwed friends pull off her loosened garters and attach them to their hats, making the whole party laugh. The women surround the bride, clucking like protective hens, leading her up the stairs to the bedroom. The inn's best bed has been decorated by the same hand as the taproom to resemble a country maid's bridal bower. Greenery twists round the canopy, and ribbons are tied round each of the four posts.

The women undress her together, all ribald jests and nudges. Dressed in her nightgown, she climbs into her bed. She meets the eyes of Will's mother, who smiles a small, tight smile at her. They can hear the men next door undressing Will, and then they burst through into the room with a clatter.

'Too limp, them ribbons,' shouts one voice as the whole party staggers in. Will is pushed forward until he is half sprawled on the bed, and he looks up at her with an apologetic grin.

'Give him the sack, put some stiffeners in him,' shouts another.

Hen and Will climb into the bed. Beatrice, his sister and Hen's bridesmaid, and his groomsman, a young lawyer named Steven Aubrey, sit at the foot of the bed facing away from them. Steven holds Will's stockings and Beatrice Hen's, and the crowd counts them down. 'One, two, three!' They throw the stockings over their heads, and Beatrice's throw is true. The stocking lands on Hen's nose.

'I shall be married!' shouts Beatrice, and her mother manages to look cross and relieved all at once.

A cup is passed forward over the heads of the guests, and they share the sack posset.

'Sack to make him lusty, sugar to make him kind,' intones Hattie from just behind her.

It is strong and sharp and sweet. Hen giggles, twisting with a tipsy embarrassment. Will just looks excited, and absurdly happy.

'Drink it quickly and they'll leave us alone,' he says, making the company laugh.

'I'd sip it then, love, if I were you,' Hattie calls out, and some of the women nod appreciatively.

Hen looks sideways at Will, and then drains the posset in one emphatic rush.

CHAPTER THIRTY

January 1647

𝒯HE GIRL STIRS BESIDE HIM. GOD'S WOUNDS, HE CAN'T remember her name. Florence, or Marie, or some popish moniker or other. The light creeping through the heavy curtains is enough to read by, and Sam reaches again for Hen's letter. Goodness knows how it found him here.

Married, no less. And to that fellow Will. A bit bookish, but sound. Dear Hen. I hope she is happy with him, he thinks. If that sod plays her false...

Florence or Marie stirs again, throwing the coverlet back in her sleep. Her white back is bare. He can't quite remember her face and it's now hidden under the riot of unpinned curls. Still, he thinks with a twinge, a decent arse.

He suddenly feels a bit cheap. Bored and shallow and dissatisfied. He loathes this courtly living. All these former soldiers cooped up together in a chateau that looks extraordinary but they can only afford to heat in certain areas. They lounge about, cold and bored, vying for favour from a prince with no kingdom and a queen wed to an imprisoned king.

He throws the cover back over the girl. It's fucking freezing in here, he thinks. He may be on decent terms with the prince, but the French bugger doling out the rooms knows everyone's pedigree down to a freckle, and the merchant's son is at the end of a wing, in a small room with two exposed walls and windows that leak icy wind. He shivers and moves nearer to Florence or Marie.

Still, there may be a duel soon, and that will liven up the day. Rupert's followers have humped themselves sore and drunk themselves sober since they withdrew here from their bit part in the French war with Spain. Sam is getting a bit bored, especially now the best girls have worked out that none of them have a clipped coin between them.

Prince Rupert himself, still recovering from his head wound earned in someone else's war, grumbles and bursts into rages, so that even Sam has to remind himself that he loves his chief. They say that he's quarrelled with his old enemy Lord Digby again, and there may be a fight. Sam has no fears for Rupert in that encounter.

But all the politicking and the grubbing for favours is making him feel shabby. And there's not even any hunting to slough off the boredom, with the snow keeping them hemmed in this demi-England on the outskirts of Paris.

Lord, what he'd give to be in action again.

Dear Hen. She sounds so happy in her letter. The girl turns and eyes him from under her tangle of hair. She mistakes his grin for something else, sliding a leg across him. Oh well. He lays down the letter. Why not?

~ ~ ~

First they hear the tramp of boots. Hattie runs to the window at the back, which looks across the rooftops to the street behind. A troop of men, swords drawn and purposeful, surround the Overtons' house.

'Mary,' she says. 'They've come for her.'

Hen, there visiting, scoops baby Anne onto her lap, ignoring her wriggling. She presses her nose into Anne's hot neck and kisses her shoulder. She is tired. All the delights of the marriage bed keep them awake late into the night. Some four weeks into their marriage and she's still snatching at sleep during the day. Nights are for kissing and talking, for sex and the long, sated aftermath of tangled limbs and lazy conversation.

They can hear shouting, and the sound of someone crying.

'We should see if we can help,' says Hattie.

Hen nods, reluctant. She is selfish; she knows that. But she is so stupidly happy, she is in no hurry to tarnish her mood, to wade into someone else's fight. Already the sounds remind her of that day they came for her father.

They grab shawls, and Hattie pops baby Anne on her hip, wrapping them both against the cold. By the time they have run down the stairs, out into the street, and up the alley behind the house, a small crowd has collected. A soldier has hold of Mary's arm and is dragging her towards his chief. Mary holds her little baby, and two older children cling on to her skirt.

Mary looks old, frantic. She is remonstrating with her captors. Printer's ink stains her hands and there are smudges of black on the baby's cheeks where she has pressed away tears with inky thumbs.

'With himself in prison, how else am I to feed the little ones? Tell me? What would you have me do? *What would you have me do?*' She screams the last question, her self-control deserting her in the face of her captor's placid face. Someone in the crowd laughs, and Hen wants to find him and slap his face so hard his eyes pop.

'Printing this filth. What did you think would happen? Whore,' the officer spits at her. At a command, two of his men take her and tie her to two cudgels, even though she is still holding on to her baby.

'Stop!' shouts Hattie. 'Stop, you rogues. Can't you see she is with child?' One soldier turns to look at Hattie and then, with a casual flick of his boot, kicks Mary in the stomach as she lies there on the cudgels, feet dangling in the mud.

Claire Barker, just arrived in time to the see the kick, looks stricken. She falls to her knees in the slush and mud, and starts to pray, looking intently at Mary.

'Hattie,' cries Mary, sobbing still. 'You'll look after Dick and Martha?' The little boy and girl, neither much past five, cling on to each other, crying. The girl looks like her mother: square-faced and dark. Tears and snot make her face glisten wetly. Hattie hands Anne to Hen and gathers in the children, pressing their wet faces into her shawl.

The soldiers begin to move off, dragging Mary behind them so she bumps and grinds across the stones and through the muddy puddles. She holds the baby above her with straight, shaking arms, trying to keep it from the filth. All around her the soldiers swear and spit.

'Strumpet.'

'Whore.'

'Is that the devil's whelp in your belly?'

'I'll go with her,' says Claire, and she walks off behind the miserable cavalcade, singing a psalm with tuneless persistency.

'Hen, I'll take them up. You go in and gather what you can.' Hattie takes a grubby hand from each child and leads them off. Through the open doorway, past the broken door, Hen finds the press. It has clearly been dealt some vicious blows by the soldiers. There are sheets still hanging up to dry, and elsewhere there lies a small pile of finished newsbooks. It looks like Mary had been stitching the dry sheets when the soldiers came. Sheets are trampled on the floor, torn into pieces. A newsprint charnel house.

Hen finds the children's clothes and empties out what little she can find in the larder. She reaches for one of the drying pamphlets. Footsteps. She crumples the paper and shoves it in with the children's things. It's only Charlie, Claire Barker's husband.

'Fix the door,' he grunts, and she nods, stepping past him on the street.

Back at Hattie's, the two children are diving into a bowl of broth.

'Two more to feed, Hattie?' Hen sits next to them, Anne twisting on her lap in an attempt to get to the interesting new faces.

'What choice did I have?'

'True. I'll do what I can to help.'

'Hush, Hen. You and Will are starting out. Come and help when your mother's jewels are not laid up in lavender. Your company is all I need. Trade's brisk, at least. People need to eat.'

She bustles off to get the children more to eat, and Hen watches her. She wonders what it was like for Hattie before the war. Alone with her sottish, bullying husband. And now, suddenly, a noisy riot of a house with children in it, and no one to tell her when to come or go.

As Hattie turns back towards her, Hen sees the flush in her cheeks. Little Anne reaches demanding hands up to her, squawking loudly. With mock exasperation, Hattie scoops her up.

'Can I not have a moment's peace, little otter?' Anne giggles, delighted, and pulls her nose. 'Ow!' shouts Hattie, and the little Overton children look up from the broth to smile.

Later, Claire comes back. Hattie takes one look at her face and sends the children out to feed the pigs. Anne is asleep on a cushion in the corner, arms flung above her head in complete surrender.

'She lost the baby,' says Claire, sitting heavily at the table.

'Poor Mary,' says Hen.

'God's will,' says Claire.

Hattie just grunts. She's losing patience with God's will, Hen thinks, though they don't speak of it. There are some subjects even the best of friends can't touch. They tried going to one of Claire's meetings once. Hen was excited, beforehand. Tales of the famous woman preacher abounded, of her astonishing ability to fast and speak to the Holy Spirit. But the hours spent listening to the sermons left both of them cold, unmoved by the spirit and arses aching from sitting.

Hen went hoping to hear the pure voice of God, but left bewildered. One sermon, delivered with passion by a bearded tanner, insisted that learning was the mark of the devil and that books obscure the Word. God's truth is in the mouths of the simple and the honest, he said.

Hen shifted uncomfortably all through his long harangue. How can God despise learning? Did He not give us minds?

Afterwards, walking back with Claire, Hattie and Hen watched her bouncing joyousness with envy. Claire was so utterly filled with the glory of God, with the Holy Spirit, and with love, that she almost glowed in the dim light. But after they had dropped her off, sitting by the fire in Hattie's hall with a cup of hot spiced wine, Hattie had turned to Hen and said in a conspiratorial whisper: 'Is it just me, Hen, love, or was that just plain unmuzzled boring?'

Hen smiles to think of it. Outside they can hear the children laughing and the squeal of a pig being teased.

'Blood everywhere, there was, and they wouldn't let me clean her up,' says Claire, and she is crying now, with a weary compassion at the misery of it all.

'Bless your kind heart, Claire,' says Hattie, and pats her hand.

'I'm not surprised that they arrested her,' says Hen. 'The stuff she was printing! Oh my word. Levelling, no doubt. The pamphlet's title alone: "A Regal Tyranny Uncovered".'

She pulls out the rescued sheet and smooths it down. The ink is smudged but still legible.

'Listen to this,' she says.

For by natural birth all men are equally and alike born to like propriety, liberty and freedom; and as we are delivered of God by the hand of nature into this world, every one with a natural, innate freedom and propriety – as it were writ in the table of

every man's heart, never to be obliterated – even so are we to live,
everyone equally and alike to enjoy his birthright and privilege;
even all whereof God by nature has made him free.

Hattie whistles. 'No wonder they came for her.'

'It's what the moderates like my father always feared,' says Hen. 'That you tip the lid off the pie and don't like what's inside.'

The women stand and look at the parchment. It's terrifying – intoxicating, even – having it there. All the power punched into those words.

'Poor, brave Mary,' says Claire. 'What was she thinking?'

Hattie nods. 'Brave all right. What a thing. Read it again, Hen.'

She does, and the words' majesty seems only to grow. Hen looks up at Hattie, the butcher's wife, and feels the truth of it all. She shies away, frightened.

'No mention of women,' says Hattie.

'It's implied,' says Hen. 'Besides, who knows best about tyranny than us? The innate freedom writ in your heart, Hattie. You can think on that when your husband's home.'

'You think it will help when he's got the belt out?' She smiles, thinking it through. 'Aye, perhaps it will help.'

Claire turns her back on the paper and walks away from it.

'What about Mary? She was spitting fury at the prison governor,' says Claire. 'Accused him of "enslaving the common people of England in vassalage and bondage". Told him he was a tyrant, a usurper. Told him he was trampling on her "laws and rights".'

Knowing Mary, they can all imagine the scene.

'I do admire her so,' says Hen.

She tries to imagine what her father would make of her friendship with a levelling agitator. He is much in her mind of late. And this morning's scenes remind her of that dreadful day four years ago when they came for him.

~ ~ ~

London, used to divisions, is more fractious than ever in the first months of Hen's marriage. It's a time of dissent and grand ideas. Parliament's ongoing tussle with the army is the backdrop. Unpaid and mutinous, the army squats beyond the city walls, and those inside begin to fear that it may soon bite the hand that's too slow to feed it.

The 'reformadoes' set the tone too – wandering veterans, mostly royalists, drawn to London by poverty and desperation. Alongside the usual tussle of living, there is a plague of dissent and arguing, all inflated and fed by the voracious presses. The godly, who were once themselves the dangerous thinkers, are now the moderates. It is not enough to despise the bishops and altar rails. To be dangerous means despising the very bricks of a church. It means the Holy Spirit working through the poor and the dispossessed. It means a harkening back to the rights and liberties of the English peoples, now trampled by Parliament as well as the king. And, increasingly, it can mean thoughts too dangerous to be spoken louder than a whisper. The word is there, though, floating on the currents of news and opinion that bubble around the city: Republic.

Late into the night, Will and Hen try to make sense of it all. He is sympathetic to the political independents with their insistence on finishing the war and remaking the state with limited reference to the king. He is less sympathetic to the religious independents, believing that one uniform state church, godly or otherwise, is the best route to healing the nation's deep and festering wounds. But then, Hen counters, the call of the Holy Spirit has never meant much to him. He hurries through his prayers to reach for his star charts.

Hen's views are more inchoate. She agrees with much of the radical thought, but shies from the consequences of the logic. It is one thing to agree with the theory that men are equal under God, but what does that mean in practice? She remembers her father's fear of anarchy. To work out where you stand is no easy matter, especially when the ground keeps shifting.

And then, suddenly, Hen's ground disappears from under her feet.

Hattie and Goodwife Simmonds confirm it. She is pregnant.

She hasn't seen Goody Simmonds since their eyes met over Anne's broken body. When the confirmation comes, Hen stands and shrugs off their concern. She is not acting how she should, she knows. She runs home to wait for Will.

Their new rooms, where he comes when not sleeping in his Temple lodgings, are in a quiet street not far from Fetter Lane. They have little stuff. One chest of linen and pewter – mostly wedding presents from his side. A bed and a table. But she loves it here, not for itself, but because it reminds her of him. He is in the air here, even when he is somewhere else. And sometimes, at night, Will sneaks out, even when he should be keeping his hours in the Temple.

She waits for him as evening approaches, not bothering to light the candles. When at last he comes in, he finds her in the dark, sitting hunched in the corner. She runs to him, burying her face in his shoulder, sobbing so violently that he has to coax it out of her.

'But Hen, that's wonderful!' he says, and draws away so she can see his smile in the gloom.

She is furious, raging at his blindness. 'Wonderful! Do you know the last thing Anne said to me? "I'm frightened," she said. And my mother – I killed her, Will. Wonderful? You looby!'

He is aghast at her fury, visibly at a loss for what to do.

'Inside here!' She strikes her stomach. 'It's growing, do you understand? Growing. And it wants to kill me. It will try to. And then I'll have to leave you, Will, and Hattie, and Anne. And the baby.'

'You're being unreasonable,' he says, and she finds herself at a new pitch of fury. How dare he! *He* should carry it. Already it's making her weak. She understands now why she feels so sick, why every day she sinks into a bone-deep weariness that no amount of sleep can relieve.

That night, they sleep at opposite corners of the big bed, both horribly aware of the cold, dark space between them.

Outside St Mary's, knots of soldiers talk, agitated and passionate. Ned wants to be alone and so walks down to the shore. The water this far upstream, at Putney, is somewhat clear. It is yet to reach the sewage and stink of London. There's a metaphor there, but Ned can't quite grasp it. His head is all raddled with claim and counter-claim. Arguments spin, befuddling him.

Suddenly, a voice behind him. 'Well, Ned. I don't know about you, but I feel as though my head is doused in sack.'

It is Captain Shelby, from Whalley's regiment. They became friendly in Bristol after the siege two years past.

Ned shakes his hand, glad to see him. 'Well, John. And where do you stand?'

'Lord alone knows. When the levelling officers speak, I am all fired up. Did you hear Colonel Rainsborough? "I think the poorest he that is in England hath a life to live, as the greatest he." I hear that and the fire in my belly shouts, yes! This is what we have fought for. This is God's providence. A vote for each man, justice for all, freedom of conscience. And then I hear Ireton railing that such thoughts will lead to anarchy, that property rights and political franchise must go hand in hand, and my head convinces me he is right, and I pull back.'

Ned nods. He feels this sway too. Three days of debates – called by Fairfax and Cromwell – to hear the growing swell of dissent within the army, men and officers both. The arguments pull back and forth in an orgy of passionate rhetoric. No man here can doubt that they are arguing for England's future. A strange triumvirate is at play in the search for peace: King, Parliament and Army. The king, now held by the army, is obstinate yet slippery. He is backed into a corner, alone, and yet seems bent on engineering a stalemate. He agrees terms with one face and scoffs them with another. Parliament is crippled by factionalism, exasperated by the king and frightened of the army it created. Its attempt in the summer to disband the army brought the soldiers down on London. And though they showed their customary restraint, the tramp of their boots down the Strand echoed from the Tower to Westminster. And now, on this brisk autumn day in the year of our Lord 1647, here is the army, camped not six miles from Westminster, debating its very soul and the terms on which it will look to peace.

'My father,' says Ned, 'used to say that no matter how much you love both sides of the coin, when it is spinning, you have to call it.'

'He called it wrong, as I recall.'

'Yes, but his thinking was sound. The coin is spinning, John. We have to choose.'

'Well, Ned, I choose to fight for my arrears of pay, and my men's, and leave the politicking to others. I want to go home, Ned.'

'But if all the good men leave the politicking to others, we are left with fools and knaves.'

Shelby nods his agreement. They watch Colonel Rainsborough walk past. The highest ranking of the Leveller officers is passionate, battle-hard and fierce. The men love him. 'He is neither fool nor knave,' says Ned.

'You served with Holles?' Shelby asks.

He nods. Denzil Holles, who stood beside him at Edgehill, is now the prime mover in the MPs' bid to disband the army. If a man like Holles, who Ned admires, wants them broken up, there must be something to his side of the argument.

'He's a good man, John. He argues that all the apparatus set up to fight the war – the parliamentary committees and the local committees – are contrary to the spirit of liberty and hatred of arbitrary power that led us to war in the first place.'

'The committees are as bad as the king.'

'Exactly. Arbitrary taxes and levies – just the same, but in a new guise. Yet he cannot dismantle the committees without dismantling the army they service.'

'But we must be paid first,' says Shelby. 'If they won't pay us with swords in our hands, why should they pay us when we have laid them down?'

Ned nods. 'But there is no money,' he says.

'Lord, Ned, are you on their side?'

He protests not. Protests his loyalty to the army. But he is in a muddle. And there is only one point of clarity in his thinking: the king. Everyone talks of the liberty of the English people; the king, the army grandees, the MPs, the Levellers, the radical sectaries, the prophets, the Anglicans – each defines it differently. Ned sees the tangle of thoughts and ideas like a Gordian knot, smothering the chance of a settlement, strangling peace. One sword could cut through it. What if, Ned whispers to himself, that sword took the king's head? Because unless the king disappears, they will be beating each other about the heads with blunt edges until the Second Coming. But who can kill a king but God?

CHAPTER THIRTY-ONE

November 1647

*O*N A CHILL NOVEMBER DAY, NED STANDS BY SIR PHILLIP Skippon as the army grandees lose patience with the levelling soldiers.

The king has escaped from Hampton Court. No one knows where he is. The army is mutinous, grumbling. But the officers, by and large, have forsaken the men. The king first, grievances second. Fairfax has called for seven regiments to assemble at Corkbush Field. Two more arrive, against clear orders and without officers, waving a copy of their latest demands: 'An Agreement of the People'. The soldiers have copies of the agreement in their hats. Close up, the black type can be seen clearly: 'England's freedoms, soldiers rights'.

The mutinous regiments know they have crossed a line. The men are defiant, but clearly nervous. For a moment, they contemplate each other, men and officers. Silence hangs over the field. Next to Ned, Skippon's horse blows through its nose, and its impatient hooves rake the frosty turf.

It is Cromwell who breaks them. Cromwell, filled with a spluttering fury, who charges in among them, sword drawn, grabbing copies of the agreement and trampling it underfoot. He is puce with anger, his ugly face transformed. Such is his righteousness, his reputation and his air of carrying Providence in his palm, they crumble a little before him. He is a one-man forlorn hope, carving a path for his allies to come in behind him and round up the Leveller ringleaders, swords drawn. Without their leaders, the men lose heart and sink a little lower to the ground.

Fairfax and Cromwell are implacable. They work together, those two – the fox and the toad. The Leveller ringleaders are told to draw lots in front of the army for the one who will be scapegoated.

Watching the lot-drawing is as good as a play. The first man steps up, trembling and white, reeling backwards in exaggerated relief as his lot comes out long and thin. The second pulls himself forward, will trumping fear. Long. The third looks younger than the others. He's a private too. He pulls. Short. His face crumples with disbelief. That his life could be pierced by so slender, so tiny a stick, makes no sense to him.

Cromwell himself strides forward and grabs him by the wrist, forcing him against a post his troopers have driven into the ground. The private looks wildly about him, as if there has been some terrible mistake. He sees only the solemn faces of his comrades, silently watching. To give him credit, he straightens his back and looks straight ahead.

'England's freedoms—' he starts to shout, but Cromwell nods and the muskets fire a ragged volley that cuts him short mid-word.

He falls to the floor, and Cromwell turns to face the rebel

regiments. Bullish, pugnacious, he stands there in an unspoken challenge. They turn away.

~ ~ ~

By the end of the year, Hen is reconciled to the life inside her. She talks to it, on quiet evenings, singing sometimes and beating out time on her belly. Will laughs at her, calling her cracked. She sings and thrums, and lies listlessly through short winter days, waiting for her fate. She has resolved to meet it firmly, to walk towards her own gibbet with her head high.

Hattie visits often, pulling a tottering baby Anne up the stairs to Hen's rooms, where she climbs where she shouldn't and pokes fingers into every crevice. They talk about childbirth obsessively. Hattie says that fear makes the pain worse. Hen smiles, but wonders, then what is she to do? She is afraid, so the pain will be worse, so she is more afraid.

'You'll be there, Hattie?' she asks, endlessly and urgently.

'Of course, Hen. Of course.'

When the day comes, and her pains start, they come on slowly. She finds herself unexpectedly giggling at the ebb of each contraction when she registers Will's face set in exaggerated concern. Hattie arrives at last. Baby Anne has been deposited on Mary Overton, freed from prison for now, and eager to repay the moral debts accumulated last time.

Hattie bustles into the room, kisses Will and sends him away. She kneels in front of Hen, who finds that leaning over the back of a great chair gives some relief. Hattie holds on to her hands, looking at her anxiously.

'Well now, how is it?'

'Smarts a bit,' says Hen.

Hattie laughs. Hen snorts with laughter too, just as another wave takes her down. Somehow, though, the pain is a relief after all the waiting. As the night moves on, the room fills with the gossips. They chivvy her and try to make her laugh. Lucy is there, and Frances Cooke, and Will's sister Beatrice, newly married to another London lawyer and wide-eyed at Hen's pain. Two or three of her new neighbours come by, bearing sweets and biscuits, spiced wines and hot possets.

Hen walks around the room – she finds that moving helps. The groaning stool sits in the corner, but she's not ready for it yet.

'Taking its time, this one,' says Frances towards dawn.

'What size is your brother's head, Beatrice?'

'It's not his head she'll worry about after this one.'

'Easy, honey, easy,' says Hattie as Hen crumples under a fresh wave of pain. They are closer together now, and strong, so strong. The midwife, fresh from another birth, arrives.

'Just in time,' says Hattie.

'Well. Full moon. They pop like spawn this time of month. She's lucky I didn't just go home to bed, that tired I am.'

Hen stifles a scream. She hops from foot to foot. It's a terrible burning now. She lies on her back, and the midwife brings a candle between her legs. It's worse lying down, and Hen is racked with pain.

'I can't. I can't. Make it stop.'

'They always say that when it's near.'

'It's not. It wants to kill me. Hattie. Make it stop.'

'Hush, now. Hush. I can see the head. The head, girl.'

Hattie and the midwife lift her by the elbows and take her to the stool, where she squats and howls. She is a beast, an animal. She watches them cajole her with feral, detached eyes.

'Now, girl,' says the midwife.

'Now, Hen. Go on, my darling. Push it out.'

Hen feels as if her body is pushing itself inside out, as if a sharp blaze of light, star-like, is burning its way down her back and through her groin. The star turns inside her; she can feel it. A sudden new pain, sharper than the rest, splits her between the thighs. She screams for her God, calling His name, begging Him for His mercy.

'There! There!' Hattie is near weeping with excitement, and the gossips crowd round, urging her on, a shrill chorus.

A slithering, a wetness, and it is done. Here comes a surge of joy as strong as the pain. The midwife lifts it up, and she sees its face as if she's always known it, scrunching up for a scream.

'A boy!' the cry goes up. 'A boy!'

~ ~ ~

Later, towards noon, they all file out, flush with the joy of watching this tiny miracle. They kiss her, one by one, Hattie last. He's swaddled in Hen's arms, and she can barely raise her eyes from his face long enough to say goodbye. He snuffles and sniffs the unfamiliar air.

'Shall I send him in?' Hattie asks.

'Who?'

'Will, you looby!'

Will! He rushes in, unshaven, red-eyed, and pauses suddenly

on seeing them. He looks ridiculously young, and she finds herself laughing at his face, at its peculiar mix of awe and excitement. She looks down to their baby's sleeping face and traces his father in his oddly malleable features. Hen looks from one to the other and feels a surge of love so powerful it can only escape her exhausted body in silent sobs. And then there were three, she thinks.

Will takes a hesitant step forward. He is so male, he must feel out of step in this room, steeped as it is in all the mysteries of birth and pain.

'A boy!' he says in a hushed voice.

'Did you expect a cat?' asks Hen, smiling as the tears stream down. He sits down next to her on the bed and folds his arms round both of them.

~ ~ ~

When war breaks out again in the spring, Hen is furious. She takes it personally, as if the machinations of kings and grandees and the movements of armies are all designed to compromise the safety of baby Richard. She is pleased that there is no money, so she has to nurse him herself. Wrapped in a bed with him feeding, his limbs limp with pleasure, she curses everyone involved.

Across London there is a weariness and sadness. When will things be ever be normal again?

Burying her nose in his neck, wallowing in the smell of him, she whispers: 'How can you smell sweet and sharp all at the same time, hey, baby? Like a blackberry. My blackberry baby. Hey, hey, I will keep you safe, my blackberry.' And there it is. She kisses him guiltily. Her first lie.

CHAPTER THIRTY-TWO

Summer 1648

SAM'S FAVOURITE SPOT IS THE BOWSPRIT. HE STANDS EASILY
now, practised in riding the waves. He is halfway along, the
sprit narrow under his feet, and the white-flecked water rushing
underneath. His hand grips on to a rope, or a sheet, or a stay,
or whatever it is these absurd sailors call it. He flexes his knees
and spreads his toes inside his boots, finding his balance without
thinking, laughing as the spray rains down on his bare head.

'Huzzah!' he shouts at the sea. 'Huzzah!' His voice is whipped
away by the wind, which pulls and tugs at his shirt, and buffets
his face. Lord, how he loves it. The ship, gallant thing, rises to
meet a fearsome wave, trembling at the top of it, before crashing
down the other side, threatening a dunking. Air whooshes in
his stomach, putting him in mind of the swifts that danced over
Marston Moor.

It's like riding a charger over a fence that's too high. These
are choppy seas in the channel. The sailors tell tales of waves the
size of palaces, which toss the boat like a child's top. I'd like to see

that, thinks Sam. The sailors think he's cracked, standing out here in rough weather. The ones whose job it is to furl the heavy sails along the sprit grumble about him. They call the sprit the widow-maker, and curse him for his joy in their penance. But the devil take them. He relishes this heady rush of wind and sea and fear.

He leaves aside the thoughts that plague him; that plague them all. This ragtag navy, which mutinied against its parliament, and now carries the Prince of Wales across the sea, is scarcely fit for the job. There is bad blood already between the mariners who sail the ships and the gentlemen who will fight them – largely those loyal to Rupert.

Behind him, the sailors go about their unfathomable and endless tasks, knotting things and cleaning things and climbing things. Out here, there is only the rushing of water and air. It is the nearest place to heaven that Sam can imagine. I wonder, thinks Sam, if this is what Ned is seeking from his God. This joy! He realizes that he is crying – the wind is pulling the tears from his eyes. He throws his head back and laughs at the sky.

~ ~ ~

Ned grunts with a kind of pleasure as his sword finds flesh and pierces through it. Each kill, each stricken royalist, each gutted Scot, each spitted Kentish traitor is proof. The Lord is smiling upon us again. We are His saints marching to His wars. His angels are at our wings; His breath is in our hearts. And we will prevail, again and again.

Afterwards, as the battle heat grows tepid, they talk. There is only one explanation for their tumult and bickering last year, and for this glorious winning certainty now. Last year they were talking to the man of blood, Charles, and God had turned his face from them. This year they are fighting, and God is with them again. Hugh Peter, Cromwell's own chaplain, says that kingship is craved only by the weak and the fallible. What man would set himself up in opposition to God and call himself a king? The state itself is sinful. Did Gideon not say to the Israelites: 'I will not rule over you, neither shall my son rule over you; the Lord shall rule over you.'

At Putney last year, even Cromwell had warned against imagining fancies and calling them God's will. But this summer he has no misgivings.

They win battle after battle. They crush all before them. His glory shines on them. His will is clear. At prayer meetings, Ned watches grizzled veterans cry. He watches them raise their hands to the sky, thanking the Lord for His benevolence, for His choice of them as His saints. They decry the king as a false idol, a usurper of the Lord's rightful authority. The Lord has chosen them to bring him low. They sing psalms of joy with the blood still crusted on their swords. Ned too cries without shame when the Spirit comes to them, standing shoulder to shoulder with his brothers.

~ ~ ~

Hen props Blackberry up with some cushions, watching for his easy, familiar smile. Rewarded, she turns back to Hattie and Mary Overton. They have created a prison for baby Anne and Mary's youngest, trapping them behind a table against a wall with some spoons and pots to bash. They talk over the noise.

'Now,' says Hen. 'Let me look.'

She reads the sheet they have given her.

'Perfect,' she says. She suggests one or two changes and then reads it out.

'*Since we are assured of our creation in the image of God, and of an interest in Christ equal unto men, as also of a proportionable share in the freedoms of this Commonwealth, we cannot but wonder and grieve that we should appear so despicable in your eyes as to be thought unworthy to petition or represent our grievances to this honourable House.*'

She pauses, looking at Hattie and Mary. They return her gaze. This is powerful stuff. She feels giddy suddenly, as if the ground ahead of her has fallen away unexpectedly. The phrase spins. Equal unto men. Equal.

She looks down and the words scramble across the page. She takes a deep breath and continues reading: '*Have we not an equal interest with the men of this nation in those liberties and securities contained in the Petition of Right, and the other good laws of the land?*'

She lays down the document and the three of them lean back. It sits between them, and they all stare at it.

'They will not listen,' says Hattie.

'And does that mean we should not speak?' Mary's frustration can sometimes spill into aggression, and Hen lays a placatory hand on her arm.

'Of course not.'

She makes a decision. She does not look over at Blackberry, but she knows exactly where he is.

'I will help you,' she says. 'But I will not sign it.'

Hattie looks shocked, and Mary is cross.

'It is Will,' she says. 'I will not harm his prospects just when he is starting to gain a name.'

They cajole and entreat her, but she sticks to the story. They all know it is a lie, but they are fond enough of her not to bring it into the open. At last they leave, and she gathers up Blackberry, crying into his back so he cannot see her tears.

'I will not leave you,' she tells him. Shame and fear rack her. She has been tested, called to stand up for her beliefs. And she has failed.

~ ~ ~

On the day of the army's purge of Parliament, Hen huddles inside, curtains drawn, lying on the floor and playing with Blackberry. Ned warned them it was coming. The soldiers are lining the streets of Westminster, turning away MPs who still want to talk to the man Charles. His new war is dead, his navy sent scuttling back to Holland. And still they want to talk to him. England's rivers flow red, its fields are soggy with blood, and still he lives and plots and schemes.

She agrees with Ned. The king must be held to account. Will thinks so too. She wishes that they would find their bollocks, these men, and just assassinate the king. Play the Brutus and strike him until his own blood runs in atonement. But they say now that there must be a trial, that the king must be openly accused of his crimes, so all the world knows that tyranny will not go unpunished. The glory of Parliament is at stake, they say.

She shivers, imagining how London will be if the trial happens.

She imagines the violence on the streets, the threats gathering in shadows as the men play their daft legal games.

When did she become so frightened? She watches the blue veins scribbled under Blackberry's translucent scalp. She did not understand before how love can incapacitate you. She starts at shadows; she reaches for Blackberry in the night just to hear his breathing.

Is that the soldiers' boots she can hear? She fancies she can see the walls trembling. Blackberry starts crying and fussing, pulling at his ear. She settles him onto her breast for a feed, listening for sounds of danger. He gives her a half-smile, still feeding. She smiles back, but it doesn't reach much further than her lips.

How can there not be a reckoning? How can the three Challoner children be unscathed when so many are dead? How can Blackberry be alive and thriving when so many others wither as soon as the cord is clamped? She has started to believe that God must be saving something for them, some terrible retribution for their luck. How did Job stand upright? How did he not just curl into a ball and whimper?

Blackberry rolls off her breast and sighs, contented and entirely secure. She wraps him up and climbs out of the bed, leaving him swaddled on the blanket. Automatically she checks for the rise and fall of his chest.

She crosses over to the trunk and lifts out her case of pistols. Dear Sam. Where is he? Was he with Rupert and his ships, which they chased back across the sea?

Ned taught her to use the pistols before he left for the recent fighting. She tries to remember, and the commands pop into her head in his deep, sombre voice. Powder. Shot. She pours a measure of powder down the barrel, and then pops a bullet in, pushing both down with the ramrod kept in the case. Priming powder in the flash pan. Flint in the jaws. She pulls the catch to half-cock, listening to the sear clicking into position. Ned says that when you fire a pistol, there is a pause between the pull of the trigger and the blast of the bullet. The spark from the flint striking the frizzen must touch off the priming powder, which sets off the main charge, which forces out the lead ball. A chain reaction, consequence following consequence with no chance of stopping the sequence once you have started. What was the trigger for all of this mess? she wonders. Strafford's execution? Laud and his blasted altar rails? The death of Charles' big and glorious brother Henry, who would have been king? Where to stop? Perhaps when Adam turned to Eve and took the apple.

She lays down the pistol where she can reach it. She is exaggeratedly gentle, despite the half-cock. Having Blackberry has given her a new sense, a heightened awareness of danger. She can't saunter by the river without imagining him toppling in, or walk by a window without imagining him toppling out. As she lays the pistol down, a dozen images flash through her head of ways it could accidentally discharge itself, hurting her boy in her zeal to protect him. God likes those kind of cruel jokes.

~ ~ ~

The moon hangs stark and white over the sea, a silver trail marking their way. At another time he might savour it and conjure poetical fancies about the lunar path leading him home to England. But it's too bright and too dangerous, and the sharp, choppy waves of the Channel are swilling that greasy, French pottage around his stomach. A miserable, cold and nauseous way this is to start an adventure.

The fishermen call to each other in their peculiar dialect, urgency evident despite their exaggerated quietness. He looks up and sees the low-lying, treacherous ground of the estuary marshes.

The bottom of the boat where they huddle is wet, with water that stinks of old fish and seaweed. He feels the nausea rising again, and he fights to keep it down.

At last, at long last, he hears the crash of breakers, the unmistakable sound of surf grinding stones. They come closer, the wind on their quarter and the land dark and silent ahead of them. Suddenly, the sails shudder. Sam, with his rudimentary grasp of sailing, realizes the wind has shifted, and that soft, dark mass ahead of them is now a real danger. Bringing the boat off again with the wind blowing straight to shore would be hard enough in the best of boats – but this unweatherly tub could be in trouble.

The Frenchmen are arguing behind him. At last, the biggest comes forward and puts his hands together as if in prayer.

'Swim,' he whispers. 'You swim'.

Sam nods. This will be the least of the dangers to come. He looks towards the dark smudge ahead. Not too far, and he's sodding soaked through already. He slips over the side into the icy, black water. The waves roar about his ears, and the cold slams the air out his body in a shocked gasp. He strikes out for land.

~ ~ ~

It is the king, Ned realizes with an intake of breath. Here he is, made flesh, stepping out of a curtained sedan chair. He shivers, the chill January air catching him. A small reminder, if they needed it, of the mortal ordinariness of this man they are taking to his trial.

He is even smaller than Ned remembers, hunched over. Colonel Thomlinson hands him into his barge, a work-a-day craft of little gaudiness, which seems in keeping with the general tone of the day. The barge tosses on the choppy Thames, as if impatient to be off. It slaps against the St James's steps, and Colonel Thomlinson reproves the waterman, whose eyes are fixed on the king's face. The king!

Streaks of white stripe the king's long hair and unkempt beard. His face is as grey as the water, hatcheted with lines. If you knew nothing about this man, you would see the stress etched in his skin, sense the misery in his hunched shoulders.

Ned pulls himself straighter in his seat at the prow of the guard boat and fashions a scowl. It would not do to have his men see this weakness in him, this strange sympathy. His troop fidget in their seats, fighting to keep their eyes straight ahead and away from the king's person. They're nervous on the water, some of them, used to the certainties of soil beneath their boots. And here is the king, in person, to add to their fretfulness.

The king thanks Colonel Thomlinson for handing him into the barge, and then sits. In the second guard boat, Ned hears his chief, Colonel Hacker, calling out a warning.

Shit. Ned curses himself for his inattention. A flotilla of small craft is heading towards them. He raps an order and his men hoist muskets to their shoulders.

'Keep off!' shouts Ned. 'Or we will fire.'

They keep coming. The faint sound of cheering crosses the water. 'God save the king! God save the king!'

Ned looks down into the barge, where the king sits straighter now, gripping the sides of his seat with whitened knuckles.

'We will fire,' Ned shouts again. The king looks up at the sound of his voice, and their eyes meet. He cocks an eyebrow, as if to say: 'And now what, boy?'

The order to fire lodges in Ned's throat. He feels his cheeks burning. The king's eyes are steady, his brows still raised. There is a hint of a smile at his mouth. Ned forgets to breathe.

The colonel calls out from behind him, and he wrenches his eyes away.

'We're just pulling along a few yards, captain. Cover them, and fire if entirely necessary, but not before. We don't want to provoke anything.'

A good man, Colonel Hacker. Godly. A pleasure to serve.

Skippon will have nothing to do with this trial. He has withdrawn. At the last, some of the older men are becoming squeamish. Fairfax too, by all accounts.

The small craft bob alongside as the king is pulled along to his lodgings for the trial. If Ned finds it was one of his men who leaked the king's route from Windsor, there will be blood. The king is to be lodged in Cotton House, a merchant's house next to the Palace of Westminster, where the court is convened. It has been chosen because it will allow them to keep him secure on the daily walk across to the court, where Ned and his men will help protect proceedings.

The court functionaries will be processing to the palace now, according to the timetable Ned has seen. Will is there. He has helped John Cooke, the solicitor-general, prepare the case. They are dressing it all with processions and pomp and finery, to give this thing the outward show of legitimacy.

Will thinks it is necessary; Ned is not so sure. The army is all the legitimacy that this trial needs. The men are camped outside the walls expectantly, looking in at the lawyers' dance.

No one noticed my father's trial, he thinks. There was no pomp then. No solemn processing. Ned remembers Hen's mad ride across the country to find him and bring him home. She would not do it now. Motherhood seems to have diminished his fiery sister. She didn't want Will to be involved. But we're all involved, one way or another, Ned thinks.

They're landing now, and the king is taken into Cotton House to prepare. Ned watches him walk away, up the steps and through a plain, wooden door. What is he thinking? Is he sorry?

Ned takes his men through the rear approach into the Palace of Westminster. In the hall, they join the guards lining the walls. At the front, on a small raised platform, John Bradshaw, the lord president, sits on a scarlet chair, flanked by his two assistants. They wear their barristers' robes. Ned allows himself a small smile. Will has told him that Bradshaw's headgear is not really a hat but an iron helmet shaped as a hat and covered in black felt. He had it specially commissioned when he was catapulted out of the ranks of junior judges above more cowardly heads and into the raised scarlet chair.

A second red velvet chair awaits the king within the bar. The commissioners and barristers, all dressed in their black robes, cluster like ravens waiting to pick over the king's words.

The scarlet coats of Ned and the other New Model officers stand out in this place of dark wood and black cloth.

The clerk calls for silence and begins to read the Commons Act, which commissioned the court to try the king. He reaches the part that caused the ructions when the act was passed two weeks since.

'The Commons of England assembled in Parliament declare that the people under God are the origin of all just power. They do likewise declare that the Commons of England assembled in Parliament, being chosen by and representing the people, have the supreme authority of this nation.'

It is no less shocking now it is familiar. Ned tries to think back to the days before the first war. We would never have even dreamed such thoughts – that the people are the origin of all power, not the king, and that Parliament can claim the divine authority once monopolized by the king. Were we fighting for this all along, but knew too little to articulate our cause? Or has our cause grown monstrous with each pint of blood spilled?

He imagines his father's reaction to the claim. 'The fucking people! The lumpish, lead-pated blockheads who mill about whining. And they are the source of just power?' Ned can picture his father's face growing puce, the invective soaring. He almost laughs, then remembers where he is.

The clerk is calling out the names of the commissioners, the men who have convened this court. As each man is called, he is to stand and answer to his name.

The clerk sonorously calls out: 'Sir Thomas Fairfax.'

Silence. Then from the gallery a woman's voice shouts: 'He had more wit than to be here!'

The ravens crane their necks around, eyes swivelling. A woman is bustled out, and there is a rustling of feathers as word of her identity spreads: Lady Fairfax herself.

Ned is glad that he does not have to police the great and the good that were allowed into the gallery. Manhandling aristocratic ladies is not for him, although Lucy would like the tale. Perhaps he will stretch the truth and tell her it was him gripping Lady Fairfax's arms. What harm?

The other commissioners stand and answer to their names. Henry Ireton, Oliver Cromwell, Thomas Pride... Most are filled with conviction. Now they are here, the job must be done. Others are more tremulous, as if the awfulness of their undertaking is only just becoming clear. Their eyes flit to the door, their legs twitch with the urge to flee.

The king is late, and the ravens mutter among themselves. Ned sees Will, deep in a book, and feels a sudden rush of affection for his friend. He looks just as he did at Oxford, engrossed in an almanac of stars. The other lawyers meld into one. It takes a familiar face to rise above a uniform.

Suddenly, here he is. The king. He looks more as Ned would expect now, in this setting. He is imperious, haughty. He sweeps into the court. All Ned can see is his arrogance, not his bravery. He is dressed in black, with a collar of brilliant white lace. A diamond-studded silver star holds his cloak. He walks to his seat and sits, not deigning to look to the right or to the left of him. He keeps on his tall, broad-brimmed hat.

Suddenly he stands again and slowly turns. He looks at the soldiers guarding the hall. He looks into the enclosures at the back, brimful of curious spectators, and the gallery where the privileged few sit. He looks at them all, and Ned wonders if he is the only one who quails at the king's stare. The people's claim seems hollow, hopelessly brash. This is the Lord's anointed one. What are we doing here?

There is a shuffling of papers. Ned does not want to look anyone in the face, so he finds a point on the wall opposite to stare at and fixes his gaze on it.

There is a frightened ripple of conversation in response to the king's challenge. The court crier calls for silence. Into the silence, John Bradshaw, the lord president, speaks.

I bet he's practised this a thousand times, thinks Ned. I'll bet he pulls his best judge face at the mirror. We're all boys here, playing a game.

'Charles Stuart, King of England; the Commons of England assembled in Parliament, being deeply sensible of the calamities that have been brought upon this nation (which is fixed upon you as the principal author of it), have resolved to make inquisition for blood, and according to that debt and duty they owe to Justice, to God, the Kingdom and themselves, and according to that fundamental power that rests in themselves, they have resolved to bring you to trial and judgement.'

John Cooke stands and unrolls a parchment containing the charge.

Suddenly the king speaks. 'Hold,' he says.

Cooke ignores him and continues to unravel the document. 'Hold.'

Cooke resolutely refuses to look at the king. There is a strong silence in the hall, a universal holding of breath.

'Hold.' The king reaches out with his silver-tipped cane and raps Cooke on the shoulder. Once, twice. At the third blow, just as the king is saying 'Hold!', the silver ball at the end of his cane falls off and clatters to the floor.

From Ned's vantage point he can see it rolling to a point on the floor between the king and the lawyer. For a pause as long as a century, the two men eye each other. Ned cranes forward to see, and has the sense that the entire crowd is doing the same. Necks are stretched, and toes are stood on, all the ravens and ghouls and soldiers leaning forward to where the king and Cooke stand immobile, watching each other. Cooke does not bend. And the king, to astonished murmurs, bends his knee. He stoops, the king of England, Scotland and Ireland, in front of John Cooke, the farmer's son, and he picks up his own silver bauble.

~ ~ ~

At Hen's house, they snatch news of the trial where they can. Patience, Will's sister, is staying with them. Lucy is there too, waiting until after the trial to set up home with Ned. Since Ned was commissioned to guard the king, Lucy has puffed up like a bullfrog. Every sentence she utters that winter begins with: 'His Majesty told my husband . . .'

Hen doesn't believe half of it. She has watched Ned talking animatedly to Lucy about his dealings with the king, and seen how he colours slightly when his sister catches his eye. No doubt he's close enough to give the tales a flavour of truth, but to hear him talk you would imagine him to be the king's greatest confidant. Lucy hangs off his every word, though. She wears her reflected glory like emeralds.

Hattie, who drops by often, bearing choice cuts and home brew, has to turn away whenever she hears the phrase, afraid of catching Hen's eye and collapsing into laughter. Hen does not begrudge Lucy her triumph, however. She likes it that her sister-in-law is kinder to Ned at present, even if she is irritated by the cause.

Today Lucy's smug sheen is almost unbearable. She has confided some news to Hen in round notes that suggest this is a confidence widely shared.

'Yes, I am with child.' She strokes her still-flat stomach often and ostentatiously.

Blackberry throws his pottage across the room, where it hits the wall and splatters. Lucy looks at him, wrinkling her nose.

'Perhaps if you just…' she begins, an expert suddenly now she has a child in her. She catches sight of Hen's face and trails off.

'Come on, my darling.' Hen coaxes a little into his mouth, and he grins with his new and startling teeth.

'Will says that the king still refuses to plead,' says Patience, turning the subject hastily.

'His Majesty told my husband that he would not,' says Lucy. 'Not recognizing the legitimacy of the court, you see. He says that it is enshrined in Magna Carta that an Englishman can only be tried by his peers. He is the king and has no peers, therefore he cannot be tried.'

'Why does he bother?' says Hen, irritated. 'They will kill him whatever he says.'

'Kill him?' shrieks Lucy. 'Abdication, surely. Exile at worst.'

Hen turns round to look at her, ignoring Blackberry whining at the disappearance of his spoon.

'Lucy. You don't really think that. What were the charges Cooke laid out? That he is a "tyrant, traitor, murderer and a public and implacable enemy to the Commonwealth of England". And you think they will slap his wrists and pack him off? Perhaps to Ireland, where the Earl of Ormonde is marshalling his army of papists? Or to France, where the Prince of Wales leaves off his whoring long enough to pimp for arms? Please.'

'But the court has no legitimacy, Hen. His Majesty told Ned.' Lucy pets her bottom lip, forgetting it is Hen not Ned who needs mollifying.

'The Magna Carta also says that no one is above the law, not even the king,' says Patience, who looks unhappy at her inept attempt to lighten the atmosphere. 'Will says that a sovereign's power is held in trust and can only be exercised in keeping with our traditional liberties.' She looks like a schoolboy reciting his Cicero, and Hen smiles at her.

'But who is to decide what is what?' says Lucy, sniffing.

Hen spoons more pap at a reluctant Blackberry. 'So it may be subjective,' she says. 'What is a traditional liberty? Blackberry would say it's not having his tyrant mother force this gloop on him. But the late wars and the men killed? There is no world, real or imagined, where that can subjectively be termed in the people's interest. So he has broken the trust. And so…' She ends on an interrogative.

'So the king must die,' finishes Patience.

'The king must die,' Hen says. Blackberry swallows a loaded spoon, and she claps, laughing as he claps back at her.

~ ~ ~

As the trial progresses, two things become clear to Ned. The first is that the king is winning the war of words in his constant refusal to recognize the legitimacy of the court. And the second is that, by winning, he is signing his own death warrant. Without his acceptance of the charges, there can be no face-saving compromise. He will not abdicate in favour of his younger son.

'It is the liberty of the people of England that I stand for,' says the king. Ned is reminded of childhood games. Beneath the verbosity, the king shouts: 'I'm liberty,' and Cooke shouts back: 'No, I'm liberty!'

Ned grows irritated. As the days progress, everyone knows that the king's life has been forfeited by his customary obstinacy. And yet they insist on carrying on with this legal masque.

Will insists that the end is not already writ, and that important precedents are being wrangled here. The lawyer and the soldier will not agree. God's will must be done in this, thinks Ned. His will alone is what counts, for all our earthly posturing.

At last, the only possible sentence is passed. As the king is led from court, the soldiers forget themselves. There are hundreds of them. He has escaped before and Parliament's agents are warning of fresh attempts to break him out. But the troopers are in mutinous mood. They shout and jostle him. Ned wades in to push them back. Some spit at the king, shouting for his head. One solitary voice cries: 'God save the king!' and the nearest officer strikes him with a cane.

Ned uses his parade voice to call them back to order. The

king is bundled into his sedan chair, and looks back at Ned as he blusters and shouts at his unruly men.

The two porters carrying the chair have removed their caps as a sign of respect. The soldiers surround them and abuse them, shouting until the frightened men put their caps back on and pick up the chair. At last the chair moves off. One of the porters has a cut lip, and blood trickles down his chin.

Ned and his men watch the chair go. Behind him, he hears a voice he recognizes. Turning, he sees Hugh Peter, Cromwell's chaplain. His eyes are fixed on the departing chair. In his raised hand is the Bible, the one he carried from Marston Moor to Naseby and onwards.

'*Let the High Praises of God be in their mouth and a two-edged sword in their hand, to execute vengeance upon the heathen and punishments upon the people.*'

Ned drops to his knees. The cold, sodden mud seeps through his trousers. He listens to Peter's familiar tones, feeling the Word seep into him. He wants to be sure again, to know that glorious absence of doubt, that holy certainty. He hears his men thud down next to him.

'*To bind their kings with chains, and their nobles with fetters of iron; to execute upon them the judgement written; this honour have all His saints. Praise ye the Lord!*'

~ ~ ~

London simmers.

Voices cry from the shadows: 'Long live the king!' Bands of drink-bold men wander the streets. Soldiers tramp and look for trouble. From beyond Hen's window, strange shrieks and shouted slogans intermingle. Inside, she huddles close to the fire, singing tuneless half-snatches of songs to Blackberry.

Suddenly, shockingly, there is a tapping on the door.

'Who's there?'

No one answers. She puts Blackberry down and moves closer to the door. Her heart slams against her chest.

'Lucy?'

A tapping again, fainter this time.

She drags the chest towards the door, so it can open only fractionally. Turning the handle, she pulls it towards her. A figure sits, back slumped against the wall. She brings her candle closer to the gap. At first she can only see the blood, and a tangle of hair. Then the head lifts towards the light, she sees his bloodless face.

Sam.

CHAPTER THIRTY-THREE

January 1649

FOOTSTEPS APPROACH THE DOOR. HEN RUSHES OVER AND opens it a fraction. Lucy.

'Well, let me in,' she says.

'It's Blackberry. He's ill. A rash.'

Lucy pulls back from the door. A hand instinctively goes to her cheek. She has a horror of smallpox. Hen has seen her close her eyes to avoid seeing disfigured faces, as if the act of observing could somehow draw the sickness down upon her. Lucy's fingers stroke her own cheek softly.

'Will he…' She trails off.

'I don't know,' says Hen, pleading with God in her heart to close his ears. Let not this lie be held against me, Lord. Let it not be twisted into prophecy.

'I'll go to Ned. He'll find somewhere for me.' She pauses, her voice brightening. 'Near His Majesty, perhaps.'

Hen holds the door tight, her loathing of Lucy consuming her. Something shows on her face, and Lucy seems suddenly uncertain. Humble, almost.

'I hope Blackberry—' she begins to say, but Hen slams the door and turns back into the room.

Hattie, crouched low over Sam's body, sniffs at the wound in his side. The blanket beneath him is sodden with blood.

There is a smell of roasting meat in the room. Hattie walks to the fire and rakes out a piece of beef from the coals. With the tongs, she presses it against Sam's wound. He grunts with the pain, unconscious despite the sizzling and spitting of the beef. Blood leaks down his side still, mingling with the juices from the meat. The smell of crisping flesh and the pools of blood combine to make Hen feel dizzy and faint.

She sits heavily in a chair beside the bed. Blackberry is asleep next door, oblivious.

Hattie sits up, passing a hand over her forehead and leaving a trail of blood.

'Well?' Hen asks.

'I don't know,' she says. 'You should call in someone, Hen.'

'No.'

Hattie gets up, wiping her hands on a reddened cloth.

'Well, then.'

'Sorry, Hattie. I'm just . . .'

'Scared? Listen, love. Don't tell me more. Clean edges, that's a sword cut. Not deep, but perhaps deep enough, we shall see. And I'm not blind, Hen. Stranger, my arse. Good Samaritan my arse.'

They both turn to look at Sam's face. His eyes are closed; hair sticks to his clammy forehead. He is white as Kentish chalk, with purpling like a bruise round his mouth. For all that, he is still the spit of her. She crosses over to him and pushes the stray hair back from his face.

'What's he doing here?' says Hattie.

'I don't know. He hasn't spoken. Just fell in like this. I came for you. Sorry, I shouldn't have. I'm sorry.'

'Well,' says Hattie. 'I've left Anne long enough.'

She seems to relent at the misery on Hen's face. 'If it were me alone, Hen, I'd not mind. But I've the child to think of.'

Hen's eyes flick to Blackberry and then back to her friend.

'Sorry,' she mumbles again, hunched in her chair. 'No one will know. Lucy thinks we've the pox, and Patience has been called home to her mama. It's just me and the boy.'

Hattie reaches over and cups her cheek. 'Don't worry.' She pulls her stuff together into a bag. 'Listen, my darling. He can't be moved for a few days. That wound has some breaking to do. If he comes through, get him out of here.'

Hen nods, numb with misery.

'Sorry, Hen. But have you thought on it? About Blackberry?'

'Of course. You think I don't know that Blackberry is at risk? He's my life, Hattie.'

'Come, honey. Let us not quarrel. But think on this. If they did what they did to Mary for printing some seditious words, what would they do to you for sheltering a traitor? They are all filled with their righteousness, Hen, and scent the king's blood. They're like a pack on the trail, and what do you think they will do to those who get in the way of the kill?'

~ ~ ~

'Henrietta.'

A voice, sharp and familiar, pulls her to wakefulness. She is in the narrow bed with Sam, holding on to him, trying to keep him warm.

Ned. He stands over them, a familiar silhouette in the gloom.

She sits up, confused. A metallic taste like blood is in her mouth, and her arm is sore where she has been lying on it. There, between them, is Sam, still lost but with some colour now. She strokes his hair.

'Ned. I was sleeping.'

'So I see.'

'What are you doing here?'

'Lucy said Blackberry was sick. I came to help.'

'Oh.'

She looks beyond Ned to the window, to the dull glimmer of a winter dawn. She gets out of bed, shivering at the cold. She pads across the room to where Blackberry is sleeping. It must be nearly time for him to wake. Sleeping, he looks like his father, serious and still. Awake, there's too much life in him to resemble Will. He bubbles with it, pours it into mischief or climbing. Sam was like that as a boy.

Ned taps his foot, impatient.

'I assume there is nothing wrong with Blackberry,' he says.

Hen shakes her head.

Blackberry stirs, waking. He looks straight at her and grins sleepily. She scoops him up, his flushed face pressing into her neck. 'Hey hey, my Blackberry. Hey hey.'

He looks over her shoulder to where Ned stands and points at him. 'Neh,' he shouts happily. 'Neh!'

Ned smiles, despite himself.

'Yes, clever bird,' Hen coos into Blackberry's ear. 'Uncle Ned!'

'Henrietta,' says Ned in the voice his men have learned to fear. 'What's Sam doing here?'

'I don't know. '

Ned shakes Sam's shoulder. 'Sam!' he shouts. 'Sam.' Sam stirs, and his eyeballs seem to shudder under the lids, but he does not wake.

'Ned! He's hurt.'

'Hurt how?'

'Hattie thinks it is a sword cut,' she says.

'Lord, help us. How long has he been here?'

'Two nights.'

'Has he spoken?'

She shakes her head. 'Not much. Nonsense. He has been feverish.'

He pulls back the blankets. The blood on the sheets is crusty and dark, but there's no new redness on the bandages.

'Lord, Hen,' says Ned. 'There was an attempt to free the man Charles two nights past. Beaten off, but they melted away.' He looks into Sam's face intently, as if he can read it.

'The MPs are to meet soon,' he says over his shoulder to Hen. 'They may kill him as early as tomorrow.'

He pulls back from Sam and walks over to the window, looking sideways along the street. Outside they can hear the sounds of the City stirring. It's a muted sound of carts rumbling and echoing footsteps. A troubled, frightened City.

Hen ducks under his arm to see. The cold air on her face wakes her, and she breathes deeply. He speaks behind her, and she can feel the vibration of his chest pressed into her back. He kisses the top of her head, unthinkingly aping a gesture her father used to make.

'He must have been part of it. Oh, Hen. What is he doing, mixed up with this… this villainy?' He looks back across the room. 'He looks so much older. I suppose we are used to each other, and the ageing. But seeing him like this, it's…'

'I know,' she says. 'Hattie says not to move him.'

Ned begins to speak slowly into her hair, as if to a small child. 'Hen, he tried to rescue the man Charles. He knows where his fellows are hiding. Hen, I must take him in.'

She breaks away from him. 'Ned, you cannot mean it. They'll kill him.'

'And how many has the man Charles killed, Hen? How many times has he defied the will of our Lord, and led us all like sheep into misery and slaughter? And Sam wants to let him go free so he can do it again. No, Hen. No.'

'Ned. I say again, you cannot be serious. He is our brother. And they will kill him.'

He hugs his cloak round his shoulders. His eyes are screwed tightly shut.

'I have my duty.'

'He is your brother. And what of us, Ned? Will they not notice his patched-up wound, do you think? Will they not think of me, and Blackberry?'

The boy wriggles to be free, and she sits him down on the floor. Off he crawls, impatient.

'Hen. Be reasonable. Charles has been found a murderer and a tyrant.'

'By whose authority, Ned? It seems to me that your Rump Parliament is as tyrannical as Charles ever was. Who is Ireton? Who is Cromwell? Where is your precious Fairfax? Hiding in his wife's skirts. You know this is all a farce.'

'It is God's will.'

'Are you as implacable as your God, Ned?'

'Our God, Henrietta, has made clear His will.'

'And it is His will that you kill your brother? Are you Cain, now, Ned? You will do to Sam what our father died thinking you did to him?'

Ned looks across at her, and she watches the pain spread on his face. Good. He is so unyielding when he thinks he is right.

He walks across to Sam, pushing Hen to one side. Wordlessly, he runs his hand down his brother's cheek. Hen sees then that he is crying.

Softer, she says: 'Surely, Ned, we have a duty to those who love us. What about your duty to me, to Will, to…' She pauses, Lucy's name sticking on her lips. 'To our parents?' she finishes.

'And what about your duty, Henrietta?'

'Me?'

'Will you teach your son that the only thing worth fighting for is survival? You sit in here cowering. You're so terrified that you have forgotten how to stand upright.'

'It's not true.'

'Isn't it? If Charles escapes, Hen, through Sam's deeds and our complicity, what kind of world will it be for Blackberry?'

'What kind of world will it be anyway, Ned? You all talk of this regicide as the end of it all. But what comes next? How will we be governed? None of you know. Are you fighting for the same cause you started out in, Ned? When did you turn Republican? I don't recall that in forty-two.'

'Enough of this. You're just a woman; you can't understand.'

She turns to him and he sees a flash of the old fire. 'Just a woman? So I cannot understand as well as you?'

'No, Hen. You cannot. How many comrades have you watched die, slowly and in pain, because of the man Charles? I had a friend, at the Battle of Maidstone, whose stomach was shot open. He tried to scoop his own guts up and pack them back in, Hen. And the look on his face, you would not believe it. Wonderment. Pure confusion. A pointless half-arsed battle in a pointless half-arsed place.'

'You've always got half an eye on the next world, Ned. He's gone there; be happy for him. I don't care. I don't know him.'

'That's not worthy of you. God gave us this world, Hen. No one said it is easy, but we have a responsibility to make it reflect His own image.'

'We're doing well, hey, Ned? Is He venal, stupid and blood-drunk too?'

'Hen!'

She waves away his remonstrance impatiently. She paces the room, searching for something, anything, to convince him.

'Responsibility. Duty. What of love, Ned? Didn't our Lord overflow with that?'

'He does not love one more than another, Hen. You'd have me save Sam's life and let all the others be damned?'

'Yes.'

'No!'

They stand and look at each other.

A voice breaks in. 'Pudding cat!'

They look over towards the bed. Sam is awake. Grinning, even, for all love.

Hen rushes over, and kisses his bloodless face and grimy hands.

He looks over her head to where Ned stands. 'Thirsty,' he says, and Hen tips water into his dry mouth. She props him up on some cushions, noting how broad he has become, her skinny brother, how muscle has packed on his frame. The sun has burnt his face and forearms but left his body an ethereal white.

'Oh, Hen,' he says. 'It's mortal good to see you. You look lovely.'

'Did they wound your eyes with your belly, Sam?'

'Aye, and perhaps knocked me about the head while they were at it, the sods, for this all seems a dream.'

'For the love of Christ!' Ned spins on them, furious. 'Are we at a fucking masque? Are we exchanging tittle-tattle? Henrietta. Sam is a traitor. Do you understand? A God-cursed, imp-spawned traitor?'

'Good to see you too, Neddy,' drawls Sam, and Hen jumps anxiously to her feet. She cannot remember the last time she saw Ned lose control. He looks murderous, vicious. Oddly young. She stands between him and Sam, waiting for a blow.

She watches Ned find his control. He walks to the chair, Will's chair, and throws himself into it. His hands grip the armrests and his head presses into the chair's back, as if he is restraining himself.

'What a time for jokes,' he says. 'You always were a damn sight too full of levity, Sam.'

'And you were always a damn sight too severe,' counters Sam.

'Were you involved in the attempt to move the king? Where are your friends? Tell me now, and I need not take you in.'

'You have your notions of duty, brother, and I have mine.'

'You will talk at the end of the questioning. Everyone does. Please, Sam, please. Just tell me now.'

Sam spreads his hands wide, glancing at Hen. 'Well then, brother,' he says. 'Here it is.'

Ned leans forward in the chair, relief clear on his face.

'Prince Rupert has taught me, himself, the secrets revealed to him by the imp, his dog Boy.'

'Go on,' whispers Ned.

'Aye. Necromancy, brother. Shape-shifting. To get here, we assumed the shape of a gull, and took wing across the sea towards—'

'Sam! By the Cross you are trying me.' Ned turns away so Sam can't see his face, and the despair he knows it will betray. It was a faint hope that Sam would help him find his fellow plotters, and then vanish quietly.

Sam puts his head back, smiling broadly.

'If you two have quite finished,' snaps Hen. 'You,' she raps at Sam, 'no more japes. We need to find a way out of this. What's to stop one of the men you are shielding from giving up your name, Sam? And how long do you think it will take them to come here looking for you? What about my son, Sam? My Blackberry?'

He looks up at the mention of his name, raising chubby fists to her, smiling wildly.

There is shouting from the street. 'Sir, sir! Captain Challoner, sir.'

Hen and Sam turn to stare at Ned. He curses softly and crosses to the window. It is stiff, frozen shut with ice crusting the panes from the inside. Even so, the shock of the cold air draws a gasp.

'What?' he shouts down to the sergeant waiting in the street below.

'Sir, the MPs are said to have reached a decision. It will be soon. Today, perhaps, or tomorrow. We must—'

'Yes, yes. Meet me downstairs,' says Ned. 'God save us.' He must get back. He turns round to them, relieved that there is an excuse to put off this decision. 'This is not over,' he says. 'Not over.'

CHAPTER THIRTY-FOUR

*T*HE DAY WHIRLS BY. NED LETS IT GO, CONCENTRATING ON his job, and on keeping his men mindful. He's too busy to decide. A few of the men bother him. They are keyed up, pumped. They laugh too loudly and bounce as they march. It is intoxicating, this regicide. This tearing down of the temple walls.

Roberts, a young boy blooded in the small fights of the second war and the New Model's divine certainty, is the worst. Ned fears he will do something rash, something shaming. His parents were killed in the siege of Brampton Bryan. The wars have created too many boys like Roberts – rootless and twitchy. Boys who believe only in the power of a musket.

As they guard the king's person, Roberts' eyes keep swivelling, turning back to where the man himself talks quietly to his chaplain, William Juxon.

It's hard not to look, to stare at this man who walks with death. The man bears it well. He is calm, self-possessed. His enemies are rootling about London, trying to persuade people to sign the death warrant. There is a safety in being one of many names on the paper that will kill the king. Fairfax, they say, has locked himself away. He is washing his hands of the act.

Ned watches Charles and thinks of the two men, both pinioned in a corner. Fairfax, who Ned has admired so fervently, is choosing to do nothing. Should he not, having won the war, fight for the peace?

And here is the man Charles, surrounded by enemies, deserted by friends, and he knows what he must do. He knows that his only recourse now, his only escape, is to show them all how a king must die.

~ ~ ~

Hen steps out of the baker's shop holding Blackberry. She has that wired tightness to her face she remembers so well from when Blackberry was a tiny scrap who screamed all night for milk. Tiredness so strong it seeps into your bones, changing the very structure of your face.

She had managed to calm her fear, quelling it with lies and platitudes, but now it is back. She feels it in her trembling legs and sweating palms. And suddenly her heart is beating so violently and so fast that she cannot breathe. She clings on to Blackberry, trying to find some calm. The street swirls beneath her.

An oyster-seller shouts and calls, his words too familiar to be distinct; two women stand gossiping, their shawls pulled tight against the cold and their cheeks chapped and red; a veteran clumps past on a wooden leg, his crutches catching in the mud and the mutterings falling from him like imprecations to a deaf deity; a beggar sits on the corner, huddling under the overhang of the tenement above. She is poorly dressed and thin; beside her sit two children – one baby and one toddler. One shivers violently, and the other sits motionless, her face so white as to be translucent, and her lips blue with the cold.

Hen focuses on them, trying to count her blessings and calm her breathing. Blackberry, swaddled, warm and red-cheeked, wriggles on her hip. The beggar woman catches her eye and holds out a hand. Hen reaches into the bag and tears off a chunk of bread, still warm, and hands it over.

She watches, appalled and fascinated, as the woman eats it ferociously. The mother doesn't look to where her children sit watching her eat. The older child turns and looks at Hen with dull, unseeing eyes beneath a ragged dark fringe. The woman finishes the bread with a sigh and, seeing Hen standing there still, stretches out a hopeful hand.

Hen shakes her head and walks on.

The woman's indifference is chilling. That despair and hunger and cold could override all pity, all care for her children – this Hen could not imagine until now. She hears the coward's voice in her own heart asking her the questions: And where would you break? What makes you think that you would be any better?

Another brick to add to her fear. She had thought that the existence of love was what made her vulnerable; that she was most afraid of her heart breaking. But now she sees a greater terror: in a place where her love has failed, and she exists without it. She fears her inner coward; she fears reaching the limit of love and crossing over to a place beyond.

~ ~ ~

Yesterday, the king said goodbye to those of his children who remained in England: Prince Henry and Princess Elizabeth. Colonel Hacker tells Ned the tale as the troops line up to be inspected on another freezing dawn. The dawn of the day they will kill the king.

Grizzled New Model veterans openly wept, says Hacker, as the king sunk to his knees next to the young princess and told her not to grieve for this, his glorious death.

Ned nods, distracted.

'We're worried about the young prince,' says Hacker as they turn back towards the rooms serving as their mess. 'He promised his father not to usurp his older brothers and become Parliament's puppet king. But that promise is not enough from an eight-year-old surrounded by enemies.'

'Mmm.'

'We are worried they may try to kidnap him, the royalists. Use him as a pawn. Find new ways to undo what we have done. We need him yet.'

'The royalists, sir?'

'Yes, Ned. Are your wits addled this morning? The royalists – remember them? Their cursed London spies. The ones who not three days past tried to get into the king's rooms, the audacious puppies.'

The ground heaves beneath Ned's feet. He thought that time would make the decision for him. That the king's head could roll into the basket and take Ned's great choice with it.

In the mess Ned finds Skippon sitting alone by the fire. His former chief has been distancing himself from the trial. He tells Ned that he has found, at the last, that he wants to be among his fellow soldiers. That his feet brought him to their mess despite himself. He looks at Ned as if seeing him for the first time.

'What troubles you, Ned?'

'What are my troubles worth in these times?' he replies.

'Come, Ned.'

Ned is silent. He did not know, before now, how very much grief can feel like fear. The same physical punch. The same nausea. The same enveloping sense of a stubborn presence that will never give ground to a lighter future. He watches the flames. He thinks about his God.

At last he speaks: 'Sir, if someone you loved committed a great sin, against God and his country, and to be quiet meant bearing the silence on your conscience, but sparing his life, what would you do? I speak, of course, hypothetically.'

Skippon is quiet.

Ned babbles into the silence: 'I mean, is it selfish, sir, not to want to bear the guilt of speaking up?'

'But it is not your own guilt that matters, Ned. It is the sin. And not to bear sin is a mercy, not only to the good but to the sinner. Is it not, then, a mercy, a kindness for the one you love, to know the consequence of his sin?'

'But,' says Ned, anguished even by saying it aloud, 'what of my love for him? What of the pain of dealing the blow?'

'You were talking of selfishness before, were you not?'

Ned acknowledges the truth of Skippon's words with a shrug.

'And remember,' says Skippon, 'that if we cannot stand before our own consciences, how shall we be able to stand before the God who knows all things? Conscience is but God's deputy in every man's breast.'

Ned feels the weight of the words settle on his shoulders.

'Sir,' he says, 'I have something to tell you.'

~ ~ ~

The crowd is eerily silent. You bastards, thinks Hen. You cowed, stupid bastards. You were not so quiet when it was my father being killed. You were not so squeamish then.

She stands by Will and grips his hand. Blackberry is with Hattie. Sam is sleeping. There is a blush of pink in her brother's skin now, a sparkle in him of one who has kissed the scythe and lived. Ned has not come back. Now that they are standing here, watching the king's execution, what would be the point? Please God, let him let it lie. Please God, let him find some pity in his heavy soul.

She hears a murmur, like the rustling of linen. There he is – the king. Christ, but he looks small. They have led him out through the window of the Banqueting House, onto the scaffold built hastily outside and shrouded in black. He looks around him. The street is packed to bursting. The roofs are lined with people. There is a power in the silence of so great a crowd, and everyone can sense it pulsing. The awe hovers in the sky above their heads, whistles in the air that they breathe.

Will and Hen stand among the regicides, invited by John Cooke. Jesus weep for us. How did it come to this? What if Father could see this? What if he could see where I am? Ned

443

here somewhere wielding a sword that killed the king's power. I, clutching the beloved hand that wrote the words that will kill the king's body.

Charles looks around at the crowd, up at the men hanging from the tiles, across at the boys perching on impossibly small ledges, and the children hoisted onto shoulders. Is that a half-smile on his lips? Is it remorse? Pity?

~ ~ ~

Ned looks around at the crowd and fears trouble. It is too quiet, too solemn. He starts to remember the raucous, laughing crowd that watched his father die, and checks himself quickly.

What if this ominous, shuffling crowd turns? What if, amid all this talk of 'the people', the people themselves cry out, and the word they cry is 'No'?

He sees young Roberts muttering to himself, making himself brave. He is rocking back and forth on his heels. Ned considers reprimanding him but lets it go.

Ned turns to look at the man Charles, who is standing and looking out over the crowd. He is courageous, that much is clear. His path is fixed, his decisions made, and he is facing the consequences with shoulders set square. Ned catches his own thoughts as they drift past. It is as if he has looked in the mirror and found a stranger. Am I learning lessons now, from this man who has drenched the land in blood?

What do I know of God's will, after all? Am I wrong? Oh Lord, oh Jesus.

What have I done?

~ ~ ~

Hen looks at the king and thinks of his children. Princess Elizabeth, they say, has not stopped weeping. Prince Henry vowed that he would be torn to pieces before he did Parliament's will. She imagines the pugnacious stance of an eight-year-old trying to be a man, his pinched white face and his little-boy bravery, and she feels herself begin to cry.

Stupid, stupid. Why cry for a stranger's boy when her own is still in peril? Why do You make it so difficult, Lord God? Why do You crush us? Why do You grind Your heel when we are already prostrate? Is it because we killed Your son?

The king starts to speak. The crowd is held back by the soldiers. They inch forward to try and hear him, but the pikes push them backwards again.

At last, Hen spots Ned. His back is to the king and he scans the crowd, watching for rebellion. There's something odd about his face, something troubling. She tries to decipher it, but the king is speaking, and she supposes she ought to listen. Only the regicides can hear him clearly; the rest are too far.

'A subject and a sovereign are clear different things,' he is saying. His words are pulled away by the icy wind.

The man with the axe steps forward at last, fingering the edge. Charles' voice drops lower. Hen can't hear his words, but Ned can, there at the front.

'Take care they do not put me to pain,' he says, his voice more tentative than Ned has ever heard it. Oh Lord take pity on him, Ned finds himself thinking. On us all.

A voice behind Hen says: 'We ordered a small block. For a small man – you see the joke?' But no one laughs and Hen is not the only one to turn and look at the speaker with contempt, so that he mumbles something and looks at his feet.

The king hands Juxon his garter. 'Remember,' he says.

King Charles looks awkward as he kneels. He has to lean too far over, and it makes him look undignified at the last. The axe flashes up to the sky and falls with the dull thwack of a man's soul dispatched. With it comes a long, keening sigh from the crowd which rolls down Whitehall, through St James and beyond Westminster to where the Thames coils, frozen and still.

CHAPTER THIRTY-FIVE

AFTERWARDS IS A DAZE. EYES SLIDE AWAY FROM EYES; WORDS die on lips. Everywhere she looks, there is a blinding uncertainty. An old man, with tears running down the lines of his face, raises his eyes to the heavens. Is he looking for thunderbolts, or paeans from the angels?

The king's headless body lies awkwardly on the scaffolding. His head is carried away, rattling around a threadbare basket. Someone made that, Hen thinks. Someone whittled and bound and worked that basket, watching it grow. Expecting apples, perhaps. Or loaves. Instead, a king's sightless eyes stare up from its depths.

The mood begins to shift as they disperse, shepherded away by troops of horse. A few boys break free from the cordon and run forward to dab handkerchiefs in the king's blood, which drips down the black cloth of the scaffold. One goes down under a flurry of nailed boots, but more escape, pocketing their prizes and melting into the crowd.

There's a reckless wonderment now. They can look at each other again. Their feet shuffling through the slush whisper: We killed a king, we killed a king.

A raven circles above, cawing: You killed your king, you killed your king.

Their voices return, and there's a low murmur. The same question rattling around different mouths, taking different forms: 'And now what?'

Hen holds onto Will's hand and looks up into his face as he says: 'Are you bearing up, my darling?'

She nods, the lie of omission curdling inside her.

He says: 'I must go back. I'm sorry. There are some loose papers to deal with.'

She feigns disappointment. 'What more use your papers, Will? He's dead, isn't he?'

'Come with me,' he says. 'We should be together. It won't take long.'

She looks past his shoulder and sees Ned, standing to one side of a handful of soldiers. He looks detached, incongruously still against their evident sense of purpose. An older man is talking to the troop, all flailing arms and urgency.

Ned looks crushed. He is motionless and hunched amid the buzzing crowd. Her heart leaps in sympathy for him. And then catches.

Hen turns to Will, kissing him quickly. 'I love you,' she says.

She makes her way through the crowd, pushing and shoving against the flow. As she nears Ned, he sees her. He takes a step forward, then glances sideways. He shakes his head, and she pauses. He looks to one side again, to where the handful of soldiers stand with their backs to him, watching their colonel harangue them.

Unobserved, he mouths: 'Go. Go quickly.'

~ ~ ~

She pushes through bodies. Her elbow rams the head of a short woman who swears at her. She steps on toes and curses chase her as she cleaves her way through the mass of people. The river? Too crowded and slow. No. Think. It's frozen solid. She can't imagine the soldiers skittering along the ice in their great boots. They will have to fight this crowd. Dare she risk it?

She remembers the last time the Thames froze. She was ten, or thereabouts. Ned was twelve, and still happy. They went down at Temple stairs with their father and ran around on the ice, laughing at each other's slipping and sliding. They drank hot, spiced wine from the stalls and ate sausages, huddling around the ice fire. They had watched the mummers and the archery contests. The winner had bright red hair, she remembers. It seemed to burn against the frosted ice.

Ned and Sam had competed in a race of their own invention. It involved running to a mark and dropping to their knees, and then sliding along the ice as far as they could go. She remembers the cold in her toes, and the helpless laughter as they slid past her, Sam pulling theatrical faces, Ned grinning at her. Until at last they had stopped sliding, keeling over onto the ice, arms outstretched like fallen angels, laughing at the sky.

The memory takes her down to the river. It is already dusk. A gloomy, short winter's day. She edges down onto the steps; the wind rattling up the frozen river steals her breath. There are dark figures on the ice. She pauses on the bottom step, the now familiar fear returning. 'What should I do?' she shouts to the silent sky. 'What should I do?'

~ ~ ~

Ned's troop rounds the corner into the street where Hen lives. It is near dark and the linkboys' torches throw leaping shadows on the ground. The crunch of their feet and the clanking of their swords send people scuttling into the dark corners. Ned catches sight of Roberts' face in the light from a flame just as one old man hurries for cover. He recognizes the boy's smile, his satisfied sense of his own power. I was him once, thinks Ned. He feels as old as Methuselah.

He has told them that Henrietta is away, staying in the country with her husband's parents during the disturbances. Will is at the Temple, killing the king. He said that Sam was there alone. Unaided. He's hoping – praying – that Sam will have left already. Somehow he will cover up signs of any complicity, any succour from his sister. He will protect her. Lord, he prays, help me protect her. Guide me.

They come to the door.

'Show us the way, Ned,' says Colonel Hacker, and he finds himself nodding.

He finds himself gripping the door as it is pulled away from him. He finds himself stumbling backwards as a woman rushes out. She is tall and wide, and her skirts, he notices with staggering slowness, barely reach the tops of her big, incongruous boots.

'Excuse me, madam,' Ned says, but there is something not right here, something altogether awry. Something familiar and all wrong about her form in the darkness.

Roberts pushes past him, taking the stairs two at a time. He is eager, bristling. He needs to prove himself. Ned chases the boy up the stairs, shaken out of his reverie, the discord still tugging at his brain.

~ ~ ~

Hen watches his figure walk quickly down the dark street. The soldiers ignore him, thank the Lord. If they looked closer, they would see the undone ties at the back of the dress – the only one that would fit him, the one she had worn today to watch the king die. They would see the largeness of his feet, the stubble underneath the overhanging cowl of the shawl. If they'd had time, they could have made him more convincing. Still, it's dark now and easier for a woman, even an unconvincing one, to flit through the advancing soldiers.

She shivers in her thin underlinens. There is a clattering on the stairs. She grabs the nearest thing – the old shirt Sam was wearing. It is stiff with dried blood, but she pulls it over her head. They will take if for a nightshirt. Perhaps it will fit Will. As she pulls it down over her head, she smells Sam – earthy and familiar. Could she smell him when they shared a womb, she wonders?

~ ~ ~

Ned bursts into the room, just behind Roberts. And there, in front of him, in an oversized, bloodstained shirt, is Henrietta. She looks like the girl he remembers – fierce and proud.

She starts to speak, hands raised, looking not at Ned but at the boy beside him, who is shouting. Shouting words that Ned does not catch. But then there is a flash, which he doesn't understand, and the sound of a shot. And suddenly she is falling, falling, and the fresh blood spreads fast on her brother's shirt.

CHAPTER THIRTY-SIX

May 1649

*T*HERE ARE WOMEN EVERYWHERE. BAREFOOT WOMEN WITH mud grimed into the cracks of their heels. Tattered women with patched-up cloaks that billow like sails. They are thin, these women. They have sharp, angled cheekbones and desperate faces. They huddle in groups; walk abreast; sit crying in corners.

To Ned, used to being surrounded by men, it is like moving though a shadow world. They pull at his coat, jeer at him as he passes. He is frightened, he finds. Sea-green ribbons flutter from their clothes, the mark of the radicals. A tumble of grey and misery and green. Their desperation sticks to him like treacle. He wades through them, clutching his secret dispatches with painfully tight fingers.

They want food for their children. They want their husbands and sons released from the army, paid and sent home. They want the release from prison of the Leveller martyrs, men who raise the possibility of a new world and a new order. Men who say the unsayable: that equality before God is possible, and desirable. Most of all, they want to be heard. They have marched on Parliament before, these women, and been sent home with jeers and taunts by the MPs. Go home to the dishes. Send your husbands. Rightly, thinks Ned, as he pushes his way through. Women have no place in public life. It is hard enough, in these times, for men to grapple with the future.

They shout slogans and jostle at him. He feels himself caught by their passion. He finds himself next to a pretty young woman. She looks prosperous, as if she is strolling along to the river for a picnic. She sees Ned looking at her and stares back as she opens her mouth wide to shout and call. Something about arbitrary power. The rule of law trampled. He can see her pink tongue and the blackness at the back of her throat.

What a time he has picked to arrive at Westminster. He should have visited Lucy first, cooed over her growing belly. She would never march with these women. Never expose herself in this way to censure and ridicule. Henrietta, however… The thought brings him to a sudden halt. His heart beats wildly, loudly, muffling the sound of the women's cries. Women behind him bump into him as he stands there, making him stumble.

He ducks sideways into an alleyway, looking for a way round the demonstration, and trips over something. He looks down to see the body of a child. A small boy, stripped naked. His stomach is bulging; his face is peaceful. If Ned had not seen starving children in Bristol, he would have missed the signs. The sharp-ridged ribs above the swollen belly. The hollowed-out cheeks and the dark-rimmed eyes.

Ned feels the nausea rising. Last night's pie sits like a reproach on his stomach. It cost a small fortune. The price of food has soared. Famine grips a land already soaked in blood. Is this the taste of hell before we shape His kingdom?

Ned squats on his heels beside the body of the dead boy. He feels sweat breaking out on his forehead and prickling at his armpits. He tries to force down the boy's eyelids with a shaking hand, but they will not close. The boy is beginning to turn, lying here amid the rubbish. Jesus, keep us. Jesus, keep me.

In his other hand is the petition, thrust at him by one of the women. He smooths out the creases in the paper. He reads:

Since we are assured of our creation in the image of God, and of an interest in Christ equal unto men, as also of a proportionable share in the freedoms of this Commonwealth, we cannot but wonder and grieve that we should appear so despicable in your eyes as to be thought unworthy to petition or represent grievances to this honourable House.

Lord, grant them wisdom, thinks Ned. What have we unleashed if women can write these words to Parliament? Equal unto men, the strumpets. Where will it end?

He pushes himself upright, tapping his fingers on the bag carrying the dispatches, abstractedly drumming out a marching tune on the dark leather. He must avoid the women or push his way through. He must deliver his letters. Yet he stands still. His legs are moulded to the earth, trapping him in this alleyway with a dead boy and an urgent, undelivered message.

His regiment is in Bristol. The Levellers are deep in its rank and file. Some of the officers are close to mutiny. They talk of arrears of pay and abuses by the army grandees. They rage at the raising of troops to conquer Ireland. They spit at the Council of State, the body set up by the Rump Parliament to govern in the absence of the king. It fits awkwardly in the king-shaped hole, like a piece of ill-made puzzle jammed in arbitrarily.

Ned must get his message through. He must let the grandees know how it stands in Bristol. Who is safe, and who is suspect. He thinks of the pamphlet he carries, which circulates in his regiment. He feels it banging against his thigh, feels the heat of it through the leather. Not the king's fault, but ours. That is what it says. Our fault. My fault.

He knows it by heart, has pored over it by candlelight, recited it to the clip-clop rhythm of his walking horse.

He whispers the words to the dead boy: 'Oh! The ocean of blood we are guilty of. Oh! The intolerable oppression we have laid upon our brethren of England. Oh! How these deadly sins of ours do torment out consciences.'

The boy is silent. His open eyes are a reproach. They stare sightlessly at the evening sky.

Ned whispers it again. 'Do you think he is right, boy? The one who wrote the pamphlet? Are we guilty? Am I guilty?'

The boy does not answer, and Ned finds himself becoming angry. He shakes the boy. He hears the crack of ribs and drops the body down again into the filth. He weeps then, tears dripping down onto the boy's greying skin.

'Ned.'

Will's voice is flat. It tells Ned nothing. He looks down to see Blackberry twisting his arms round his father's legs in the doorway.

'Un-le Neh,' says Blackberry, reaching out two chubby arms, demanding to be lifted.

Ned leans down and picks him up, suddenly overwhelmed by the smell of him. He feels his knees quiver. There is a possibility of fainting, and he leans against the wall, Blackberry in his arms.

'Can I come in, Will?'

Will looks at him with an impassive face. He says nothing, but walks back into the room, leaving the door open. Ned carries Blackberry through. Standing in the corner with wide, frightened eyes is Will's sister. Patience, is it?

She looks terrified. Ned almost checks behind him to see who it is that she is afraid of. He stops himself.

'Patience,' says Will, 'could you take Blackberry?'

She nods and comes forward to take the boy. She avoids Ned's eyes with a heavy effort. Only when she has closed the door behind her does Will speak.

'What are you doing here, Ned?'

'I wanted to see you. I am here for two days. Then leaving for Bristol. I have volunteered to fight in Ireland, under Cromwell. We will embark soon. I am not sure for how long.'

'Want to kill some papists now, Ned? Not enough blood spilled here for you?'

Ned feels an angry retort spitting on his tongue. He has become adept, he thinks, at controlling his thoughts and his actions. He breathes. 'It is true,' he says, trying to keep his voice low and calm, 'that I want to be in action again.'

'Why?'

He shrugs. 'It is my job.'

That is not it. Not it at all. How can he say it to Will? He wants clarity again. He wants certainty. He wants to feel God's breath on his cheek as the papists flee His wrath. He wants orders. A chain of command. He wants the roar and thunder of battle to push his thoughts from his head, like air from a pig's bladder. He breathes in.

'And how are you, Will?' He wants to reach across and touch his friend's shoulder. He clasps his hands behind his back.

Will shrugs. 'I am alive. Not living, perhaps. Breathing. I have Blackberry. Otherwise, I am not sure I would bother. Breathing, I mean. Last night, Ned, there was a shower of meteors. Did you know that? And I looked out of the window, and I felt... nothing. Complete and total nothing.'

'It will pass.'

'Will it? Since we buried her, Ned, there is only one emotion that I feel with any depth. Hate. Lord knows how I hate.'

'Will, I...'

Will holds a hand up imperiously. 'Hate, Ned. I have been scoured clean of love. Just a pinprick left for my son. Nothing else. Do you want to know who I hate, Ned?'

Ned nods, mutely.

'The dead king. The living queen. The Members of Parliament. The women who walked past my window moaning about empty bellies. The judges. Hattie, who has done nothing wrong, but who cries and cries and makes me envy her tears. Sam, for being here and putting her in danger. Then writing a jolly fucking letter from Prince Rupert's hind tit about his daring escape. He should be getting my letter back about now, Ned, so

I suspect he'll be a bit less fucking jolly.'

Will walks over to the table, where a flask of wine is sitting. It is not yet noon, but he pours out two generous measures. He hands one to Ned, who drinks deeply, feeling the burn in his throat. He is not used to strong drinking any more. He drinks again, watching Will above the rim, throwing off his measure.

'I hate the boy who shot her. I hate you, of course, Ned. That goes without saying.' He drops into a courtly bow. Ned twists his glass in his hands.

'I hate myself the most, I think, Ned. There was I, playing at lawyers, while she was getting shot. While she was trying to protect the ones she loved. You too, of course. Not just Sam. Protect you from yourself.'

Ned closes his eyes. He has become proficient at blocking out the image of her puzzled face as she fell. The hand she put out to him, stained with blood. The film already forming on her eyes.

'She is with Jesus now,' says Ned gently.

'Damn your eyes, Ned. Damn you to Hell.'

'Will, I…'

'With Jesus. And you know that how, Ned? Hasn't half this blood been shed because you and the other lot were fighting over who gets to go to heaven? Jesus, Ned.' Will laughs; a strange, mirthless thing.

'It's almost funny. If your father was right and you were wrong, there must be a long queue for judgement. The sheer numbers you lot have sent to be judged. And if you were right and he was wrong, my Henrietta could be in hell right now. Burning.'

'No. No. She is elect.'

'Funny how you bastards always think you know who is elect

and who is damned. You don't think He judges, but you do it all the time.'

Ned drains his drink. 'I should go,' he says. It is unbearable to see Will like this. Gentle, clever Will.

They walk towards the door. 'Tell me this, Ned,' says Will. 'Do you feel guilt for her death?'

Ned pauses on the threshold. He hears someone screaming in the still air. His head feels tight, as if a headache is coming on. 'I did not pull the trigger,' he says at last.

Will smiles, and its bleakness twists Ned's stomach.

'Goodbye, Ned,' he says, slamming the door with a thud that echoes.

Ned puts his hand on his sword hilt as he walks away, running his thumb over its edges. He tries not to think about Henrietta. He tries not to think about Sam. He will leave London behind soon enough. He will feel the salt spray on his face and know that there is a sea between him and the politicking. The great earthquake of the king's death has levelled the land. He had thought that it would be clearer, what came next. He had thought that, with the king gone, a new Jerusalem would rise. It turns out that earthquakes leave behind rubble and sewage and frightened, bickering men.

He tries not to think about Henrietta. He tries not to remember her white, puzzled face as she fell.

It will be good to be in battle again, to draw this sword in earnest. It will be good to have orders that are clear, precise. Dig this trench. Set this watch. Use this password. It will be good to do His work. To hear God's pure voice calling in the darkness.

HISTORICAL NOTE

A few years ago, I was living on Fetter Lane. It is a typical central London street – a jumble of hideous concrete buildings, glass-fronted offices, a newsagent, a mellow wood-panelled pub and a dodgy boozer for the Friday night bingers.

It was a magical place to live. At weekends, the old square mile of London and a few streets beyond empty out. The offices are shuttered; the pubs are hushed. The streets are left to a handful of bemused tourists, a few lucky residents and sightless, grey statues. The City is quiet, and you can hear the echoes of London's deep layers of history.

Idly researching my street one day, I came across the story of Waller's Plot. The two merchants involved, Richard Challoner and Nathaniel Tompkins, were hanged outside their front doors – one on Fetter Lane. The aims of the plot are murky, but I have tried to be true to what facts there are. I have borrowed the names of the merchants and invented their characters and families. Edmund Waller's character I have inferred, rightly or wrongly, from his poetry.

I have long been fascinated by the English Civil War, and perplexed by its absence from our national story. French and

American souls are informed by their revolutions; we are more diffident about ours. Perhaps the Restoration made all the ructions and schisms seem like a macabre dream. Perhaps the religious zeal that drove the political radicals is hard to tolerate in a more secular age.

But the fact remains that the ferment of ideas generated in those twenty years informed all the West's later movements for liberty and the rights of man. The very early seeds of feminism are evident in women's writing during the period, albeit tinged with godliness. The British instigated an extraordinary attempt to define and claim freedom in an era of hitherto unchallenged monarchy.

It was costly. In *Going to the Wars*, Charles Carlton estimates that 190,000 people died in England and Wales alone – both directly on the battlefields and as a result of the disease and hunger which follow armies. This from a population of five million. It was unprecedentedly bloody and brutal, with atrocities on both sides. Our neat caricatures of Roundheads and Cavaliers distort a much more interesting, complex reality.

For those who would like to read further, the best recent introductions to the era I have read include: *The English Civil War* by Diane Purkiss; *God's Fury, England's Fire* by Michael Braddick; *The English Civil Wars* by Blair Worden; *Civil War* by Trevor Royle. John Adamson's *The Noble Revolt* is a radical reinterpretation of the causes of the war.

Other books I found invaluable include: *Birth, Marriage & Death* and *Dangerous Talk*, both by David Cressy; *The Tyrannicide Brief* by Geoffrey Robertson; *The Verneys* by Adrian Tinniswood; *A Royal Passion* by Katie Whittaker; *The Ends of Life* by Keith Thomas;

Samuel Pepys by Clare Tomalin; *Charles 1* by Richard Cust; *Black Tom* by Andrew Hopper; *The Impact of the Civil War on the Economy of London* by Ben Coates; *Puritan London* by Tai Liu; *Merchants and Revolution* by Robert Bremner; *Women all on Fire* by Allison Plowden; *London and the Civil War* by Stephen Porter. *The King's Smuggler* by John Fox is a fascinating book on Jane Whorwood, a secret agent for Charles 1.

On the military side, these books were very useful: *A Military History of the English Civil War* by Malcolm Wanklyn and Frank Jones; *Naseby* by Glenn Foard; *The Battle for London* by Stephen Porter and Simon Marsh; *Cromwell's War Machine* by Keith Roberts; *Prince Rupert* by Frank Kitson; *Going to the Wars* by Charles Carlton; *War in England* by Barbara Donagan. All mistakes and misinterpretations are mine alone.

This is a very limited bibliography. As well as numerous secondary sources, it excludes countless letters, eyewitness accounts and diaries. I have been reading about the English Civil War ever since I studied it for A level, when I was inspired by a wonderful teacher – Annabel Smith. A second brilliant history teacher and Civil War expert, Serrie Meakins, kindly read the work early to check for errors, and found a couple! Thank you to both of you – history needs its inspirational teachers.

Other huge debts of gratitude are owed to Andrew Gordon, my agent. Without his advice and support, this book would still be mouldering, half-written, in the 'if only' pile. Thanks too to my editors at Corvus, Maddie West and Anna Hogarty, for all their enthusiasm and hand-holding.

I have been cajoled and encouraged to publication by various friends and colleagues – in rough chronological order:

Surmaya Talyarkhan, Clare Moore, Jeanette Burn, Megan Skipper, Annabelle Honess Roe, Anne Ashworth, Gráinne Gilmore, Robert Cole, Anne Spackman, James Harding, Bill and Sandra West. Thank you to all of you for the wine, ego-stroking, babysitting and professional breaks that contributed, sometimes indirectly, to the writing of this book.

Thanks to the old block I'm a chip off – my dad, Bob Senior. My beloved sisters, Glencora and Elishna, deserve a special mention in a book about sibling bonds and tensions – I am almost sure we would have been on the same side! Hector, my nephew, thank you for being a fellow history buff. Lara and Romilly, my daughters, I love you to the stars and back.

Thank you to Lisa, my mother, for everything; and for teaching me how to read.

Thank you to Colin for everything else; and for teaching me how to write about love.